Starting Ove

A grin spread over Lindsay's face, and Cici's, and Bridget's. Then Lindsay grabbed the laptop with its scrolling pictures, hugged it to her chest, and cried fervently, "Oh my God, I love this house!"

Cici fell on her, embracing both her and the laptop. "Me, too!"

"I love it more!" exclaimed Bridget as she flung herself into the melee.

They separated after a breathless moment and sat there with fingers entwined, letting the enormity of the moment sink in.

"Okay," Cici said at last. "This is serious."

"Totally."

"Absolutely."

"It's a huge risk."

"Imagine that!" Lindsay grinned. "Taking a risk at our age!"

"If we're going to do this, we're going to have to be committed. We've got to promise each other we'll give it at least a year."

Bridget said, "It *is* like starting over. Like getting a bonus life. We can do this, I know we can."

Cici raised her right hand and insisted, "One year."

Bridget repeated solemnly, raising her hand, "A year."

And Lindsay followed suit. "A year."

They clasped hands in midair, eyes shining, the excitement in the air as thick as honey.

"Okay then," Cici said. She pulled her legs into a semi-lotus position, took up her legal pad, and picked up her glass of wine. "Let's make a plan."

And so they did. ❧

Berkley Books by Donna Ball

A YEAR ON LADYBUG FARM

AT HOME ON LADYBUG FARM

LOVE LETTERS FROM LADYBUG FARM

A Year on Ladybug Farm

Donna Ball

BERKLEY BOOKS, NEW YORK

THE BERKLEY PUBLISHING GROUP
Published by the Penguin Group
Penguin Group (USA) Inc.
375 Hudson Street, New York, New York 10014, USA
Penguin Group (Canada), 90 Eglinton Avenue East, Suite 700, Toronto, Ontario M4P 2Y3, Canada
(a division of Pearson Penguin Canada Inc.)
Penguin Books Ltd., 80 Strand, London WC2R 0RL, England
Penguin Group Ireland, 25 St. Stephen's Green, Dublin 2, Ireland (a division of Penguin Books Ltd.)
Penguin Group (Australia), 250 Camberwell Road, Camberwell, Victoria 3124, Australia
(a division of Pearson Australia Group Pty. Ltd.)
Penguin Books India Pvt. Ltd., 11 Community Centre, Panchsheel Park, New Delhi—110 017, India
Penguin Group (NZ), 67 Apollo Drive, Rosedale, North Shore 0632, New Zealand
(a division of Pearson New Zealand Ltd.)
Penguin Books (South Africa) (Pty.) Ltd., 24 Sturdee Avenue, Rosebank, Johannesburg 2196,
South Africa

Penguin Books Ltd., Registered Offices: 80 Strand, London WC2R 0RL, England

This book is an original publication of The Berkley Publishing Group.

Cover photos by Ewa Ahlin/Johner/Glasshouse and SuperStock
Cover design by Judith Lagerman
Text design by Tiffany Estreicher

First edition: March 2009

Library of Congress Cataloging-in-Publication Data

Ball, Donna.
A year on Ladybug Farm / Donna Ball.—1st ed.
p. cm.
ISBN 978-0-425-22587-5
1. Female friendship—Fiction. 2. Shenandoah River Valley (Va. and W. Va.)—Fiction. 3. Dwellings—Maintenance and repair—Fiction. I. Title.
PS3552.A4545Y43 2009
813'.54—dc22 2008034288

PRINTED IN THE UNITED STATES OF AMERICA

10 9 8

This book is for Shannon, Libby, and Janet . . .
Who sat on my porch, listened to my stories,
and said, "You should write a book."
And for Gisele, who went for a walk one
morning and brought back a fawn
And for Karen, who never stopped believing
And for Jennifer, who extended her reach
And for Jackie, who brought us all home.
You are the women of Ladybug Farm.
Cheers!

In the Beginning

1

In Which the Ladies of Huntington Lane Go Looking

August

"Well," said Cici, stepping slowly out of the car. "It certainly is big."

"And old," agreed Lindsay, getting out of the passenger side.

Bridget got out of the backseat and drew in a breath. "Good heavens. It's—Monticello!"

Cici and Lindsay glanced back at her, then turned their eyes forward again. Cici pushed her sunglasses up into her hair to better assess the megalith of faded brick and painted Corinthian columns that sprawled before them. In the foreground stood a tangled and overgrown rose garden. In the background, sheep grazed in a meadow that seemed to sweep all the way to the Shenandoah mountains. On the deep front porch, which was partially obscured by giant boxwood tangled with Virginia creeper, a woman in a blue pantsuit waved to them. The three women waggled their fingers back.

"Okay," said Bridget, "we're just looking, right?"

"Of course we are," said Lindsay.

"Absolutely," agreed Cici.

"I mean, this isn't serious."

"Don't be silly."

"Not even close." Cici flipped the sunglasses back down over her eyes, finger-combed her honey blonde bangs back into place, and straightened her shoulders. "Let's go."

Three doors slammed in a rhythmic concerto, three purse straps were slung over shoulders, and three pairs of legs strode forward. Viewed from a distance, they could have been sorority sisters in their designer jeans and walking shorts, slim tanned arms swinging gracefully at their sides, casually coiffed hair glinting in the sunlight. Bridget, the oldest of the three by a couple of years, was shorter and slightly rounder than the other two, but no one could pull off a pair of kitten-heeled sandals and fuchsia toenail polish like she could. Lindsay wore her auburn ponytail pulled through the band of a baseball cap, and a close-fitting T-shirt that barely skimmed the top of her jeans. There was a time when, as a college student, she couldn't have afforded the special-edition Vera Bradley Sunshine and Shadow quilted back-pack bag she carried by one strap across her shoulder, but no more. Cici was blue-eyed and covered in freckles, head to toe. She had the legs of a dancer, which looked twice as long and twice as lean in her CKs, and was tall enough to have been a basketball player. But she wasn't. In fact, none of them were what they appeared to be from a distance.

It was not their clothes, their sizes, or their accessories that gave them away as they came across the lawn toward the wide front steps of the big house. It was the way they moved: with ease and confidence, and a kind of unconscious pride in being female that no one has when she's twenty. You're not born with a walk like that. You have to earn it.

They had already gotten their degrees—in liberal arts, education, business, and good old-fashioned survival. They had not only written mortgages, but had paid them off. Each one of them could soothe a teething baby, write a letter to the editor, and bake a soufflé—usually all at the same time and without interrupting anyone's dinner to complain about it. They had elected seven presidents, picketed for paid day care, campaigned for national health insurance and secured parental leave policies at workplaces across the nation. They had saved the ozone layer, the whale, and the Southern hemlock, all while keeping their streets safe from drunk drivers, their schools safe from drugs, and their sons safe from war. They had raised families, raised funds, and raised their share of hell.

Now they were moving on.

Just as, upon close examination, a few of Cici's freckles might have been revealed to be age spots, the ladies could not help noticing that the painted porch, which had looked so stately and inviting from a distance, was actually cracked and peeling. Bare wood was showing through in places on the steps. Cici scuffed up a square of paint with the toe of her sneaker and murmured, "I can fix that."

The woman in the blue pantsuit came forward with a big smile and her hand extended. "Hi, I'm Maggie Woodall with Woodall Realty?" She said it with an uplift in her voice, like a question.

"Cecile Burke," replied Cici, returning a firm handshake. "People call me Cici. I'm the one who called. These are my friends Lindsay Wright and Bridget Tyndale."

They exchanged greetings all around and Bridget said, "It was good of you to come out on a Sunday."

"Not at all, not at all! That's what I do!" She beamed at them as she handed out business cards, a heavyset woman with a short red haircut and eyeshadow the color of her pantsuit. "I'm so glad you called. This is such a unique property, I just love showing it. Cici, didn't you say you were a real estate agent back in Baltimore?"

"Just outside," agreed Cici, and dug out one of her own business cards.

This seemed to make Maggie very happy. "I offer three percent on referrals," she said. Her smile traveled from one woman to the other. "So. Which one of you ladies is looking to relocate?"

"She is," Lindsay said

"She is," Cici said.

Bridget apologized, "We're really just looking."

Maggie's professional smile barely wavered. "Well then. Shall we go inside?"

Lindsay was already snapping the shutter of her digital camera. "Is it okay to take pictures?"

"Of course. You won't see anything like this anytime soon. Sixteen acres, fenced and cross fenced, plus outbuildings, livestock, and attachments, as we say in the business." She turned what looked like an old-fashioned skeleton key in the brass-faced lock of a tall set of carved mahogany doors and stepped aside to usher them in, her arm flung wide like a game show host. "Here we are!"

"We're really just looking," Bridget began as she stepped inside, and then didn't say anything else. Neither did Cici, as she followed her over the threshold, and even Lindsay lowered the camera and just stood there, looking around.

The central feature was a curved staircase, easily wide enough for four people to pass at once, that swept into the room from a landing twenty feet high. On the landing was a round window of blue stained glass. A matching window was on the ground floor, at the opposite end of the room. There were tall clerestory windows and a walk-in fireplace surrounded by antique brick in a fan arch. The ceiling, Cici noted, looked like pressed tin, and the floor was wide heart pine. The view through the windows was of rolling green and blue purple mountains, and the smell was of aged wood and sunshine . . . and dust, of course. Lots and lots of dust.

"I'm afraid you won't find the place exactly spic-and-span," apologized Maggie. "It's been closed up for over a year while the lawyers tried to decide what to do with it after the death of the owner, Mr. Blackwell. He was ninety-two, bless his heart, and lived here all his life. They did an initial cleanup when they cleared out the house, but I don't think anyone has been back in here since then. No living relatives, you know, and the will stated the proceeds of the property sale will go to various charities and local churches."

Something crunched underfoot as they moved forward, and Bridget looked down. "What's that?"

The floor was littered with hundreds, if not thousands, of tiny shelled corpses. "Ladybugs," explained Maggie matter-of-factly. "They've just been horrible the past couple of years. Somebody told me the university released them to try to control some kind of aphid problem, and they started breeding out of control until they became more of a problem than the aphids! They're just everywhere."

Bridget made a face and tried to step around the bodies, but with no success. She moved toward the window, where a flock of ladybugs took flight as she passed. Bridget gasped and ducked, covering her platinum bob with her hands. "The warm weather causes them to be more active," Maggie observed, "but we get them all year long, even in the dead of winter. So, are you ladies on vacation?"

"Hmm," Cici agreed, moving around the room. The ceiling had to be fourteen feet high, and the windows had the wavy look of leaded glass. "We drove up through Lancaster, and are taking the scenic route back home."

"Oh, Amish Country. Don't you just love it? All the floors are heart pine," Maggie pointed out, "and the wainscoting on the walls is wood, not framed plaster. That's one thing about these old houses. They didn't take any shortcuts."

Lindsay raised the camera and started snapping shots of the staircase. "Isn't that gorgeous?" Maggie said. "Can't you just see ladies in big hoopskirts going up and down those stairs—just like Tara!"

"How old is the house?"

"Well, probably not as old as Tara," admitted Maggie. "I think it was built around 1900 by Abraham Blackwell, and it never left the family. The Blackwells were in phosphates, quite well-to-do. The house was a real landmark in its day. Copper pipes, gaslights, indoor bathrooms, all the best of everything. Hear tell, it even has its own ghost! Don't you just love those glass doorknobs?"

Cici grasped the doorknob of a glass-inset door that led to a small enclosed porch, and the knob came off in her hand.

Maggie looked dismayed, but Cici shrugged. "I can fix that," she said, and loosely pushed the knob back into its opening.

"Well," declared Maggie cheerfully, "shall we go upstairs?"

Six sun-filled, high-ceilinged, wide-plank-floored bedrooms and several thousand ladybugs later, they descended the staircase. Bridget kept absently brushing at her shoulders and hair, as though trying to rid them of ladybug scales. Lindsay snapped a shot of the stained glass window and of the big, dust-fogged chandelier overhead.

"All the wardrobes stay," Maggie pointed out, "since the one thing they didn't tend to do in the 1900s was build walk-in closets. There's some other furniture stored in one of the attics, too, I think, but all of the good stuff was sold at auction."

"There's nothing to putting in a closet," Cici said, "and the rooms are definitely big enough."

"You could take that little hallway that connects the two rooms at the back and turn it into two nice-size closets," Lindsay pointed out, adjusting her lens for another shot. "One for each room."

"Of course the wardrobes are beautiful," Maggie said. "They add a lot of character."

"We're really just looking," Bridget insisted gently, as though she felt she needed to soften the blow.

"Can you imagine the work it would take just to keep this place clean?" observed Lindsay. "How would you even dust that chandelier?"

"Mr. Blackwell had a woman live in, but you could probably get away with having somebody come in a couple of days a week. It's really not that hard to find household help around here."

"Not to mention the heating bill," Cici said. "What is it, an oil furnace?"

"Actually, no. It's quite ingenious, really—a wood burning furnace in the cellar heats this whole house. With the fireplaces, of course."

"So as long as you don't run out of trees you're all set," Bridget said, and Maggie chuckled.

"To tell the truth, the first thing I would do is put in central heat and air," she admitted.

Lindsay turned on the bottom step to get a shot of the landing, catching the newel post with her hand as she did. The carved pineapple post cap came off in her hand and she flailed for balance. Maggie gave a little cry and lunged toward Lindsay as the pineapple flew from her hand. Bridget ducked, and Cici caught the cap in midair. Lindsay saved herself, and her camera, by grabbing the newel post, which gave an ominous crack, but held. Maggie breathed an audible sigh of relief. Bridget exchanged a wide-eyed look with Lindsay. Cici raised an eyebrow, gave the carved pineapple a little toss in her hand, and said, "I can fix that."

Maggie displayed a brave, rather forced smile, and tried to summon enthusiasm by rubbing her hands together. "Well then. Shall we have a look at the kitchen?"

They passed through an elegant dining room with a medallioned ceiling, twin built-in, custom-made china cabinets, and an enormous, elaborately carved walnut table. "The table stays," Maggie pointed out. "Isn't it gorgeous? It was built for this house, and to tell the truth, it's so heavy no one could figure out how to move it." She paused and smiled apologetically. "I don't know what happened to the chairs."

She pointed out the French doors that opened onto the

broad wraparound porch. Lindsay admired the pale green paint and the matching silk wallpaper below the wainscoting—a historic color, Maggie told them. She pushed open a set of old-fashioned swinging doors to the kitchen.

Bridget walked to the center of the enormous room, drew in a breath, and pressed both hands to her cheeks, turning full circle. "Oh, my goodness," she said.

The floor was paved in brick worn smooth by time, and the antique brick on the walls was oiled to a sheen. There was a raised cooking fireplace at one end of the enormous room where they could imagine placing a downy sofa and a couple of chairs for cozy winter evenings. The center island was soapstone, and the countertops were tiled in cottage white and delft blue. The backsplash behind the deep farmer's sink was a mural in the blue willow pattern. There were two big stoves, two dishwashers, a giant refrigerator, and an upright freezer. "Obviously, the kitchen has been upgraded over the years, and the appliances are industrial grade," Maggie said. "The Blackwells did a lot of entertaining in their prime."

Bridget touched one of the stoves reverently. "Oh my God," she said. "This is a Viking."

"Bet you could whip up a casserole or two on that, huh Bridge?" said Lindsay with a grin.

"Of course all appliances are included," Maggie said. "And there's a butler's pantry."

Bridget dashed off to explore it, and in a moment they heard a muffled squeal of delight.

"I hate the tile," Cici said, but she was grinning, too. It had been a long time since either of them had seen their friend this happy.

In a moment Bridget returned, breathless with excitement. "Unbelievable," she said. "The silverware drawers are lined with blue velvet. There's a pie safe with a lock! And just outside there's a walled herb garden. Some of the herbs are still growing. There's a rosemary bush as big as a tree!"

Maggie was looking very pleased with herself, and Cici knew what she was thinking, what any real estate agent worth her commission would think: The kitchen sells the house.

Unfortunately, not in this case.

"Let me show you around the grounds," Maggie said cheerfully, and led the way.

She did a lot of chatting about an overgrown rose garden, which would take nothing, simply nothing, to bring back to glory, and Lindsay, who was Queen of the Roses back on Huntington Lane, identified several antique species. She seemed duly impressed.

"Do you ride?" asked Maggie, gesturing toward a big barn with a sagging shed and a rusted-out metal roof. "This is a great place to keep horses."

"Don't know one end of a horse from the other," Cici said, stepping high over tangled knots of fescue grass. She shaded her eyes toward a stone building set in a sunny tangle of wisteria vines behind the house. "What's that?"

Maggie led the way. "It's an old dairy," she said. "This place is just full of history. They used to make their own butter and cheese, and up until the 1950s, actually sold it. People used to come from as far away as DC to buy Blackwell cheese."

She pushed open the recalcitrant wooden door of the building and gestured them inside. "Isn't it adorable?"

The interior was cool and smelled faintly of milk products and sweet grass. Sunlight poured in from two overhead skylights and from the rows of windows that lined either side of the building, catching dust motes and soaring ladybugs in its beams and bleaching squares and rectangles on the flagstone floor. The building apparently had once been divided into partitioned sections, like stalls or small enclosed rooms, but some of the walls had fallen over and had been dragged to a pile in a far corner; others were sagging on their supports.

"It would take some work," admitted Maggie, "but wouldn't this make a darling guesthouse? And it's solid as a rock. Well, it is rock, through and through!"

Lindsay walked carefully around the rubble, turning this way and that to observe the fall of light, and her face was filled with wonder. Both Cici and Bridget knew what she was thinking, but Bridget said it aloud.

"Well, here's your art studio, Linds."

Cici said, "You'd have to get electricity down here, but it probably already has plumbing. The dairy operators would have had to have some way to hose the place out." She moved to test the sturdiness of one of the upright posts that had once framed an interior doorway, giving it a little shake. It crashed to the floor in a cloud of dust, causing everyone to jump back. "Not a problem," said Cici, brushing off her jeans.

"You can fix that," finished Bridget and Lindsay in chorus, and all three women shared a grin.

They walked back toward the house, intending to thank Maggie for her time and veer off toward the car. Instead, they started wandering, separately and together, around the overgrown lawn, through the house, over the porch. They peeked into the decrepit barn and pried open the door on an old potting shed. Standing on a slight rise behind the house,

Maggie pointed out an orchard of peach, pear, and apple trees, now in such bad need of pruning they were practically unrecognizable, as well as a tangled hill of grapevines that had overgrown their support posts.

They found a wrought iron fence that enclosed absolutely nothing, and a moss-covered statue of a girl with a flower basket standing beside a black reflecting pool. They imagined white wicker furniture on the wide covered porch and a gazebo in the garden, and painted iron chairs with colorful cushions underneath the spreading oak tree. They meandered through the warren of downstairs rooms and the big sunny bedrooms upstairs, and speculated in wondering tones about the time in history when people could afford to lead such lives. Cici even went down to the cellar and came back, peeling cobwebs off her eyelashes, to report that not only were there copper pipes throughout, but the wiring wasn't nearly as antiquated as one might expect. Morever, there was a stone wine cellar, and several other rooms that had no doubt been used for storage. The heating system, however, remained a mystery.

When they finally were ready to move back to the car, the sun was low on the late-summer horizon, and they spent a good ten minutes apologizing to Maggie for taking up her Sunday afternoon. "It's a wonderful house," Cici assured her. "But none of us is ready to buy yet, and even if we were, it's way out of our price range."

"Not a problem," Maggie insisted. "You just remember what I said about referrals. I'm sure there are lots of people in Baltimore who are looking for the perfect family getaway."

"Well, exactly," said Bridget. "This is really a family house, isn't it? No place for a single woman."

"It's so far away from everything," agreed Lindsay.

"It certainly is quiet," agreed Maggie. "But I love living out here. The community is so friendly and close-knit."

"Well, we appreciate your time." Cici offered her hand as they reached the car.

"We were really just looking," Bridget apologized.

"Oh wait!" Lindsay untangled the camera strap from around her neck and handed it to Maggie. "Do you mind taking a picture of us in front of the house? We like to keep a photo journal of our vacations. Come on, girls, it'll only take a minute." She grabbed Cici and Bridget by the hand and tugged them back to the house, posing them one above the other on the steps, leaning forward, faces close together, grinning into the camera.

The photograph captured in the background a brick-faced, Corinthian-columned house, its paint a little cracked, its brick a little faded, but all in all aging beautifully. In the foreground were three women with the corners of their eyes crinkled by the sun, their lipstick a little faded, their faces full of the joy of adventure, and also aging beautifully.

When that photo eventually made it onto the first page of a brand-new scrapbook, mounted in 3-D with puffy torn-cotton clouds on a cerulean background, the scrolled caption would read, "In the Beginning..."

2

In Which a Dream Is Born

Eight Months Previously

"Sweetie?" Cici came in from the kitchen, drying her hands on a dish towel. "How about a cup of tea?"

From her place in a corner of the deep window seat, Bridget looked like a small black-and-white kitten, curled in upon itself and all but lost in its surroundings. She shook her head silently, staring out the window. An early winter dusk had settled over the suburban street, and there wasn't much to see. Almost as though she suddenly realized that, she cleared her throat, pulled her gaze away, and directed a small, vague smile toward Cici. "No, thank you."

Lindsay took a cashmere throw from the sofa and draped it over her friend's knees. "You already have a cup, Bridge," she reminded her, and picked up the untouched cup of tea on the windowsill. "It's cold."

"I've got a pot of decaf on," Cici suggested, "if you'd rather."

Bridget pulled up her black-stockinged knees, drawing the throw beneath her chin. "I don't think so."

Cici and Lindsay exchanged a helpless look. "How about a sandwich, then? There's plenty of chicken and roast beef. Maybe some fruit? Honey, you've got to eat."

"No," Bridget replied softly, gazing at the window again. "You go ahead, though."

Lindsay put down the cold cup of tea, pressed her hands against the sides of her black pencil skirt, and said, "I don't know about you two, but I'm having Scotch."

Bridget looked at her, and the smile that curved her lips was very close to genuine. "Now you're talking," she said.

Lindsay poured, Cici served, and Bridget made room for them on the window seat. Cici patted Bridget's knee as she scrunched up her long legs and squeezed into the opposite corner. "Where are the kids?"

"Oh." Bridget sipped the Scotch. "Kevin had a seven o'clock flight. Katie and the girls went back to the hotel. It's been a hard day on them, and they're leaving first thing in the morning."

Cici looked incredulous. "Do you mean they're not staying the weekend?"

Lindsay punched her in the leg and gave a warning frown as she kicked off her shoes and slid in beside her. Bridget glanced at the liquid in her glass. "Oh, I know. It sounds a little selfish. But they came so often while Jim was sick, and they both have jobs, and lives of their own . . ."

"Excuse me!" Cici said. "Their dad just *died.* I think they could spare one evening to spend with their mother."

"Cici, will you shut up one minute?" This time Lindsay kicked her with a stockinged foot.

"Oh, come on, you know it's the truth. And I'm sorry Bridge." She gentled her voice as she squeezed Bridget's knee. "You know I love Kevin and Kate, and Katie's little girls are just too precious for words. But are we all really so wrapped up in our own little self-important worlds that we can't even take a little time off for death?"

"Cici, for the love of—"

"No, it's okay, Linds." Bridget sighed and sipped her drink. "She's right. Kids'll break your heart every time. You were smart not to have any."

Lindsay gave a little snort. "What, are you kidding? I've got thirty-two." Lindsay had been a middle school teacher for twenty years. "And when they're not selling drugs or giving each other blow jobs in the bathroom, they fill my life with joy, make my heart sing, and impart meaning and hope to a bleak and unforgiving world."

Bridget smothered a half laugh. "Lindsay, you're awful." And then she sighed. "You know what else is awful? I'm glad the kids are gone. They get on my nerves. I don't know them anymore, I hardly even know how to have a conversation with them, and I'm not . . ." She paused and sipped her whiskey. "Entirely sure I like them."

The silence from the other two was understanding and nonjudgmental. They sat and drank without talking for a while, comfortable together in the way that is only possible between those who have known all the best and most of the worst of each other.

Their friendship had begun twenty-three years ago, when Cici, who lived on the cul-de-sac at 118 Huntington Lane, had sold Lindsay the house at 115 Huntington Lane, which was next door to Bridget, at 117. Bridget's dog had promptly bitten Lindsay's husband, and Cici, in an attempt to try to avoid a lawsuit and preserve her commission, had taken them all out to dinner. As it turned out, Bridget's husband Jim was held up at work and Lindsay showed up at the restaurant without the person for whom the entire outing was arranged, because, as she announced without hesitation to the other two, her husband was a jerk and didn't deserve to eat.

Two hours and twelve mai tais later, the three women had shared far too many secrets and laughs to ever be mere neighbors again. Less than a year later, Lindsay had divorced her husband, and even though the offending pooch had gone on to his Great Reward years ago, Lindsay still sent Bridget flowers on the dog's birthday.

Together they had founded the Huntington Lane Reading Group, the Huntington Lane Neighborhood Watch, the Children's Food Drive, and the Animal Rescue League. They had taken twenty-eight vacations together, and had spent every Christmas together since the time they met. When Bridget's son Kevin had chased a ball into the street and been struck by a car, neither Cici nor Lindsay had left the hospital for the three days he was in a coma. Afterwards, quietly and without being asked, they took over the running of Bridget's household, shopping, cooking meals, picking up Katie from school, until Kevin was home from the hospital and life was back to normal again. When Cici moved her mother into her home to care for her during her last months of life, Lindsay and Bridget had taken turns providing respite care. When Lindsay totaled her car during an ice storm one January, it was Bridget and Cici that the nurse called from the ER at two in the morning.

But those were not the things that made a moment like this possible, as they sat in easy, comforting silence in the cold dusk of loss. Such a moment was the result of a thousand cups of coffee, an endless stream of phone calls, shared diets, bad dates, and ruthless assessments of how the two-piece swimsuit *really* looked. They had gone from homework hotlines to hot flashes together, and everything in between. When Bridget said she wasn't sure she liked her children anymore, what she really meant was that the only people she wanted with her right now were the two women at her side. Lindsay and Cici understood that, and that was why they did not have to say anything.

When her glass was almost empty, Bridget sighed, looked around the room, and said, "I can't stay here. How can I stay here?"

Cici said hesitantly, "Do you mean—do you want me to sell your house?"

Bridget shook her head vehemently. "I love this house! I don't want to sell my house. But how can I stay here? How can I take care of everything by myself?"

Both Lindsay and Cici, who had been taking care of everything by themselves for years, looked a little confused. "Like what? What things?"

"Oh, you know." She made a clumsy, wavering gesture with her hand that encompassed the room, and then briefly blotted a tear from one eye with her knuckles. "The gutters. The storm windows. The lawn. Everything."

"Oh, is that all?" Cici waved it away. "You can learn how to do that stuff. I'll show you."

"I don't want to learn how to do it," she said, sniffling. "I'm afraid of ladders. I hate mowing the lawn."

"I don't blame you," Lindsay said, patting her hand. "Mowing the lawn sucks. We'll get you a boy."

Bridget covered her face with her free hand and sobbed. "I don't want a boy!"

Lindsay moved in and slipped her arm around Bridget's shoulders, hugging her close for a minute. Then she said, with her voice muffled into Bridget's hair, "Do you mind if I get one?"

Bridget choked on a cross between a laugh and a sob, and wiped her face with a corner of the cashmere throw.

Cici said gently, patting her hand, "Honey, I think you're a little drunk."

Bridget sniffed again and held out her empty glass. "Not yet."

Cici took the glass and got up to refill it. She returned with the bottle, and a box of tissues.

Bridget leaned back with her hands wrapped around the glass. "I just wish . . ." She exhaled a soft breath. "I just wish we'd had more adventures, you know? Jim used to talk about sailing to Bimini, tying up at the marina and living off the boat, catching our dinner right out of the ocean every night . . ."

"Sweetie," Cici pointed out gently, "you get seasick."

"I know. But it didn't matter, because I knew . . . I knew he was never going to do it. And I was right. God, it's just so sad."

Cici passed her a tissue. "I guess we all have things like that, that we talk about doing, and dream about doing, but we never really get around to doing."

"Like me and my art studio," Lindsay said. "Some sun-filled loft where I can do nothing but paint all day, take in a few students on the side, you know, just to pay the rent . . . I've been threatening to do it—"

"And talking about it," Cici pointed out.

"Ever since I got out of college, but somehow I never actually got around to it." She shrugged a little and took a sip from her glass. "Everyone does that."

Bridget nodded. "Like my restaurant. I've always wanted to do it, and I'd be good at it, you know? Jim and I even talked about it, and we could have used some of our savings to get started, but there were always so many other things to take care of first."

"Then why don't you do it now?" Cici said suddenly. "What's stopping you now? You just said how sad it was that people don't follow their dreams. Well, here's your chance. You can make a whole new life for yourself."

But long before Cici finished speaking Bridget was shaking her head. "No, I couldn't do it now. Maybe when Jim was here, to help . . . but I can't do it by myself."

"Of course you can!" Lindsay insisted. "Come on, Bridget, Jim would want this for you, and it would be good for you to get involved in something that you care about. And we'd help you, wouldn't we, Cici?"

"No," Bridget said. Her voice was soft, but it was firm. "I know what it would take to start a business like that, and it's more than I can afford. Not to mention the time and the energy . . . I can't do it alone," she repeated. "I just don't have the courage."

"Bridget, that's crazy," Lindsay said, squeezing her hand. "You're one of the bravest women I know. It's not a matter of courage, it's a matter of just doing it."

"So why don't you open your art studio?" Bridget asked.

Lindsay hesitated, licked her lips, seemed about to protest, and then allowed a small smile. "Because it's scary," she said. "You're right, it's scary when you're alone."

Cici said, topping off their glasses, "Tell you what. Why don't we all move in together, then nobody will be alone. Bridge can cook and do the housekeeping, and Lindsay can support us all with her painting."

"And what will you do?"

Cici grinned. "I'll fix things. The gutters, the plumbing, the shelves, whatever. You've got to have somebody to fix things."

Lindsay sighed and clinked her glass with Cici's. "Ain't it the truth?"

Bridget smiled a little wanly. "This sounds like one more thing we can put on our list of things we talk about but never do."

"So?" Cici lifted a shoulder. "Talking is good. Talking is great. Talking is what women do best. So let's talk." She leaned back into her corner, sipping her whiskey. "Where would this house be?"

"Florida," said Bridget. "By the ocean."

"Dry rot," objected Cici.

"Too many old people," agreed Lindsay. "How about Seattle?"

"Yuk!" Bridget shook her head. "Too rainy."

"But lots of bookstores."

"And coffee."

"And men."

"But they're all geeks."

"But *rich* geeks."

"And a rich geek in hand is worth two in the pocket."

"Depends on which pocket."

Then they were laughing, and pretty soon they were laughing so hard they couldn't talk, and before long they were laughing and crying, and spilled whiskey mixed with spilled tears as they tumbled together in an embrace. "I love you guys," Bridget sobbed. "I love you."

"You're going to be okay, Bridge. We're going to get you through this. You're going to be okay."

So they held each other and cried together, and after a long time Bridget's muffled voice said, "Tennessee."

Cici pulled away, looking at her in some puzzlement. "What?"

Bridget wiped her swollen eyes, and Lindsay pushed back the strands of pale hair that were caught in the moisture on Bridget's face. "Tennessee," she repeated thickly. She fumbled for a tissue and blew her nose. "It's got mountains, beautiful farm country, horses . . ."

"Dollywood," added Lindsay.

"Elvis," supplied Cici.

And they all smiled.

So that was how it began, as a game to comfort a grieving friend on a dark winter day, just one of those things people fantasize about but don't really intend ever to do. But it was brought out more and more often during the coming months. Cici would run across a listing that would send them off to the Internet for a virtual tour: plenty of room for Bridget's herb garden here, but the kitchen was too small; this one had a swimming pool but they hated the bedrooms; that one was big enough but had no garden space. Then they started spending Sunday afternoons riding around, looking at properties; not every Sunday, but occasionally. It was something to do, a way to help Bridget through a difficult time, nothing more. Or at least that's what they told themselves. But gradually, without any of them really being aware of it, they started to take the idea almost seriously. Somehow the game traversed the line in their minds between fantasy and reality and became something very close to a plan.

And until that Sunday afternoon in the Shenandoah Valley, none of them even realized what had happened.

3

In Which a Plan Is Made

Back to August

Back at the Holiday Inn in Staunton, Virginia, an hour's drive from Blackwell Farm, they piled together on the king-size bed in Cici's room in their crop-legged PJs and robes, watching the photos Lindsay had taken that afternoon scroll across the screen of her laptop. They drank white wine from water glasses and shared a box of Lancaster County chocolates while Cici, wearing oversize reading glasses, scribbled absently on a legal pad, and Bridget, having recently discovered the joys of wireless Internet access, surfed the Web for information about their surroundings.

Lindsay said, without taking her eyes off the slide show on the computer screen, "Amish country. What's next for us? Red hats and early-bird dinner specials?"

"Maybe for you two." This from Cici, who spoke without looking up from her figures. "I was planning to be a cancan girl on the Moulin Rouge."

"I like the early-bird specials," Bridget said.

"We could go to the Moulin Rouge," Lindsay said. "We used to have great vacations. Ireland, the Grand Caymans, remember that cruise we took to Antigua?"

"I've been to the Moulin Rouge," Cici said. "You'd hate it."

"Oh yeah?" Both Bridget and Lindsay looked at her with interest. "When?"

"In 1996," Cici said. "That two-week tour we took of France? You two went on the excursion to Giverny, I went to the Moulin Rouge. It was a rat hole."

Lindsay groaned. "Now I know we're getting old. Not only is the best part of our lives behind us, we can't even remember it."

"Speak for yourself, Missy." Bridget tossed a foil-wrapped chocolate at her, which Lindsay caught and began to unwrap.

"It's true, you know," she said. "Women were never meant to live past menopause, evolution-wise speaking. Once a woman's childbearing years are over, her usefulness to the species is over. So if society treats us like castoffs, that's why."

"I resent that," Bridget said.

"So do I," Lindsay answered, "but it's true."

"Then tell me this," Cici said. She appeared to be making some kind of graph on the legal pad, with long straight lines and lots of shading. "Who's going to be raising all those change-of-life babies if all the women past childbearing age are dead?"

"Poor planning on the part of the evolutionary process."

"Not to mention on the part of the change-of-life mothers."

"And who do you suppose is going to be taking care of all the old men if all the old women are gone?"

"Oh they'd be eaten by a mastodon long before then."

Lindsay sighed. "In a way, life was a lot simpler before we all started living so long."

Then, noticing the brief wanness that crossed Bridget's face, Lindsay squeezed her foot and smiled apologetically. Bridget shook her head. "Actually, I was just thinking you're right. You know that old saying—Lord, let me run out before my money does? It's hard."

Cici was looking at the slide show. "I think that was my favorite part of the house," she said. "That stained glass window on the landing."

"The marble fireplace in the bedroom," Lindsay said, as the next photograph came up. "I've always wanted a fireplace in my bedroom. "

"Well, you could have your choice in this house. They all have them."

Bridget turned back to her own laptop. "It says here ladybugs are a sign of good luck. They used to be called "The Beetles of Our Lady" because in the Middle Ages the farmers believed they came in answer to a prayer to the Virgin Mary to save their crops from being destroyed by insects. That's how they got the name ladybug."

Lindsay said, tossing the foil wrapper from a chocolate toward the waste basket, "I'm eligible for retirement this year."

Cici raised an eyebrow. "Are you going to take it?"

"I'm fifty-one years old," she replied morosely. "Who retires at fifty-one?"

Cici said, "Shut up with your fifty-one, already. Talk to me when you're fifty-four."

Bridget raised her hand. "Fifty-eight."

"My hair is falling out," she complained.

"You've got gorgeous hair."

"Everything I wear makes me look fat."

"You're a size six for Pete's sake!"

"I'm growing hair on my chin."

Cici adjusted her glasses and peered closely at Lindsay. "So you are."

"I hate my life."

"Welcome to the club. So. Are you going to retire?"

"God, I'm tempted." She stuffed another chocolate into her mouth, and chewed thoughtfully for a moment. "But I can't live on half pay. I can barely live on full pay. And what would I do? It would be like starting all over again."

"I'd take it in a heartbeat," Cici said.

"Are you kidding? You have a great job! You set your own hours, you get to walk around in other people's houses all day, and every now and then you rake in a big fat commission."

Cici just laughed.

"Well, what would you do if you didn't sell houses?"

"Anything," replied Cici. "This is a stupid job. There's no point to it. I mean, there was a point to it when Lori was at home. It's the kind of thing you can do and still raise a child, and you're right—sometimes you can make a pretty good living. But with Lori gone . . ." Cici shrugged.

Cici's daughter Lori was a sophomore at UCLA whose phone calls were growing almost as infrequent as her trips home, and whose tuition and living expenses were being completely funded by her father. The fact that her father, a Hollywood entertainment attorney whose glamorous lifestyle and celebrity clients only added to his charm, suddenly wanted to be her best friend no doubt contributed to Lori's infrequent communications with her mother, not to mention her mediocre grades. But if Cici was hurt by this she worked hard at not showing it . . . except, of course, for the occasions upon which she referred to her daughter affectionately as "the ungrateful little brat."

"It's just a stupid, tiresome job. When you go home at the end of the day you don't have anything to show for it. You haven't made anything, you haven't changed anything, you haven't mattered. Something with my hands, that's what I'd do. Something I could *see*."

The people who knew Cici well—a short list, which was undisputably topped by Lindsay and Bridget—understood that she was a walking contradiction. With her cell phone pressed to one ear while she e-mailed with her BlackBerry and struck through clauses on a contract with her free hand, she was the quintessential twenty-first-century woman: She could build a high-rise in a Chanel suit and Jimmy Choos, give lessons in multitasking, and freeze the heart of the coldest competitor with a single unblinking gaze over the rim of her ebony-framed reading glasses.

But that persona was like a bodysuit that she pulled on at eight in the morning and peeled out of at five in the afternoon, when she would like as not pick up a sledgehammer and a hard hat and spend her happiest hours working alongside the construction crew on her latest house remodeling project. She mowed her own lawn—hatless, and in baggy shorts and running shoes, which was no doubt how she had gotten most of her freckles—she shingled her own roof, she built a gazebo in her own backyard while the neighborhood husbands, having been repeatedly and cheerfully turned down on their offers of help, gathered around with bottles of beer to watch and shake their heads in wonder.

If there was a petition to be drawn up, a plan to be presented, or a dispute to be resolved, Cici was your go-to girl. She coached soccer, headed the Arts and Music Society, and was chairwoman of the Library Fund Drive for ten years in a row. She was on boards and committees. She brought in guest speakers and organized charity balls. She was Cici, and she got things done.

But over the past few years it had become impossible not to notice that the Chanel suit came out less often, and the hard hat more. She joined fewer committees and took more vacations. More days than not, her BlackBerry never left her briefcase. She said that no woman past the age of fifty should be required to multitask. The truth was, she just wasn't interested anymore. And neither Bridget nor Lindsay was really surprised to hear her say she was bored with her job.

"Oh my goodness, girls, listen to this!" Bridget sat up straighter, tapping a key on her computer as she read from the screen. "Blackwell Farm, Blue Valley, Virginia. Once listed on the *Virginia register of historic places*..." She glanced up to see their reactions, and then went on, "Blackwell Farm was once known for its regional cheeses, fruit jams, and *wines*. Its small runs and high quality made Blackwell Farm wines a favorite with collectors and restaurateurs alike in the sixties." She looked up. "I wonder why Maggie didn't tell us that?"

"She probably didn't know." Cici replied. "I'll tell you something else she didn't know. The tiles in the kitchen were hand-painted originals. The marble floor in the sunroom was real Cararra. And there's a difference between *glass* doorknobs and crystal ones, and every interior doorknob in the place is cut crystal. That house is worth a fortune."

"They're *asking* a fortune."

"Not really. A few cosmetic repairs, some updates, and a smart investor could double her money inside a year. And remember, there are no heirs. No one is motivated to fight for the asking price."

The other two stared at her.

"It's an eight thousand square foot brick house," she explained patiently, "with antique heart pine floors, eight fireplaces, imported fixtures, a soapstone and brick kitchen *with* state-of-the-art appliances and imported tile work, a wine cellar, sixteen acres of valley with outrageous mountain views, outbuildings, orchards, a guesthouse—"

"Dairy," corrected Bridget.

"Studio," corrected Lindsay.

"It's not a bad investment," Cici said. "Some hotshot Washington consultant or software mogul wouldn't blink at paying three, four million for a place like that."

Two pairs of eyebrows shot up. "But it's falling apart!"

"Well, there's that," Cici admitted. "But if it were fixed up . . ."

"I don't think it would take that much to fix it up," Lindsay said. "After all, the old guy lived there until—what did Maggie say?—a year ago? That means it's at least fit for human habitation."

"That kitchen," Bridget said wistfully. "You'd feel like Emeril Lagasse cooking in a kitchen like that."

"You'd have to hire a team of tractor drivers just to clean up the yard," Lindsay said.

"High school boys," insisted Cici.

"But wouldn't it be something to bring that orchard back to life? And look, right here." Lindsay hit the Pause button on her keyboard and a photograph of tangled spiky bushes overgrown in grass froze on the screen. "Those are raspberry bushes. And that whole hill behind them is covered in blueberries."

"Raspberries are $6.99 a pound," Bridget said. "Wouldn't it be something just to walk out in the orchard and pick your own?"

"Or open it to the public and let *them* pick their own—for $4.99 a pound," Cici said.

Bridget nodded. "Pick-your-own farms can make six figures a year."

"Where did you hear that?" Lindsay demanded.

"On the Internet."

"She's right," Cici said. "With the organic produce/natural foods craze, small farms are actually becoming profitable again."

Lindsay looked from one to the other. "You're not seriously suggesting that we finance the restoration of a hundred-year-old house with a farm stand?"

Nobody said anything for a moment. Then Cici answered carefully, "Actually, I don't think anyone is seriously suggesting anything. But as long as we're fantasizing . . ."

She turned the legal pad around so that they could see the chart she had made and the numbers written there. "Okay. Just talking, here. This is what I think we can get the place for." She pointed with her pencil to the top number.

"And this is what I think I can get for each of our houses." She pointed again, one by one. "Mine, Bridget's, Lindsay's. The total . . ." The bottom number made Bridget gasp.

"Now, the rest of this is just speculation and estimate. We know it's going to need central heat, and upgrades to the bathrooms. Restoration of the outbuildings, including the dairy,

I'm figuring at fifty dollars a square foot. It might be less depending on the cost of labor out here. Cleaning up the gardens and orchards, maybe two hundred hours at minimum wage. Of course we'd have to do an awful lot of the cosmetic work ourselves. But if you add up all the numbers, and subtract the outgoing from the incoming..." She drew a line under the final figure.

Two pairs of eyes went big. "Oh my God," Bridget said. "We can afford this."

"It would be close," Lindsay pointed out.

Cici nodded and sat back, picking up her wineglass and trying to look casual. "But nice to know you have options. Just in case anyone was wondering."

They just sat there for a time, lost in their individual thoughts.

Then Lindsay said, "I've never been much of a farm girl."

"Me either," admitted Bridget.

"Not one of my fantasies," Cici said.

Lindsay poured more wine. "But what an adventure it would be, huh?"

They turned their attention to the pictures scrolling by on the computer screen.

"I love the light from those windows."

"Imagine waking up to that view every morning."

"That little porch off the dining room is just enchanting. With the stone floor and the sunlight coming through the trees like that, it feels like a secret garden."

"Remember how quiet it was out there? You couldn't even hear traffic."

"I don't know if I could get used to that."

"Boy, I could," Cici said.

The other two grinned and agreed, "I could, too."

Cici said, "Bridge, what does the Internet map say is the nearest town?"

She typed. "Blue Valley, Virginia, population 1,236. And it's thirty-five miles away."

"Let me rephrase that. Where's the nearest town with a Publix grocery, a Barnes & Noble, and a Home Depot?"

Bridget clicked some keys. "There isn't one."

Lindsay rolled her eyes. "Well, for that we could go to rural Alaska, or the Australian Outback, or some eight-hundred-year-old village on a cliff in Tuscany."

"Or," Bridget said softly, "we could stay right here, where we've already found a place we love."

The silence that fell over them was filled with wonder, and thick with possibilities. They looked at each other. They looked at the pictures on the computer screen. Cici said, "Oh my God. We're really considering this."

"It would mean leaving everything we know," Lindsay said. "Our jobs, our friends, our homes . . ."

"You hate your jobs," Bridget said, trying to subdue the rising excitement in her voice, "and working part-time at the library is not exactly the most fulfilling thing I've ever done. And do you think our friends won't be beating a path to our door when they hear about this incredible place? Think of the house parties we can have!"

Cici said, "But consolidating three households, selling furniture, deciding what to take and what to leave . . . it's mind-boggling."

They thought about that for a moment, then Bridget

declared somberly, "You're right, it would never work. For one thing, we could never agree on a China pattern. And we're likely to come to blows over the living room drapes."

A grin spread over Lindsay's face, and Cici's, and Bridget's. Then Lindsay grabbed the laptop with its scrolling pictures, hugged it to her chest, and cried fervently, "Oh my God, I love this house!"

Cici fell on her, embracing both her and the laptop. "Me, too!"

"I love it more!" exclaimed Bridget as she flung herself into the melee.

They separated after a breathless moment, and sat there with fingers entwined, letting the enormity of the moment sink in.

"Okay," Cici said at last. "This is serious."

"Totally."

"Absolutely."

"It's a huge risk."

"Imagine that!" Lindsay grinned. "Taking a risk at our age!"

"If we're going to do this, we're going to have to be committed. We've got to promise each other we'll give it at least a year."

Bridget said, "It *is* like starting over. Like getting a bonus life. We can do this, I know we can."

Cici raised her right hand and insisted, "One year."

Bridget repeated solemnly, raising her hand, "A year."

And Lindsay followed suit. "A year."

They clasped hands in midair, eyes shining, the excitement in the air as thick as honey.

"Okay then," Cici said. She pulled her legs into a semi-lotus position, took up her legal pad, and picked up her glass of wine. "Let's make a plan."

And so they did.

4

Auld Lang Syne

December

The annual Huntington Lane Christmas Party, jointly hosted by Cici, Lindsay, and Bridget in Cici's home, was an event without parallel. Friends, neighbors, colleagues, and their families shopped all year for the perfect outfits, the just-right shoes, the unprecedented hostess gifts. The ladies themselves held their first organizational meeting in September, and from Labor Day onward the clock was counting down toward what was to be, each and every year, the party that would leave all previous parties in the dust.

A graceful draped rope of tiny blue lights lined both sides of Cici's driveway from the street to the house. A miniature Christmas tree, decorated in twinkling blue and white lights, adorned the fish pond that was the centerpiece of her front lawn, while overhead, every branch of every deciduous tree was wrapped in tiny white lights and hung with oversize, interior-lit, blue glass ornaments. The front porch was swagged with greenery and studded with white lights and pink poinsettia leaves, and the double entry doors show-cased twin wreaths in which glittery white lights and blue satin ribbon were woven in and out of bouquets of white roses.

The foyer was dominated by a fourteen foot, snow-white Christmas tree done completely in crystal ornaments and blue lights. Every doorway was swagged in fake-snow-frosted greenery that was interwoven with blue satin ribbon and tiny white lights. To the right of the tree was a bar, draped with white satin and decorated with sprays of white roses and a half dozen blue candles, where a bartender made certain every guest was immediately greeted with a cup of creamy Southern Comfort eggnog. Hidden stereo speakers provided traditional Christmas music as a background to the "oohs" and "ahhs" and the happy greetings of guests who only saw one another once a year.

In the study, Cici's office furniture had been pushed against the wall and covered by floor-to-ceiling drapes of theatrical scrim, which were backlit by red and green up-lights and draped with swags of evergreen tied with elaborate red bows and clusters of sparkly ornaments. In the center of the room was a twelve foot evergreen decorated in gold balls and red and green lights. Surrounding it, Cici had built a circular serving table that was draped in gold lamé and lit by dozens of gold candles on mirrors. Behind the table another bartender prepared pomegranate margaritas while guests plucked shrimp from the Christmas-tree-shaped tower decorated with red pepper ornaments, and filled their gold-colored hors d'oeuvres plates with everything from homemade cheese straws to olives wrapped in prosciutto.

The dining room buffet was an L-shaped spectacle of

white satin, silver ornaments, and red glass. Rows upon rows of glittering white lights were tucked into nests of greenery and draped through folds of satin, while red glass ball ornaments reflected the sparkle and clusters of red roses accented each serving dish. The beef Wellington was a work of art with its crispy pastry crust and savory spinach filling, complemented by an asparagus casserole for which Bridget would never reveal the recipe. The flaky rolls had been three days in the making. Mushrooms had been stuffed and frozen a week in advance. Crispy crab cakes on a heated platter surrounded a silver bowl of remoulade sauce. New potatoes had been tossed with a hot tomato vinaigrette mere moments before serving, and were kept warm with a chafing dish. Vegetarian selections included a broccoli quiche, tomato tarts with black olives, and a six-layer cheese, red pepper, and pesto torte. The dessert buffet featured a Christmas tree decorated with sugared fruit and surrounded by a colorful wreath of decorated cookies—all lovingly handmade of course—bowls of truffles and dipping chocolate, three different layer cakes, and the *pièce de resistance*—individual custard cups, trimmed in silver paper and filled with peppermint cream.

Bridget presided over the dining room like a proud mother at a virtuoso's concert—thrilled and excited at its success, but always a little nervous as well. When Cici stood beside her she squeezed her arm happily. "Everyone's having a good time, aren't they? Can you believe we pulled this off on top of everything else? Did you try the crab cakes? They're not getting soggy, are they?"

"Oh my God, you outdid yourself. I tried everything and it is all out of this world. They're going to have to cut me out of this dress. Can you believe we pulled this off on top of everything else?"

Lindsay edged up to them through the crowd at the buffet table, a dessert plate in her hand. "Did you taste the tomato tarts?" she inquired, popping a sugarcoated grape into her mouth. "And I don't even like tomatoes! Bridget you are a genius. God, I love our parties, don't you?" She sighed and looked around happily. "Can you believe we pulled this off again this year on top of everything else?"

The "everything else" had, of course, been selling three houses, holding two giant yard sales and an eBay auction, traveling back and forth to Virginia four times, drawing up contracts, sorting and packing and trying to prepare, both physically and emotionally, for a move that would change everything about their lives. In the midst of it all, Christmas had come, and with it, their last chance to say good-bye.

Bridget's house had sold first, and everything she owned was currently packed away in cartons awaiting her temporary move to a furnished apartment on January first. Lindsay's contract called for her to complete the school year, which, with saved vacation and sick time, meant that the earliest she would be able to leave was the last week of March. The buyers of her house had children in school and did not want to make the move until the end of the school year, either, so it would all work out. Cici's buyers would only wait thirty days to take possession, so she would be joining Bridget in the apartment by the middle of January. No one wanted to move to the country in the dead of winter, and even if they had, they wouldn't have gone without Lindsay. The adventure had begun together, and it would continue together.

They had made an offer on Blackwell Farm, and it had been accepted. The closing documents had arrived only that morning, and since their real estate attorney happened to be a guest at the party—as well as a dear friend to all of them—they had decided to have a ceremonial signing tonight, at the last gathering they would ever host in this house.

"The decorations are the best ever, Linds," Bridget said.

Lindsay licked the peppermint cream off of a chocolate truffle. "Couldn't have done it without Cici."

Bridget grinned. "And her house."

Cici slipped an arm around each of their waists. "This is the best Christmas party yet."

Bridget's expression grew wistful. "And we've given a few of them."

They stood together for a moment against the background of festive lights and holiday glitter in a vignette that could have made a Christmas card: Bridget in misty green chiffon shot through with silver threads, Lindsay in sparkly sapphire blue, and Cici in a strapless black taffeta that flared out into a swing skirt accented by a timeless ivory cummerbund. Their hairstyles were curled and upswept, their manicures flawless, their makeup dramatic, their jewelry elegant. And on their faces were perfectly matched smiles of tender remembrance.

Across the room Cici spotted her daughter Lori, the cascade of her coppery hair spilling over the spaghetti-strapped shimmering metallic slip dress that barely covered her slender hips and perky A-cup breasts. She was standing in a group of people laughing and talking, but whether she was conversing with them or the cell phone earpiece cleverly hidden by her hair no one could tell—not even the people who were talking to her. Cici couldn't help smiling even though she had spent most of Lori's two weeks home alternately wanting to strangle her and trying to find her. So many Christmas trees in this house. So many Barbies and skateboards and iPods and piles of shiny wrapping paper scattered across the floor.

Lori had conceded to come home for Christmas, ostensibly to say good-bye to the house in which she had grown up, but mostly because Cici had threatened to donate to Goodwill any items from Lori's room that were not claimed by December 31. That afternoon she had come upon one of the boxes Lori had packed, and the battered stuffed bunny lying atop one of them—battle-weary veteran of an entire childhood of tea parties, sleepovers, temper tantrums, and broken hearts—had made her eyes flood with tears. She was leaving more than a house behind. She was leaving a lifetime. And so were they all.

As though reading her thoughts, Lindsay said softly, "Good times."

"So many of them," agreed Bridget, and her voice sounded a little shaky.

Cici was surprised to find her own throat thick with emotion as she said, determinedly, "But better ones ahead."

The women released a collective breath, and Cici saw in their eyes an expression that had become familiar over the past months, that she had seen over and over again in the mirror—a kind of sparkling excitement and dazed amazement that was usually reserved for people half their ages; people who had lives filled with adventure and accomplishment and discovery ahead of them and who couldn't believe their good fortune. They were doing this. It was crazy, it was unreal, it was outrageous, and they were actually doing it.

"Girls, you are the *best*! And I hate you every one, I really do." Their friend Paul, whose syndicated "In Style" column was a must-read in metro newspapers up and down the Eastern Seaboard, rested one arm on Bridget's shoulder and another on Lindsay's as, careful not to spill his glass of chardonnay, he air-kissed them each down the line. "You're going to make a bleepin' fortune on that broken-down pile of bricks and all you have to do is move to the middle of East Nowhere, abandon every shred of modern civilization, and live like savages for a couple of years. I'm so jealous I could slap you. Would that I had your courage! And will you tell me what we're supposed to do for Christmas from now on? Bridget, the crab cakes were divine, and the beef Wellington simply melted. Melted, I tell you, right on the tongue. How can we live without you?"

Bridget laughed. "Well, you can't, which is why you're going to have to come visit."

"Oh promise you'll invite me! I'm sure I must have *something* to wear to the country."

"And speaking of which . . ." Paul's partner Derrick slipped up behind Lindsay and kissed her on the back of the neck. "That dress is you, my dear. You've never looked more lovely. It breaks my heart to think of your talent and extraordinary beauty languishing in that misbegotten cultural desert."

"And what about my beauty?" demanded Cici.

"And my talent?" insisted Bridget.

Lindsay sighed elaborately and caressed his cheek. "Why are all the good men gay?"

"Not all of them," corrected Derrick, smiling across her shoulder at Paul. "Just most of them."

"What I want to know," insisted their neighbor Rosalee, joining them, "is what in the world you think you're going to do with yourselves out there in the wilderness? Cici, this is the best party ever, and it just makes me want to weep when I think it's the last one *ever.* How can you do this to us? Oh, give me a hug!"

"The house I can understand." Jena, a broker at Cici's firm, joined the conversation and the embraces. "Prices are skyrocketing all along the I-81 corridor and getting the place at below appraisal was just brilliant. But three women living together? Are you crazy? You'll be pulling each other's hair out and chasing each other around the kitchen with serving spoons before a month is out."

Derrick said, "I don't know. Paul and I have lived together for ten years and we never chased each other with serving spoons."

"Well, there was that one time," corrected Paul, leaning back into his embrace.

Lindsay laughed. "Believe me, that house is so big we won't even be able to find each other half the time. Did you see the pictures?"

And so it went, the compliments and the good-byes, the disbelief and the regrets and the eager urging for details. Promises to keep in touch. Curious inquiries about the new families moving into the neighborhood. Sentences that began with "Do you remember when..." It was not, of course, as though they would never see each other again. Each of their friends demanded an invitation as soon as the guest rooms were ready and groaned with envy as they described the house, the porch, the meadow, the view. It wasn't an ending, they all tearfully insisted, it was a beginning.

Still, it was hard to say good-bye.

Cici slipped away from the crowd and approached Lori, who was happily chatting to a display of Christmas cards that framed a doorway. Snatching the earpiece from her daughter's ear, she said, "She'll call you back" and dropped the device into the capacious pocket of her skirt. Lori whirled. "Moth–er!" This was followed by an eye roll. "Very mature."

Cici kissed her bangs and dropped an arm around her shoulder. "Merry Christmas to you, too, darling. Are you having a good time?"

Again a slight upward shift of the eyes. Cici wished she could remember when young girls outgrew that mannerism. Age twenty-one? Could she hold out until then? "The crowd's a little old for me, Mom."

"You've known most of them all your life. It won't hurt you to be nice for one evening."

"True." She shrugged. "It's just hard being nice every single minute." Then she grinned. "Tell Aunt Bridget the quiche was awesome. Of course it would have tasted even better with a margarita."

"Don't they teach math at UCLA?"

"Of course."

"Then maybe you can help me figure out exactly how many months it is you have left until you are of legal drinking age?"

"Mom, you are *so* quaint."

"Thank you, sweetheart. Long one of my goals." She tidied the strands of shiny copper hair her initial embrace had disarranged, and her smile softened as she did so. "You look pretty tonight."

"So do you," Lori replied generously.

"So. How does it feel, saying good-bye to the house you grew up in? Are you going to miss the old place?"

Lori thought about this. "A little, I guess. But everything changes. And it's not as though I hadn't already moved out."

Cici nodded sagely. "Very sensible. So you're not mad at me for selling?"

Lori gave a dismissive wave of her hand. "Of course not. I know all about that midlife crisis stuff. It's just like Dad driving around in a Porsche and dating models half his age."

"Nothing," replied Cici evenly, "is like your dad dating models half his age."

She grinned. "It's okay, Mom, even he knows it's stupid. But it's like my social psych prof says, it's a life passage. And at least you didn't marry the pool boy or run off with your Italian lover."

Cici lifted an eyebrow. "I didn't know those were options."

"It has to do with reinventing yourself. Men do it because they're afraid of losing their virility. Women do it because, once their children leave the nest, they don't know what their role in life is anymore. Some women go to spin class. You bought a hundred-year-old farmhouse in the middle of nowhere. It's no surprise to me."

"Well, as glad as I am to know you're learning something in social psych class, let's go back to that Italian lover I could have run off with."

Lori laughed. "See? No surprise. You're a nut, always have been."

Cici hugged her. "I love you, baby."

"Love you back."

"I wish you were coming with me."

Lori looked very seriously into her mother's eyes. "Mom," she said, "I have a life."

Cici didn't know whether to laugh or to cry, and she struggled hard to keep from doing either. "But you're coming this summer, right? Aren't you dying to see the place?"

"Well, maybe not *dying*... it sounds like an awful lot of hard work to me. But I'll definitely try to make it out for my birthday. There's an airport there right?"

Cici realized she had no idea where the nearest airport was in relation to her new home. Had she ever in her life lived further than an hour away from an airport? "Oh sure," she replied airily. "Paved roads and everything. And it's all horse country out there. Maybe we could talk about keeping a horse for you to use when you visit."

This time Lori's expression was a little sad. "Mom," she said gently, "I'm really too old to bribe with a pony."

Cici opened her mouth to reply, snapped it shut again, and instead hugged her daughter fiercely. "I miss my baby," she whispered, squeezing her eyes tightly shut.

"I miss you, too, Mom." Lori leaned back and smiled through what Cici was surprised to see was a shimmer of tears. "But we're both big girls now, huh?"

Cici sniffed and carefully blotted her mascaraed lashes with the tips of her index fingers. She tried to mimic Lori's brave smile. "You bet."

Lori gave her mother's fingers a reassuring squeeze, then held out her hand, palm up. "Cell phone," she said.

Cici hesitated, then grinned, dug into her pocket, and plopped the device into Lori's open hand. "Let's get back to the party," she said.

❧

Holding a drink, Kevin slipped his other hand around Bridget's arm and nodded an apologetic smile to the group surrounding her. "Mom, okay if we borrow you for a minute?"

Bridget excused herself and let Kevin lead the way to Cici's downstairs guest room, which tonight was serving as a coat closet. Kate, who had just returned from putting the girls to bed next door, had cleared off three chairs. She was sitting in one of them, her hands folded, her knees crossed, her expression reserved. Kevin quietly closed the door behind them. "Have a seat, Mom," he said.

Bridget glanced around, smiling a little. "Why does this feel like an intervention?"

"Nothing like that," Katie insisted quickly, patting the chair next to her. "We just wanted to talk to you for a minute. Sit down, Mom."

Curious, Bridget did. Kevin straightened the bottom of his suit jacket before sitting on it, straight and stiff, just like he had been taught in law school—or wherever it was that he had picked up all those rigid, pompous mannerisms that always reminded Bridget of some stuffy British barrister on public television. Pompous, at his age. And what about Katie? The single mother of twin preschoolers, working sixty hours a week at a Chicago accounting firm, her lipstick was perpetually chewed, her face puffy, her eyes always strained. She was barely thirty. She should be having the time of her life. Bridget's heart ached for her children, but in the end, what could she do?

As though in answer to her unspoken thought, Kevin said abruptly, "Mom, Kate and I have been talking it over, and we think you should go live with her."

Bridget's eyebrows shot up. "With Kate? In Chicago? Why in the world would I want to do that?"

Her children exchanged a glance in which Kevin was apparently elected spokesperson. The way he squared his shoulders and jutted out his chin reminded Bridget so much of his father that she felt a stab of longing in her chest. He said, "Mom, we know losing Dad has been hard on you. You've never been alone before. And God knows, he didn't exactly leave you a wealthy woman . . ."

Bridget said sharply, "Your father was a college professor. He did the best he could."

"What we're trying to say," Kate intervened quickly, "is that we know this whole plan of moving to the country is just your way of trying to build a new life for yourself. But it's just not necessary, Mom. I mean, moving in with two strangers—"

"Sinking all your assets into a broken-down old house and leaving the only life you've ever known—"

"It's not as though you don't have a family, or anyplace to go. You don't have to do this," Kate repeated. She took a breath, tightened her fingers in her lap, and declared, "We'll take care of you."

Bridget's first reaction was astonishment. What did she mean, they would take care of her? What was she, a hundred and eight years old? And her second reaction was a flare of anger at the grim determination on Katie's face as she made the announcement, as though having considered all the options and weighed all the evidence they had come to the reluctant conclusion that yes, they had no choice but to step up and take care of their mother, no matter how inconvenient, how great the sacrifice.

She wanted to say, *Damn right you'll take care of me, Missy. When I'm old and sick and too tired to feed myself and too weak to dress myself, you'll do it for me just like I did for you. You'll tie my shoes and wipe the drool off my chin and change my diapers just like I did for you about a hundred and thirty-seven times a day for the best years of my life. You'll put a roof over my head when I can't afford to do it myself and you'll put groceries in my cupboard when my only other choice is to eat cat food and you'll take me where I want to go when the state takes my driver's license just like I did for you for the first twenty years of your lives and by God you'll do it with a smile on your face.*

But then she saw the strain behind the bravado in Kate's eyes, and the fear disguised as determination in Kevin's, and her heart softened. They had lost their father at the same time she had lost her husband. They, too, were trying to find their place in a world without him. And the sudden realization that the one person they had always depended upon—their mother—might need them to take care of her was more than an inconvenience. It was terrifying.

She said, "Thank both of you for worrying about me. But it's not necessary, really. I'm fine."

Kevin said, "It's not Cici and Lindsay, you know that. We love them like family, always have. I've looked at the contracts and they seem fine, but I don't think you realize what a potentially devastating risk this is. I know they're your best friends, but owning property together—"

"You could lose everything," Katie said, "including their friendship. It's just crazy, Mom. Come to Chicago. There's a three-bedroom apartment becoming available in a few months in my building, and with your help we could afford to move. Meanwhile, there's room for a rollaway in the girls' room. It would mean so much to me, Mom, not only financially—I mean, you know how we've struggled since the divorce—but to have you there to help out, now and then, you know, and on weekends, maybe I could finally have a life again. And it would be great for the girls to have their grandma with them. It would be great for everyone."

"You haven't signed the closing documents yet," Kevin reminded her. "It's not too late. So let's do it, okay? Let's tell Cici and Lindsay you've changed your mind and you're going to Chicago instead."

Bridget spent a long moment looking from one to the other of her children, so filled with conflicting emotions that she didn't know where to start. Were these really her children? How had they grown into these strangers whose thought processes Bridget could barely begin to fathom? Kate had not bothered to ask her mother's advice when she decided to marry a man she'd dated less than three months, nor when she decided they "had nothing in common" on her twin girls' second birthday. But now she wanted her mother to fix everything. And Kevin, whose perpetual bachelorhood was merely an excuse for the kind of selfishness that included scuba diving in Belize and a designer apartment with a view of the Washington Monument, thought he could settle the problem of his inconvenient mother with the same brusque efficiency with which he settled a court case. Who *were* these people?

The answer of course was simple: They were her children, whom she loved with all her heart.

She said gently, "Katie, I love my grandbabies, but I told you when they were born that I did not want to raise them. And I'm sorry you can't afford the three-bedroom apartment. Maybe prices would be cheaper if you moved out of the city."

Before Kate could draw a breath to reply, Bridget turned to Kevin. "Kevin, honey, you are a dear, dear boy. But you don't have to be the daddy now. You don't have to take care of things, and you don't have to fix things, and for heaven sakes you do not have to be responsible for me. All you have to do, both of you, is to live your best lives, right now, just like I am. Someday I am going to need you, and when that day comes I want you"—she pointed a finger at Kate in mock sternness—"to have a house in the suburbs with a mother-in-law suite, a maid, and a pool. And you"—she turned the finger on Kevin—"to have a wife who loves you as much as I loved your father.

"In the meantime..." She smiled. "You're right, I do have a family. And it includes Cici and Lindsay. We're about to go off on a marvelous adventure together, and we've earned it. Some day, if you work hard and live right, the two of you might get a chance to have as much fun as I'm having. So be happy for us, okay?"

She stood, then, and extended her hands to her two rather dazed-looking offspring. "Now, unless you're planning on serving me with papers for a competency hearing..." She paused only slightly to toss Kevin a look of mild inquiry. He quickly stood up and grasped her hand. "Let's get back to the party, shall we?"

❧

His name was Peter Shepler, and he insisted everyone call him Shep. He was over six feet tall, slim and muscular with iron gray hair and a nose like Richard Gere's. There had been a time in Lindsay's life when the mere sight of him could stop her breath.

Now all she could notice was that he had had a lot of work done on his teeth. His smile was about three shades whiter than the brilliant white satin she had used for the buffet. She thought about complimenting him on it, but wasn't sure that would be polite.

He looked down at her now with that sad, tender, sweet expression in his eyes that once upon a time had melted her heart like chocolate in the sun. "So," he said, "after all these years, it's good-bye."

Lindsay actually remembered a very distinct good-bye some five years ago, when he had married another woman. But she merely smiled and agreed. "It looks like it."

His gaze swept her face, her hair, and barely skimmed the glitter-dusted curve of her cleavage before returning to her eyes, the tenderness in his smile never wavering. *Subtle, Shep. Very nice.*

"You're finally getting a chance to paint full-time, just like you always wanted," he said. "You're going to have gallery owners beating a path to your door."

She smiled. "I don't know about that. But there aren't too many times in life you get a chance to go after a dream. This is mine."

He nodded. "I'm happy for you."

"Thank you, Shep."

"I remember that weekend we spent in Charleston. You did some fabulous paintings there."

Back in those days, he had been the principal at the school where she taught. She had been madly in love with him for almost a year before he noticed. It had taken another three years for him to finally convince her he would never make a commitment. A month after she had accepted a teaching position in another school, he announced he was engaged to be married—to someone else, of course.

She said, "Actually, I only took photos. I never travel with painting supplies."

He looked surprised. "Are you sure? I distinctly remember you painting the bridge at Magnolia Gardens."

"That's a pretty popular scene to paint. But I never got around to it."

"Not even a sketch?"

"Not even."

"Funny how the mind can play tricks."

"I guess."

"Anyway, you're going to be great. And I'm envious."

She said, "I'm a lucky woman," and meant it.

She sipped her wine. He said, after a time, "I love the Shenandoah Valley."

"Me, too."

"Maybe I'll drive up some weekend, after you get settled." Still the same bedroom eyes.

Damn him to hell.

"We'd love to have you," she said. "How is Estelle, anyway?"

He flinched. "Still in rehab."

"Oh." She did not look away. "I'm sorry to hear that."

He gave her an apologetic smile. It was another one of his tricks, that little quirk of the lips, half begging, half flirting, that used to work every time. "It just seems so strange, knowing you won't be here. That I'll never bump into you on the street again, or see you at a soccer game or band recital. That . . . you just won't be here."

That almost got her. Suddenly she found herself thinking about all the things that simply wouldn't be there anymore. The familiar desk in room 312, the giant hemlock in her backyard, the eighty-year-old clerk at the Shop-and-Go who always gave her the wrong change. The Cineplex, the creaky board in her bedroom closet, the teller at the bank who called her "Miss Wright" because three of her four children had been in Lindsay's class, cranky old Mr. Daughtery who lived on the corner and refused to clip his overgrown hedges despite the fact that they were a traffic hazard . . . she had lived here for twenty-three years. What was she thinking?

Shep reached out, lightly touched her arm. "We were good together, Linds," he said softly. "Whatever happened to us?"

She looked at his fingers on her bare arm for a long time, and slowly the panic that had begun to gather in her chest dissipated. She looked at his face. She smiled. "You got married," she said, "and I got smart."

She glanced over his shoulder, and saw Cici and Bridget standing across the room. They raised their glasses to her, and she returned the salute. "It was great talking to you, Shep. Now," she said, turning her smile back to him, "if you'll excuse me, I have to get back to the party."

❧

Delores and her secretary, Sheryl, were waiting for them in the media/game room downstairs, where the baize card table had been claimed as a temporary office. "Let's get this show on the road," she declared as they came in, "so I can get back to what I do best—drinking."

Years of chain-smoking had given the attorney's voice a gravelly tenor, and she had a habit of chewing on the tip of her pen when cigarettes were not an option. Her spiked silver hair and crocodile-tanned skin spoke of a woman who wasn't afraid of living, and her shrewd black eyes didn't miss a trick. She had handled Cici's divorce, Jim's estate, and Lindsay's contract dispute when she left her former school system early due to the aforementioned incident with Shep. She was a woman who knew how to get things done.

"So." She peered at them across the spread of papers as they sat down. "Last chance to back out. You're really going to do this thing?"

Almost as one, they burst into laughter. "Are you kidding me?" "Silly question!" and "Let's get on with it, Delores! We're missing the party!"

"All righty, then. The closing documents are pretty straightforward. I'll go over them as you sign, and Sheryl here will witness. I'll fax them to Virginia first thing in the morning and we're done. Here's your Agreement to Enter into Joint Venture." She distributed three copies of the document between them. "It covers everything from how much each of you is required to contribute to household expenses each month to how many pets you're allowed to have."

"I still think this is unnecessary," Cici said.

"How many pets are we allowed to have?" Bridget asked.

"As many as we want," Lindsay said.

Delores answered Cici. "It's like a prenup. Everyone thinks they're unnecessary until they don't have one."

Cici murmured, "Well, I guess I can relate to that."

Delores said, "You've been lucky. Everything has gone smoothly up to this point. But what if things start going bad? How much more are you willing to invest? Where are you going to draw the financial line?"

Lindsay said, "What line? It's drawn. All I've got left is my retirement fund, and I'm not touching that."

Bridget spread her hands. "My financial life is an open book. All I have to live on until Social Security kicks in is what's left of Jim's life insurance, unless we're talking about selling my jewelry." Absently she fingered the emerald and diamond ring which had been Jim's last anniversary gift to her. It was extravagant, but he hadn't been able to afford an engagement ring when they had gotten married, and this had been his way of making up for its absence.

Cici said, "And I'm not borrowing money from my ex. I don't care if he is richer than God. So there you go. We've invested all we can afford to."

"Exactly." Delores tapped a clause on the document with a sharp red fingernail. "All written down plain as day in paragraph 12-A." She flipped over a page. "Heirs and assigns, fair use of property... okay look at paragraph 15, term of contract. We talked about your agreement to give this situation a year before reassessing. We still good with that?"

She glanced around the table, and received three nods. "Okay, so at the end of a year, any one of you can offer your share of the property to any of the other two, or jointly agree to offer the entire property for sale to a third party at a mutually agreed upon price, or renegotiate this agreement or any part thereof in any way you choose. Understand?"

"It all sounds so lawlerly," complained Lindsay.

"Can't help it, dearie. I'm a lawyer. Now I need a date of termination. Shall we say January first?"

They consulted each other with a questioning glance, and shrugged. "Sure." "Suits me." "Sounds fine."

Delores scrawled the date on her copy of the contract, while Sheryl went around the table and did the same to everyone else's. "Okay, ladies, get out your pens. Let the signing begin."

Six minutes and a flurry of signatures later, they all sat back and looked at each other in a kind of stunned astonishment. Just like that, it was over.

And it had just begun.

Spring

Starting Over

5

Moving On

Nine months to the day from the evening they had spent at the Holiday Inn with two laptops, a bottle of wine, and a legal pad between them, making their plans, a caravan of shiny SUVs pulled into the rutted and overgrown gravel drive that led to Blackwell Farm. They were loaded down with suitcases, pots and pans, nonperishable food items, art supplies, tools, pillows, linens, photo albums, electronics, toiletries, and all of those essential items that one snatches first from a house fire and refuses to trust to the movers. They had been driving for five hours, but the journey had taken most of a lifetime.

Lindsay, leading the procession, stopped fifty feet into the drive, sprang out of the car, and opened the back hatch. Bridget pulled in behind her, followed by Cici. From the top of a pile of boxes that was almost over her head, Lindsay slid a large, colorfully painted sign out of the van. Bridget came up quickly to help her. Between them, they carried the sign back to the end of the drive, followed by Cici with the hammer.

"Left," Bridget advised, standing back as they positioned the sign in the midst of the weeds where the drive met the road. "No, left and back about three feet. It's too close to the driveway."

"There's a big rock."

"Leave room for the flower bed."

"How about here?"

"It's crooked. Go back a little."

"There's a ditch there!"

"Wait, I can do this . . ."

Straddling the ditch, Lindsay held the sign while Cici hammered it into the ground. "We'll set it in cement later," Cici said, and they joined Bridget to admire their work.

Cut in a sweeping scroll design, the sign was painted pastel yellow and decorated with three bright ladybugs. In flowing script, the lettering said, Welcome to Ladybug Farm.

The three shared a grin and a high five, and hurried back to their cars.

They had seen the house in November for a final walk-through before finalizing their offer, but had not been back since. They pulled their three cars in a semicircle in front of the house and got out one by one. They stood there for a moment in silence, taking it all in.

The good news was that the surroundings were even more beautiful in the spring than they had been in August when they had first toured the house. Baby grass the color of a chiffon ball gown swept in graceful arcs and curves around the house, and the red clover and yellow dandelions that dotted it were like colorful embroidery. The pear trees in the orchard were covered in snowy blossoms, and the apple trees were just beginning to show their pink flowers. The giant tulip poplars that surrounded the house were alight in brilliant green, and the big white flowers for which the trees were named were just beginning to unfurl. There was a crazy quilt of purple Siberian iris and bright yellow daffodils spilling across the path that led to the dairy, and the dairy itself was draped in purple clusters of fragrant wisteria. Wild dogwoods dotted the face of the distant mountains, which faded from dark to light in shades of blue and green.

The bad news was that winter had not been kind, either to the house or the yard. A hickory branch, big enough to be a small tree, had fallen on the barn, taking out part of the roof and one of the loft doors. A pile of sodden leaves and a network of thorny vines had blown onto the front porch, and mossy green mildew decorated the railings. The paint on the steps had flaked up in huge hunks, and there was more wood showing on the white columns than paint. The multigabled roof of the house had an odd, patchy appearance, and it took them a moment to realize that that was because quite a few of the clay tiles were missing. Rows of naked windows gazed down upon them like so many empty, forlorn eyes. A panel of torn screen on the little side porch flapped forlornly in the breeze.

Dead vines clung to the brick chimney and stretched their parasitic fingers toward the upstairs windows. As Lindsay's dismayed eyes followed the path of the vines upward, she was struck by something odd. "Look at that," she said, pointing.

"Look at what?"

"That top window there. The curtain is closed."

"So it is."

"But it wasn't a minute ago."

Bridget and Cici looked at her. "Are you sure?"

"Positive. When we first got out of the car all the windows were open. Now that one has a curtain over it. What is that, anyway, the attic? Someone must be in there."

Cici thought about that for a minute, then shrugged. "Probably just a ghost."

"Maybe it was Maggie," Bridget suggested. The real estate agent had promised to meet them there to do a walk-through of the house and review some of the general maintenance and operating procedures.

"Well," Cici said, rubbing her hands together with forced enthusiasm, "the movers are going to be here at two, and we've got a lot of work to do."

"Kitchen first, bathrooms second, bedrooms last," Bridget said. "Who's got the broom?"

"Bathrooms first," Lindsay said, "I've really got to pee."

"Then you'd better hope that was Maggie you saw in the window," Cici said, "because the water isn't turned on."

As they mounted the steps of the house they saw a wicker basket with a bow sitting in front of the door. Bridget oohed and ahhed as she unpacked the basket—a bottle of wine, a geranium plant, a homemade loaf of banana bread wrapped in waxed paper, and a card. Cici read the card out loud.

"Welcome home, ladies! I'm sorry I couldn't be here but my daughter went into labor this morning. I'm going to be a grandmother! I will check in with you tomorrow. If you have any problems, you can call my brother-in-law, Farley, at 7834. Good luck! Maggie."

Lindsay raised an eyebrow "A four-digit phone number?"

"This is the country," Bridget said. "All the exchanges are the same."

"Do we know what the exchange is?"

They looked at each other blankly.

"Well. Okay." Cici tucked the card back into the envelope. "How hard can it be to turn on the water? It's a gravity water system, that much she told us, so there's no pump to worry about. The shutoff valve has got to be at the cistern."

Again the blank looks.

"It's a big concrete thing set into the ground," Cici explained impatiently. "Maggie said it was on the hill behind the barn, remember? Come on, let's find it."

Three-quarters of a sweaty, briar-scratched, bug-bitten hour later, Bridget tripped over an iron handle sticking out of the kudzu-covered ground. The handle was attached to a round concrete lid, and with all three of them putting their weight behind the effort they were able to shift the lid off of a dark, cold hole that smelled like a wet basement. "Ladies," said Cici, panting as she sat back on her heels, "I give you the cistern."

While Lindsay and Bridget scrunched up their faces and averted their eyes in horror, Cici thrust her hand into the black hole and fumbled around for the shutoff valve. "Eureka!" she cried, and in a moment they heard the whoosh and gurgle of water rushing into pipes.

"We have water!" exclaimed Lindsay.

"We did it!" cried Bridget. "I feel like a regular pioneer!"

"Well, it might not be as showy as making fire," admitted Cici, unable to restrain her pride in the accomplishment, "but damn good for a bunch of amateurs. Come on, let's get the lid back on."

They wrestled the cistern cover back into place and hurried back to the house. With a flourish, Cici produced the big skeleton key and opened the door.

"Oh . . . my," Bridget said, and they moved slowly inside.

Somehow they had forgotten how neglected the interior was. The windows were foggy with dust, the floors dull. There was a huge spiderweb cloaking the entire bay window, and the winter winds had blown a fine coat of gritty ash from the fireplace over everything. Hundreds of thousands of ladybug shells littered the floors and were piled in the corners of the windowsills.

Lindsay blew out a breath. "Well, okay," she said. "We knew what we were getting into."

"Right." Bridget clapped her hands together decisively. "I've got buckets, mops, and three gallons of bleach in the car."

"I've got brooms, dustcloths, and a vacuum cleaner," Cici said, turning toward the door.

"I've still got to pee," Lindsay said.

"Around the corner on the right."

Cici and Bridget started for their cars, but before they even reached the front porch Lindsay called, "Hey! There's no electricity!"

Cici tried the switch by the door. "The power company was supposed to be out yesterday."

"They're probably just running behind," Bridget said. "They've had the work order for weeks. They'll be out today."

"Uh, girls . . ." Lindsay came around the corner, looking grim. "No water, either."

"Are you sure?" Cici went to the kitchen, which was even darker and dustier than the front room, and turned on the faucet. Not so much as a gurgle. She turned it off again, looking thoughtful.

Then her face cleared. "Wait! I'll bet there's a whole-house shutoff valve in the cellar. Of course there is. Let me get a flashlight from the car."

Bridget stood guard at the cellar door as Cici crept down the stairs, her flashlight beam bouncing in the darkness. "Be careful!" Bridget called. There were some bumps, a small crash, and Cici swore. "Are you okay?"

"Wait. I think I found it."

Bridget sprang back from the door as the whole house was filled with a terrible rattling, thumping noise. Lindsay came around the corner, her hands over her ears. "Is it supposed to do that?" She had to shout to be heard.

"It's just air in the pipes," Cici said, brushing cobwebs out of her hair as she came up from the cellar. Already the noise was beginning to subside. "But that should do it. Let's check the faucet."

They pushed through the swinging door of the kitchen to the sound of an ominous rumbling that seemed to be coming from the sink. Without another warning, the faucet suddenly exploded into the air. Metal handles, screws, and fixtures flew in four different directions. Bridget screamed. All of them ducked. A geyser of water erupted into the air, splashing off the ceiling and running like a river across the brick floor.

Their horrified paralysis lasted only a moment, and then they rushed forward, slipping and splashing, to the sink. Bridget and Lindsay flung themselves on the geyser, trying to stem the flow with their hands. Cici dropped to the floor and flung open the cabinet beneath the sink, pulling herself underneath. She found the cutoff valve, wrenched it with both hands, and slowly, inevitably the fountain dropped from the ceiling, to a three foot pulse, to a gurgle, and then a drip. Cici crawled out from under the sink, and pulled herself to her feet.

The three women looked at each other, gasping. Their hair hung in dripping strands around their faces, their shirts were soaked through, and they were standing in water that covered their shoes. When she was able, Cici said, "Pressure valve."

Lindsay said, "I think I wet my pants."

Bridget just looked at her, a shell-shocked expression on her face. "How can you tell?"

And they went in search of towels.

Fortunately, the kitchen explosion seemed to have relieved the pressure in the pipes, and water was flowing freely to all other outlets—including the water heater, where it immediately flowed out again, creating another lake in the laundry room to match the one in the kitchen. Cici turned off the valve to the water heater and added "water heater" to the grocery list that Bridget had tacked up on the pantry wall. They spent the next four hours mopping, scrubbing, disinfecting, and polishing. They swept up twelve dustpans filled with ladybugs and two trash bags of leaves. They washed and wiped and polished the windows until they glittered with sparks of sunlight. Two o'clock came and went, but the movers did not. They scrubbed toilets and bleached grout. They ate banana bread with peanut butter from Lindsay's stash. They wore out two mops on the floors, and poured out twelve buckets of muddy water. No power company truck pulled into the driveway.

At six o'clock, Cici trudged out onto the porch with Maggie's gift bottle of wine in one hand and a cordless drill in the other. She sank to the top step, shoulders slumped, the wine bottle dangling between her knees, too tired to move another inch. After a time, she became aware that Lindsay had come out to sit beside her.

Lindsay's ponytail was straggling, her cheek was smudged, her shirt torn. There was a Band-Aid on her index finger, and she was rubbing a blister on her thumb. She said, "Bridget found rat poop behind the stove."

With a deliberate effort, Cici said, "I . . . don't . . . care." She lifted her arm and brushed away a ladybug that was crawling on Lindsay's collar, and let it drop heavily again.

A silence, while they both seemed to gather their strength for further conversation. Lindsay said, "I guess we'll be going back to the Holiday Inn tonight."

"I guess."

The mere thought of getting back into a car, any car, and driving an hour for a room seemed almost to defeat them both.

In a moment, Lindsay nodded toward the drill that Cici held motionless in one hand. "What's that for?" Her voice was dull and flat, as though exhaustion had made the words themselves heavy.

With an effort, Cici roused herself. "No corkscrew."

Cici placed the bottle of wine on the step between her feet, tore off the foil cover, and inserted the drill bit into the cork. Lindsay watched without comment as she drilled halfway through the cork, braced the bottle between her feet, pulled upward with both hands on the drill, and popped the cork free.

"You're a regular little MacGyver, aren't you?"

Cici looked at the bottle for a moment. "No glasses," she said.

Lindsay held out her hand. Cici passed the wine bottle to her. Lindsay brought the bottle to her lips, drank, and passed it back to Cici. Cici did the same.

"I don't understand," Lindsay said after a time, "how the moving company can lose an entire thirty-five foot van complete with the personal possessions of three separate households."

Cici seemed to ruminate on that for a while. "It's not exactly lost," she said. "It's just not here."

Lindsay retrieved the bottle. "I finally got hold of the power company on my cell," she said. "They have no record of our work order. They said it would be a couple of weeks."

Cici drank again, and returned the bottle.

"Also called the phone company. Guess what we don't have?"

"Phone service?"

"Broadband Internet. Apparently it's not available in this area. Neither is cable television."

"Jesus. Where are we? The Yukon?"

"Nah. In The Yukon you can get satellite Internet."

They drank in silence for a while. The birds fluttered, chirped, and scolded raucously from the branches of a poplar tree that hung over the porch, and they could hear Bridget still bustling around inside through the open door. But otherwise the quietness was so intense it was almost a texture—as light as silk, as soft as velvet. After a while they felt it seep into them—the smell of grass, the rolling valley, the absolute stillness.

"If silence was a color," Lindsay said softly, "it would be green."

Cici leaned in and bumped her friend affectionately with one shoulder. "Stop talking like a dumb artist."

Lindsay blew out a slow, tired breath. "Did we make a mistake?"

Cici didn't answer for a time. She looked at the afternoon sun glinting on the dogwoods on a hillside, at the brilliant blanket of green that covered the distant mountains. And she looked at the tangle of overgrown vines in the orchard, the rotting tree limbs that littered the yard, the tumbled-down barn. She said, "I don't think we can fix this place up in a year."

"I don't think we can even clean it in a year."

"On the other hand..." Cici retrieved the bottle, and drank. "With no cable and no Internet, what else have we got to do?"

Lindsay sat up a little straighter, looking around. "Do you smell that?"

Cici tested the air, her brow wrinkling. "It smells like—"

"Dinner," called Bridget cheerfully. She pushed through the screen door carrying a big footed tray. "Canned tomato soup with fresh herbs, wild dandelion salad with strawberry vinaigrette, pan bread, and strawberry cobbler!"

The other two hurried to help her with the tray. "What in the world?"

"But how—"

"The stove is gas," she replied, beaming. "The herb garden is thriving, and that sunny hill behind the house is just covered in strawberries. I picked the ones that were ripe, and there was a enough for the salad *and* a cobbler!"

"Where did you get this?" Lindsay cupped the half-unfurled rosebud that was displayed in a small silver vase in the center of the tray, leaning close to inhale. "Oh, my God, smell that! It's an Old English rose!"

"They're blooming in the garden," Bridget said matter-of-factly, "but you'd better get out there and give them some attention pretty soon or all you'll have left is a weed garden."

The exhaustion that had weighted Cici's arms and stiffened Lindsay's legs only a moment ago evaporated into the spring air as they spread a quilt on the porch and set out the picnic. They sat cross-legged on the floor around the quilt table while Bridget dished out soup and salad into Haviland china and poured wine into star-cut crystal stemmed glasses.

"Oh, Bridge, your mother's Baccarat," Lindsay said reverently, holding hers with both hands. "You don't even use these at Christmas."

"First of all, this is a much more important occasion than Christmas," she said, settling down beside them. "And secondly, that's going to change. No more saving the good stuff for a special occasion. From now on, every day is a special occasion." She raised her glass. "To us."

Cici smiled, and so did Lindsay, and the tiredness ebbed out of their faces as they touched glasses to Bridget's. "To us."

There was a whirring sound, a blur of wings streaking between them, and a small yellow bird swooped toward the golden-crusted pan bread, snatched up a crumb, and flew away again. They didn't even have time to register astonishment before it was over. Bridget jumped to her feet and ran toward the direction in which the bird had flown. She gasped.

"Oh, my goodness, girls, you have got to see this."

Cici and Lindsay joined Bridget at the corner of the porch, where she was gazing in awe at the poplar tree. On every branch and limb, twittering and hopping from leaf to leaf, were tiny yellow goldfinches. Hundreds of them. Perhaps a thousand.

"It's like living in an aviary," Lindsay said wonderingly.

"They look just like the ones people pay hundreds of dollars for and keep in cages," said Cici.

Bridget laughed and spread her arms. "Name me three other women in this country who get to have dinner with a thousand goldfinches tonight!"

"In this hemisphere," said Lindsay, still in awe.

"In the world," agreed Cici.

They grinned at each other again, and clinked their glasses. And they did not go back to the Holiday Inn that night.

6

In Which Help Arrives

Lindsay opened her eyes the next morning slowly, groggily. The three of them had made the best of a bad situation by constructing a pallet on the floor out of their combined bedding and huddling together for warmth, but the night had not passed easily. Her back felt as though it would break in two, Cici's elbow was digging into her ribs, and a big man wearing a ginger-colored beard and camouflage gear was staring down at her, holding a soda can. She blinked. He was still there.

Lindsay punched Cici in the arm. Cici muttered something and punched her back. Lindsay hissed, "Cici! Bridget! There's a man in our living room!"

Cici groaned, "Don't listen to her, Bridge. She sees ghosts."

Bridget opened her eyes, gasped, and sat up straight, hugging her pillow to her chest. "Cici!"

Cici turned over, rubbed one hand over her face, and opened her eyes. She looked the ginger-bearded man in the eye, and didn't move another muscle.

The man spat a stream of tobacco juice into the soda can, and said, "It's a boy."

Bridget said hoarsely, "Wh–what?"

"Maggie said to tell you it's a boy."

A beat of silence, and then Cici said, still not moving, "You must be . . . Farley."

The huge man gave a curt nod of his head, and spat again into the can. "Said I was to come see what you needed."

Slowly, carefully, Cici stood up, bringing the blanket with her. She cleared her throat, ignoring Lindsay's efforts to tug the blanket away as she wrapped it around her shoulders. "Do you mean besides a phone, electricity, hot water, and our furniture?"

The man spat again. "Ain't got no phone on me." He walked over to the light switch beside the front door, and toggled it upward. The brass-filigreed drop pendant in the foyer immediately sprang to life, as did the chandelier on the stairway.

The three women stared at each other. "But—the power was off. We tried every room in the house."

Said Farley, "Where's the water heater?"

Within the hour, Farley had replaced the pressure valve and the fixtures in the kitchen, and had patched the water heater with parts from the dusty, dented pickup truck he had parked at their back door. Bridget had made coffee with her French press and was flipping strawberry pancakes on her iron griddle. Apparently the entire cargo area of her SUV had been filled with the contents of her kitchen, a fact for which they all had reason to be profoundly grateful.

"I'm sorry we can't offer you a seat, Mr. Farley," Lindsay said, handing him a mug of fresh coffee. "But our furniture seems to have been delayed somewhere between here and Baltimore. We have evaporated milk for your coffee."

"Take it black." He spat tobacco juice into the can and sipped the coffee. "Mighty fine coffee, ma'am, thank you."

Bridget and Lindsay exchanged a look that reflected a kind of dread curiosity about the commingled tastes of chewing tobacco and coffee, and suggested that neither one of them would feel entirely comfortable drinking from that mug again.

"I wonder if you could recommend a good plumber and a good electrician," Cici said. "In case of emergency, you know."

"I do plumbin'," he said. "Do electric, too. Carpentry. Build about anything you want."

"That's wonderful," Cici said, looking relieved. "And you live near here?"

"Down the road a piece."

"Have you been here long?" Bridget asked, sliding pancakes onto a plate.

"All my life."

"So you knew the Blackwells?"

"Yep."

Lindsay encouraged, "You probably have all kinds of stories about this place the way it used to be."

He sipped his coffee and appeared to consider that. Finally he said, "Nope."

The three women looked at each other a little uncertainly. Bridget placed a plate of pancakes on the island before him. "Won't you have some, Mr. Farley? If you don't mind standing to eat, that is."

"Can't." He finished off the coffee. "Thank you kindly, though."

He started toward the back door. Cici said quickly, "Thank

you so much for your help. How much do we owe you for your work?"

He stopped, and for a moment she thought she had insulted him. "Ten dollar," he said.

Her eyebrows shot up. She couldn't help it. "Ten dollars? But that wouldn't even cover the cost of the parts!"

"Ten dollar," he repeated.

She hurried to get her purse.

While she was gone, Lindsay said, "I don't suppose you would know any high school boys looking to do some yard work, would you? We sure could use some help cleaning up this place."

He thought for a minute. "Nope."

Cici returned with a ten dollar bill in her hand. "Thank you again, really."

He removed a worn leather wallet from his back pocket and carefully tucked the bill inside. "Be back with my ladder to fix your roof," he said.

"But—we don't have the tiles," Cici said.

"Cost you ten dollar."

"Oh. Well, yes. Okay. Thank you very much."

He touched the brim of his camo cap, nodded to them, spat into the soda can, and left.

They waited until they heard his truck rumble down the drive before observing, "Strange."

"But nice."

"And cheap."

"Strange."

"I think this is good news," Cici decided, picking up the plate of pancakes and spearing a bite with a fork. "A plumber, an electrician, and a carpenter."

"All for ten dollars," Bridget said, and put another plate on the island.

Lindsay dug into the pancakes. "At least we can shower now."

"We still have to replace the water heater."

"Yeah, but now we know who to call to install it."

Cici toasted them with a forkful of pancakes. "Things are looking up."

No sooner had the words been spoken than they heard a loud rumble and screech coming from outside, followed by what sounded like the gunning of a heavy engine and the whine of tires. Cici went to the back window but saw nothing. She went to the front of the house, and Bridget, shrugging, dished up more pancakes.

Cici had a bright, if rather strained, smile on her face when she returned. "Well," she said, rubbing her hands together, "the good news is our moving truck is here. The bad news is, it's in the ditch. And," she added, with a shrug of wry resignation, "so is our sign."

Lindsay finished off her coffee, set the mug on the counter, and squared her shoulders in determination. "Okay then. Let's go start carrying boxes to the house."

Bridget paused with her first taste of the strawberry pancakes only inches from her lips. "Good times," she murmured. "Oh, yeah." She gulped a bite of pancakes, put her plate aside, and hurried to help.

❧

Their beds were made, the kitchen unpacked, and the Ladybug Farm sign was restored, albeit rather crookedly, to its place beside the drive. The remainder of their possessions—

boxes, furniture, lamps, wardrobes—were huddled in random corners throughout the enormous house. Even deciding what belonged to whom was a task so daunting that it seemed to hover on the edge of impossibility. One by one, they wandered out onto the porch and sat there on the steps, drinking up the cool, sweet taste of the night air and sharing the silence of utter exhaustion until slowly, in stages, the ache in their muscles and the fuzziness in their heads were replaced by a kind a wonder, a still and reverent awe.

"I never knew," Lindsay said softly after a while, "that it got this dark anywhere in the world."

"Or this quiet," agreed Bridget, almost in a whisper.

The light that spilled from the uncurtained windows behind them illuminated the porch in a pale yellow glow, cast their silhouetted shadows on the steps, and was swallowed up in the blackness that was the lawn. Overhead, the sky was a network of stars, more stars than any of them had ever imagined existed before, a hundred million dancing globes suspended in the viscous liquid of space, a three-dimensional spectacle of near and far, small and large, brilliant and muted. There were no stars in the suburbs. There was no darkness, and there was no silence. To sit there, suspended in the midst of such a rare and unanticipated gift, made them feel almost guilty, as though if they breathed too deeply of the sweet-smelling air or lost themselves too totally to the mesmeric canopy overhead they might take more than their share, and leave less for those less fortunate.

"It makes you think," said Cici after a time, "about how the first men must have felt, hundreds of thousands of years ago, squatting outside their caves, looking up . . . dwarfed by all this."

"It must have been terrifying."

"Makes you understand why they worshiped the sun."

"Funny thing though," Cici said. "In the city, the dark was something to be afraid of. You know, dark alleys, dark parking garages, dark corners. Out here it just seems . . ."

When she floundered, at a loss for words, Bridget supplied, "Magnificent."

"Yeah," agreed Cici with a slow smile. "Huge, and magnificent."

"Kind of like what we've just done," said Lindsay.

"It was huge all right," said Cici. "The magnificent part . . . I don't know yet."

"It's not like we moved to Africa," Bridget pointed out.

"Africa, Virginia . . ." Lindsay shrugged. "I've slept in the same room for twenty-three years. Tonight when I get up to go to the bathroom, I won't know where it is. My doctor, my dentist, and my grocery store are in another state. The guy at the mini-mart doesn't know me. There *is* no mini-mart. The air smells different. This isn't home."

Bridget released a slow, soft breath, and agreed, "Yeah."

Cici leaned back on her palms, gazing at the stars. "It's scary, what we've done."

"Yeah," agreed Lindsay.

"The world is a scary place," Bridget said, in a moment. She slipped one arm through Cici's, and the other through Lindsay's. "I'm glad you guys are in it."

The other two smiled tiredly, and leaned inward, and they sat like that in a silence that no longer seemed quite so deep, until it was time to go to bed.

7

Settling In

Lindsay loved lists. She liked to make plans, write them down, check them off. Doing so gave her a sense of order and accomplishment. And in a project as big as this one it made her believe, however temporarily, that accomplishment was actually possible.

So, on the morning of the tenth day, she sat at the breakfast table with Cici and Bridget, a pot of coffee and a fragrant plate of blueberry muffins between them, contentedly going over her list. At a yard sale before leaving Baltimore, they had found a battered white wicker dining room set, which, with a little spray paint and a cheerful daffodil-patterned tablecloth, was perfect for the side porch off the dining room. Wrapped in warm terry robes against the cool mornings, they had breakfast there each day, watching the mist rise off the meadow and the chickadees and indigos and goldfinches hop from branch to branch, gathering their own breakfasts. Sometimes a hummingbird would zip across the table between them with a sound like a giant mosquito, which had prompted Bridget to put up the bright red feeders she had brought from home. They got into the habit of lingering over coffee and watching, with a kind of stultified awe, as blue and green iridescent-winged creatures darted back and forth to feast on sugar water.

The first item to be checked off Lindsay's list had been "telephone service." As it turned out, it had been connected on time and as promised by the telephone company, but, for reasons unfathomable to anyone, all the telephone wiring inside the house had been disconnected and wound into a neat coil that hung on a nail inside the cellar door. When Cici had made that discovery a mere two days previously, it had taken less than an hour to reconnect the wiring to the telephone box, thread it back through holes in the walls and floors, and connect it to the one land line phone they had had the presence of mind to bring with them.

After being deprived of communication with the outside world for so long, they were like starving women at a feast. They called Paul and Derrick, who laughed at their stories about communication woes in the country and promised to visit soon, but both of them sounded rushed and busy. They called friends and neighbors, most of whom were at work. Cici called Lori, who was in a hurry but said she would call her right back.

That was when they all realized that no one had remembered to ask the telephone company what their new telephone number was.

Lori said, "So you have a phone, but no actual phone number?"

"Directory assistance will look it up for you," Cici replied impatiently. "The important thing is, you can call any time! Gosh, I've missed you! It seems like forever since I heard your voice."

"It was only a couple of weeks ago."

"When are you coming to see us, sweetie?"

"Mom, I was just home."

"I'll have you know that was last year, and it wasn't to *this* home."

"Well, that's just it, isn't it?" replied Lori blithely. "That's not exactly my home. It's yours."

Cici opened her mouth to answer, but didn't know what to say.

"Mom, I've got to get to class. Was there anything else?"

"No," Cici said in a moment. "I just wanted to check in. And don't forget you promised to fly back here for your birthday."

A hesitation, and Cici compressed her lips.

"About that . . ." Lori had the grace to sound abashed. "I might have to change the plans . . . maybe we can talk later?"

Cici set her teeth and began to count to ten.

"Mom? You there?"

She forced a smile that she hoped softened her voice, although it hurt every muscle in her face. "Sure, sweetie. I know how hectic college life is. You just let me know."

"Thanks, Mom. I love you."

"Love you, too, baby."

Cici replaced the receiver with firm and careful deliberation. Bridget glanced up from her diligent search through the telephone directory in the hope that their telephone number might be listed there.

"Everything okay?"

"Five thousand four hundred and eighty-three," Cici said without turning. "That's how many lunch boxes I packed. Sixty-eight thousand, nine hundred and eight Flintstones vitamins, seven hundred fifty soccer practices, sixty-two crepe paper costumes . . ." She turned, and made a sweeping gesture toward the telephone before she stalked away. "The telephone," she declared, "is yours."

Bridget called Kevin at work. "You should have seen the place when we got here," she reported happily. "The shingles were falling off, there was a dump truck load of fallen branches in the yard, and it took two days to get through the first layer of dust! Cici says we're going to have to replace the wiring before we can install the central heat and air, and we haven't even started on the barns and the landscaping. Sometimes we can get the news out of Roanoke, but mostly we don't have any television reception and absolutely no Internet. It's like going back in time!"

Kevin said seriously, "I've consulted with a couple of my colleagues here, and I think we have cause to challenge your agreement with Lindsay and Cici. In fact, I'm not at all sure your purchase contract was bulletproof, so it's entirely possible that you all could get your money back if you want to."

Bridget actually moved the receiver away from her ear and looked at it for a moment as though she did not recognize the voice on the other end. "Why would we want to do that?" she said.

"Obviously, you didn't know what you were getting into when you offered on the house. I doubt if parts of it are even up to code, and—"

"Oh, Kevin, really, stop it. I love this place! How could anyone not love it? There's enough here to keep me busy for the next decade at least! Why would I want to leave?"

On the other end of the line, Kevin sighed. "Well, Mom, all I can say is I hope you appreciate what good friends you have."

She laughed. "Of course I do! I love them." And then she frowned a little. "Why? What do you mean?"

"Just that there aren't a lot of people in this world who would do what they did for someone who isn't even related. I mean, they both had great jobs, friends, and lives back in Maryland. But they gave that all up."

Bridget caught her underlip between her teeth and glanced around uneasily. "That was what they wanted to do. What we all wanted to do."

The silence that followed made Bridget realize how chilly the spring morning was, and she shivered. "Sure, Mom," Kevin said gently. "Whatever you say. Listen, I've got to be in court in half an hour. You let me know if you change your mind about that place, okay? I really think we can make a case."

"Kevin, you don't really think—"

"Seriously, Mom, I've got to go."

"Okay, honey, sure. You take care now, you hear?"

"Bye, Mom."

Bridget hung up the phone, but it was a long time before she felt as cheerful as she had been before she dialed his number.

Lindsay dialed two of her friends from school before she realized they were still working. She had used her accumulated leave to depart six weeks early, but her colleagues would be frantically readying their classes for the year-end placement tests this week. For a moment she felt a stab of nostalgia. The mountains of paperwork, the parent–teacher conferences, the unutterable smells coming from the cafeteria… no sane person would miss them. She supposed it had something to do with the way zoo animals would return to their cages even when the gates were left open, and prisoners would re-offend in order to return to the familiarity of their cells. For good or bad, the smell of chalk dust was all she had ever known.

She called her sister in Fort Lauderdale instead, which was a predictable mistake.

"So how is everything in rural wherever?" Edith wanted to know, sounding busy.

"I wish you could see it. This has got to be the most beautiful place in the world. Everything is so green, and in the morning, the way the fog settles just above the treetops… I can't even describe it, it's so pretty. We have raspberry bushes and blueberry bushes and strawberries already getting ripe. The rose garden is unbelievable, and—"

"I've been meaning to ask you," Edith interrupted. "Do you have Mother's onyx brooch?"

Lindsay blinked. "What?"

"You know, the brooch she used to wear on her winter coat. It had diamond chips all around it. I know I saw it after the funeral, but I never did find it among her things."

Lindsay said, "Mother died three years ago. Why are you asking me about this now?"

"I just thought in the move you might have found it."

"How could I find it? I never had it."

"Well, you know she always wanted me to have it. She must have said so a dozen times."

"I never wanted it. If you can't find it, it's probably still on her winter coat."

"Well, I can't stay on the phone all day. I've got a bridge game, and Harold's going to be home from golf any minute wanting something to eat. I'm glad you're having a good time. Bye."

Since that day of gorging on mass communications, none of them had used the telephone once. They still did not know their telephone number, though they promised themselves they would stop by the telephone company office to inquire the next time they were in town. And no one could remember why it had seemed so important that they have telephone service in the first place.

The days had a different kind of rhythm here. They rose early, but they were never in a hurry. They never lacked for something to do—as evidenced by Lindsay's list, which took up more and more pages of the blue-lined legal tablet—but they never felt guilty for simply sitting and gazing at the mountains. The very texture of their lives was different. Accustomed to going from their air-conditioned homes to their air-conditioned cars to their air-conditioned workplaces, they now slept with their windows open to all the sounds and scents of the night, dined in the open air, and worked all day in the sun. Once they had been accustomed to staying up for the eleven o'clock news and being shocked into groggy wakefulness by the shrill blare of an alarm clock; now they awoke with the sun and were in bed, exhausted, by dark. They had been on Ladybug Farm little over a week, and the lives they once had lived seemed like someone else's memories.

"Okay," Lindsay said, turning over a page in the tablet.

"Not bad for the first couple of days. The downstairs is completely unpacked, the living room window frames are scraped and painted, and the staircase is finished."

They had spent the past two days on their hands and knees and, one enormous curved stair at a time, used steel wool and sandpaper to scrape away the layers of dark, dull wax. Washing away the residue with mineral spirits, they applied a fresh coat of wax to each of the twenty-four stairs and the landing, and then buffed each stair to a high sheen by hand. The results were spectacular, but the effort had taught them a valuable lesson about the physical toll an excess of ambition could take.

"I don't suppose . . ." She looked at the other two tentatively. "Anyone is interested in tackling the living room floors?"

The expressions her friends returned was the only answer she needed. "Right," she said quickly, making a strike on the pad. "We'll come back to that one."

"You know what we really need to do," observed Cici, cradling her coffee cup in both hands as she leaned back in the cushioned wicker chair. "We need to take a weekend and go antiquing. I'll bet there are some great places around here where we could pick up some things that would really suit this house."

The other two nodded agreement. As the interior of the house slowly began to take shape they couldn't help but be struck by the enormity of the decorating task that lay before them. Bridget's grand piano went into the front bay window. Cici's damask wing chairs were arranged before the fireplace and Lindsay's grandmother's Queen Anne table went beneath the stained glass window. An occasional table here, a mirror there, and it hadn't taken long to realize that their meager possessions were dwarfed by the oversize rooms of the mansion.

"The landing really cries out for a grandfather clock," observed Bridget with a sigh.

"Paintings on the walls," Lindsay said. "That's what we need."

"That's what we have a resident artist for," Cici pointed out, and Lindsay grimaced.

"I mean real paintings," she said. "You know, from the period. The house should tell a story."

Before moving, they had agreed that, while their personal bedrooms could be decorated in any style they chose, the downstairs areas of the house should remain true to the period. That was one reason that the downstairs rooms were so sparsely furnished.

Bridget said, examining a chipped nail, "Remember when we used to have time to do things like antiquing?"

"Anyway," admitted Cici reluctantly, "we shouldn't get any more furniture until we refinish the floors. And before we do the floors, we really should paint."

"But before we pick a paint color we should decide on draperies," Bridget pointed out.

"I think I'll start taking down the wallpaper in my bedroom today," Lindsay said, reaching for another muffin.

"I'd love to get started painting the porch," Cici said.

"That's going to be a nightmare project."

"I know. But it's kind of like—my gift to the old place, you know? Like when a woman goes in for a little shot of Botox, just a little around the eyes and the frown lines, and she walks out feeling twenty years younger. It's all in the attitude."

They nodded in thoughtful agreement, sipping their coffee.

"I finished cleaning out the herb garden," Bridget announced after a moment. "You can mark that off the list. We'll have tarragon, basil, and dill by June. And today I'm going to clear a vegetable plot. I bought a dozen seed packets the day after we bought the house, and I've been waiting all these months to get them in the ground." She stood. "I'm going to warm up my coffee. Lindsay, can I pop that in the microwave for you?"

"Oh, thanks." Lindsay handed her the plate with her buttered muffin on it, and dutifully marked "herb garden" off the list. "I really should start working on that rose garden, too. What do you think about moving that statue from the side yard and placing it at the end of the path in the rose garden?"

Cici looked surprised. "There's a path there?"

Lindsay nodded. "I think there used to be a bench or something at the end of it, but it must have rotted away. Gosh, I'd love to have a landscape design of how this place used to be."

"Well, I'll be glad to help you move the statue, but it's going to take about a ton of concrete cleaner to make it look presentable again. And I thought the next thing on the list was getting the dairy cleaned out so you could move your art things in there."

"There's no rush on that. I don't exactly know how I want to set it up, and it's going to be awhile before I have time to paint."

"That's odd," said Bridget, returning from the kitchen. "The microwave doesn't work." She set Lindsay's plate in front of her, the butter on her muffin still unmelted. "Sorry, Lindsay."

"I'll check the fuse box," Cici volunteered.

"Better her than me," Bridget confided after she was gone. "That basement gives me the creeps."

"It's not so bad," Lindsay murmured absently, turning another page. "I think the wine cellar is kind of quaint."

Bridget said softly, after a moment, "Does it ever scare you, what we've done? I mean, it's so . . . big."

Lindsay looked up, and reached across the table to squeeze her friend's fingers. "No," she lied. "Never."

Bridget returned a smile that recognized the bravado, and appreciated it. She sat back, sipping the lukewarm coffee. "You know what would really be spectacular? To get the reflecting pool cleaned out and the fountain running again."

"I can't imagine what that would cost."

"Probably just a pool pump. I was flipping through the telephone book last night and saw there was a hardware store in town. I bet they have pumps."

"Girls!" Cici's voice, muffled as it came from the cellar stairs and through the open door. "Come down here! You've got to see this!"

"Oh God." Bridget rushed to her feet, only half kidding. "She's found a body."

The two women hurried inside and, slippers clattering on the stairs, rushed into the dimly lit cellar.

"What is it?" Lindsay demanded.

"Are you okay?" Bridget insisted.

Cici gave an impatient shake of her head, holding the hem of her robe off the dusty floor as she led the way forward. "I fixed the fuse," she told Bridget. "But that fuse box is the first thing we're going to have to replace if we expect to have central heat and air. But look." Turning a corner, she pushed open an arched, stained plank door. "This is what I wanted to show you. I never even realized it was here. I guess the movers must have found it when they were storing our stuff down here and forgot to close the door all the way. I only noticed it because of the daylight coming through."

"Good heavens," said Bridget.

"Well, will you look at that?" Lindsay entered the room slowly, gazing about.

Cici had flipped the switch that illuminated the overhead light fixture, revealing a small chamber with a painted iron bed, a dresser, and a nightstand. The interior light was not really necessary, though, because of the glass-paned door that opened to the exterior of the house. A set of steps, all but concealed by an overgrown boxwood, appeared to lead to the back garden.

The bed was neatly made up with a patchwork quilt, and on the dresser was a worn leather Bible. Bridget carefully opened the front cover of the Bible and read the faded brown handwriting inside. "Ida Mae Simpson, 1951," she said softly. "Wow." She glanced around. "It's like whoever lived here just . . . walked away."

On the left-hand wall there were two doors. Cici opened one of them to reveal a small bathroom.

"Probably this whole cellar was the servants' quarters," Lindsay said, "until they decided to turn it into a wine cellar. And this room they would have kept and updated for the modern-day housekeeper." She sighed. "Imagine being able to live like that. I feel like I'm in one of those PBS specials. You know, *Upstairs, Downstairs* or something."

"I think you're right about this being the old servants' quarters." Cici opened the second door, and found a light switch on the interior wall. A narrow staircase opened upward into the house. "Probably this opened into a hallway originally until they decided to build this room around it."

"Oh!" exclaimed Bridget. "That must be the staircase that goes from the kitchen to the attic. I never realized it went down, too!"

"That's because there are doors on every level to conserve heat," explained Cici. "This must have been the maid's quarters, or maybe the chief housekeeper's. She would have access to all the floors from here, plus the kitchen garden." She nodded toward the outside doors. "Nice digs, for hired help."

"Come on," said Lindsay, catching Bridget's hand and pulling her into the stairwell. "Let's check it out."

Cici flicked a switch that illuminated a bare bulb one floor above them, and Lindsay tossed a grin over her shoulder. "I just love this house!"

They traced the staircase all the way to the attic, a long, dusty-floored room that they had only briefly explored before. The small windows at each end were so caked with grime that only a pale wash of sunlight made its way through, and the expanse was mostly in shadows. There were some pieces of abandoned furniture—a rocking chair with broken rungs, a child's wooden table, a painted lampshade—and odds and ends piled in various places against the wall.

"We really need to spend a day up here straightening this place up," Lindsay observed, plucking a few cobwebs from her hair.

"I wonder what's in those boxes," said Bridget, making her way toward a haphazardly piled row of boxes—some cardboard, some wooden—that lined a long wall.

"Mice, probably," replied Cici, and Bridget withdrew quickly.

"It's like living in a castle," said Lindsay with a wondering shake of her head. "You never run out of things to explore."

"Say, Lindsay," grinned Bridget, elbowing her in the ribs. "Do you think this is where your ghost hangs out?"

Lindsay drew a breath to reply, and then they all froze as a sound floated up the stairs, muffled and distant.

"Hal-loooo!"

Bridget's eyes grew big. So did Lindsay's. The voice came again.

"Yoo-hoo! Anybody home?"

Cici went to the window and looked out. "It's Maggie's car," she reported with visible relief, and they hurried downstairs to greet their guest.

Maggie insisted she just stopped by to see how they were settling in, but was easily persuaded to stay for coffee and muffins. She had brought Farley with her, and while she told them how to find the nearest hairdresser and where the Laundromat was, Farley rumbled around the barn until he found a box of tiles that matched the ones missing from their roof, and proceeded to make repairs. As usual, all he wanted in return was ten dollars.

"It's his disability insurance," confided Maggie. "He's convinced that if he charges more than ten dollars for anything, the government will take it away. Lord, when that man goes, we'll probably find a couple thousand ten-dollar bills hidden behind the walls of that trailer of his!

"Now," she went on chattily, "have you had much chance to get out and look around? Finding everything you need? You know the best prices are at the supermarket on the highway, but Jason's Grocery in town has the best smoked bacon in the state, and he cuts his own meat. His milk is delivered twice a week, but you need to be careful to check the expiration date on his dry goods—I don't think he moves them fast enough to keep them fresh. I know I showed you the bank and the post office, but if you need a good mechanic..."

And so as they sat on the porch sipping coffee and nibbling on muffins, Maggie filled them in on the details of their new community. Cici could get whatever building materials she needed from J&J Lumber three miles west of town, and they delivered the same day—for free. Doug Hasting's Chevron was fine for gas and oil, but never let him fix your car. The town library had a Charlottesville telephone directory, which would be helpful for finding contractors, and high-speed Internet. And Family Hardware on Main Street was worth spending an afternoon browsing even if you didn't need hardware.

Bridget said, "Oh, that reminds me! When we were checking the fuse box this morning we found a room in the cellar we didn't even know was there. We think it was the maid's room. There was a Bible there from 1951—I think the name was Simpson."

Maggie nodded. "It probably belonged to Ida Mae. She took care of this place for, oh, as long as I can remember. She used to make fruitcakes at Christmas and take them to all the neighbors. I think she went to Mountain Rest Nursing Home after Mr. Blackwell died."

"Maybe I'll send it to her there. It looked like a family heirloom."

"That'd be real sweet, honey." She finished off her second muffin and said, "Now those were just delicious. Where did you get the pecans?"

When Bridget confessed she bought them, Maggie gave a

dismissive wave of her hand. "You won't be doing that anymore! See all those trees up and down your driveway? Pecan trees! And all behind the house here are hickory and black walnut. Some people make a hickory nut cake, but give me black walnut any day—as long as you can keep the squirrels away from them! Be careful not to get the juice on your hands, though. You'll never get the stain out. That was what the Indians used to dye their clothes."

She cocked her head and said, "Well, that sounds like Farley coming down off the ladder. He'll be wanting to get back." She pushed back her chair and stood while Cici hurried to get a ten dollar bill for Farley.

Bridget and Lindsay walked with her around the porch to the front of the house. "You ladies certainly do have your work cut out for you," Maggie said, stopping to gaze back appreciatively as she descended the steps. "But my, this is a marvelous old place, isn't it?"

They agreed that it was. Then Lindsay said, "We sure could use some help with the yard work. I don't suppose you know a high school boy looking to pick up a little extra cash."

"No, I can't say that I do. But I'll ask around for you."

Farley was already in the car, and Cici was squinting up at the roof, admiring the job he'd done.

"Oh by the way, I love your sign," Maggie called as she reached the car. "It's a little crooked, though. I'll have Farley fix it for you when we go by." She opened the driver's door. "Ladybug Farm. Is that the cutest thing? Welcome home!"

They waved as she drove away, and then turned back to gaze up at the big old mansion. "Home," repeated Lindsay. "Wow."

And Bridget added, with a note of wonder, "Imagine that."

Cici was silent for a moment, nodding thoughtfully, and then she grinned. "I think I can get used to it," she decided.

Linking arms, they mounted the steps and went inside.

❧

While Bridget spent the morning scouring and rearranging the pantry, Cici drove into town for her first visit to the lumber store, and Lindsay decided to tackle the wallpaper in her bedroom. She had spent the winter flipping through decorating magazines and browsing the home improvement stores, and had arrived at Ladybug Farm armed with wallpaper stripper, glazing medium, two gallons of primer and two of base coat, and two painstakingly chosen shades of paint: Misty Arbor and Apple Blossom. To the untrained eye, the two colors looked very much the same, but Lindsay knew better. When she was finished the room would have the feel of a woodland bower, dappled with misty morning sun.

She moved the furniture to the center of the room and covered it with tarps, then taped down first a layer of plastic, followed by brown paper over the hardwood floors. With the help of a PaperTiger and a spray bottle of adhesive remover, the cabbage rose wallpaper came off strip by strip, and with surprisingly little resistance.

She was thrilled until she realized that underneath the wallpaper was another layer of paper. Newsprint had been used to even out the walls before applying the wallpaper, and it appeared to have been applied with permanent glue. In some places they had apparently run out of newsprint and had used sheets of newspaper—even writing paper—instead.

For a while she was intrigued by the scraps of printing she could make out: *July 1921 Chicken House Destroyed by Fire*; *December 1928, New Fire Engine Arrives*, and advertisements for Carter's Pills and Borax, 20 cents. She even tried to save a few pieces intact, thinking they would make a nice collage or framed artwork for one of the downstairs rooms. But by lunchtime she was sticky with glue and her clothes were splotched with the water she was using to soften the papers, the room was littered with trash, and only half a wall was finished. It was clear to see that the project was not going to be as simple as she had assumed.

When Cici returned from town with a dozen two-by-fours sticking out of the back hatch window of the SUV, Lindsay was relieved to take a break to help her carry them upstairs. "I thought I'd start framing out the closets in that hall between your room and Bridget's," Cici explained, walking backward up the stairs with the bundled ends of a stack of two-by-fours in her gloved hands. "The lumber store said they could deliver the rest of the materials this afternoon."

"Great," said Lindsay. "I can unpack my suitcases. Of course, now I'll be lucky if I can even find them."

Cici glanced into Lindsay's room as they passed. "What a mess."

"You're telling me."

They placed the lumber in the connecting hall between the two rooms, and Cici wandered into Lindsay's room to take a look at her progress. "You've got your work cut out for you," she said, kicking away wallpaper scraps as she entered the room. “That underlayment looks like it’s been put on with mucilage.”

“What is that?”

“That’s the glue they used to make from—well, from horses. It’s almost impossible to dissolve.”

Lindsay grimaced. “Terrific.”

“You could repaper it.”

“I don’t want wallpaper. I wanted my own faux finish.”

“Wow, look at that.” Cici bent down to pick up a scrap of paper. “They used old newspapers.”

“Other things, too. I found some store receipts from 1912.”

Cici laughed. “That’s great. I always wanted to paper my walls with my bills.” She bent down again and picked up another paper.

“What’s this? It didn’t come off the wall did it?”

Lindsay turned to examine the paper she held. It was a little battered, torn at the corners, and crisp with age, but completely readable. “Oh my goodness,” Lindsay said, taking it slowly from Cici. “Do you know what this is? It’s a landscape map. A complete layout of the gardens!”

“How funny,” Cici said. “Only this morning you were saying you wished you had one.”

Lindsay gave her a startled look. “You’re right,” she said, “I did.”

“Look here.” Cici pointed on the map, “The paths were flagstone. I bet if we dug down a little they would still be there. And there was a wall around the whole rose garden. What is that—river rock?”

“There’s a stream at the edge of the property,” Lindsay said. “I didn’t know that, did you? I’ll bet that’s where they got the rocks.”

"Come on," Cici said eagerly, "let's go check it out."

"Beats scraping wallpaper," Lindsay agreed. "Let's go!"

❧

The streambed was in fact a virtually endless source of the kind of large, flat polished stones that, when arranged into a low wall, would transform the rose garden into a work of art. Lindsay remembered seeing an old wheelbarrow in the potting shed, and couldn't wait to start hauling rocks to the garden. Cici found a hoe and started chopping away at the weeds and years of earth until she uncovered, just as she had predicted, the first flagstones of the original garden path. By the time they put away their tools for the day they were streaked with sweat and dirt, and they knew their muscles would ache in the morning. But an entire section of flagstone path had been uncovered, and one layer of shiny dark river stones outlined the rose garden.

"It's never ending," Lindsay said, bringing a glass of wine to join Cici on the front steps that evening. She groaned a little as she sat down on the top step beside her. "The list of projects just keeps growing and growing."

"Yeah," Cici agreed, smiling. "It's hard to know what to do first."

They wore jeans and sweaters against the chill of a spring evening, and Lindsay carried a lightweight knit throw over her arm. She spread it over her knees and Cici's, and leaned back on one palm as she sipped her wine, admiring the glitter of the single evening star against a purple sky, and the chittering and trilling of the birds in the background.

"It was fun, though," she said in a moment, contentedly.

"Like an archaeological dig. And then to see the garden start to take shape like it used to be."

"Tomorrow we'll move the statue."

"Meanwhile I'm sleeping in a bedroom with half a wall covered in newspaper."

"I don't know about you," Cici said, "but I've slept in worse."

"Like I said, it's hard to know where to start."

The screen door squeaked open softly behind them as Bridget came out. She wore a floor-length terry robe and had her hair wrapped in a towel. In addition to her own glass of wine, she carried a platter of chocolate chip cookies. "If you don't mind a suggestion," she said, "a new water heater would be first on my list."

They loved the deep, claw-foot tubs. Unfortunately, they required so much hot water that only one of them could take a bath per evening. The other two had to be content with a lukewarm spritzing from the shower attachment. A new, higher capacity water heater was the only solution.

"I know," Cici said with a sigh. "But we're going to have to go to Charlottesville to get it and . . . I just don't want to leave, you know?"

The other two murmured agreement as Bridget joined them on the steps, setting the cookie platter between them. Leaving this oasis of timelessness and peace for anything that resembled a city seemed to them all as reckless as trying to breathe water.

Bridget tugged a corner of the throw over her knees, and picked up a cookie. "I called the nursing home, by the way, about Ida Mae Simpson. She's not there anymore."

Lindsay helped herself to a cookie and passed the platter to Cici. "Oh? Where did she go?"

Bridget gave her a patient look. "Where does one usually go from a nursing home?"

"Oh. That's too bad."

"Well, I guess she was pretty old."

They sat quietly for a moment, munching cookies, sipping wine, and listening to the rise and fall of crickets' breath as the indigo twilight deepened to a smoky gray. The cool air, such a delicious contrast to the warmth of the afternoon, carried the promise of dew. Their flesh prickled with cold, but they did not consider going inside.

"What do you miss the most?" Bridget said softly.

Lindsay said, "I don't know. It's funny, but I kind of miss school. The kids, you know. What about you?"

"The Internet, maybe. And good coffee ice cream."

"Eaten right out of the carton," Lindsay agreed.

Bridget turned to Cici. "What about you, Cici? HGTV? The Sherwin-Williams store? What do you miss the most?"

Cici leaned back on one palm, gazing out over the darkening mountains, and she smiled, lifting her glass. "Not a damn thing," she said.

Lindsay drew in a deep breath of night air. "Yeah," she agreed softly, "me either."

Bridget said, "Who needs coffee ice cream?"

They touched glasses, and drank to wanting nothing.

8

In Which Bridget Gets into a Jam

For Cici, there was little more beautiful than the way the early morning light stretched across the kitchen. It had a rosiness that suffused the ancient bricks and brought out shades of gold and cerulean that were embedded in the mud from whence they came. Yet there was a mistiness to the light, a softness that combined with the sweet, damp air of early summer and reminded her of just how many sunrises this kitchen had seen, just how untouched it had remained. To walk into this kitchen, to see the way the light graced the soft blurred patterns of the Delft tile and the weathered soapstone and the worn brick floor, made her feel ageless.

On this particular morning, Cici came into the kitchen in her pajamas and robe, stretching sore muscles and combing back her hair with her fingers, to find it filled with strawberries. There were bowls piled high with them on the island. A wicker basket overflowed with them on the counter, surrounded by half a dozen tin pails and an enormous galvanized tub, all filled with strawberries. The aroma swelled through the kitchen and seeped out into the corridor: strawberry, strawberry, strawberry. When Cici licked her lips she could taste them.

Cici said, "Let me guess what's for breakfast. Strawberry blintzes."

"With strawberry compote, strawberries and cereal, and strawberry muffins for dessert," added Lindsay, popping one in her mouth as she carried a bowl of freshly hulled strawberries to the stove. "Apparently, it's strawberry season."

Bridget was at the sink, washing a sieve full of strawberries. "These were going to go bad if I didn't do something with them. I just couldn't stand to let them rot. So I'm making jam!" She shook the water off the strawberries in the sieve, poured them into an empty bowl, and handed them to Cici. "Help me hull these."

Cici took the bowl, flicked a ladybug off the rim, and went to pour herself a cup of coffee. "There are enough strawberries here to make jam for the whole state."

"Everything grows so well here," Bridget replied. "I think it's the ladybugs."

Lindsay asked, eating another strawberry, "Do you know how to make jam?"

"There's nothing to it. It's just fruit and sugar."

Cici poured herself a bowl of cold cereal and sliced strawberries over it. Every other slice went into her mouth. They had been enjoying the strawberries for weeks as they ripened, but still every taste was a surprise. Like most consumers in the United States, they had forgotten what strawberries were supposed to taste like. They knew the smell, and the color, but the taste of the ordinary supermarket strawberry out of the carton was like cardboard. The strawberries of Ladybug Farm were so sweet they were a confection unto themselves; they practically melted on the tongue and infused the senses with the taste of sunshine, the essence of strawberry.

"Well, all I can say is that if you can bottle this taste, you've got yourself a gold mine." Cici poured milk over her cereal, then dipped a strawberry into the milk and ate it with her fingers.

Bridget turned from the sink with a happy, speculative look on her face. "Wouldn't that be something? To bring back the Blackwell Farms jams?"

"Well, I don't know if we're ready for a national ad campaign," Lindsay said, "but it would be a shame to let all this fruit go to waste. Do you have a big enough pot, Bridget?"

Bridget hauled out a stockpot, two Dutch ovens, and a crockpot, and they spent the next hour washing, hulling, and slicing strawberries. Bridget filled the pots, covered the fruit with sugar, and the entire house began to fill with the aroma of strawberries as the fruit came to a simmer.

"Now," declared Bridget, giving the countertop a final swipe with the sponge, "all we have to do is let the fruit cook down and thicken, and we have jam."

Cici said, "Shouldn't we be washing the jars?"

Bridget's face, for a moment, displayed absolutely no expression. Then she said, "Get dressed. We're going to town."

❧

The little town of Blue Valley snuggled up against the base of a hillside that was awash in deep violet thrift, which made one wonder whether the town had been named because of the flowers, or whether the thrift had been planted to honor the town. It was the latter, in fact. The Mountain Gardenias Gardening Club had planted the thrift as part of the Centennial Celebration ten years earlier and the result had astonished even the originators. The bristly blue-flowered plant had dug in its roots and spread up and down the back side of Main Street, so that the impression, as one first came over the hill into town, was of a French watercolor.

The town was laid out in a *T* shape, with a single stoplight where one could turn right off of Main Street and be on Harrison Street, and left off of Main to be on Riker Street. On Main and Harrison, there was a white clapboard Methodist church with a steeple and a bell. Across the intersection on Main and Riker was an identical Baptist church. On Sunday mornings the cacophonous pealing of the two bells woke everyone within a five-mile radius.

Over the years, locals had begun referring to Harrison Street as "the Methodist side" and Riker Street as "the Baptist side." The library, for example, was on the Methodist side. The quilt and notions shop was on the Baptist side. Jason's Grocery was on the Methodist side, and Henry's Bait and Tackle on the Baptist. Main Street was home to Harrison's Fine Furniture, which took up two of the four blocks, Dana's Family Clothing, Johnson's Pharmacy, the Dollar Store, and Family Hardware and Sundries, established 1901.

Sundries was one of those ambiguous words that did not begin to describe the extent and variety of Family Hardware—the vast majority of which was not hardware at all. The sidewalk in front of the store was crowded with a display of wooden rocking chairs, porch swings, and hand-carved birdhouses. Inside, the wood floors were dark with age and barely visible amidst the shelves and stacks of merchandise that overflowed every available space. There were galvanized washtubs and vacuum cleaners, new and refurbished, alongside homemade soaps and hand-dipped candles, which were haphazardly displayed next to lantern globes and cotton wicks. There were stacks of cotton dish towels, electric skillets, rabbit hutches, wire traps, rodent bait, and fertilizer. Portable television sets were arranged on a shelf next to wheelbarrow tires. There were decorative crock butter churns, hand-painted flower pots, and plumbing supplies, in addition to light switches, junction boxes, and R-16 cable. There were chain saws and snowshoes, camping supplies, and antique dolls displayed in a glass case. There were music boxes, Burt's Bees shampoos and hand lotions, and yes, glass canning jars.

"Look at this," Lindsay exclaimed softly from behind a stack of hand-stitched quilts.

Cici, dragging herself away from the study of a rather nice original oil painting of sheep in a pasture, murmured, "It's Aladdin's cave."

Bridget came around a corner laden with gardening gloves, lip balm, bath salts, and a bizarre-looking white wicker contraption that was shaped like a hoop with a platform in the center and a chain at the top.

"What in the world?" queried Cici.

"It's an iced tea butler," Bridget replied, pleased with herself. "It hangs from a beam on your porch, or from a tree limb, and you put your iced tea or lemonade on the platform, with the glasses in the little cup-holders here, and the napkins and teaspoons go underneath. Every cultured Southern lady should have one. And it's only fifteen dollars!"

"Look," repeated Lindsay, from the next aisle.

She was caressing an oak cabinet with a brass handle on the side that was squeezed in between an iron baby crib with peeling white paint and a stack of Black Kow garden manure. She moved aside several wicker baskets filled with seed packets and lifted the lid, revealing an old fashioned turntable underneath.

"Oh!" exclaimed Cici. "It's an old Victrola!"

"Doesn't it belong in our front room," said Lindsay, "in that corner underneath the stained glass window? Can't you just see it there?"

"You've got a good eye," said a male voice behind them. "I believe that's right where old Mr. Blackwell used to keep it."

They looked around at a tall, sandy-haired, impossibly skinny man in blue jeans and a plaid shirt. He had a ruddy face and friendly, faded eyes that somehow identified him immediately as the shopkeeper. It did not, of course, explain how he knew who they were.

"Nice old piece, too," he went on. "My granddaddy used to have one just like it. I remember him and my grandma dancing to it of an evenin', even after they got their place electrified. That's the good thing about the Victrola, don't you know, you can have your music even when your power's out. Do you want to hear it play?"

Without waiting for a reply, he slid the cabinet out of its cubby on squeaky casters, and opened a side door. "See here, it comes with a couple of records. Extra needles, too. I've got another whole box of records in the back somewhere, if I can find them."

Cici, Lindsay, and Bridget slanted looks toward each other that were a mixture of astonishment and uncertainty. They watched the man place a disk on the turntable and crank the handle. When the turntable was spinning, he lowered the needle arm onto the record and the slightly tinny sounds of Caruso singing *La Traviata* filled the store. Their eyes went wide with delight.

"Did this really come from the Blackwell house?" Bridget asked.

"Sure did. Estate auction. This is the last piece I've got left from it. Let you have it for, oh, seventy-five dollars."

"Sold," said Lindsay. She held out her hand. "I'm Lindsay Wright. These are my friends Cici and Bridget."

"Rick Jones," he replied, shaking Lindsay's hand and nodding to the other two. "Folks call me Jonesie. Pleased to meet you ladies. Been wondering when you'd be in. Anything else I can get for you? You got your hands full with that old place. Need any nails, shingles, screws? If we don't have it, we'll get it for you."

"Do you have water heaters?" Cici queried.

"What size you need?"

She told him.

"Gas or electric?"

Cici looked at the other two, they shrugged, and she decided, "Electric."

He nodded thoughtfully. "Well, now there's three of you ladies, doing laundry, washing hair, and all. Like as not, you'll have company now and again. If it was me, I'd get two heaters, and make 'em gas."

Cici, who was quite accustomed to dealing with salesmen, contractors, and other commission-based workers, smiled politely just to let him know who was in charge, and repeated firmly, "One water heater. Electric."

"Up to you," he agreed amiably. "I'll have it delivered for you Thursday morning. Anything else you need?"

"Actually," Bridget said, "We could use some canning jars."

"And some rocking chairs," Lindsay said. And at Cici's questioning look, she explained, "For the front porch. It's a rocking chair porch with no rocking chairs."

"Somebody misses the mall," Cici murmured.

At the register, they met Mrs. Jonesie, a woman with spiked iron gray hair in a John Deere T-shirt whose name was Rita. She asked Bridget what kind of jam she was making, and when Bridget told her her face lit up.

"The Blackwell Farm strawberries were always the best in the county. It's got to be the soil. And to think they're still putting out with nobody taking care of them these last years. You got plenty of pectin? We carry it, on the back shelf."

No one but her friends noticed Bridget's slight hesitation, or the almost imperceptible note of shrillness to her laughter. "My goodness, is there anything you don't carry?"

With two of the rocking chairs snugged against the Victrola in the cargo area, and the third securely strapped to the top of the SUV, the ladies waved good-bye to the Joneses, and Bridget put the car in gear. "Pectin," she muttered under her breath. "I knew I left something out."

Lindsay stared at her and Cici leaned forward from the backseat. "What are you talking about?"

"Pectin. It's the stuff that turns fruit into jam. It makes it thick." Bridget backed carefully out of the parking space.

"And you don't have any? Why didn't you say something?" Cici demanded.

"And let that woman know how stupid I am? She probably wins first prize at every county fair with her jams."

"Bridget!" This was an accusatory chorus from both women, and Lindsay added, "Go back and get some!"

"No point," Bridget replied with a sigh. "We already cooked the fruit and sugar. It's too late to add it now."

"Do you mean to tell me we have ten gallons of strawberry *mush* sitting on the stove?"

"Actually," answered Bridget morosely, "I think it's more like twelve."

❧

While Lindsay and Cici unloaded the rocking chairs and wrestled the antique Victrola into its place beneath the stained glass window, Bridget carried the canning jars into the kitchen. With her face pulled into a grimace of self-disgust, she dipped a wooden spoon into a pot of the strawberry mixture and watched it drip back into the pot like a thin soup. She picked up the pot to dump it into the sink, and then she noticed something.

On the work surface beside the range there was a book that had not been there before. She put the pot down and looked more closely. It was more than just a book. It was a recipe book, with a faded blue cover and pages that were dark and crisp around the edges with age. It was open to the section on "strawberries."

Bridget snatched up the book and turned toward the door, drawing a breath to shout for Cici and Lindsay. But then she stopped, glanced down at the book in her hands, and again at the door. Cici and Lindsay had been with her all morning. Neither of them could have left the recipe book there, even as a poorly timed joke. But if they hadn't done it, who had?

Bridget flipped through the pages. Some were stained, as

the pages of any good cookbook should be, and on others notations had been made in a thin spidery handwriting: "reduce to half," "serve with sweet cream," "substitute pecans"—the same kinds of notes that Bridget's own recipe books contained. The recipes themselves ranged from the oddly old-fashioned—"Milque toast for the Invalid"—to the outright bizarre, like "Brains and Eggs." Bridget turned to the front page, and saw the publication date was 1939. And in the same faded, elegant script was written the name Emily Blackwell.

"Oh . . . my," said Bridget softly, and sat down at the island. She turned back to the section on strawberries, and began to read.

❧

"The moral of this story," said Cici, raising her glass, "is 'when life hands you strawberry mush, make coulis'!"

They sat on the front porch in their brand-new rocking chairs, sipping wine, watching the evening roll in like a slow-moving wave. Crickets chirped. Purple shadows rippled in the grass. The breeze smelled like honeysuckle. The subtle rhythmic thumping of three rockers against wood boards was like the tympani of complementary heartbeats. And seventeen jars of jewel-colored strawberry syrup—which when laced with framboise could legitimately be called coulis—lined the pantry shelves.

"I should have thought of it myself," Bridget said, shaking her head. "After all, what is coulis anyway except fruit puree with liquor?"

"I wouldn't know," Lindsay said. "Until today I'd never heard the word *coulis*. Now I'm hearing it in every other sentence."

Bridget sipped her wine thoughtfully. "Do you think a house can talk to you?"

Lindsay made a snorting noise. "This one can. And what it says is, 'Feed me, feed me!' just like the man-eating plant in *Little Shop of Horrors.*"

"Very funny."

"It's true. Everywhere you look, there's something else this house needs. You restore the stairs, and the floors look like crap. You paint the trim and that only makes the walls look dirty. You weed the rose garden and you have to resod the lawn. It never ends."

Cici said, "I should have gotten another water heater."

Lindsay rocked forward; Bridget rocked back. Both of them glanced at Cici.

"I was just thinking about how you were too proud to admit to Mrs. Jones that you'd forgotten the pectin," Cici went on. "I think maybe I should have listened to her husband. I thought he was trying to prove he knew more than a bunch of women, and I wanted to prove that he didn't, so I stuck to my guns. But we need another water heater."

They rocked in silence for a while, while the tide of darkness seeped across the lawn, and lapped at the steps. The mountains in the distance looked like purple clouds stacked against an indigo sky. A handful of stars were sprinkled across the horizon like carelessly tossed jewels.

Bridget said, "How do you suppose the cookbook got there?"

"I think it was Lindsay's ghost," Cici said.

Bridget said, "I think the house was talking to me. It wanted me to have Emily Blackwell's recipes, just like it wanted Lindsay to have the map of the gardens."

"I don't think the house cares whose recipes you have. I think it just wants to suck every drop of life's blood out of us. It's even got Cici buying it two water heaters."

"Oh, Lindsay, hush. Nobody hauls a hundred and twenty-eight river stones by hand unless she wants to. You love this place, you know you do."

Lindsay smiled to herself, sipping her wine. Piece by piece, the rose garden was beginning to reveal what it must have looked like in its glory. When the flagstone paths were fully uncovered, the statue was cleaned and centered, and the river rock wall was rebuilt around it, the garden would be a work of art. Next year she would plant baby's breath around the wall and lavender along the path. It would be like a living bouquet.

"It's like a blank canvas," she admitted. "The only limit to what you can create is your imagination."

"Speaking of which," Cici said, "I'm ready to help get your art studio started whenever you are."

"Oh, don't worry about it. There's not that much to do, and I have to finish my bedroom first. I think I'm going to do a Venetian plaster treatment." Over the past weeks she had tried painting, paneling, and re-wallpapering, none of which had produced satisfactory results. The project, like everything else in the house, had become an exercise in patience.

"I wonder if Jonesie sells Venetian plaster."

"I wouldn't be a bit surprised."

They laughed, softly, into the night.

"This whole house is kind of like a love affair, really," said Cici after a moment. "You know, they say when you fall in love the body releases enough hormones to keep the feeling going for three to five years."

"Those would be the hormones that make you stupid."

"Right. And five years later you wake up in bed with some sweaty, hairy creature you never met before in your life."

Lindsay said, "Do you think we'll still be here in five years?"

No one answered, but the sound of the question turning over in their minds was almost palpable. So absorbed were they in their thoughts, in fact, that it was a moment before the sound of music—sweet, lilting, and a little tinny—registered with them. It took a moment longer to realize that the music was coming from inside the house.

They stopped rocking at once, listening, eyes wide in the darkness. "What is that?" Lindsay whispered.

"'Roses of Picardy'," Bridget whispered back.

Lindsay stared at her. "How could you *possibly* know that?"

Cici stood slowly. "It's the Victrola," she said.

Bridget stood, too, pressing close to Cici. "I don't think those things play by themselves," she whispered.

Lindsay inched to her feet. "Maybe this one does. Maybe . . . it's glad to be home."

Cici gave her one disparaging look, and then cast her gaze around the dim and shadowed porch, looking for a weapon. She found a twisted laurel branch that they had used to prop open the door while moving boxes in and out, and weighed it in her hand. It wasn't very heavy, but it was better than nothing. She moved toward the door. Bridget whispered, "Not without me, you don't!"

And Lindsay hurried to join them. "You're not leaving me out here alone!"

Cici turned the doorknob carefully and they edged inside.

They had left a single lamp burning on a low table by the fireplace, and the big room was filled with shadows. The music wafted out of the darkened corner of the room where the Victrola was located. The sound of it made gooseflesh rise on Cici's arms. She fumbled for the light switch beside the door. The pendant overhead bathed them in a welcoming pool of light, and the staircase chandelier chased away all but the deepest shadows in the remainder of the room. They moved slowly forward, turning on lamps as they went. The lid of the Victrola was open, the turntable spinning, "Roses of Picardy" spilling from the speaker. Nothing else was amiss.

Their quick search of the house turned up nothing, and they met at the Victrola just as the scratchy old tune was winding down. Lindsay lifted the needle arm from the record. She said, "I don't ever want to hear another word about 'Lindsay's ghost.' It's everybody's ghost now."

"I don't know," Bridget said. "You're the one who brought a haunted Victrola into the house."

Cici said uneasily, "We should probably lock the doors and windows."

Since moving to the country, their suburban paranoia had gradually fallen away, partly because of the intoxicating and addictive nature of sleeping with windows open to the fresh air, and partly because many of the doors had not come with keys. Even now, with clear signs that an intruder had entered the house, they were reluctant to return to the habits that seemed to belong to another place, another time.

Bridget said, "We might be locking it in with us."

"Great, Bridge. Thanks, Bridge." Lindsay hugged her arms. "I'm going to sleep so much better now."

Cici frowned a little. "There's no 'it.' This"—she made a

vague circular motion toward the Victrola—"is spring-operated. Obviously we left the needle on the record when we were moving it, and there was enough tension left in the spring from the demonstration at the store to play the record."

"And it started up all by itself?"

"Sure," Lindsay said, eager to agree. "Things like that happen all the time. Gravity."

Bridget drew in a breath. "Okay. I believe that."

Cici was still scowling at the Victrola. "Then you're crazy."

They were silent for a time, brooding. Then Bridget decided, "I think it was the house. And I think it's saying, 'Welcome home.' "

And at the looks the other two gave her she went on insistently, "Think about it. We have electricity even though the power company never turned on the power. A recipe book appears out of thin air to save our strawberries. And we have background music to make our evenings more pleasant. All of these are good things. The house is welcoming us home."

"Bridget," replied Lindsay after a respectful moment, "you are definitely crazy."

"Entirely certifiable," agreed Cici.

But neither of them could think of a better explanation, and that night, no one locked her windows.

Summer
Growing

9

In Which the Earth Moves and the Roof Caves In

"Miz Burke, can I just show you one thing?"

The ladies had only been in the house for a few months, but already they knew that those words, particularly when uttered by a workman, were never followed by good news. Cici and Lindsay were using paint scrapers and sandpaper to ready the front porch for painting; Bridget was in the garden. When the heating-and-air contractor poked his head out the front door and pronounced those fateful words, Cici looked at Lindsay, gave a small shrug of resignation, and followed him back inside.

The garden path was still only half restored, but the living room walls had been painted a pale shade of antique gold and the trim—including an endless chair rail and an acre of pressed tin ceiling—had been refreshed with gloss white. The floors were still rather dull and battered looking, but the rock wall in the garden was now eight inches high. Lindsay was still debating how to finish her bedroom walls, but Cici had completed the closets for Bridget's and Lindsay's rooms. No one had time to shop for furniture, so they ate all their meals at the wicker table on the porch, or sitting on stools at the kitchen island. The problem with taking on such a huge project, they soon discovered, was focus. No matter how much they accomplished, nothing ever seemed to really get done.

The central-heating and air-conditioning project had begun three weeks previously, at which time afternoon temperatures rarely surpassed the high seventies. To date, a forced air furnace had been wrestled into the cellar, several hundred feet of silver paper tubing coiled and snaked across the cellar floor, and random holes had been cut into the ceiling on every floor. There was as of yet no sign of an actual air-conditioning unit, and the temperature now rarely dropped *below* the high seventies. Cici couldn't help wondering, as she followed the contractor down the stairs into the brick-floored cellar, whether the reason he was taking so long with the job was because the cellar was the only place in the house where it was cool enough to work.

"The situation is," he explained as they descended into the bare-bulbed dimness, "this house wasn't built to carry air-conditioning. Probably wasn't even built for electricity. Looks like the wiring was added later. How old is this place, anyway?"

"A hundred and six years," replied Cici.

He gave a low whistle. "They sure don't build them like this anymore. Solid. Anyway, here's your problem."

He made a sharp right at the bottom of the stairs and crossed to the fuse box on the wall. He opened the door, switched on the high-powered beam of his flashlight to illuminate the inner workings, and stepped back to allow her to appreciate the problem for herself.

Cici looked at the fuse box, looked at him, and said, "Okay."

He said, "You're gonna have to run a new wire. We can't hook up anything to this. There's no room."

She stared at him. "You couldn't have discovered that before you cut holes in the ceiling?"

He shrugged. "Generally, when we come to do a job, we're counting on electricity."

Cici frowned impatiently. "Look, I don't mean to be unreasonable, but it has been three weeks and it's getting hotter by the day. How long will it take you to run the wire and install the air-conditioning unit?"

He was shaking his head before she finished speaking. "You're gonna need an electrician for that."

Again, she stared. "But—you're a contractor, right? Isn't that what it says on your card? Heating-and-air contractor? Isn't that what contractors do? They contract with whoever they need to get the job done?"

He snapped off the flashlight beam. "Call me when you get the wiring done."

And he left.

❧

The electrician said, "Miz Burke, can I just show you one thing?"

Cici, who was on the third from the top rung of the stepladder with a roller dipped in glossy white exterior paint poised against the ceiling of the front porch, glanced down at him. He was greasy-haired, ruddy-nosed, and the script across the pocket of his half-tucked blue work shirt suggested that his name was Cal. He had, however, introduced himself as Lenny, of Lenny's All-Electric in Silverton County.

Lenny had brought a crew of three with him, and so far they had walked around the perimeter of the house together, muttering and nodding, squinted upward at the roof a good deal, and done a lot of leaning against walls while Lenny/Cal had taken readings with his voltage meter. Previously Cici had been asked to interrupt her painting to look at the fuse box, which was in desperate need of being upgraded to a circuit breaker system, and the outside meter, which apparently was improperly grounded. Every time she looked at the estimate, which originally had been requested only to cover running the wiring for a heat pump, went up another thousand dollars.

Cici carefully climbed down from the ladder, wrapped the roller in plastic film, covered the paint tray, removed her gloves, and followed Lenny/Cal inside.

At eleven a.m., the temperature was already eighty degrees—seventy-eight inside with all the windows and doors open. By noon it would be uncomfortably hot on the ladder, and by one the paint would be dry before it left the roller. Cici suppressed a groan as she heard Lindsay's brand-new, state-of-the-art riding lawn mower sputter to a stop somewhere in the backyard, and grind its engine repeatedly in an effort to start again. It would definitely be too hot to mow the lawn in another hour, even on a riding mower.

Lenny/Cal led the way across the living room into the small enclosed sunporch that adjoined it on the back side of the house. The low ceiling and marble tile floors suggested this room might once have been an open patio. Now the banks of windows on three sides—all of which were encased in wooden frames that were suffering from dry rot and covered in flaking white paint—filled the room with morning light and made it hot enough to bake bread. Even the ladybugs that swarmed across the window panes were dropping, shells-down, onto the sills from apparent heat exhaustion. For this reason, the ladies hadn't yet found a use for the room, and it was empty now except for the three men in sweat-stained blue uniforms with names stenciled on the pockets who variously squatted on the floor and lounged against the wall near an electrical outlet whose faceplate had been removed.

"See this here?" Lenny/Cal hunkered down and pointed at something in the outlet with the tip of his screwdriver.

Cici saw nothing, but she made a sound of interest as she blotted her forehead with the back of her arm.

"What you got here," explained Lenny/Cal with authority, "is your reversed polarity. Same all through here. Way I figure it, this room was built onto and whoever did the wiring did a half-assed job. If I was you I'd check the rest of the house, too. Who knows what we're like to find."

The other three men nodded sage agreement.

Cici said, "And how much will that cost to fix?"

He looked thoughtful as he straightened up. "Well now, that all depends. We go through, have to pull wires, replace all the outlets... parts, labor, three men upwards of two weeks... that's not counting construction work, mind you, if we have to cut into walls... could run oh, two, three thousand more."

Cici gazed at him without expression. "Okay," she said in a moment. "Let me see if I've got this right. The original job you were hired for was going to cost six hundred dollars. Next thing I know we're replacing the fuse box for a thousand dollars, and burying a ground wire for another thousand. Now you're talking about another three thousand dollars. Let me ask you something. How much does an electrical outlet cost?"

"Well now, I'm not saying it's for absolute we'd have to replace them all—"

"They're $2.98 each," Cici supplied for him, "and it takes approximately three minutes to change one out. Even if you replaced a hundred outlets in this house at your outrageous rate, we're talking less than five hundred dollars, now aren't we?"

He started to sputter. "Well, I don't know how you're figuring that. Besides, that's not even counting the wire—"

"Which is fifty cents a foot for 120," she returned, "and which I did not ask you to do." Sweat trickled down her sides and began to chafe behind the knees of her paint-splattered jeans. "Mr.—um"—she glanced at his shirt pocket and decided—"Lenny, I think we need to come to an understanding, here. All I want is a separate 220 circuit installed for a heat pump and air conditioner."

"You're gonna have to upgrade your box," he insisted defensively.

"I understand that," she replied, as patiently as she could. Another trickle of sweat crawled down her spine and she twitched her shoulders against it. "What I don't understand is why it's going to cost a thousand dollars."

He grinned at his three compadres. They grinned back. Then he grinned at her, hitched up his pants, rocked back on his heels, and began to explain. "Now there, young lady, there's a lot about electric you don't know. Lots that can't be found in your Sears, Roebuck catalogue. You start dealing with live wires, you're gonna be talking about some money. You take an old house like this, she could go up like kindling, you don't know what you're doing. Why, I remember one time—"

Cici took a breath. "Lenny," she said, very calmly, "this is not your fault. I think what we have here is a simple misunderstanding, so let me see if I can clear it up. First of all, I am not a young lady. I am a big-city woman who's low on hormones and low on patience and you don't have any idea how much I want air-conditioning right now." His grin began to fade. She took a step forward. "So here's what you're going to do. You're going to go out to your truck and you're going to get some wire and some tools and you're going to hook up a 220-volt circuit for my new air conditioner, and you're not going to worry about new outlets or pulling wires until I tell you to, okay?"

He shifted his sullen gaze from Cici to his crew, and then back again. He muttered, "Got to go into town to get the parts."

Cici said, staring him down, "Then you'd better get started."

As one, they shuffled past her out of the room. When they were gone, Cici pulled up her T-shirt and wiped her face, then followed them. She reached the front of the house just as four truck doors were slamming, and Lindsay came in from the kitchen. She looked as hot and sweaty as Cici felt, and her face was spattered with grass clippings. She tugged off her baseball cap, lifting one shoulder toward the front door. "Where's the electrician going?"

Cici sighed. "Who knows? But I'll bet you ten dollars that's the last we'll ever see of him."

"Unless his crew comes back to murder us in our sleep. Did you get a good look at those guys? I swear I've seen some of them on the bulletin board at the post office."

"Oh." Cici scrubbed another film of sweat off her face with the hem of her shirt. "Maybe I'd better be more careful who I piss off from now on."

"Cici! Lindsay!" Bridget's voice, shrill and imperious, came through the window. "Will you come out here please?"

They started toward the back door. "Why didn't you just call Farley?" Lindsay asked.

"I guess I'll have to. I just hate to ask the man to rewire the house for ten dollars."

"Well, when you do, tell him to bring his tractor."

Cici pushed open the back door. "What for?"

"To pull our lawn mower out of the swamp."

"What swamp?"

"The one in our backyard. There's an inch of standing water and a bog over my ankles." She pointed to her bare feet. "I lost a tennis shoe."

Cici stared at her, but Bridget's insistent voice came again. "Cici! Lindsay! I'm not kidding!"

Far more concerned about the sudden appearance of a bog in the backyard than with either the electrician or whatever was on Bridget's mind, Cici opened her mouth to question, but Lindsay just shrugged and hurried off after Bridget.

❧

They found her, as expected, in the garden. The ten-by-ten spot she had originally cleared for vegetables had quickly grown to twenty-by-thirty as repeated trips to Family Hardware yielded flat after flat of seedlings. It had all begun when she went out one morning to check on the progress of her three tomato plants, and discovered they were gone. Rabbits, she was certain. She went into town for replacement plants and tomato cages, and returned with not only the tomatoes, but a six-pack of yellow squash—and each pack contained three plants. Squash takes an enormous amount of room, but the ground was soft and easily tillable, so Bridget simply enlarged the garden spot, planted eight new tomato plants and all the squash. The next day half the squash plants had been plucked out of the ground. Bridget went into town for deer repellent and returned with a packet of seed corn, a flat of bell pepper plants and another of cucumbers. Once again she enlarged the vegetable plot to accommodate three rows of corn, two hills of cucumbers, and a row of bell peppers.

She accused moles of making off with the cucumbers, but replanted them and enhanced the garden with eight climbing bean plants, three pumpkin vines, and a selection of zucchini and winter squash. Barring any more mysterious disappearances, they would soon be harvesting enough produce to supply a town twice the size of Blue Valley.

And that was what brought them up short as they made their way past the abandoned reflecting pool, through the walled garden that protected nothing, and emerged from beneath the rotting twig arbor into the sunny vegetable garden. There they just stood, and stared.

"Well, now that's weird," Lindsay said at last.

"That is definitely one rabbit I don't want to meet in a dark alley," agreed Cici.

Where once there had been stalks of foot-high corn, there were now only empty holes. Where once had stood a neat row of bell pepper plants, there was now dirt. Every other trailing cucumber plant was missing. The huge yellow squash blossoms that had been so cheerfully promising yesterday were no longer. And standing in the midst of it all, wearing a floppy hat and a thunderous look, was Bridget.

"Are you going to try to tell me a deer did this?" she demanded. "What kind of deer pulls corn stalks out of the ground?"

"A hungry one?" suggested Lindsay, then shrugged apologetically as Bridget turned the look on her.

"I don't know, Bridget," Cici said, stepping carefully around the rows to reach her. "What do we know about deer except that they used to eat hostas out of Mrs. Livingston's yard? These are country deer. Maybe they like corn."

"Sure. So they just pull it out of the ground and take it home to transplant."

"Maybe it's not deer."

"Maybe it's the ghost."

"Maybe," suggested Bridget darkly, "it's a person."

Cici lifted her eyebrows. "Why would anyone want to steal produce from *us*?"

"Especially when it's not even ripe," Lindsay pointed out.

Bridget's scowl grew uncertain. "Well, all I know is it needs to stop."

"We could put up a fence," Cici offered, albeit with obvious reluctance.

"We could call the sheriff," Lindsay said, "but if it turns out to be a deer . . ."

"It's not a deer!" Bridget insisted sharply.

Cici patted her shoulder. "At least you saved most of the corn. And we had too many peppers anyway."

"What kind of deer eats peppers?" Lindsay mused.

"Wait!" Bridget exclaimed, her face clearing suddenly. "Cici, do you still have that nanny cam you bought when you thought that maid was dipping into the bourbon?"

"Maybe . . . I guess so . . . I don't remember selling it. It's probably in a box somewhere in the cellar. The maid quit before I ever set it up."

"It runs on batteries, right?"

"Oh no," said Lindsay. "You're not going to put a nanny cam in the garden? This sounds like something Ethel and Lucy would do!" And when Bridget turned the full force of her glare on her, she added quickly, "I'll help you set it up."

❧

While Bridget and Lindsay trolled the cellar for unopened boxes from the move, Cici went to examine the bog in the backyard. She had a dreadful suspicion even before Farley puttered up the drive on his tractor to pull the lawn mower out of the mud and confirmed her fear.

"Septic," he said, unhooking the chains from the lawn mower. "Roots."

Cici had grown used to reading between the lines of his taciturn conversation, but this one gave her pause. "I'm sorry?"

He just grunted.

"Is there a—um, septic person I can call?"

"Yep."

"Do you know his name?"

"Yep."

"Who is it?"

"Will Peterson. Bear Gap Road."

As she so often did after successfully finishing a conversation with Farley, Cici sighed. "Thank you." She pulled a ten dollar bill out of her pocket and he took it silently.

"Won't do you no good." Farley tucked the bill into his wallet.

Again, a sense of dread crept upon her. "Why not?"

"Gone to Baltimore."

"Oh. When will he be back?"

He looked at her for a moment as though the stupidity of the question surpassed understanding. "Ain't no telling. Sometimes a week, sometimes two."

"Isn't there anyone else?"

He said, "Nope." He climbed aboard the tractor. "Ya'll coming to the pig-pickin'?"

Now it was her turn to stare blankly. "The what?"

"Fourth of Ju-ly." He pronounced it with the accent on the first syllable of July. "Parade and pig-pickin', downtown. Starts at one o'clock. Maggie said I was to ask you special. Ain't got no fireworks," he added, somewhat morosely, Cici thought.

"Oh. Well, yes, of course we'll come. Thank you." She felt compelled to add, "I'm sure it will be wonderful, even without fireworks."

She wanted to ask him about wiring the house for a heat pump, but he started the engine of the tractor and puttered down the driveway without another word.

All things considered, it was probably just as well.

10

In Which the Ladies Find Religion

"What do you suppose a pig-picking is?" Bridget asked

Lindsay tossed her a look of mock disdain. "Where are you from, anyway? The big city? Everyone knows a pig-picking is where they turn a little pig loose in a maze and a bunch of boys try to catch it."

"I think that's a greased pig chase," Cici said.

"Well, it's something like that."

Cici pulled into one of the few remaining parking places on Main Street, half a block away from the Dollar Store. "Remember," she cautioned, "we can't stay long. I want to try to get the front porch floor painted this afternoon."

"You sure know how to celebrate a holiday," Bridget said.

"It's way too hot to paint," agreed Lindsay. "What I want to do is find someone, anyone, who will sell me a window air conditioner."

"You try to plug in an air conditioner and you'll blow every fuse in that house."

"Come on, girls," Bridget said, opening the car door, "let's try to forget about the heat for a while and enjoy the parade."

"No fireworks," Cici reminded them with a fair imitation of Farley's glum expression, and they all grinned as they got out of the car.

The smell of charcoal and hickory smoke greeted them, causing them each to suppress a groan of anticipatory pleasure. The sidewalks were lined with booths decked in red, white, and blue bunting, selling everything from crocheted teapot cozies to memberships in the Women's Club. The Lions Club had the most popular booth, featuring homemade ice cream scooped from churns packed in dry ice. The ladies joined the line of men, women, and children dressed in cotton shorts and colorful shirts and found themselves sharing some of the restless anxiety as, in the distance, they heard the drumming of the marching band beginning its warm-up. No one wanted to miss the opening of a parade.

They purchased dripping sugar cones—peach, strawberry, and black walnut—and followed the hurrying crowd to the roped-off intersection of Main, Harrison, and Riker Streets. Veteran parade-goers had arrived early and set up lawn chairs and coolers on the curb. Now they sat with paper plates filled with barbecue and sticky-faced children bouncing up and down with excitement, proud owners of the best seats in the house. Others had camped out on the grassy lawns of the two churches with checkered tablecloths spread out for picnics and games of dodgeball and blindman's bluff going on to pass the time until the parade started. There were tables and booths everywhere one looked, most of them selling food, and from the lawn of the Baptist church came a slow coil of smoke and the enticing aroma of savory cooked pork.

"Wow," said Cici, looking around as she licked melted ice cream from the bottom of her cone. "It's like a scaled-down version of Macy's Thanksgiving Day Parade."

"Or maybe a miniature Rose Bowl," offered Lindsay, catching drips from the piled-high scoop of strawberry ice cream with her tongue. "This is heaven in a cone."

"We are not going home without some of that barbecue I smell," Bridget said.

With a drumroll and a slightly flat blare of trumpets, the nattily dressed marching band opened the parade with their own rendition of "Stars and Stripes Forever." There were high-stepping girls with flaming batons, and no one seemed in the least alarmed when one of the batons, having sailed to the heavens and executed three midair turns, landed in the middle of the crowd somewhere. There was a little excitement while the flames were stamped out and the baton was returned to its rightful owner, but the marching band never missed a beat.

The riding club was represented by riders in turquoise Stetsons atop white horses in jingling harness, and Miss Blue Valley made her entrance riding on the back of a Mustang convertible, wearing a blue satin gown, evening gloves, and what appeared to be a fox stole around her shoulders. Sweat stains had damaged the blue satin beyond all hope of repair.

There was a vintage fire engine and a contingent of Army Reservists in full uniform, which elicited wild cheers and applause from the crowd as they passed by, followed by a World War II cannon pulled by a pickup truck. There were representatives of various clubs and civic organizations carrying banners, and mascots wearing chicken suits and pig suits and dog suits, waving to the crowd. The whole thing ended with Shriners in tiny cars, and it was impossible not to laugh and cheer with the rest of the crowd when the last of them passed by.

They stopped by a booth selling fried pies and homemade pound cakes, and received an invitation to join the Women's Literary Society. Bridget bought a folk-art painted birdhouse and received advice on organic pest control for the garden, as well as a great many helpful—although not necessarily relevant—thoughts on what kind of mole, rabbit, deer, or goat might be devouring her sprouts. Cici bought a vintage marcasite ring that that she thought Lori might like for her upcoming birthday, from a booth that was raising funds for new computers for the elementary school; it was there that she met the mayor and his wife. Lindsay saw Jonesie selling his wife's lemon cakes to raise money for new band uniforms, and promptly placed an order for electric fans, which he promised to deliver the first thing in the morning.

But by far their most lucrative find was when they crossed the street to the Baptist lawn and discovered a pig, roasting in a pit under a bed of glowing wood coals while a bluegrass band played and men in overalls served parts of that pig, with your choice of red (sweet) or vinegar (sour) barbecue sauce, complete with baked beans, potato salad, and a side of slaw, for five dollars a plate.

"And now we know," announced Cici as they stepped into line, "what pig-picking is."

Maggie was behind one of the tables, pouring lemonade, and she happily introduced her husband Lee as the overalled barbecue chef by her side. When they inquired about the pig, Lee was pleased to explain how it had been roasting in a closed pit all night, supervised by the men of the Rotary

Club, who kept each other awake with tall tales and, he added with a wink and a nod toward his wife, maybe a six-pack or two. It was an annual event, and the money they raised was divided equally between the mission funds of the two churches.

"What's the deal with the fireworks?" Cici wanted to know. "Farley seemed awfully disappointed."

Lee gave a snort that was half derision, half amusement. "Guess he should've planned better, then."

"Farley usually drives down to this little place in South Carolina to get a special deal on the fireworks," Maggie explained. "It's not that we have a big display, just a few little things for the children, you know. But this year he waited too late to go and they were all out of the good stuff."

"Got plenty of sparklers though," chuckled Lee, ladling up baked beans. "Ya'll be sure to stay for that."

"They told him they'd have a new shipment in by the middle of next week," added Maggie.

Lee just shook his head, still chuckling.

Maggie wanted to know how they were settling in, and they regaled her with stories of their house-restoration efforts while she helped fill their plates.

"So now we have a forced-air furnace sitting in our cellar and no air conditioner, and I don't think we'll ever see that electrician again," Lindsay said.

"Not to mention we're going to have to have some serious septic tank work done," Cici said. "Farley gave me the name of a fellow, Will Peterson, but said he was in Baltimore for a couple of weeks."

Maggie frowned a little as she filled three paper cups with lemonade. "Baltimore? Will Peterson can't even afford to go to Stony Gap." And then her face cleared. "Oh! He must have said 'gone to Baltimore.' As in . . ." She lifted one shoulder and looked at them meaningfully. "You know."

Cici looked at Bridget and Bridget looked at Lindsay. They all looked back at Maggie.

Maggie glanced at Lee, who just shrugged and wedged a huge piece of Texas toast onto the plate he was preparing. She lowered her voice and leaned toward them confidentially. "You *know*. He drinks. Sometimes for weeks at a time. Most of the year, he's just as fine a fellow as you could meet, but if you happen to be in the middle of a job when he goes off on a bender, Lord help you. No, no, you don't want Will, do they, sweetie?" She poured herself a glass of lemonade, looking thoughtful. "Why don't you girls put in your own circuit box?" she suggested. "Nothing to it, really, just make sure you turn off the main breaker for the house before you get started."

"Easy as pie," Lee assured them, mounding coleslaw onto the plate. "Ya'll want sweet or sour?"

Lindsay said, "Sweet for me," and Lee ladled red sauce over the shredded pork on her plate.

Cici said, "Don't you have to have a licensed electrician do something like that to pass code?"

Maggie gave a dismissing wave of her hand. "What code? Around here, we figure it's your property and you can do what you want with it. Farley can take care of your electric work," she added, growing thoughtful again, "but you're really going to need a heating-and-air contractor, not to mention a new septic tank. What you need to do," she advised, "is go to church."

Lindsay accepted a heaping plate of hot barbecue pork. "Church?"

Maggie nodded. "The Baptists have the carpenters, the Methodists have the plumbers. Baptists have a good heat-and-air man, Methodists have the best stonemason. And for your grading and septic work, it's Methodist all the way."

"But I'm Presbyterian," Lindsay said.

"And I'm Lutheran," said Bridget, looking concerned.

"Unitarian," Cici admitted with an apologetic shrug.

Maggie gave them a sympathetic smile as she produced the last overflowing plate. "Well, now," she assured them gently, "I'm sure you'll do just fine." She held out her hand. "That'll be fifteen dollars."

❧

So, on Sunday, Bridget and Lindsay went to the Methodist church and Cici went to the Baptist church. They wore their most conservative suits—Bridget's navy blue with a white blouse and ruffled collar; Lindsay's a camel color with a short jacket and pleated skirt; and Cici in smoke gray and a black blouse. Their hair was pulled back, their jewelry modest, and their expressions determined. They looked like members of a law firm setting off for a power lunch.

Lindsay volunteered to stuff envelopes for the March of Dimes in the spring, and Bridget agreed to serve on the Food Committee for the Mission Society's annual banquet in the fall. They were introduced to two contractors, a high school guidance counselor, the librarian, and Deke Sanders, who owned Sanders Grading, Hauling, and Septic Repair.

Cici sang "Amazing Grace," listened to a sermon on the

evils of moral complacency and video gaming, and was heartily embraced by Maggie—as well as by several other people she didn't know—who swept her off to the Fellowship Hall to drink Kool-Aid and munch lemon cookies. There she wrote a check to the Building Fund, and was introduced to the pastor and his wife, several councilmen, the church pianist, and Sam Renfro, of Sam's Heating and Air.

"You know," decided Lindsay as they kicked off their high heels and peeled out of their hoisery at home, "it's not such a bad thing to go to church every now and then. In case of emergency, you know."

Cici said, "You don't call having no air-conditioning and a backed-up septic system an emergency?"

"I know what she means," Bridget said. "You know, in case you get sick or something." The last time they had been together in a church, had been for Jim's funeral.

Cici took off her jacket and tugged her blouse out of her skirt as she started upstairs. "I suppose," she agreed, a little reluctantly, "at our age you have to think about things like that. Besides, it's a good way to get to know the new community."

"One thing," Lindsay cautioned, following her up the stairs. "I think the pastor was a little annoyed that you didn't come with us to the Methodist church."

Cici admitted, "Maggie *did* ask where you two were."

The three of them stood on the stairs and puzzled over this for a moment.

"I don't see how all of us can be at both churches at the same time," Cici said.

"A house divided against itself cannot stand," Bridget pronounced solemnly.

"On the other hand," ventured Lindsay, "the Methodist church does have an eight o'clock service."

"And the Baptist church has one at nine thirty."

"Do you mean," Bridget queried, only slightly incredulous, "we should go to *both* churches?"

Cici shrugged and continued up the stairs. "I don't see that we have much choice. We can't afford to make anyone mad at us now. Besides, what are we going to do if we ever need a new roof?"

11

A Few Minor Adjustments

By Wednesday, there was a hole in their backyard big enough to drive a truck through, and thirteen linear feet of their ceiling had been removed. Cici had just put the final coat of glossy white paint on the porch ceiling and was standing back to admire her work when she heard the inevitable words:

"Ms. Burke? Could I show you just one thing?"

She wiped her hands on a damp rag and went through the screen door into the front room, joining Sam Renfro, the heating-and-air contractor from the Baptist church, as he stood beneath the gaping hole in the ceiling, craning his neck upward to examine it.

"Looks like you boys are making good progress," she commented, trying to keep her tone upbeat. A box fan roared in the window, pushing warm air back and forth, and the backhoe that was scraping away at the lawn was a steady throb in the background. She had to raise her voice to be heard.

Sam said, "See there?"

Cici tilted her head back as far as it would go, but had to admit, "No. What?"

He extended his tape measure, locked it, and thrust it into the hole, tapping the floor joists with the metal end. "Six inches, max. There's no way we can run your ductwork through here."

She stared at him. "But you already tore out the ceiling."

He looked grave. "Yes ma'am, and I'm real sorry about that. It was fine until we got right here. I'm guessing when they put in the bathroom they ran the plumbing in through here and closed it up."

Cici drew a breath. "What can you do?"

He thought about that for a minute. "We could tear out the ceiling, lower the whole thing by about a foot. You've got the room. Of course, who knows what we're going to find in the rest of the house."

Cici blew out her breath. "Right. Who knows."

He said, "I really hate to tell you what I have to say now."

He looked so genuinely regretful that Cici felt her spirits sink another notch.

"That furnace them other fellows sold you," he said, "it's about half the size you need for this place. It wouldn't even heat the downstairs come winter."

The two of them stood for a time, looking at the ceiling and listening to the backhoe. Then Cici said, "Well."

He agreed, "Yeah."

"How much more money are we talking about?"

"A lot."

"I appreciate your honesty."

He said, "You know, a house like this, it's stood here all

these years, my guess is they must've had a few hot summers."

Cici's worried frown turned puzzled. "I guess."

"What I mean is, take that wood-burning furnace you got down there. It'll heat the whole house on three cords of wood a winter. I know that for a fact because it's my cousin that delivers the wood out here every year. Less than three hundred dollars a year, you can't beat that."

"No," said Cici, taken aback, "you can't."

"And the best heat pump, it's not going to cool your house more than fifteen, twenty degrees below the outside temperature," he went on. "It stays cooler than that in your cellar."

"You're not suggesting that we move to the cellar for the summer?"

"No ma'am. What I'm thinking is it would be a lot cheaper to move the cool air you've got to where you need it, than to try to make cool air out of hot and then move it, if you follow what I'm saying."

"I'm not exactly sure I do."

"What if we tried to kind of suck the cool air up from the basement through the same vents your furnace uses?"

The furrows on her brow deepened. "How?"

"I'm thinking some kind of whole-house exhaust fan."

"Like an attic fan?"

"Something like that."

"How big a job would that be?"

"Well, I'm going to have to do some figuring on that," he admitted. "Meanwhile, I can get you in business with some ceiling fans. That ought to help some."

"Okay, that sounds good. The sooner the better on those fans."

The backhoe stopped grinding. It was an ominous sign. Sure enough, in less than thirty seconds there was a rattling knock on the screen door and Deke, the backhoe operator and septic tank expert from the Methodist side, stood on the porch in his muddy boots.

Cici turned to greet him, and Sam eyed him with the polite reserve due a neighbor from the opposite camp. "Deke," he said.

"Sam," returned Deke in a similar tone.

Sam said to Cici, "I'd best get back to my measuring."

And Deke said, "I don't want to track in dirt, Miss Cici, but I was wondering if you could come out here for a minute. I just wanted to—"

"Show me one little thing." Cici sighed, heading for the door. "I know."

❧

"So," Cici wound up the story long-distance, "it seems the roots of a hundred-year-old hickory tree have infiltrated the septic system and we have to have a whole new drain field dug."

"Jeez, Mom, it sounds awful." But Lori, three thousand miles away, sounded as rushed and as distracted as she always did when she talked to her mother. Cici knew that the only reason she didn't hear music blaring in the background was because it was blaring in Lori's other ear from her iPod, and she could picture her daughter balancing the phone on one shoulder as she tried on earrings or held up dresses or did whatever it was that twenty-year-old girls did instead of worrying about septic tanks and drain fields.

"Oh, it's not so bad," she said. "We can flush the toilets once a day, we just can't do laundry or empty the bathtubs."

"Eeew, gross! It's like a third-world country or something! How can you stand it?"

"Listen to this." Cici held the phone toward the open window.

She returned the receiver to her ear in time to hear Lori say, "I don't hear anything."

"Exactly."

"Whatever."

"When are you coming to visit?"

"When are you getting the toilets fixed?"

Cici laughed.

"Mom, I love you, and you know I'm dying to chat but—"

"You've got to run, I know. Where're you off to on your big day?"

Lori's voice became infused with genuine excitement, "Dad got us into the absolute coolest pool party in L.A.—and he bought me a brand-new swimsuit to wear to it! It's gold lamé with a beaded top and three strands of Swarovski crystal on each side of the bottoms from front to back, you know, it's just to absolutely die for. All kinds of models and actors and producers are going to be there, including—you won't believe it!—Hugh Grant!"

Cici bit her tongue until she thought she actually tasted blood. "Sounds fabulous, sweetie," she managed at last. "Although I really can't understand why you'd rather spend your birthday at a pool party with Hugh Grant than digging up septic tanks in Virginia with your mom."

She laughed. "I love the ring, Mom," she told her, "and thank Aunt Bridget and Aunt Lindsay for me, too, will you? I'll write them a note."

"I know you will, sweetheart."

"I wish I had time to talk to them but—"

"I know, you've got to run. Have a wonderful time."

"I'll call you!" Lori sang.

"I love you," returned Cici, but the line was already dead.

Cici let the screen door squeak shut behind her as she went out onto the porch and took her place in the rocker next to Lindsay. The last light of day had faded to a deep purple twilight, silhouetting the poplar leaves in stark black against the sky. Crickets trilled in and out. Their rockers thumped softly on the freshly painted boards of the porch. On cue, as it had been for the past ten evenings just as the last daylight left the sky, there was the distant whine of a bottle rocket, a muffled pop, and an umbrella of red, green, and gold light cascaded against the eastern sky.

"Ooh, nice," observed Bridget, rocking.

"Umm," agreed Lindsay, passing Cici a cool glass of chardonnay. "How's Lori?"

"Terrific." Cici took a significant swallow of wine. "She's going to a party with Hugh Grant."

"No kidding!"

"There's going to be nothing but wild sex and free drugs."

"At a Hollywood party?" exclaimed Bridget, feigning shock. "Surely not!"

And Lindsay added, "Thank God we never had anything like that when we were in college."

"She's wearing a swimsuit"—Cici pointed out with great deliberation—"that's held together at the bottom with three strands of Swarovski crystals."

Lindsay and Bridget sipped their wine in silence for a moment. Then Bridget said, "Guess she won't be doing any actual swimming, then."

"It won't matter," Lindsay said, "since the swimming pool is probably filled with champagne."

Cici sighed. "My daughter is going to a pool party with Hugh Grant. I'm sitting in a sweat pit with a thirty foot hole in the backyard and a ceiling that's falling down. What's wrong with this picture?"

"It's a little cooler tonight," Bridget offered.

"And the fireworks are nice," Lindsay said. They watched as a red flare spiraled upward and exploded into a canopy that covered half the night sky. Everyone made an appreciative sound for that one. "Actually, I think I like this better than having them all on the Fourth of July."

Farley, having finally obtained his fireworks, had decided to prolong the pleasure as long as possible by setting off a few each night from his backyard. The residents of Ladybug Farm had front row seats for every show.

"She wanted me to thank you for the book, Bridge," Cici said, "and she loved the CD, Lindsay. She's going to send notes."

"She always writes such sweet notes," Bridget said.

"She's a good girl," Lindsay added.

And Cici admitted, "I know." She sipped her wine and appreciated the spectacle of another light show, this one red, white, and blue, blossoming against the sky. "Would you go back to being twenty if you could?"

Lindsay said, "For Hugh Grant? You bet your sweet booty. Of course," she added thoughtfully, "he might be disappointed. After all, I wouldn't be nearly as good-looking as I am today."

Bridget chuckled. "You couldn't pay me to go back. Lord preserve me from ever being that stupid again."

"It all seemed so simple then," Cici agreed. "Remember? You made a plan, you mapped out your life, and you figured all you had to do was sit back and watch it unfold. Your job was done."

"Hmm." Lindsay sipped her wine. "I was going to study at the Sorbonne."

Bridget said, "I was going to go to Africa and build irrigation systems. But first I was going to marry a priest." When the other two looked at her she explained with a wistful sigh, "I was wild about *The Thornbirds* back then. I must have read it twenty times."

Lindsay lifted her eyebrows. "It was a book?" She rocked back thoughtfully. "What do you know about that?"

Cici said, "When I first started working, right out of college, I was actually refused an apartment because I was a single woman. They wouldn't even let me fill out an application."

Bridget sipped her wine, and seemed a little embarrassed as she reported, "When Jim and I were first married and things were tight, you know, I applied for a job as a secretary at a glass factory. The manager wouldn't hire me until he got my husband's permission."

"Jesus," Lindsay said.

"You should have slapped his face and walked out," Cici said.

"You should have taken the apartment manager to court," Bridget said.

Both of them just smiled, sadly, reminiscing.

"Hell no," Lindsay said after a moment. "You couldn't pay me to go back."

In the distance there was a fanfare series of pops, accompanied by a lively explosion of red and white sparks near the horizon line. They appreciated the show while it lasted.

The startled crickets, silent during the fireworks, started chirping again. Cici said, "Well, I guess that's it for the night."

"I wonder how many more fireworks he has left?"

"Maybe he should save some for New Year's."

Bridget changed the subject. "I have a theory about the garden thief," she said.

Cici and Lindsay looked at her with interest. The nanny cam, cleverly set up in a tree to record everything that happened during the night, was unfortunately not equipped with night vision. So when two more stalks of corn had gone missing, a review of twelve hours' worth of tape had shown nothing but foggy darkness.

"If you'll notice," elucidated Bridget, leaning forward a little to capture their attention, "all the thefts occur on the hedge side of the garden."

"I wouldn't exactly call that tangle of blackberry vines and honeysuckle a hedge," Lindsay objected.

"But it's always the same row," Bridget insisted. "Right there, next to cover. I think whatever—or whoever—it is, is sneaking through the hedge at night and pulling stuff out of the ground, then hiding back in the hedge before anyone can catch him."

There was nothing but the sound of rocking chairs and crickets for a while. Lindsay and Cici sipped their wine. Cici said, "I don't know, Bridge. Sounds pretty weird to me."

"You still don't have a motive," pointed out Lindsay.

"I'm working on it," Bridget pronounced darkly.

A ladybug dive-bombed into Cici's wineglass. She plucked

it out absently and flicked it away. She said, "It's going to take the rest of the summer to get the air-conditioning installed."

"Wouldn't be so bad if we could take a shower."

"We can take a shower," Bridget pointed out, with an obvious effort to remain positive. "We just can't use more than five gallons of water doing it."

"We haven't even gotten the estimate on what digging the new drain field is going to cost."

"Whatever it is," Lindsay said, "it's more than we can afford."

They were silent for a while, rocking, listening to the crickets.

"I guess," Bridget said in a moment, "this is the best part about not being twenty anymore. We know that plans hardly ever work out the way you planned them."

Lindsay raised her glass in the dark. "Here's to not looking back."

Cici rocked forward and raised her glass as well. "Here's to Hugh Grant," she said.

"And here's to catching the hedgerow garden thief and prosecuting his sorry ass to within an inch of his life," added Lindsay.

Bridget raised her glass as well. "I'll drink to that."

They drank, and sat back and listened to the crickets until it was time for bed.

12

On Farming

Lindsay came downstairs a little after seven, as she always did, yawning and belting her short pink terry robe around her waist as she made her way to the kitchen. She stepped over tools and neat piles of materials, as she always did, and said, "Morning, Sam. Morning, Deke. Morning, Farley" as she always did, and made her way to the coffeepot, as she always did. "Morning, Bridge."

The kitchen was redolent of cinnamon and butter, with warm base notes of fresh ground coffee, as it always was. Privately, Lindsay thought Bridget was spoiling the workmen by providing them with coffee and sticky buns each morning—and no doubt prolonging their stay—but being Bridget, she could hardly be expected to do anything less. Besides, Lindsay enjoyed the sticky buns as much as the men did.

A chorus of "Morning, Miss Lindsay," "Morning, ma'am," and "Good morning, Linds" greeted her, just as it always did.

She poured her coffee, added cold milk, drank a generous portion, and noticed for the first time that everyone was standing at the window in the breakfast room that overlooked the front porch, staring out. She said, coming over to them, "What are you looking at?"

No one answered. They just kept looking. And that was her first hint that this was not a morning just like any other.

"Oh my God," she said, staring through the window. "Cici's going to have a fit."

Just then Cici entered the kitchen in her robe and slippers. "Morning, Bridge. Morning Lindsay," she said.

Neither woman could quite tear their eyes from the window. "Good morning, Cici."

"Morning, Farley. Morning—" And she stopped, staring as they stared. "Oh my God. What is that?"

"They're sheep, ma'am," replied Sam politely.

"But—they're on my porch!"

"Yes'm," he agreed with a thoughtful nod of his head. "They surely do appear to be."

"But I just painted that porch! Look what they're doing! They've ruined the paint! There's mud everywhere! They're eating the wicker! Oh, my God, there are a hundred of them!"

"Twenty-five," corrected Farley, but Cici was already gone.

She flew out of the kitchen and into the front room, banging her ankle against a pile of two-by-fours and half hopping, half limping to the bank of windows that overlooked the freshly painted front porch. The flow of sheep covered the wraparound porch, from breakfast area to rocking chairs, and spilled down the steps into the front lawn, a big, muddy, ragged, wooly mass of grumbling, shifting, *baaing* life. They seemed to be wedged between the rail and the wall, as though, having made their way up there, they couldn't figure out how to get off.

"Shoo!" Cici cried, banging on the windowpane. "Get out of here!"

Not a single sheep even looked up.

"Problem is," Farley explained mildly, following her, "sheep don't know how to back up."

Cici tossed him a half-frantic, half-incredulous look, and flung open the door. "Get!" she demanded to the sheep, clapping her hands. "Go on, get out of here! Scat!"

Lindsay and Bridget crowded around her at the door. Sam and Deke followed with slightly less enthusiasm, coffee cups in one hand and sticky buns in the other.

"Reckon we could get a rope around the neck of the lead sheep," suggested Sam. "Pull him over the rail. The others might follow."

Deke shook his head. "Gonna have to take the railing off."

Farley said, "I could go home and get a dog."

Cici looked from one of them to the other with an expression that was, for the moment, completely unreadable. Then she turned and plunged into the fray. Grabbing a handful of wool, she jerked and hauled and tugged and pulled, crying, "Scat! Go! Scoot!" until the shifting mass of dirty sheep fur began to rumble with agitation, swaying from side to side, plunging and bleating. Lindsay and Bridget set aside their coffee cups, and, with an exchanged looked of resignation, waded into the sea of sheep. Following Cici's lead, they each grabbed a sheep and began to tug and shout until suddenly one of the sheep broke free and sprang, as though on steel coils, up and over the railing. A mass riot followed. Bridget lost her balance and sat down hard on the floor, hands over her head, squealing incoherently. Lindsay yelped as she took a hard hit in the shin. Cici stumbled backward, gasping, as sheep began to jump over the railing, spindly black-stocking legs flailing, just like in a cartoon.

"Jesus!" exclaimed Lindsay, rubbing her shin as she limped inside the doorway. "I thought sheep were supposed to be peaceful!"

"They're killers!" screeched Bridget, hands over head. "They're killer sheep!"

Sheep continued to pour over the railing, splintering boards, leaping over each other, landing splay-legged on the lawn and trotting off, *baahing* hysterically, in sundry directions.

"Stupid critters," acknowledged Sam, sagely.

Deke said, "What're you going to do with them now?"

Cici looked in dismay at the ruined porch, and the shaggy muddy creatures who were now making ruin of their lawn. "The garden," she managed.

"Oh my God, the garden!" Bridget struggled to her feet. "We've got to keep them out of the garden!"

"What you need is a dog," volunteered Farley.

Lindsay caught Bridget's hand and pulled her down the steps toward the garden. "Get the dog!" she cried.

For the next twenty minutes the women formed a human fence in front of the vegetable garden, shouting and flapping towels at the sheep who ventured too close while Sam and Deke, catching on to the urgency of the situation, eventually put down their coffee cups and stood ready to haul the particularly obstinate sheep to the back of the flock. By the time Farley roared up with a bedraggled, dirty, black-patched dog balancing in the back of his pickup truck, they were filthy, sweaty, and hoarse with shouting, and the sea of sheep was still surging.

Farley slammed the door of the truck and unlatched the back gate. He said, "Ya'll better stand back."

The three women looked at each other dubiously. Then they looked at the tomato plants, spilling over their cages with fat red and yellow fruit, the thick coils of bean vines splayed along long wires, the dark green corn stalks towering over their heads, bright yellow squash ready to be plucked. They said as one, "No!"

The word was barely spoken before the dog slunk out of the truck and, with belly close to the ground and eyes locked on the flock, he froze in place. In the blink of an eye he darted to the left, and the sheep shuffled and bunched. He flowed to the right, and the flock swayed. The women watched, almost as mesmerized as the sheep, as the dog crouched, head down and eyes fixed on the sheep. He took one step forward. And another. And suddenly all hell broke loose.

The flock charged. Hooves and muddy wool and divets of earth flew everywhere. Bridget screamed and ducked as a sheep flew over her head. Lindsay ended up sprawled on her back. Cici dove for cover between two rows of corn. She could hear Sam and Deke yelling their astonishment and cheering the dog on. And as suddenly as it had begun, it was over.

The ladies got slowly to their feet, brushing mud off their knees and rubbing bruises, looking cautiously around. The sheep were miraculously on the other side of the hedgerow, behind the fence, munching grass as though nothing had ever happened. The dog had retreated to the shadow of Farley's truck, where he sat at attention, his gaze fixed upon the sheep. Sam returned from his examination of the hedgerow and pronounced, "Right here's your problem. Hole in the fence."

Farley said, "I'll fix it for you. Ten dollar."

Cici's voice was filled with wonder. "How in the world did you train that dog to do that? You didn't even give him a command."

Farley just looked at her, expressionless. "Didn't train 'im. He just knows."

Bridget said, "Do sheep eat radishes? And tomato and cucumber plants?"

The three men just stared at her.

Lindsay said, rubbing a bruised hip, "Whose sheep are they, anyway?"

Farley replied, "Yourn."

It was several beats before Cici could manage, *"What?"*

And Bridget parrotted, "Ours?"

"Came with the farm," confirmed Farley. "I been keeping an eye on 'em, over the winter you know. Put out some hay. Won't charge you none. They ain't much trouble. Need shearin'."

"So that's what that clause in the sales contract about 'outbuildings and livestock' meant," mused Lindsay.

"Sheep?" Cici's voice was close to a screech. "How in the world are we supposed to take care of sheep?"

"Sheep!" cried Bridget, delighted. "We have sheep!"

Farley said thoughtfully, "You can have the dog."

Bridget whirled from her enraptured survey of the sheep in the meadow, her eyes growing even wider. "Are you serious? You'd really let us have that incredible dog?"

"Ten dollar," said Farley.

"Oh good God," said Lindsay, sotto voce, "she's out of control."

Cici said, "Bridget, I think we should talk about this."

"You can't have sheep without a sheepdog" was Bridget's reply. And to Farley, "What's his name?"

Farley thought about that for a moment. "Dog," he decided.

Bridget blinked, but her smile didn't waver. "Well, we'll worry about a name later." She approached the dog, hand extended. "Come here, you sweet thing. You want to live here? Are you going to be my sweet dog?"

Cici said, "Bridget, be careful."

And Lindsay, "I wouldn't—"

There was a ferocious sound, a blur of fur, and Bridget jumped back with a cry, cradling her bleeding hand.

Farley said, "He don't much like people."

Cici said, "I'll get the first-aid kit."

Lindsay rushed to Bridget, giving the dog wide berth. "Are you okay?"

Farley repeated firmly, "Ten dollar."

And Bridget said, "I'll get my purse."

❧

The good news was that the dog did not have rabies. The bad news was, at least as far as Cici and Lindsay were concerned, that he did not run away. Every morning the dog would spring over the fence as though his paws were filled with helium, herd the sheep into a tight little bunch and move them, with his spooky eyes and creeping gait, from one side of the meadow to the other. He would then retire to a place under the front porch, where the wary passerby might or might not be warned by a rumbling growl before he sprang from the shadows to rip at cuffs and sneakers. Shortly before sundown he would sally forth once again, sail over the fence, and repeat the exercise, moving the sheep to a part of the meadow that he had apparently predetermined after twelve long hours of precise mathematical calculations. It was, they all had to admit, amazing to watch.

On the other hand, no one had counted on sheep, much less a psychopathic sheepdog, when they signed on the dotted line.

"It's a *farm*," Bridget insisted joyfully, "and what's a farm without livestock? This makes us real farmers!"

Lindsay said in a tone that brooked no argument, "Maybe it makes you a farmer. I'm an artist. I don't do sheep."

"Sheep," repeated Cici with a small shake of her head, still not quite believing it. "How could that possibly have slipped by me?"

"Isn't it like real property?" offered Bridget hopefully. "You know, attached to the premises?"

Cici returned a look that said, *Nice try*. Out loud she said, "Windows are attached to the premises. Rosebushes, maybe. But sheep? I think that's pushing it." At Bridget's crestfallen look, she added, "For heaven's sake, Bridge, we don't know anything about sheep! We're city girls, and this is a huge responsibility."

"I saw a movie one time about a sheep station in Australia," Lindsay added thoughtfully. "The sheep would swell up like ticks from bloat and the farmer would have to go around puncturing their stomachs with this huge needle to keep them from exploding."

Bridget's eyes went wide, and Cici stared at Lindsay.

"What I'm saying," Cici said, when she could tear her eyes away from Lindsay, "is that sheep can be delicate, and a lot of work. Don't we have our hands full just trying to put this house back together? Are you sure you want to take on more?"

Bridget raised her chin. "I'll take care of them," she promised. "And the dog, too. They'll be my responsibility. You two will never even know they're here."

Lindsay looked at Cici. Cici looked at Bridget. "Sheep," she said, shaking her head again.

And Lindsay repeated, her tone heavy with resignation, "Sheep."

❧

Bridget immediately checked out every book on sheep and sheepdogs the library had to offer, and over the next several days was rarely seen without a text in her hand. Occasionally she would glance up to offer such arcane wisdom as "April is the best month for lambing in this region" and "A good sheepdog can work a 2,500-acre ranch all by himself." But for the most part she spent her time completely immersed in the written world of animal husbandry.

It was therefore no surprise for Cici to come into the kitchen for lunch and find Bridget sitting at the island, hair pulled back against the heat, reading glasses on, lost in a book. Fresh-picked tomatoes were scattered across the island around her, and something wonderful was simmering on the stove.

Cici lifted the lid and inhaled the fragrance. "Smells divine," she said. "What are you making? Pate?"

"Chicken livers sauteed with garlic and white wine," replied Bridget, without looking up, "for Spike." The dog had gone through three different names in as many days; Spike was the latest. "Farley said he loves chicken livers, but I can't get him to eat anything I make."

Cici replaced the lid on the pan. "I don't think dogs are supposed to have wine."

In the background, the sound of the backhoe had stopped, since today was the day the septic tank crew was laying pipe. But Lindsay's sturdy riding lawn mower puttered on, as she was determined to get the entire front lawn clipped before the earth-moving equipment started up again.

Bridget said, sighing, "It says here it's too late in the year to shear the sheep. But we're going to have to have their hooves clipped or they'll go lame. I have to find a farrier."

Cici took out a cutting board and began to slice a firm, ripe tomato. Since the tomatoes had started coming in, tomato sandwiches for lunch were the highlight of the day. They all agreed that none of them had ever tasted a tomato as sweet, as rich, or as purely tomato as those that came out of Bridget's garden. A single sandwich made worthwhile every moment of that dreadful morning they had spent in their nightgowns protecting the garden from the sheep.

Cici spread a generous swath of mayonnaise on two slices of white bread. "You don't really think it was the sheep who were pulling up your plants by the root, do you?"

"What else could it have been? Remember, they were coming through the hole in the fence, and we practically caught them red-handed on the nanny cam."

"Hard to say what you caught on the nanny cam," Cici reminded her. "Besides—"

She broke off as the sound of a high-pitched screech cut

across the grinding of the lawn tractor. The dog started to bark furiously, and the screech came again, and again. Cici dropped the knife and rushed to the window, and Bridget ran to the back door. They each arrived in time to see Lindsay racing away from the path of the lawn mower, which was chugging around in ever widening circles. She was screaming and swiping madly at the air as she ran, the dog barking and circling her wildly. As they watched, she tore open the front of her shirt and wrestled out of it, tossing it away. She ran toward the house in her bra and denim shorts, slapping at her bare shoulders and thighs. Sam, who had gone to his truck for a tool, turned to stare. The men who were laying the pipe came around the corner to investigate the commotion and stopped dead, staring. Bridget flung open the back door and tossed a tomato at the barking dog, who scampered away about five feet but continued to bark furiously.

Lindsay cried, "Bees!"

Cici ran to her, slapping a kitchen towel through the air to knock away any lingering insects, and pulled her inside. Bridget ran to the freezer and pulled out the ice bin. Cici demanded, "Are you allergic?"

"No, I'm stung!" cried Lindsay. "Look at me, I'm stung!" Red welts were beginning to rise on her arms, chest, shoulders, and even her bare belly.

Bridget made soothing sounds as she gingerly applied ice packs to the stings, and Cici searched through the bathroom vanity for antihistamines. But for the most part all they could do was wince in sympathy and murmur things like "Oh, honey" and "Oh, you poor thing" while dabbing with ice and cortisone cream at the angry red knots that rose up on her face and neck and arms.

And suddenly a stricken look crossed Lindsay's tear-streaked face. "Oh my God, I just took off my shirt in front of all those men!"

Bridget and Cici returned a sympathetic look. "Well, at least you were wearing a pretty bra," Bridget offered.

Sniffing, Lindsay looked down at her soft white torso. "But my stomach is flabby."

Cici smoothed back Lindsay's hair. "I wouldn't worry about that, honey. I'm sure no one noticed."

"They were too busy looking at your bra," added Bridget.

"Well, that's it for me," Lindsay declared wetly, her voice muffled through the ice pack she pressed against her face. "I'm never getting on that lawn mower again. I don't care if the grass grows over our heads. I could have been killed!"

The other two murmured agreement, smoothing her tangled hair away from her face. "Don't you worry. As long as you're all right, that's all that matters."

A timid knock came on the back door, and Sam poked his head inside, carefully averting his eyes from Lindsay's half-naked torso. Lindsay quickly dragged a towel around her shoulders to cover up.

"Um, I just wanted you to know we stopped your lawn mower," he said. "Guess you ran over a pretty big yellow jacket nest. But they're about settled down now."

They had not even noticed that the sound of the lawn mower had stopped.

"Oh," said Cici. "Thank you, Sam. We appreciate your help."

Sam looked uncomfortable. "Well, it's not all good news. We couldn't exactly get to it before—with the yellow jackets and all—and by the time we were able to grab the throttle . . .

well." He stepped away from the door with a resigned gesture toward the yard, which more or less invited them to see for themselves.

Cici and Bridget followed him out to the porch curiously, and in a moment Lindsay, adjusting the towel around her shoulders, cautiously joined them. Sam led the way to the side of the house, and stopped. He didn't have to say anything. As one, the women drew in a breath.

The garden, which Bridget had so painstakingly cultivated all spring and summer, which they had protected from the hedgerow thief and marauding sheep, was in shambles. Proud stalks of corn had been crushed as though by a thresher. Poles and pole beans were tumbled together in a tangle. Tomato plants were sheared off at the roots; squash and melons decapitated. In the midst of the ruins sat the lawn mower, looking like a tank in the aftermath of a battle.

"Oh . . . my," said Bridget softly.

No one had anything to add to that.

❧

A gentle rain began to fall at dusk, tapping on the porch roof and pinging in the gutters, smelling like sweet hay and earth. Greedy birds fluttered back and forth between the feeders and the poplar tree, bright yellow and deep indigo finches, bossy red cardinals, black-and-white chickadees, storing up reserves against the time when the weather would be too wet to fly. The mist muted the colors of the landscape to a dusky gray green, broken in spots by groupings of pastel hollyhocks and proud white phlox in their formal flower beds. Rolling meadow faded into foggy mountains, which faded into cool gray sky.

The women gathered on the porch for their evening ritual, comfortable in cotton drawstring shorts and tank tops without bras, their hair caught up off their necks with elastic bands and short strands sticking out willy-nilly. Their feet were bare, and their makeup, such as it was, long since sweated off. During the day, when the workmen were around, they tended to wear capris or, at the very least, shorts with zippers, and shirts that covered their upper arms. But when the day was done, and they sat splay-legged in their rockers, or with their feet propped up on the railing, sipping wine and watching the evening, it didn't matter whether their armpits were shaved or their varicose veins were showing. They were at home.

"Funny," observed Cici, rocking back and forth. "It kind of makes you think how it must have been a hundred years ago, sitting on this very porch, watching the rain. I'll bet it wasn't much different from today."

"I love the colors," murmured Lindsay. "Like an impressionist painting."

"I hope the sheep are okay," Bridget worried.

"They're sheep," Cici said. "They were surviving rainy days long before we got here."

"What if it thunders?"

"Then they'll stand under a tree."

"They could get hit by lightning!"

Cici sipped her wine thoughtfully. "I don't believe," she said at last, "in all the history of the world, I've ever read about a flock of sheep being struck by lightning. Golfers, yes. Sheep, no."

Lindsay sighed. "I'm awfully sorry about the garden, Bridget."

Bridget reached across to pat her knee. "Oh, sweetie, it wasn't your fault. As long as you're okay, who cares?"

Lindsay, a little drunk on antihistamines, sipped sparkling water and sighed again. "It's like something out of *Little House on the Prairie*, you know?"

And when she received nothing but puzzled glances in response, she explained, "You *know*. Every time those poor people would get a little bit ahead, God would send locusts or hail or a blizzard to wipe out their crops and it would all have been for nothing."

Bridget nodded sagely, studying her wineglass. "The life of a farmer is never easy."

Rain dripped. A cardinal landed on the porch rail, feathers ruffled against the rain, and angrily squawked at a chickadee on the feeder. The chickadee darted away, and the cardinal took its place.

Cici said, "We were able to save some of the garden. The herbs will come back. And we'll have plenty of apples and pears and berries when they ripen."

"If the locusts don't come," said Lindsay bleakly.

Bridget chuckled. "We *do* sound like farmers, tallying up what we're going to be able to put by for the winter."

Cici turned her wineglass around in her hand, and a strained look came over her face. She said, "Well, I guess this is as good a time as any to tell you. Deke finished hooking up the septic system. We can have a real bath and flush the toilets as many times as we want."

"Yay!" cried Bridget, and even Lindsay, lost in an antihistamine haze, perked up.

"A bath?" she said.

"Add baking soda to the water," suggested Bridget. "It will help the bee stings."

"I'm going to miss him," Bridget added, and rocked back, thoughtfully sipping her wine. "I think I'll make him a basket of muffins when the blueberries come in."

"You might want to wait on that." Cici's tone was grim as she dug into her pocket and pulled out a folded slip of paper. "Here's the bill."

Bridget looked at her with a certain amount of trepidation, and then, hesitantly, took the paper and unfolded it. She gasped out loud.

"It's fair," Cici said quickly. "I checked around. It's just... unexpected."

Lindsay took the paper from Bridget, squinted at it, held it farther away, and then close. "Does that say—eleven *thousand* dollars?"

"And forty-seven cents," Cici confirmed.

For a moment the three women just looked at each other, speechless. Then Bridget cleared her throat. "Um, I don't know how to tell you this, but I don't have that much."

"I don't even have one third that much," said Lindsay, still staring at the paper.

Cici got up and poured more wine from the bottle on the wicker table, topping off Bridget's glass on her way back to her chair.

"We still have to get the hickory tree cut down," Cici said. "You know, the one that caused the problem in the first place? Deke said his brother-in-law would do it for five hundred dollars. And if we go with Sam's plan about building air shafts with exhaust fans from the cellar it will be about half the cost of installing air-conditioning, but still . . ." She drew a breath. "That's going to be at least another three thousand dollars."

Lindsay blew out a long, slow breath. "Wow."

"I suppose I could get a credit card advance," Bridget ventured.

Lindsay said, "I don't think I have that much left on my credit cards."

Cici shook her head adamantly. "At today's rates? That would be crazy."

Lindsay slanted a gaze to Bridget. "We could sell the sheep," she suggested. Then at Bridget's shocked look she added quickly, "Sorry, just kidding."

"They wouldn't bring enough to help anyway," Cici assured her, and Bridget's look darkened as she realized Cici had already researched the subject.

"Look," Cici added quickly. "I feel like this is partly my fault. When I did the cost analysis on this place, I should have allowed for the unexpected."

"Oh no, it's not your fault," Bridget said, although her tone was still distracted with worry. "How could you know?"

"We did allow for the unexpected," Lindsay pointed out. "Just not enough."

Cici nodded in sad agreement, then squared her shoulders. "Anyway, the point is, this is an investment. A business. We need to start treating it like one. We need to start thinking like men."

Bridget looked confused, but Lindsay scowled. "I don't like the way men think. Why do we have to think like men? They screw everything up."

"Not everything," objected Bridget.

"Name one thing."

"Well . . . the Declaration of Independence."

Lindsay sniffed her derision and took a gulp of sparkling water. "Oh yeah, like *that* was such a great idea. While those pompous white-wigged asses were up there making speeches and signing their names did they think about all the women and children who would be left homeless and impoverished during a war that would last, excuse me, *seven years*? Did they take a poll to see how many people were willing to put their homes on the line and have their families destroyed so that a handful of rich landowners could get out of keeping their agreements with a country that was treating them pretty damn well, all things considered? Did you know that more than half of the people living in America during the Revolutionary War were on the side of the *British*? And, oh by the way, let's compare the standard of living of the average British citizen, with their free health care and four weeks of vacation, to that of the average American today and see how many people think the Declaration of Independence was such a good idea now, huh?"

Cici stared at her. "Jeez, Lindsay, when did you start listening to talk radio?"

"It's the only station we can get before nine in the morning," Bridget pointed out.

"Name me one thing," Lindsay insisted, "one single thing that men did right."

"Okay," Cici said, "I'm game. They tamed the Wild West. Without men—big, ugly, lice-infested, gun-totin', rotten-toothed, foulmouthed, bigoted, brawling men complete with all their greed, gold mining, railroad technology, and STDs, Hollywood would not be the multibillion-dollar industry it is today and the world would be deprived of such cultural masterpieces as *Dumb and Dumber*."

"I was going to say something about disenfranchising an entire native population and destroying an ancient culture," replied Lindsay, "but I think I rest my case."

"And I think you need to cut back on the Benadryl," Cici said. "This is serious."

"I refuse to think like a man."

"Then think like a smart woman." Cici drew in a breath. "Look," she said. "None of us can afford to put out this kind of cash. But we all could afford another forty or fifty dollars a month. I say we go into town Monday and talk to the bank about a loan."

"Oh." Bridget was visibly relieved. "That's a great idea."

"I'll say," agreed Lindsay. "But I don't think it's something a man would have thought of."

"It will have to be three personal loans," cautioned Cici. "According to the terms of our joint venture agreement, none of us can borrow against our equity in the house. But I think we could get a pretty good rate, especially if we went for a short-term loan."

"Well," sighed Lindsay, "I'm glad that's settled."

They sat and rocked and listened to the rain for a time longer, then Bridget said, "They do it for us."

When Cici and Lindsay returned only questioning looks, she continued, "The pioneer men blazed trails west so they could farm more land and raise healthy children. They carried guns to keep women safe, and they cut down forests to build shelters so that their families could stay warm. And before they go into battle, they drink a toast to the women they left behind. They do it for us."

Lindsay looked at her solemnly for a moment. "Well," she decided, "I guess that's okay then."

"Besides," Cici added, "they stopped the lawn mower."

"But not before it destroyed the garden," Bridget pointed out.

Lindsay pushed herself to her feet. "I'm going to take a cool bath."

"Don't forget the baking soda."

"I hate being a farmer," Lindsay said.

Bridget smiled and sat back to watch the birds. "Actually, I think I'm starting to like it."

Cici, sipping her wine, said nothing at all.

13

In Which All Their Problems Are Solved

They wore their church suits to the bank on Monday morning. The loan officer wore jeans and a gray T-shirt with the bank logo on one pocket and Blue Valley Community Bank stenciled in green on the back. She was a frizzy-haired young woman of about thirty-five whose desk plate introduced her as Sonya Maxwell. She actually remembered them all from church—they were easy to recognize in their suits—and greeted them warmly. The ladies returned the greeting and the small talk and tried to remember whether she was a Baptist or a Methodist.

"So," said Sonya. Settling back with her hands folded across her stomach and smiling benignly, she seemed ready for a long chat. "How're ya'll liking it out there in that big old house all by yourselves?"

They agreed that they loved it, couldn't imagine a setting more beautiful, were getting used to country life, and then Cici added, "But it is quite a handful. Which is why—"

"What you need," decided Sonya, looking them up and down, "are some men. You're all just as cute as you can be. It shouldn't be too hard to find you some fellas."

Bridget smiled gratefully and said, "Thanks, but we already have some."

Sonya immediately looked interested, and Lindsay corrected quickly, "What Bridget means is that we're really not in the market for—"

"What Lindsay means," Cici corrected firmly, "is that we're much too busy with the house to have time for dating. Which brings me to the reason we're here."

"Well, when you do have time," Sonya replied magnanimously, "you just let me know. I know everybody in town, and I'm not going to steer you to anybody who can't take care of you, you can be sure of that. After all, they all have to get their mortgages through me, don't they?" She winked. "And we girls have got to stick together. So tell me, what did you all do back in Baltimore?"

There followed a fifteen-minute coffee klatch type conversation about their former careers, children, retirements, and exes; Bridget's widowhood; their decision to share a house; their accidental discovery of Blackwell Farm and their immediate passion for it. Sonya, in turn, shared her memories of the house from her childhood, cranky old Mr. Blackwell and rumors of its ghost. Cici gave up trying to work the reason for their visit into the conversation, and just sat back and enjoyed it.

"Have you found the folly?" she wanted to know.

The ladies looked from one to another. "The what?"

"Well, it's probably all fallen down by now. But there used to be a little house out in a glade in the middle of the woods, just like a little fairy castle. I saw a picture of it one time. It used to be painted green with white gingerbread scrollwork but by the time I was a kid playing around there all the paint had peeled off and the windows and doors were missing. My mother told me that's what they called them in England—silly little buildings with no practical purpose. Follies. I guess that's where the Blackwells got the idea. They used to travel in Europe a lot, especially when the vineyard was in operation. Now." She leaned forward and tapped a few keys on her computer. "How much do you need?"

For a moment all three of them simply returned a blank look, having become so relaxed in the conversation that they had almost forgotten why they'd come. Then Cici quickly assumed her business demeanor, and explained their situation and their need. Sonya listened while she typed, and when Cici had finished she said, studying the figures on her screen, "I can give you a much better rate on a home equity loan, or even a fixed rate mortgage. Are you sure . . ."

"We don't want to borrow against the house," Cici said firmly.

"We have an agreement," added Lindsay.

"A legal thing," said Bridget apologetically.

Sonya pursed her lips, typed a few more characters, and said, "Okay then, I can give you seven and a quarter variable on a personal loan, but you understand that that rate is only good for six months. You'll have to renegotiate at the beginning of the year."

They exchanged a look and a nod. "Sounds fair," Cici said.

"Good enough," agreed Lindsay.

"Sure," said Bridget.

More tapping on the keyboard, and Sonya glanced up. "I

see you've got an account here called 'Household.' Do you want the funds transferred directly into that?"

They nodded. "That would be good."

One more keystroke, and she sat back in her chair, smiling. "Okay then, you're all set. It will probably take until Thursday morning, since we're closed on Wednesdays."

Cici said, "But—you mean that's it?"

Lindsay added, "Don't you want an application form or something?"

"What for? I have everything I need to know."

Bridget said, "But . . . shouldn't we sign something?"

Sonya stood up and offered her hand. "Ya'll invite me over when you get the house fixed up, okay? I'd love to see the inside of that old place."

They each shook her hand enthusiastically, promised to do so, and left the bank with muted expressions of wonder.

"Now *that's* the way to do business!" exclaimed Lindsay when they were in the car.

"I had three accounts with the same bank in Baltimore for twenty-seven years," Bridget confided, "and I can assure you, they wouldn't even give me my own ATM password without filling out six different forms in triplicate! Much less a loan."

"All of that stuff about where we were from and what we used to do and how long we'd been married and how much we'd already put into fixing up the house," Cici said, shaking her head in amazement as she started the engine, "that was the loan application!"

"Life in a small town," Bridget said with a single, amazed shake of her head.

"Sign me up," said Lindsay, and they all grinned in agreement.

❧

It rained. It rained and it rained. The lawn mower stood idle in the shed and the grass grew higher and higher. Weeds invaded the flower gardens and even the roses hung their soggy heads. Puddles the size of small ponds formed in the backyard, and rivulets of mud ran from the newly excavated drain field.

Every morning Bridget pulled on rain gear and sloshed out to the meadow to check on the sheep, while the sheepdog—currently called Flower for the skunk in *Bambi*, whom he was growing to resemble more each day—barked and growled and darted at her legs, occasionally leaving teeth marks in her rain boots. Nonetheless, Bridget would return each morning to cook up a new recipe for chicken livers—which the dog promptly and predictably rejected. When she discovered that the sheep actually spent most of their day under a clean, dry shed at the edge of the property she relaxed a little, and started to call her morning trudge through the rain "walking the dog."

Sam finished installing the ceiling fans, repairing the ceiling, and engineering his cooling system; he went home to await the delivery of the exhaust fans he had ordered from California. Farley finished installing the new circuit box and replacing the outlets throughout the house. Now that the rain had brought cooler temperatures, Cici tackled the sunroom, prying open the painted-shut windows, scraping and sanding the walls, cutting new molding, and beginning the painstaking process of restoring the tiles. Lindsay devoted herself to her bedroom project, and the only clue the other women had as to her final design choice were the various flecks of paint that accumulated on her clothing and under her fingernails.

On the afternoon that the rain finally faded to gurgles and drips from the gutters and the sky lightened to a silver blue, Lindsay carried out a final load of trash—which included stained plastic dropcloths, empty paint cans, and buckets coated with dried white plaster—dusted off her hands, and declared, "Tah-dah!"

Bridget looked up from sweeping muddy paw prints off the front porch. "You can't mean you've finished!"

And Cici, her hair tucked under a baseball cap to protect it from paint flakes, pulled down her respirator mask as she came around the corner from the sunroom. "Is this the grand opening?"

Lindsay grinned as she led the way upstairs to her room. She paused outside the closed door for dramatic effect, and then opened it with a flourish.

She had applied a smooth coat of plaster directly over the wallpaper, glazed it with four different shades of soft, dusky green, and then polished the whole to a subtle satin sheen. Directly atop the plastered walls she had used a sculpting compound to form leaves, ferns, and delicate botanicals in bas relief, and painted them various tones of the same muted greens she had used on the walls. The effect was of a misty garden, with leaves and grasses growing directly out of the walls.

"Oh, Lindsay," Bridget said softly. Her eyes were wide as she gazed around the room. "Will you do this in my room?"

Lindsay grinned, making no effort to hide her own pleasure in the result. "It turned out okay, if I do say so myself."

Cici lightly touched one of the sculptures, and glanced at Lindsay. "Joint compound?"

She nodded. "You can do anything with it. Let it dry and seal it, and you can't tell it from plaster."

"You have got to e-mail a picture of this to Paul and Derrick," Bridget said. "Wouldn't they just die?"

"Love to," replied Lindsay, "if we ever get Internet service."

"Amazing," said Cici, admiring a delicately etched fern. "Absolutely amazing. I guess this only goes to prove that not all art is on a canvas."

Lindsay's eyes softened thoughtfully as she absorbed this. "No," she said, "I guess it's not. Thanks, Cici."

"The only problem is," Bridget said, "now all the other bedrooms look shabby. I guess we'd better start plastering over wallpaper in the other rooms, huh?"

Lindsay laughed. "Thanks, but I believe I'll pass on that if you don't mind. If I never see another putty knife or a glazing sponge it'll be too soon. Besides," she added casually—almost too casually—"I think it's about time I got started on the art studio, don't you?"

"Well, thank goodness for that," Bridget said. "I was beginning to think you'd given up on that plan."

"And after we went to all the trouble to move you to the country so you could have a dairy barn for a studio," added Cici with a grin. "Do you need help?"

"I'll let you know," Lindsay said. "Right now I just thought I would clean it out so I could store my supplies in there. Later we'll talk about putting up some shelves, but it won't need much more than that."

"I think you can heat it with electric baseboard heaters,"

Cici said. "The walls are so thick they should serve as natural insulation, and . . . what's that?"

They all heard it at once: the grinding sound of a lawn tractor roaring to life, and very close. They got to the window in time to see their own lawn mower puttering around the corner—with a complete stranger riding it.

By the time they raced down the front steps a straight, careful path had been cut in the tall grass from the back shed to the poplar tree. The dog was crouched outside his customary haunt under the porch, barking wildly and pawing the ground. Riding astride the mower was a young man with greasy brown hair that fell to his neck, an equally greasy and stained white T-shirt, and frayed jeans. He didn't look up when they came out; he just kept going in a slow, straight line, working the clutch when the mower threatened to bog down in the wet grass.

Cici looked at Lindsay. Lindsay looked at Bridget. Bridget said, raising her voice to be heard above both the sound of wild barking and roaring engine, "Do you think he's trying to steal it?"

Cici said, "If he is, he's sure got a lot of confidence."

Lindsay shouted, "Should we tell him about the yellow jackets?"

"Let's find out who he is, first," suggested Cici.

As the mower downshifted to skirt the poplar tree, the three women walked boldly out in front of it—after first dancing quickly away from the sheepdog in attack mode—waving their arms to get the operator's attention. When he looked at them, Cici made a slashing motion across her throat, indicating he should cut the engine.

When the mower stopped, so did the dog, who tucked his

tail and slunk back under the porch. They found themselves staring at a skinny, unsmiling boy with a cigarette dangling from his lower lip in a manner oddly reminiscent of James Dean. Wisps of smoke drifted around his ears.

Cici spoke up. "I'm Cici Burke," she said. "This is Lindsay Wright and this is Bridget Tyndale. We own that lawn mower. And this lawn."

He looked from one to the other of them unhurriedly, and with absolutely no sign of friendliness in his expression. He pinched the cigarette between thumb and forefinger, drew and exhaled, and said, after a measured time, "Name's Noah. Heard you needed somebody to do yard work."

"Oh!" Lindsay exclaimed. Relief replaced the consternation on her face with such swiftness that she practically beamed. "Oh, yes, you're right, we do. That's great! We're so glad—"

Cici elbowed her in the ribs. "Where are you from, Noah?" she asked pleasantly.

He drew on the cigarette, eyes narrowed. "Here."

Bridget murmured, "What did you think Cici? That he was an out of town commuter?"

Cici tried again. "Who told you about us?"

His gaze was somewhere between insolent and disinterested. "You want me to mow your lawn or not?"

Lindsay returned Cici's elbow in the ribs, her smile disguising a muttered, "*Of course* we want him to mow the lawn!"

Bridget offered helpfully, "How much do you charge?"

He spat. "Ten dollars."

Bridget relaxed, smiling broadly. "Farley sent you! See, girls?" She spread her hands; problem solved. "Farley sent him!"

"An hour," said the boy. His eyes, like his voice, were cold and flat.

Their smiles faded.

They looked from one to the other for a moment, visibly weighing their options. Bridget said, in a rather small voice, "Well, I suppose . . ."

But Lindsay held up a staying hand, her jaw set. She stepped toward the boy. "How old are you?"

He didn't reply immediately. Then, without flinching, "Eighteen."

Lindsay cast a look back over her shoulder to Bridget and Cici. If he was a day over fifteen they all would have been hugely surprised.

She said, "Have you got a high school diploma?"

He answered sullenly, "Don't need one."

"No," she agreed, "I don't suppose you do. Unless you want to make ten dollars an hour."

He scowled at her, and she advanced on him.

"Do you know who makes ten dollars an hour in this county?" she demanded. "Medical transcriptionists, legal assistants, kindergarten teachers. People with high school diplomas *and* a certificate or degree. Library assistants, firefighters, EMTs—*they* make ten dollars an hour. And do you know why? Because they went to school, they worked hard, they studied, and they did not lie about their ages. Do you know what lawn maintenance people make?"

The anger in his eyes was almost overcome by curiosity. Perhaps he had never thought of himself as being in the "lawn maintenance" business before. "What?" he finally demanded, reluctantly.

"Six dollars an hour," she replied, and he spat on the ground in disgust. "That's well above minimum wage."

His lip curled in a sneer. "I ain't working for minimum wage."

"Or you could try that burger joint out on the highway. I understand they're paying six twenty-five an hour."

His scowl was fierce as he took another drag on the cigarette. "Ain't got no car."

She shrugged.

"Eight fifty."

"Six."

"Eight dollars."

"You got it," she told him, and he looked smug until she added, "the minute you show me a high school diploma."

His scowl was fierce. She didn't flinch.

"How many hours?" he asked at last.

"As many as you can work."

He tossed the butt of the cigarette away and left it smoldering in the grass.

She said, "Well, you think about it."

She turned and walked back toward the house, her fingers crossed in her pockets. She was almost to the porch before she heard the lawn mower start up again, and her face broke into a wide, self-congratulatory grin. "We've got ourselves a yard boy!" she exclaimed happily.

Cici gave a wry shake of her head. "I hope you know what you're doing."

And Bridget added uneasily, "I don't know. He seems a little scary."

"Not as scary as that crazy dog," Lindsay pointed out, and Bridget had to agree.

Cici shaded her eyes, watching the lawn mower make a careful circuit around the overgrown flower bed. "Assuming he doesn't just drive the mower on down the highway to that Burger Shack job," she said, "it would be great if he could weed the flower beds and burn some of this brush."

"Not to mention the boxwoods," Bridget added, indicating the nine foot high shrubs that flanked the front porch.

"And when he's finished with that..."

"I think this is going to work out just fine," Lindsay decided smugly. And then she exclaimed, "Oh!" as she suddenly remembered. She whirled and cupped her hands around her mouth. "Watch out for the yellow jackets!" she shouted.

By the end of the day, the boy called Noah had mowed the entire front lawn and emptied eight bags of soggy clippings into the compost pile. At dusk, he solved the problem of the yellow jackets by the time-proven method of pouring gasoline into their ground nest and tossing a match in after it—a process to which the horrified women would have immediately and strenuously objected had they known about it before the fact. Lindsay paid him in cash for hours worked, and no one would have taken wagers as to whether they would ever see him again.

However, at seven o'clock the next morning the dog started barking and the engine started grinding, and he was back to finish the backyard. Cici made a few phone calls and discovered the boy's last name was Clete, and that he came from what a social worker might have referred to as a "disadvantaged background." His mother had died when he was a baby, and he lived in a single-wide on a half acre outside of town with his father who, Cici was given to understand from Maggie's subdued tone, drank. This wasn't much in terms of glowing recommendations, but there was some reassurance in knowing someone who knew him, and, Maggie insisted, he wasn't a "bad kid."

Bridget, who worried about how skinny he was, left orange juice and muffins on the back porch for him. Within the hour, they had disappeared. At noon she left two sandwiches, a bowl of potato salad, and a pitcher of iced tea in the same place, and was enormously pleased to find only empty dishes when she returned that afternoon to collect them.

Lindsay was feeling quite pleased with herself as she made her way down the freshly mown path to the dairy barn. The sky was a brilliant blue and the rain had brought with it a cool front that tasted faintly of autumn. It was the perfect day to work outside and, dressed in jeans, a long-sleeved shirt, and work gloves, Lindsay was ready to start reclaiming the building that would one day house her art studio.

The wisteria that had seemed so picturesque when they had first moved into the house in the spring had overgrown the door, the windows, and roof, and was encroaching upon the stone slab of the entry. Tucking her hair up under her cap, Lindsay made a note to herself about what Noah's next job would be as she ducked underneath the living canopy and pried the viny tendrils away from the door. The door squeaked on stiff hinges and scraped against the stone floor as she pushed it open.

For a moment she felt like one of those characters in a Grimm Brothers fairy tale, in which you simply *know* nothing good can happen to the protagonist once she or he has crossed the threshold of what will always turn out to be an enchanted castle. She did not remember the piles of rubble being quite so daunting, nor the debris on the floors quite so thick. Spiderwebs festooned the corners and she clawed at one that clung to her face. The two walls of windows, which had spread such a brilliant light over the building when they first had viewed it a year ago, were now clouded with a year's worth of grime and, worse, obscured by the creeping fingers of green vines that cast slippery shadows across the floors and the walls. As her eyes adjusted to the dimness, one of the shadows seemed to move, to actually slither across the floor. She stepped forward, kicking at a pile of leaves that had accumulated on the floor. The shadow scurried to a corner, formed itself into a coil, and hissed at her.

She didn't scream at first, because she was too busy choking on her own breath, paralyzed by the hot-flash strobe of adrenaline that surged through her veins. But by the time she stumbled back out into the sunlight the scream had bubbled up through her throat and out of her mouth, and she didn't stop there; she kept on screaming.

As it happened, Noah had stopped the lawn mower to empty the collection bag. Bridget had stepped out onto the porch to try to tempt the dog with another plate of chicken livers. Cici was rinsing off a paintbrush with a backyard hose. So when Lindsay screamed, everyone heard it.

Bridget dropped the plate of chicken livers and ran toward the sound. Cici left the hose running and, slipping and skidding in the mud, raced around the side of the house. Even Noah, his curiosity aroused by all the commotion, sauntered toward the dairy barn.

They found Lindsay leaning against a cherry tree, gasping

for breath and hugging her arms. "S–s–snake!" she managed.

Cici demanded, "What kind?"

And Bridget gasped, "Oh my God! Are you sure?'

To which Lindsay replied, "Of course I'm sure! Do you think I'd make something like this up?" She shuddered and answered Cici, "I don't know what kind. It didn't have an ID card. All I know is that it was huge!"

"What I mean is," insisted Cici, "was it poisonous? Some snakes are good, you know."

Lindsay groaned, closed her eyes, and sank back against the tree trunk. "And I was having such a good day."

Noah, glancing at the huddled group of women, pushed open the door and eased inside. Three pairs of eyes followed him as though he were an infantryman preparing to launch a grenade. In a moment he returned, thumbs hooked into the pockets of his jeans, and spoke around the cigarette that dangled from his lips. "Rattlesnake," he pronounced. "Big 'un. Wish I had my gun."

Lindsay's knees buckled. Bridget caught her arm to brace her. "Good heavens," she said, eyes big.

To which Cici replied, "Farley! I'll bet he's got a gun!"

She raced to the house to call him.

Five minutes later, Farley roared up in his truck, slammed the door behind him, and strode toward the dairy barn with a shotgun under his arm and a determined expression on his face. Feeling like maidens in a comic horror film, the three women pointed toward the door of the dairy. "In there," they cried, almost as one.

Farley stared down the door grimly, cocked the shotgun, and nudged the door open with his shoulder. Noah followed closely behind, his excitement almost—though not quite—disguised by his aura of slouching nonchalance. The women edged close behind—but not too close. They stood just outside the door while Noah pointed toward the corner. "There she is."

Farley shuffled his weight, planted his feet, and raised the gun to his shoulder. Cici gripped Lindsay's arm. Bridget clutched Cici's hand. They all squeezed their eyes closed and tried not to squeal like girls at the huge *ka-boom* that seemed to shake the ground beneath their feet. When they opened them cautiously again, Farley was muttering beneath his breath, his face bright red. Over his shoulder, they could see ragged daylight pouring in through a hole the size of a doggie door in the far wall. The snake, still curled in the corner, rattled its tail ominously.

"Missed 'er a little," commented Noah, deadpan.

Farley raised the gun again, and this time all three women turned away and covered their ears with their hands. Two concussive blasts later, Noah let out a triumphant, "Eeee-*haw*! You got 'er dead between the eyes!"

Farley shouldered his weapon and turned to the women. "Ten dollar," he said,

Bridget said shakily, "I'll get my purse."

Lindsay said, "I'm going to be sick."

Noah said, "What do you want to do with it?"

The three women stared at him wordlessly.

"Makes good eatin'," said Farley.

"Indians used to wear the rattles around their neck," added Noah.

Lindsay said, "I am seriously going to be sick."

"You want 'em?" asked Noah.

"What?" Cici managed.

"The rattles."

Cici glanced at the other two, took a breath, and said, "I think I can safely say—no."

"Can I have them?"

Lindsay started toward the house on unsteady legs. "Is there any aspirin?"

Cici said to Noah in a tight, strained voice, "Help yourself."

Noah pulled out a pocketknife and went to collect his prize. Farley repeated, "Ten dollar."

"Um . . . right." Bridget turned to follow Lindsay to the house. "My purse." She stopped suddenly and turned back, looking dazed. "There was something I wanted to ask."

"About the snake?" prompted Cici, when she said nothing further.

"No . . . I don't think so."

"The sheep?"

"Oh," said Bridget, still looking a little unfocused. "The dog. That was it. The dog. How does he like his chicken livers?"

Farley looked at her with absolutely no expression. "Raw," he answered.

Bridget blinked. "Oh," she said. "Of course. I should have thought of that. I'll get your money."

❧

As it turned out, the excitement was not over for the day. No sooner had Farley bounced down the drive in his truck than Deke's cousin arrived with two other men, a pulley ladder, and a chain saw in a pickup with a magnetic sign on its door that read, Tree Cutting. Within the hour the air was filled with the sound of thundering chain saws, cracking limbs, and shouting men, all orchestrated to the background of manic barking and the drone of the lawn mower. They had to close all the windows even to be heard over the din, but fortunately the day remained so cool it was no hardship.

"It's times like this," Bridget said, chopping herbs for a pasta sauce, "that I really miss my library job."

Cici was washing off the last of the overripe tomatoes they had been able to salvage from the ruins of the garden. "Somehow this is not what I pictured when I decided to move to the country either," she agreed. "The guy said they have to trim back the poplar tree by the porch," she added. "Otherwise the whole thing would come down when they felled the hickory tree."

"I hate to see the hickory tree go. I was going to make a hickory nut cake."

"It was already dead."

She sighed. "I know. It's just a shame."

Lindsay opened the refrigerator and took out a bag of store-bought lettuce, which she began to shred for a salad. "At least Noah will have plenty of work cutting and stacking all that firewood."

"Not to mention cutting back the wisteria and cleaning out the dairy barn."

"You're damn right," said Lindsay darkly. "I'm not setting one foot back in there until all the creatures have been cleared out—and that includes dust mites."

Cici chuckled and scooped a handful of chopped tomatoes into the pan Bridget had prepared. They sizzled softly and released a tangy fragrance as they struck the garlic-infused olive oil. "That should be fun," she said. "Sanitizing a barn."

Bridget used her knife to scrape the chopped herbs off the cutting board and into the pot. "What are you going to do about the holes in the wall?"

"Not a problem," Cici said, "a couple of one-by-sixes and you'll never know what happened."

"Oh yes I will," replied Lindsay morosely. "I'll never forget it. What I'd like to know," she added with a touch of weary indignation, "is why all the wildlife is picking on *me*. First the yellow jackets, then the snake . . . I hate wildlife. I don't even like the dog."

"Nobody likes the dog," Cici pointed out.

To which Bridget replied defensively, "I do." She poured a measure of red wine atop the tomato and herb mixture and set a pot of water on the back burner to boil. Then she said, "Maybe they're trying to tell you something. I read a book one time about totems and animal medicine. Every animal has a different message."

"Great," said Lindsay. "Now I not only have to worry about being stalked by them, I have to figure out what they're trying to say."

"I don't think bees officially qualify as animals," Cici said, "so you're off the hook there. Wait a minute." She turned toward the window. "The noise has stopped. Do you think they're finished?"

Bridget turned the heat down under the tomato mixture and all three of them went out onto the porch to survey the results of the afternoon's work. For the longest time all they could do was stare.

Where once the sprawling hickory tree had framed the meadow, there was now only blue sky and rolling fenced pasture beyond. The newly clipped lawn was littered with leaves and branches and massive chunks of chain-sawed trunk, as far as the eye could see. The air was filled with the bitter smell of stripped hickory leaves and green bark.

Slowly, almost as one, they walked around the porch to the front of the house. The majestic poplar tree, whose shade had once stretched over the entire west side of the house and halfway across the lawn, had been shorn off at roof level. Bare stubs of branches were all that were left of what once had been as much a part of the house as the columned porch or the mansard roof. The porch was carpeted with its green leaves, and its broken branches lay like fallen bodies from the steps to the flower beds.

"Good God," said Cici, when she could speak.

"It looks like a bomb went off," Lindsay said, her voice subdued with horror.

"It will take weeks to get all this cleaned up."

"I guess . . . nobody said anything about debris removal."

Bridget's hand was at her throat, her eyes stricken. "The birds. What will happen to the birds?"

At the bottom of the steps was Deke's cousin, proudly coming toward them with the bill.

❧

That evening they wandered with peculiar reluctance out onto the porch for their ritual glass of wine, uneasy in a place that no longer felt familiar to them. Cici had spent a long time sweeping the leaves off the porch, but the smell of them still hung heavy in the air. And they all knew what lay beyond the railing. It was like a graveyard.

For a time even their conversation was stilted. Nothing felt the same. They sat in their chairs, but did not rock, and even the wine tasted too much of green and broken things.

And suddenly Lindsay summed it up for them. "I feel exposed," she said. "The tree was like—a shelter. Now"—she gestured—"the whole world is out there."

Unwillingly, they turned their eyes toward the place the tree once had been. In the distance was a magnificent vista of the mountains they had never noticed before. They could see the rise and fall of their own drive almost to the highway, and the whole of the pasture. Had the poplar tree not been there, they surely would have noticed sooner that the sheep they did not realize they owned were grazing in a pasture that they did. Yet Lindsay was right. The tree, with its towering limbs and green canopy, had been a kind of barrier between themselves and all that lay beyond. Without it they felt uncomfortable, defenseless.

"The guy said it would come back bigger than ever next spring," Cici offered. "You're supposed to trim back poplars. They're lightning rods, and during an ice storm the branches can go right through the roof."

"I wonder how old it was," Lindsay mused.

"Not as old as the hickory tree," Cici pointed out.

"I know, but . . . I hardly even noticed the hickory tree. The poplar was like a friend."

"Well, you know the old saying." Cici sipped her wine, but the cheerful note she was trying for fell flat. "God never closes a door but that he opens a window. We got someone to do our yard work only hours before we need more yard work done than we ever thought we would."

"What if he quits?"

"Then we're screwed."

"He doesn't seem all that reliable."

"Maybe we should pay him more."

Lindsay glared at her. "Don't even think it."

Bridget said, "All that stuff you were telling him about how much people made in this county—how did you know that?"

Lindsay shrugged. "I made it up." And at Bridget's reproving glance she insisted indignantly, "When I started teaching I made twenty-four thousand dollars a year. The education of an entire generation—the future of this country—was entrusted to me, and I earned less than a sanitation worker. Now I've got some punk high school kid on a lawn mower holding me up for the same kind of money it took me four years of college and a teaching certification to earn? I don't think so."

Cici lifted her glass to her. "You go, girl."

"Well, I feel sorry for him," Bridget said. "No mother, an alcoholic father, and he's so skinny."

"Bridget, you can't be responsible for every stray in the country. First the sheep, then the dog . . ."

"Besides," Cici added, "do you really feel sorry enough for him to pay him ten dollars an hour?"

Bridget thought about that for only a moment. "No."

They were silent for a while, sipping their wine. Then Bridget smiled a little, reminiscently. "Remember the first meal we had on this porch?"

"The day we moved in." She chuckled. "Cici opened a bottle of wine with a power drill. I'd never been so tired in my life. Gosh, I can't believe it's been six months."

"A lot of things have changed."

"A lot of things haven't," Cici pointed out. "I thought we would have gotten a lot more done on the place by now."

"We keep getting distracted," Lindsay said. "What we need is a better list."

"Six months to paint the porch." Cici said with a short, incredulous shake of her head.

"And one bedroom," added Lindsay, "and the whole living room. That was huge."

"And to start restoring the garden walkway and build most of a rock wall," Bridget pointed out, "and refinish the stairs and paint all the trim and repair the molding and the doorknobs and the roof and the siding and the fence. Besides, it's a gorgeous porch."

"And a fabulous bedroom," added Cici. "Of course, we still have to refinish all the floors in the living room. And all the windows in the sunroom are rotted out. I think I can make a deal with one of the guys at the lumber store to buy some used ones cheap, but it's going to take time to replace them all."

"We should talk to someone about repairing the barn roof before winter."

"I can do that," Cici said. "All it will take is a piece of plywood."

Lindsay gave her a reproachful look. "You don't have to do *everything*, Cici."

Cici shrugged. "I don't mind."

Bridget smiled. "Remember all the plans we had when we decided to buy this place?"

"You were going to bring back the Blackwell Farms jams and restore the vineyard," Lindsay said. "Not to mention open a restaurant."

"And you were going to open an art studio and bring in students from around the country."

"And if it hadn't been for one little rattlesnake . . ."

"Besides," said Bridget, "it wasn't exactly a restaurant I wanted to open. I just wanted to cook. And who knew there would be sheep to take care of?"

"I guess it's all been a little bit more than any of us expected," Cici said. "But still, it's only been six months."

"Seems like longer," Lindsay sighed.

"Seems like only yesterday," Bridget said.

The very faintest trace of a frown creased Bridget's brow as she studied her wineglass. "Can I ask you both something? Seriously?"

They looked at her.

"If it hadn't been for me," Bridget said, "I mean, losing Jim and all, and being at loose ends the way I was . . . would you ever have done this?"

Lindsay laughed. "Are you kidding? Not in a million years. I wouldn't even have thought about it!"

And Cici agreed. "How could we have done it without you, Bridge? It never would have crossed my mind." Then she looked at her, a little puzzled. "Why do you ask?"

"Nothing." Bridget's smile seemed a little strained. "It's silly. Just some stupid thing Kevin said."

Lindsay said thoughtfully, "You know what it's like? The end of a vacation. Everything was so much fun when we started out. Now it's . . . well, a lot of responsibility."

They nodded agreement, and no one had anything to say for a while.

Then Bridget said softy, "It's so quiet out here."

They listened for a moment, trying to decide what was missing. And then they knew. It was the sound of birdsong.

Lindsay shivered and slipped her arms into the sleeves of a cotton sweater she had tossed about her shoulders. "It's cool tonight."

"Summer's almost over," observed Cici.

"I hear hickory makes good firewood," Lindsay said.

Cici gave a small, disbelieving shake of her head. "Firewood. Where did the time go? I can't even start to think about everything we have to get done before winter."

Bridget stood. "I'm cold, too. I think I'll go inside."

And then she stopped. "Oh, my." Her tone was reverent. "Would you look at that sunset?"

Lindsay stood, too, and then Cici. "Wow," she said softly. "I never noticed before."

"Me, either."

"I guess," said Bridget reluctantly, after a moment, "the tree was in the way."

They stood together, their faces painted with the pink glow of the fading sun, and watched the rich pastel colors streak across the sky until the day was done.

Autumn

Harvest

14

In Which Preservation Is Paramount

On the morning that Lindsay discovered she was fat, Bridget found a handful of canning jar labels tucked inside Emily Blackwell's recipe book, and Cici discovered a bushel basket of persimmons on the front steps.

At first they had been deeply touched by the gifts from the gardens of their well-meaning neighbors. Soon after the disaster with the lawn mower, Sam brought over a large brown grocery sack filled with green beans—from his wife, he said, who had more than she could put up. They thanked him profusely, but assured him it wasn't his fault their garden had been destroyed and that it wasn't necessary to bring them produce.

But the next afternoon, Farley brought over a basket of tomatoes and three dozen bell peppers, and Maggie sent an additional dozen eggplants. Someone from church asked if they had any corn, and when Cici answered in the negative, transferred two bushels of fresh-picked corn from the back of his truck to the back of her SUV. Their ruined garden, they quickly came to realize, had become the excuse for every woman in the county who couldn't face canning another tomato or pickling another cucumber to dispose of the excess bounty from their own gardens—and to feel good about herself while she did it.

They made zucchini bread, zucchini casserole, fried, sauteed, and roasted zucchini. They made squash soup, tomato soup, onion soup, and enough marinara sauce to open an Italian restaurant. They chopped pears for chutney and simmered them into a sweet, thick sauce and ate them whole, with juices dripping down their wrists and chins, over the sink. Everything else was put on hold for a season that wouldn't wait, and the abundance of nature's harvest took over their lives.

They bought a second freezer and installed it in the cellar. They shaved corn off the cob and packed it into plastic pint containers, blanched green beans, lima beans, okra, and field peas and did the same. And of course they couldn't ignore the bounty of their own fruit trees and bushes when they began to produce. Bridget added twenty-seven glistening jars of blackberry jam to the strawberry coulis in the pantry, and at least as many jars of cherry jelly, grape jelly, and applesauce. They wondered out loud just how long gardens could possibly continue to produce in this region, anyway.

Bridget glanced up from puzzling over the canning jar labels and stifled a groan as Cici set the basket of fruit on the counter between an overflowing basket of corn and a tall paper sack of unshelled butter beans, nudging aside two rows of fat, ripe tomatoes to make room.

"What is it?" Bridget asked.

"Persimmons, according to the note. The Baptist preacher's wife thought we could use them. I don't even know what a persimmon is."

Bridget's eyes went wide. "That's weird."

Cici gave a grunt of laughter as she edged the coffeepot out from between a tower of red peppers and yet another basket filled with corn. "Maybe to you. I gave up being surprised by what I find on our front porch about a month ago."

"No, I mean, look." Bridget waved the stack of canning jar labels at her. "I found these in the cookbook."

Cici poured a cup of coffee and crossed the room to take the labels. They were made of heavy paper, cut with a decorative edge, and were without the adhesive back of modern jar labels. Each had a colorful, faded border of fruits entwined with vines and flowers, and in the center of each label was written in brush calligraphy "Blackwell Farms Persimmon Jelly."

Cici raised an eyebrow as she returned the labels. "Cool. Now we know what you do with a persimmon."

"These weren't in this book yesterday," Bridget insisted. "I know they weren't because—"

"Get away from me with your muffins, your coffee cakes, and your French toast topped with jam." Lindsay came through the door with her face averted and her two index fingers crossed before her as though to ward off evil. "One pair of jeans, I can believe the dryer shrunk. Two, maybe. But three? I don't think so."

She marched straight to the refrigerator, opened it, and peered in. "Isn't there any fruit?"

"How about a persimmon?" suggested Cici.

"I don't even know what a persimmon is."

"Something else we have to peel, cook, and preserve," said Cici.

"Great. That's how my jeans got so tight in the first place." Lindsay closed the refrigerator door and opened a cabinet. "Isn't there anything to eat?"

Both Bridget's and Cici's eyes traced the cornucopia of produce the kitchen had become—tomatoes on every surface, baskets and bags spilling over with green and yellow vegetables, unshucked corn stacked on the counters and floor—but wisely said nothing. Lindsay closed the cabinet door resolutely.

"I'm going for a run," she said. "That's the whole problem, you know. We're just not active enough."

Cici and Bridget waited until the door had slammed behind her before they let the giggles take over.

Cici glanced again at the labels as she sat beside Bridget at the island. "Not wanting to seem ungrateful or anything, but the last thing we need is more jelly. What we need are labels for vegetable soup."

Bridget reluctantly tucked the labels into the back of the cookbook. "You don't think it's strange? A basket of persimmons is left on our porch the same morning I find a stack of handmade labels—who knows how old they are—for persimmon jelly?"

"Right. And I guess you're going to tell me the ghost of Emily Blackwell left them there."

"Well, somebody did."

"Soup," Cici insisted, nudging the cookbook. "Soup."

Bridget turned pages in the book, sipping her coffee. "We've got eight gallons of soup in the freezer. Tomato, tomato basil, tomato and okra, tomato with carmelized onion and red wine, cream of tomato, tomato chowder. Corn, corn chowder, cream of corn . . ."

"Okay, I get it. I know we're going to be glad we have it in the winter, but right now I don't care if I never see another vegetable."

"Wait. Here's something we haven't made yet. Brunswick stew."

"I love Brunswick stew." Cici leaned in to peer at the recipe. "Tomatoes, butter beans, onions, corn . . . this is perfect! We can use all these vegetables in one big stew!"

Bridget wrinkled her nose and she dragged her finger down the list of ingredients. "Venison . . ."

"Use beef," suggested Cici.

"Duck . . ."

"Chicken."

"Hog jowls?"

"Pork loin."

"It says here to slow roast the meat on a spit over an open fire."

Now it was Cici's turn to wrinkle her nose. "When was that thing written anyway? During the American Revolution?"

Bridget looked up from the book. "Wait. We've got Lindsay's propane grill stored in the barn. We haven't used it all summer."

"We've been too busy peeling vegetables."

"That's an open flame, isn't it?"

"It sure is," agreed Cici. "And while we're slow roasting the meat, why don't we grill some of those red peppers that are about to go bad?"

Bridget grinned. "Do you know how much fire-roasted red peppers go for in the supermarket?"

"This is fantastic." Cici rubbed her hands together, gaining enthusiasm for the project. "We can get rid of every last vegetable in this kitchen today! Do you know how to can fire-roasted red peppers?"

Bridget shrugged. "How hard can it be?"

Cici, remembering the strawberries, said, "Maybe we'll freeze them."

A dreamy, serene expression spread across Bridget's face as she looked around the kitchen. "We could do it. We could really clear out everything in this kitchen today."

"Except the persimmons," Cici pointed out.

Bridget's brow knotted faintly as she thought again about the labels. "I still think it's weird."

Cici finished her coffee. "I'm going to get the grill out."

"We'll have to go into town to buy the meat."

"And freezer containers. Don't forget freezer containers."

"Of course we can't do anything until we shell all these butter beans, husk the corn, and peel the tomatoes."

The two of them stared at each other, momentarily defeated. There was a knock on the back door.

The boy Noah stood there, the perpetual cigarette dangling from his lips, wearing filthy jeans and a faded blue T-shirt with a dragon on it. The temperature hoverered around fifty degrees, and there was gooseflesh on his bare arms. "Gettin' ready to start splitting your wood," he said. "Where you want it stacked?"

Bridget didn't hesitate. She snatched the cigarette from his lips and tossed it over the rail, then grabbed his arm and pulled him inside. "Do you know how to shell butter beans?" she demanded.

❧

When she lived in the suburbs, Lindsay ran two miles every day. Well, maybe not every day, but most days. Some days. The problem with running in the country was that there was no place to run to.

She started jogging around the outside of the pasture fence when the crazed border collie came out of nowhere and charged her. She groped for a stick with which to ward him off, but an apparent muscle twitch from one of the peacefully grazing sheep in the meadow caught his attention at the last moment and he veered off, leapt the fence, and charged the sheep instead. Lindsay moved carefully away from the fence and into the woods.

There was a trail that followed the stream, and she ran along it for about a hundred yards until she turned her ankle on a stone and almost fell. No harm done though. By that time she was breathing hard and her calves ached, and she was starting to understand why people didn't run in the country. Aside from the innate hazards, there was simply too much to see. And when you ran, you missed it all.

Although it was too early in the season for the foliage to have officially reached its peak fall color, the woods were awash in shades of delicate yellow, sherbert orange, and pale maroon. Interspersed with the fading green of a late summer's memory, the delicate turning of the colors of the leaves made walking down the wooded path feel like being immersed in a watercolor painting. The air tasted cool and damp, and mist clung to the multicolored ground beneath her running shoes. Lindsay shoved her hands deep into the pockets of her velour jogging jacket and slowed her stride, taking it all in.

Aside from the days spent digging up stones from the streambed, none of them had had the time over the summer to explore the property, and Lindsay had never been this deep into the woods before. The path meandered away from the stream, sometimes overgrown by weeds or blocked by fallen trees, and eventually opened onto a small, misty glade. Lindsay caught her breath.

There it was. The folly.

It hardly looked like the gingerbread house Sonya Maxwell had described. There was a round turretlike structure topped with rusted tin on one side, attached to an octagonal-shaped main room with a multipaneled, similarly rusted-out tin roof. There were three windows in each wall—although the glass was missing now—making the whole more of a gazebo than a house. The green paint that Sonya had described was completely gone now, leaving nothing but bare gray wood, and the delicate scrollwork trim was either hanging from the eaves by a single nail or rotting on the ground.

Lindsay picked her way through the briars and weeds that surrounded the structure, her breath suspended in awe as she imaged the charm this place must have held for another generation. She understood the reason for the path now, and imagined a horse-drawn wagon, filled with picnic baskets and revelers, traversing it. Or a woman in high-button boots and a bustle gown, strolling down the path with a volume of poetry under her arm, bound for an afternoon of solitary reading in this enchanted place, with nothing but the rustle of the grasses and the chirping of the birds for company.

What was it Sonya had said? That a folly was a rich man's extravagance, a building with no practical purpose whatsoever? If that was the case, this was not a folly, because it had obviously served a very important purpose in the lives of the people who had lived here a hundred years ago, and already Lindsay was envisioning how it might be brought back to life.

There was a circular porch with some missing and rotting boards, and Lindsay climbed up on it carefully. The sagging door still had a few shards of glass intact in one of its six panes, and Lindsay imaged how charming it must have been in its prime. She used her shoulder to assist the stiff hinges and pushed inside.

Dusty light filtered in from the windows surrounding the circular room. There was a sweet little marble fireplace with carved cherubs on either side, now black with smoke and age. There was a sprinkling of dried leaves on the stained marble floor, but the wind had swept most of them into a corner. Against one wall was an old settee, once upholstered in what appeared to be wine brocade that the rats and squirrels had made short work of long ago. There was a wrought iron table with peeling white paint, and an oddly mismatched cane-seated chair. And in another corner was a dingy rumpled sleeping bag, and an upturned crate upon which were arranged several objects. Curious, Lindsay drew closer.

The crate, turned on its side, formed three shelves. The top shelf held a razor, a six-pack of Coke from which one can was missing, two Snickers bars, and a bag of freeze-dried beef jerky. On the next shelf was a plastic fork and knife of the kind that came with take-out food, two cans of tuna, a blackened aluminum pan with chunks of charred food melded to the bottom, and a one-liter foam drinking cup with the Burger Shack logo on it. Next to it was a pack of cigarettes and a notebook topped by a curious-looking collection of what looked like flat stones on a leather thong. She almost picked it up until she realized what it was and jerked her hand back. Not stones. Rattles. From a rattlesnake.

Trying not to grimace, she eased the notebook away from the rattlesnake necklace and flipped it open. It was a sketchbook. Inside were random studies—a stream with rocks, a country road, various views of the mountains, a split rail fence with scrub cedar growing through it that reminded her of the one on the highway that ran alongside their house, a scruffy-looking border collie, a rattlesnake. It was not the quality of the sketches that impressed her—though they definitely showed talent—so much as the fact that they appeared to have been done with nothing more than a #2 pencil.

"Wow, kid," she murmured, "imagine what you could do if you had the right tools."

She returned the sketchbook to its place and sat back on her heels thoughtfully, looking around the room with a new eye now. A fireplace for cooking, a floor swept clear of leaves, a cane chair. Something caught her eye from one of the far windows, and she went to check it out. It was a T-shirt, hung across the low limb of a tree to dry. And beyond it, in a sunny patch of tilled earth protected by a fence made from string and sticks stuck into the ground, were the remains of a summer garden. Dried corn stalks and bean vines, a few bright squash and red peppers, empty cucumber and zucchini vines. She shook her head in mild amazement, and couldn't prevent a smile.

"Well I'll be damned," she said out loud. "The Ladybug Farm garden thief, caught red-handed."

❧

By the time Lindsay returned to the house, Cici and Bridget had, by turns, been into town twice—once for a hundred dollars' worth of meat, and again for a new tank of propane for the grill—and Noah had shucked all the corn and had almost completed shelling the butter beans. When he saw Lindsay, he stomped out to work on cleaning out the dairy, muttering something about women's work, before she could say anything more than hello to him. Within moments, she was caught up in the choreography of a century-old recipe in which, it turned out, there was very little room for error.

Cici heated the grill to three hundred degrees while Bridget prepared a spice rub for the meat and Lindsay plunged tomatoes into a stockpot of simmering water to loosen their skins. Corn and butterbeans were coming to a simmer in another huge pot.

"I don't know why I always get this job," Lindsay complained, fishing a steaming tomato out of the water with barbecue tongs. "I hate this job." She plunged the tomato into a bucket of ice water in the sink, and went after another one.

"I think the heat should be higher," Cici said, rubbing red peppers with olive oil. "Otherwise these peppers are never going to char."

"I'm trying to lose weight," Lindsay added, making a small

slice in the skin of the iced-down tomato. The skin slipped off the fruit like a sweater off a baby, and she plopped the tomato into the pot with the corn and beans. "Whose idea was Brunswick stew anyway?"

"It says to slow roast the meat," Bridget pointed out, slapping the spice rub onto the first of the two pork loin roasts. "You can't roast anything above 325."

"Maybe I'll turn the heat up just a tad, just until the peppers are done."

"Put them on the top rack and let them roast with the meat. They'll char eventually."

"I think I'll turn up the heat."

Then Lindsay said, "Listen, you won't believe what I found on my walk this morning."

Cici, cradling a bowl filled with oiled red peppers in one hand, opened the back door. Noah stood there, hands in pockets.

"What ya'll want to do with all that crap in the loft?" he asked.

Cici said, "What loft?"

And Lindsay turned from the stove. "What crap?"

While Bridget, loading heavy, spice-rubbed roasts onto a tray, said, "I thought you were splitting wood."

Noah, glowering, muttered, "Fool women. Wood, beans, dairy barn . . . Make up your minds, can't you?"

"You know what we should do," Bridget said with a sudden light of inspiration in her eyes, "is pick up some of those hickory chips from the yard and put them in the grill to smoke the meat."

Lindsay repeated, "What crap?"

Cici said, "That's a great idea. I'll get them."

Cici held the back door open as Bridget struggled through with the heavy tray of meat. Noah said, unaccountably, "Hickory spits."

Lindsay plopped the last tomato into the pot of vegetables and dried her hands on a dish towel. "What crap?" she said.

❧

Lindsay reached the top of the ladder first, followed closely by Bridget and then Cici. A trapdoor was pushed to the side of the opening that was large enough to drop a double bale of hay through. Lindsay looked around carefully before stepping off the ladder, but the floor was solid. She stood up and switched on the flashlight she had brought.

"Wow," she said.

The dairy loft was vast and steeply raftered, covered in a plank floor that looked like hickory. The smell was warm and dusty, the slow-baked aroma of old wood in the sunshine. Lindsay's flashlight beam picked out big, lumpy shapes covered with white sheets, boxes, and irregular metal objects stacked against the walls, before Bridget's light joined hers, and then Cici's.

"Who could have guessed this was even up here?" Bridget said. "I never knew this place had a loft."

"They probably stored feed for the cows here," Cici said when she joined them. "It's nice and dry, and the trapdoor would have kept the rats and squirrels from eating up the profit."

"Leave it to a teenage boy to go exploring and come up with a loft we didn't even know was here," Bridget said. "This place gets bigger every day."

Cici made her way over to one of the sheet-covered lumps

and lifted the fabric. "It's furniture," she said, and the note of excitement in her voice increased as she tossed back the sheet. "Good heavens, it's a Queen Anne highboy!"

"It matches the table in the dining room," Bridget said, and Lindsay threw back another sheet.

"Here are the chairs!" she called.

"Will you look at this game table?" Bridget cried, pushing back another dustcover. "Look at all the inset wood!"

"This chair is in pretty bad shape, but I bet it could be re-upholstered."

"What is all of this junk against the wall here?"

Cici made her way over and joined her flashlight to Lindsay's. "Bedsprings," she decided. "Old fashioned, rusted-out bedsprings."

"I wonder what's in all these boxes?" Lindsay knelt down to open one but found nothing inside but stained and rotting fabric.

"Old draperies probably," Cici said. "Not every old box is going to hide a treasure, you know."

"Well, this is a treasure." Bridget's voice, soft with wonder, came from across the room. "Look at this bed frame—it's burled walnut. And there's a dresser to match. Did you see this gorgeous gilt mirror?"

"This is better than a department store!" Lindsay exclaimed.

"This is what happened to all the furniture nobody wanted when the family redecorated," observed Cici.

"Nobody wanted this darling headboard with all the leaves and flowers carved into it?" Bridget said. "Wait, there's a footboard, too. Lindsay, you should put this in your room. It's perfect!"

"Where's Noah?" Lindsay demanded. "We've got to start getting this stuff out of here. I can't wait to see what we have! It's like Christmas!"

Cici held up a hand. "Okay, hate to be a buzzkill here, but..."

The other two groaned.

"First of all, it's going to take more than one teenage boy to get all this stuff down the ladder. In fact, I'm not even sure how they got it up here."

"This is a big project," agreed Lindsay reluctantly.

"But we could furnish the whole house out of this loft!" Bridget insisted.

"Some of it's in pretty bad shape," Cici pointed out. "It's going to take some elbow grease before you bring it into the house."

"Well," Bridget admitted, deflated. "You're right about that."

"And do we really want to start bringing heavy furniture in before we finish the floors?"

The three women looked at each other in the reflected light of their combined flashlights, and their expressions were glum.

"I hate the thought of tackling those floors."

"It wouldn't take long if we could just get to it."

"We got distracted by vegetables," admitted Bridget.

"But," said Lindsay, brightening, "that doesn't mean we can't at least explore what's here. Who knows, maybe there's a lost Rembrandt or something!"

But they hadn't pulled back more than two or three more sheets before Noah called from below, "Hey! You about finished up there?"

Lindsay went to the trapdoor and called down, "Not quite. Why?"

"Just thought you'd want to know," he answered, "that whatever you're cooking is on fire."

❧

"I would rather spend three days cutting miter joints," Cici said, stifling a groan as she sank into her front porch rocker, "than three hours in the kitchen putting up stew. And you know how I hate cutting miter joints." She leaned back heavily in the rocking chair and wine splashed over the rim of her glass onto the back of her hand. Unself-consciously, she licked it off.

"But you have to admit," Bridget said, her smile a little lopsided with fatigue, "the stew was incredible."

"The best I've ever tasted."

"It was the charred meat," agreed Lindsay, closing the front door behind her as she joined them on the porch.

"Well, Noah did tell us hickory wood spits."

"Who knew what that meant?"

"Combined with the fat from the pork—"

"And the fact that you had to turn the heat up for the peppers—"

"A few flames were inevitable."

"But no harm done."

"And I still think the hickory chips were a good idea. The smokey taste is what made the stew so good."

The flames that shot from the back of the grill had been quickly extinguished with a garden hose, and the peppers were charred to perfection. Unfortunately, to their initial dismay, so was the meat. However, a closer examination revealed that only the outer crusts of the roasts and the skin of the chicken had been blackened, and most of the meat could be saved. Three hours of simmering in the stewpot with the vegetables had turned the charcoal lumps into a tender, savory mixture of perfectly seasoned stew that they could probably never replicate.

"I think," mused Bridget, "that's what the cookbook probably meant by roasting over an open flame. It's the burned parts that give the stew its flavor."

"Maybe," Cici said. "But I'm never doing that again. We could have blown up the house."

"Not the whole house," Bridget said defensively.

"Just the back patio," Lindsay grinned.

Bridget sighed and closed her eyes wearily. "Well, at least it's done. Every last vegetable has been peeled, cooked, and preserved, and we have enough food put away to outlast the Apocalypse."

"We still have the persimmons," Cici reminded her.

Bridget groaned out loud.

"What is it with us, anyway?" Lindsay said. "Why can't we let anything go to waste? It's not like we're in danger of starving or anything. Why can't we just keep the tomatoes we can eat and toss the rest away? Why can't we leave the apples for the squirrels and the cherries for the birds? We were never like this back in the suburbs."

"True enough," agreed Cici, although a little reluctantly. "I didn't have a bit of trouble tossing out lettuce that started to wilt or carrots when they went soft. And I *paid* for those."

"It's definitely different when it comes from the supermarket," Bridget said. "There's something about seeing the produce come straight from the ground that makes it more valuable somehow. And when they're *your* cherries, and your apples and your grapes and blackberries that you picked yourself—why, it would be a crime to let the birds have them."

"I never knew what a huge responsibility it was," Cici said with a sigh, "having free food."

"Not exactly free," Lindsay pointed out. "The way I figure it, the Brunswick stew only cost us about twelve dollars a serving."

The other two turned a questioning gaze on her.

"One hundred twenty-five dollars for the meat," Lindsay explained. "Fifteen dollars for the propane, twenty dollars for the containers, not to mention the electricity for the freezer, and don't forget you paid Noah six dollars an hour to shell beans."

"It was worth it," said Cici, raising her glass.

"Definitely," agreed Bridget. "I would have spent twice as much never to have to shell another bean or husk another ear of corn. I sent a quart of stew home with him," she added, "as a thank-you."

"Good," said Lindsay, in a slightly subdued tone. "It'll probably be all he gets to eat tonight."

Quietly, she told the other two about the folly in the glade and the encampment she had found there, complete with the remnants of their erstwhile garden. When she had finished, they were all silent for a while.

Then Bridget said, "He could have stolen money, or tools, or valuables from the house. God knows, we never lock anything up. Instead he chose to steal . . . garden plants."

"He must have been living there all summer," Lindsay

said, gazing into her wineglass as she rocked. "Maybe even before we moved in."

"This is a serious situation." Cici was frowning worriedly. "We can't just let him camp out on our property. For one thing, he's a minor, probably a runaway. We have to call social services." She looked at the other two. "Don't we?"

Lindsay hesitated, then cleared her throat. "Actually, that was Reverend Holland on the phone just now."

Bridget's brow knit. "Methodist or Baptist?"

"Baptist. I thought I'd call to thank his wife for the persimmons—"

"Good idea," agreed Cici.

"And while I had him on the phone, I thought I'd see if he had any advice on the, well, situation."

"Oh." Cici sounded a little surprised. "That's a good idea, I guess. He would know who to call."

Lindsay nodded. "That's what I thought. It turns out, Noah is a chronic runaway, and it sounds like he has good reason. The father sometimes doesn't show up for weeks at a time, and when he does he apparently can get pretty violent."

Cici and Bridget made soft signs of sympathy and concern, and focused their attention on Lindsay.

"He dropped out of school, just like I suspected, but he's never been in any real trouble . . . no drugs or anything."

"That anyone knows about," Cici had to say.

Bridget waved a hand. "How many drugs could you buy on six dollars an hour?"

Cici thought about that, and shrugged.

"Anyway, he's never been in trouble with the police," Lindsay went on, "and he works when someone will give him a job, and he stays wherever he can find a place. People from the church—both churches, I guess—have tried to help him out, but whenever social services gets involved, he just runs away again."

Cici sighed. "Great."

Bridget said, "But there's got to be something someone can do."

Lindsay said glumly, "I don't know what. I've been thinking about it all day."

"And even if there was something to be done, we're not the ones to do it," Cici said. "We don't even know the kid."

Bridget gave her an incredulous look. "Cecile Burke, you're the one who spearheaded a campaign to save an entire village in Africa! What do you mean, 'we're not the ones to do it'?"

Cici frowned uncomfortably into her wine. "African villages are a lot different than teenage boys camping out in your woods."

"Well at least he has some place to camp," Lindsay pointed out. "And he's getting regular meals, thanks to Bridget, and a little cash for whatever. If we turn him in, who knows where he'll end up?"

They thought about that for a while, and none of them liked the picture. Finally Cici said, "And what do you think is going to happen when winter comes? He'll freeze out there in the woods."

"We'll have to talk to him before then," Lindsay admitted. "But until then . . . couldn't we just pretend we don't know?"

The ladies were silent for a while, watching the shadows lengthen on the mountains while a fading sun speared streaks of orange through the naked, severed branches of the poplar tree. Already the lawn, which barely two weeks ago had been littered with debris, was cleared of brush and fallen leaves, and piles of hickory and poplar wood, neatly cut into two-foot lengths, awaited splitting and stacking. But the flower beds showed the neglect of the women's late-summer preoccupation with preserving food, and the roses were badly in need of trimming. There were still pecans to be harvested, grapevines to be pruned and tied, and black walnuts littered the ground on either side of the drive—all of which would have been lost had not Noah mowed back the weeds that once hid them.

Bridget said, "He's been an awful lot of help."

And Cici added, "He certainly has been more reliable than I ever thought he'd be."

"Of course his manners could use some improvement," Bridget added.

"Not to mention his attitude," said Cici. And she fixed a pointed look on Bridget. "Neither one of which are our responsibility."

"He likes to draw," Lindsay said, and when the other two looked at her she gave an embarrassed little shrug. "He had a sketchbook. I peeked. He's really not bad. In fact, he's pretty good. Okay, I know it doesn't mean anything, and I know he's a dropout and a runaway and a garden thief, and more than likely on his way to state prison by the time he's twenty but . . . he likes to draw. That's something, isn't it?"

Bridget and Cici smiled, and leaned back in their chairs. The orange streaks in the sky grew purple, and finally gray. The shadows on the porch turned deep blue, and the air had a crisp, cool undertaste to it. The crickets and the tree frogs had retired to wherever it is such creatures go for the winter, and no birds sang after dark. The only sound was the creak of their rocking chairs, and from somewhere beyond the tree line, the warble of an owl.

Bridget said after a time, "I don't think it's just us. I think if everyone in America could watch their fruit grow from a flower and spend hours fighting the wasps for their berries there would be a lot fewer apples tossed out after just one bite, and everyone would make jelly."

"And I'll tell you something else," Cici added. "If everyone had to pack up and carry off his own garbage like we do, we could solve the landfill problem in this country in less than a decade."

"When you have to dig your own well," Lindsay remarked sagely, "you don't leave the water running while you brush your teeth."

"I don't think I've ever heard that axiom."

"It's true though. It means no one wants to waste a precious resource, once they realize how precious it is."

Everyone murmured agreement with that, and then they rocked in silence, snuggling down in their sweaters, and thinking about Noah in the woods.

15

On Children and Other Creatures of the Wild

The leaves took on hues of strawberry, lemon, and brilliant tangerine gold, the mountains burst into fiery colors almost overnight, and the cobalt days grew shorter—and colder—by the minute. The stack of hickory and poplar grew steadily higher by the back door as Noah spent his mornings splitting wood, and his afternoons dragging debris out of the dairy.

When the first dusting of morning frost stiffened the grass, Cici tried to light a fire in the fireplace and filled the downstairs with billows of blue smoke. Farley came to clean the chimneys of squirrels' nests, and charged ten dollars.

Sam arrived to install the new fans for their air-conditioning system, which, to his utter delight, worked exactly as he had predicted, blowing an arctic breeze through every room of the house and sending the women squealing and scurrying for their coats. By way of apology, he helped them start up the antiquated wood-burning furnace, which, to everyone's surprise, kept the big old house as warm, if not warmer, than a modern central heating unit.

As autumn blossomed, small offerings began to accumulate on the porch of the folly: a blanket, a warm sweatshirt, a pair of gloves, wool socks and—at Bridget's insistence—a wool stocking cap. At first Lindsay had worried that, by leaving these things, however badly they might be needed, they would push Noah into running away again. But he never gave an indication that he knew who had left them, and they never revealed that they knew his secret. He wore the sweatshirt and the gloves without comment when the mornings turned frosty, but they never saw him in the cap.

Lindsay was faithful to her daily run, which almost always turned into a walk of sheer wonder as the woodland colors grew more and more outrageous. She started taking her camera, snapping photographs to help her remember the multitude of shades and tones and hues nature could produce. But even the high-quality digital capabilities of her camera couldn't reproduce what she saw with her eyes. She promised herself she would set up an easel and capture these colors before they all faded away, but of course there was never time.

She had developed a circuit that meandered about a mile away from the house, along the trail that led past the folly, across the stream, up a hill beside a rusted barbed wire fence that was overgrown with weeds, through a tall stand of spruce, and around toward the house again. At that hour of the morning mist often still swirled through the trees, and as the sun gradually rose high enough to backlight the elm and maple leaves, they looked as though they were tipped in gold. Walking along with nothing to break the silence but the sound of her own breathing and footsteps crunching in the leaves, Lindsay often felt like she was in church.

She was returning to the house one morning a little before eight o'clock, thinking about how she used to hate getting up for her morning run when she lived in the suburbs, and how it had now become the best part of her day. She had just entered the darkest, quietest part of the woods, where tall, thick pines blocked out the sun and the carpet of needles underneath muffled even her footsteps, when suddenly there was a crashing sound behind her.

She started and whirled around, her heart thudding. She may even have let out a little cry. Then she gave a nervous little laugh at her own foolishness. There was still too much of the city in her, and what she had heard had probably been nothing more than a branch falling.

Except that it came again. A loud rustling, crashing sound in the undergrowth beyond the pines, irregular movement, but coming close. She thought about bears. She thought about mountain men with hunting caps and guns and small, mean eyes. She told herself not to be silly. She called out, scanning the dark woods, "Who's there?"

Nothing responded. And suddenly the movement again, coming fast and to her right. Something big. Did they have mountain lions here?

"Hello?"

She could see bushes part, and a shower of yellow leaves fell from a scrub tree. She started backing away, quickly. She scanned the ground for a stick or a rock, something to throw. The crashing sound stopped.

It was probably that stupid dog, she thought, but she did not slow down. In fact, she shoved her hands in her jacket pockets and quickened her pace, and when the rustling in the undergrowth started again, stalking her, she ran.

She came around a curve with the rush of her own breath blocking out the sound of her pursuer, and suddenly the creature leapt out of the bushes to block her path. Lindsay screamed and stumbled backward; slipping on pine needles, flailing for balance, she hit the ground hard.

For what seemed like an eternity she lay there flat on her back, gasping like a beached fish, helpless and staring up into the eyes of . . . a deer.

It stood as tall as a small pony, with nobby little antlers sprouting from its head and puffs of steam issuing from its flared nostrils. It was so close she could smell it—a sweet, wild, gamey smell, which nonetheless was alien enough to make her heart beat hard. It looked down at her with its big brown eyes, wet black nose twitching. For the longest time, she couldn't even move.

Then, abruptly, she sucked in a lungful of air, got her hands and heels beneath her, and scooted backward. The deer took a step toward her. She froze.

A deer. She didn't know anything about deer. But it had horns—kind of—and it was bigger than she was, and wild animals were supposed to be afraid of people. This one didn't look to be afraid of anything. Not daring to take her eyes off the creature, she swept her hands along the ground until they closed around a stick. It was a rather spindly stick, to be sure, and didn't represent much in the way of defense, but it was better than nothing.

She got her feet under her, and slowly managed to stand. The deer watched her curiously. She backed away. The deer came closer. "Scat!" she cried, and raised the stick. "Go away! Shoo!"

The deer kept coming and she kept backing up. "I'm not kidding!"' she said. "Go on, get out of here." And, because she didn't really want to strike the animal, she threw the stick over its head, into the bushes, half expecting it to chase the stick like a dog.

But the distraction worked. The deer turned toward the sound of the stick striking the foliage, and trotted over to investigate. Apparently what he found was tasty, because he began stripping the leaves from the bushes. And while he was thus occupied, Lindsay hurried away.

She hadn't gone a dozen yards before she heard hoofbeats on the path behind her. She turned, jogging backward, to see the deer trotting after her. "You have got to be kidding me," she gasped under her breath. She waved both hands and shouted, "Go away! Go home!"

The deer didn't slow down. Glancing around desperately, she saw a tangle of vines and fallen trees to the right of the path. Quickly, she scrambled over and ducked down, hoping the deer would race past and be on about his business. The hoofbeats slowed. She heard the crunching of leaves with footsteps, and then silence. Cautiously, she peeked over the barrier . . . and looked straight into a pair of big brown eyes.

"I don't believe this," she said, breathing hard. "I seriously . . . do not . . . believe this."

The deer thrust its nose forward in a nuzzling motion, and she shrank back. It took a bite out of a slender vine.

Lindsay eased over the deadfall, moving as slowly, and as

quietly, as possible. "Good deer," she whispered. The deer munched the vine, apparently oblivious. "Nice fellow. You just stay there." She edged around the animal, not turning her back on it, and crept carefully back to the path. The deer did not look up.

And the minute she started down the path, the deer abandoned his grazing, and trotted over to follow her.

Lindsay stared at the deer. The deer stared back.

"I'm in a Disney movie," Lindsay said, resigned.

The deer, somewhat to her surprise, did not respond. It simply followed her as she turned to make her way home.

❧

Bridget was measuring the living room windows for draperies when the barking of the border collie alerted her to Lindsay's return. She glanced out the window, saw Lindsay coming up the porch steps, and almost fell off the stepladder. Cici came from the workshop with an armful of quarter-round molding she had just cut for the sunroom, and saw the half-grown deer scramble up their back porch steps, while the dog stood in the middle of the yard, barking its annnoyance. The molding in her arms scattered on the ground. Noah, who was splitting wood at the hickory stump behind the house, paused in his work to watch the circus, and a slow grin spread over his face.

Lindsay tried to ease open the screen porch door, shouting, "Shoo! Shoo!" to the deer, who sniffed the floorboards with interest.

Cici bounded halfway up the steps, saw Lindsay trying to wave the deer back, and stopped short. "What in the world?" she asked.

Bridget came onto the screen porch from the kitchen. "Good heavens!" was all she said, and they stared.

Lindsay slumped against the screen door. "Can you believe this?" she demanded.

Cici backed slowly down the steps. "Not unless I'd seen it with my own eyes." She dragged her gaze from the deer to Lindsay. "How did you . . . ?"

"I didn't do anything!" Lindsay returned sharply. "It just followed me."

The deer turned and wandered down the steps, coming within inches of Cici's wide-eyed gaze, and began to nibble the azalea bushes. "It's not afraid of me," she said wonderingly.

"Or of the dog," added Bridget.

Lindsay said, "It's not afraid of anything."

By this time Noah had wandered up, hands in pockets, to better observe the developments. The deer, losing interest in the azaleas, meandered a few feet away to help himself to the remnants of the half-shriveled apples that were left beneath the apple tree.

"Maybe if we go inside," Lindsay said in a stage whisper, "he'll go away."

Cici came quietly up the steps. Lindsay opened the screen door, and the deer had bounded up the steps after them before the hinges stopped squeaking. All three women yelped with surprise and pressed themselves against the wall, and Noah doubled up with laughter.

"It's just a little ole deer," he said. "It ain't gonna hurt you."

"Well, how are we supposed to know that?" Lindsay demanded, shrinking back as the deer wandered closer.

"It don't hardly even have teeth!"

"It has hooves!" Cici pointed out.

"It's just a yearling." Noah scooped up an apple and came to the bottom of the porch steps, making a smacking sound with his lips. The deer turned, spied the apple, and came delicately down the steps to Noah. To his evident delight, and the women's amazement, the deer began to munch the apple from his hand.

"It's tame," Bridget said in amazement, coming out onto the porch to join Cici and Lindsay. "It's adorable! Do you think it escaped from a zoo?"

Noah gave her a disparaging glance. "Ain't no zoos around here."

Bridget, with the love light already shining in her eyes, came down the steps as the deer finished the last of the apple and nuzzled Noah's hand for more. "Oh, let me try!"

Before long, all three women were sitting on the steps, taking turns feeding the young deer apples and carrots and bits of lettuce from the kitchen. "Are you sure it doesn't have rabies or anything?" Lindsay said, although she wasn't nearly as uneasy as she had been before. "I never heard of a deer that wasn't afraid of people."

"Probably somebody found it as a fawn," Noah said, "raised it, let it go when it got too big to be a pet. Happens all the time. The mama deers, they hide the young'uns in the tall grass when they sense danger, then some person comes by and thinks it was abandoned. Think they're doing it a favor by taking it home and feedin' it, but what they're really doing is stealing it from its mama."

Lindsay glanced up at him, a little surprised. She had never heard him speak so many sentences in a row before, nor had she ever seen him quite as relaxed as he was at that moment, squatting on the ground between Bridget and Cici, breaking off chunks of apple to feed to the deer. He looked almost like a regular teenaged boy.

Cici said, wiping her hands on her jeans, "Well he can't live here."

Bridget insisted, "Why not?"

"Come on, Bridge," Cici said. "Sheep are one thing. The dog is another. But a wild deer is not a pet."

"Remember Mrs. Livingston's hostas?" prompted Lindsay.

Bridget looked torn.

Cici turned to Noah. "Do you think you could take him back to the woods and let him go?"

Noah stood and shoved his hands back into his pockets, his face growing shadowed again. He shrugged. "Ya'll got any rope?"

Cici got to her feet. "In the workshop. I'll get it."

"'Course," he added, his tone neutral, "huntin' season starts this weekend. Critter like that, no fear of man . . ." He brought one hand out of his pocket, cocked an imaginary gun with his thumb and forefinger, and pointed it at the deer. "Bound to make good eatin' though, young as it is."

Bridget looked stricken, and even Lindsay drew in a breath, ready to protest. Cici looked at the deer. It looked back with its big brown eyes. Cici looked at Noah, scowling.

"Well, don't just stand there," she said. "Come help me get the stuff to build it a pen."

❧

As it turned out, the pen wasn't necessary. Although they kept the deer inside the enclosure at night "for his own safety," the yearling had clearly settled into his new home, and never wandered farther from the house than the blackberry hedge on the hill. Even the border collie—currently called Fly because Bridget had read somewhere that was a popular name for sheepdogs—grew tired of barking at the deer and learned to ignore it. The women told themselves that as soon as hunting season was over they would contact wildlife officials about the proper way to rehabilitate a tame deer to the wild, but in the meantime the population of Ladybug Farm was increased by one.

As far as Lindsay was concerned, the drama of the whole affair was almost worth it for the transformation she had seen in Noah. He arrived early every morning to let the deer out of its enclosure, his pockets stuffed with dried berries and fallen apples he had picked up on the way. He led the animal back to its pen before he left at night, lingering to hand-feed it carrots from the bucket Bridget left by the back door. Although he was his usual taciturn self when others were around, she often watched him from the kitchen window, grinning as he fed the deer, stroking it and talking to it as he might a dog or a horse.

It was awhile before Noah's loquacity transferred to humans, however. On a cool bright October afternoon, Lindsay was raking out the flower beds while Noah piled kindling wood into the wheelbarrow, and the fawn stepped delicately around the edge of the lawn, nibbling on the remnants of green grass that poked through the layer of orange and yellow leaves.

"Whatcha gonna do with it when it freezes?"

Noah's voice was so unexpected that it took Lindsay a moment to realize he was speaking to her. She paused in the raking and turned around. "What?"

His scowl reflected impatience. "Deer huddle down together to keep warm in the cold. That'n's gonna freeze out in that pen at night."

Lindsay blinked. "Well . . . I guess we'll put him in the barn then."

He jerked his head toward the barn. "Roof's got a hole in it. Deckin's prob'ly rotted through."

"Oh." Lindsay was aware of the enormous significance of this moment. It was the first time Noah had ever initiated a conversation with her. But she didn't know what to say.

Noah scooped up another double handful of poplar chips and tossed them into the wheelbarrow. "How come you don't set him up in that dairy barn?"

"What?" She had never felt so inarticulate in her life.

"It's warm. Fixed the hole in the wall from the snake. What you gonna use it for, anyway?"

She relaxed a little. "It's going to be my studio."

He looked at her. "Studio for what?"

"An art studio." She smiled. "I'm an artist."

He gave a little snort. "You ain't no artist." He dumped another armload of chips into the wheelbarrow.

She was immediately defensive. "What makes you say that?"

"An artist draws," he answered simply. He picked up the handles of the wheelbarrow and pushed it toward the shed.

❧

Half an hour later, Lindsay set up a lawn chair and a camp table for her pencil kit in the middle of the back lawn, a dozen or so feet away from where the deer grazed, and directly along the path that Noah had to take to empty the wheelbarrow at the woodshed. When he passed behind her, she could hear the wheels slow, and sense his eyes on her, watching her sketch. She did not look up, but made herself concentrate on the drawing. After a while, it was not so much of an effort as she lost herself in her work and the scene began to emerge from the nubby sketch paper: the blades of grass, bent just so, the shape and flutter of autumn leaves, the velvety nose, the luminous eye, the graceful arch of a neck. As amazing as it seemed, Lindsay had actually forgotten how much she loved this.

She was not certain how long Noah had been standing over her, watching. When he spoke, she was startled.

"How do you do that?"

She glanced up at him. "Do what?"

He jerked his head toward the pasture fence, where the deer was now plucking leaves off a scrubby vine. "You're drawing him under the apple tree. He ain't there anymore. But your picture looks just like he did when he was."

"Oh." It occurred to Lindsay that all of the sketches she had seen in Noah's book had been of still objects—even the border collie, which had been drawn in profile on the hill overlooking the meadow. He drew what he saw, as most beginning artists did. His question showed insight and ambition, and she felt a smile of excitement start deep inside her—which she did not dare show, of course.

"When you're drawing something that you can't pose," she explained without looking up from the careful shading she was working on around the deer's eye, "something that you know is going to change or move, like an animal or a sunset or something like that, you make markers for positioning as quickly as you can. For the deer, I drew circles to indicate where his head was in relationship to his neck and where his eyes were on his head and where his hooves were and how long his body was before he moved. That way I made sure I had the proportions right. For everything else, you just kind of . . ." She shrugged. "Hold a picture of it in your head."

He grunted. "Where'd you learn that?"

She replied very casually, and without looking up, "Art school."

"You went to art school?"

Was that respect or skepticism she heard in his voice? She dared not turn around to find out. Instead, she picked up a stylus and carefully flicked several layers of charcoal from a point where iris met pupil on the deer's eye, revealing a white spark of light underneath. "I did," she replied.

"What's that thing?"

She held the instrument up for him to examine, but he did not take it. "It's called a stylus. You can use it to make marks or indentations in the paper for texture, or to remove color like I just did. See how that little spark of white makes his eyes look alive? Sometimes what you take away is more important than what you put in." And when he gave nothing but a grunt in reply, she added, "Something else I learned in art school."

He scooped up a handful of slivered wood kindling and tossed it into the wheelbarrow. "So how come I never seen you drawing before?"

She almost gave him the easy answer about how busy she was, how hard it was to keep up an old house like this, how few hours there were in the day, and how, after all, her studio wasn't even ready to move into yet. Instead she put down her pencil and turned to look at him, squinting a little in the sun.

"I guess I was scared," she said. And though he didn't stop his work, he moved a little more slowly and made less clatter tossing the kindling into the wheelbarrow. There was about his shoulders an attitude of acute listening. "You see, all my life I've dreamed of being a working artist. One of the reasons we bought this house was so that I would have a place for a studio, and I could work at my art full-time. But . . . I don't know, maybe this is something only an old person can understand, but sometimes you're better off dreaming about something than actually doing it. What if no one wants to buy my paintings? What if nobody even wants to take art lessons from me? What if I'm not good enough?"

She shrugged, trying not to show the embarrassment she was beginning to feel. "It's a lot easier not to try, than to try and fail, you know?"

He looked at her for a moment, eyes narrowed, and she thought that he *did* know, very well. He said, "This is the last load on your wood. You got my pay?"

"In the house." She stood up, packing away the pencils and sketch pad, and he turned to push the wheelbarrow toward the shed. Then she had an idea.

"Hey," she said.

He looked back.

"I've got a deal for you," she said. "You finish raking the flower beds for me, and you can have this pencil set. I'll throw in the sketch pad, too. It's almost new."

He looked from her to the two items in her hand, his eyes narrowed—though she couldn't tell whether the expression was from avarice or contempt.

"Forty-six pencils," she told him, "all colors. And a sharpener."

He said, "Anybody ever make any money from drawing?"

"Some do," she told him, and had to admit, honestly, "most don't."

He turned back to the wheelbarrow. "Then what's the point?"

She shrugged and put the pencil box and sketch pad on her chair. "Suit yourself. I'll get your money."

But when she returned, he was raking the flower beds, and the pencil box and sketch pad—including her drawing of the deer—were gone.

❧

"Mommmm . . ."

Cici could practically see Lori's long distance eye roll. She closed her own eyes and drew in a silent calming breath in response.

"You really just don't get how *different* college is today," Lori went on. "I mean, it's not like you only get one chance at it. So I bombed out on a few courses. I'll take better ones next semester."

Cici's hand tightened around the paper in her hand. "Lori, this letter is from the Dean of Students, who is very concerned about how seriously you're taking your academic obligations. I'm not sure how many more semesters there will be for you."

"Oh, that," Lori replied airily. "They send those out to everybody. It's a form letter."

Cici's voice was tight. "I assume your father got one of these form letters, too?"

"I guess."

"And what did he have to say about it?"

"Oh, you know Dad. He's cool."

"Lori, you can't just—"

"Anyway, Mom, it's *really* no big deal, because I switched my major and none of those stupid courses matter anyway."

Cici blinked. "Switched your major? To what?"

"Anthropology."

"You switched from business to anthropology?" She tried not to sound incredulous. "How do you even do that?"

"I'm going to Italy in the spring," she went on excitedly, "for six months! Jeff says I might even be able to go on a dig, if he can work it out with the archaeology prof who's—"

"Jeff? Who's Jeff?"

"*The Culture of Man*," she responded happily. "That's the name of his book. Also the name of the course."

"That he's teaching in Italy," Cici supplied, keeping her tone very carefully even. "In the spring."

"Right."

Cici started to say something, changed her mind, took another tack, changed her mind. Finally all she could say was, "We'll talk about this at Christmas, okay? In the meantime—"

"Oh," said Lori. "About Christmas . . ."

"You *are* coming home?" Now it was almost impossible to keep the distress out of her voice.

"It's not that I don't want to see you," Lori said, and, to her credit, she sounded as though she meant it. "And your house, and Aunt Bridge and Aunt Lindsay, and I know we've always had Christmas together and I don't want to hurt your feelings, but that's just it, you see? We always have Christmas together, and Dad was—well, he was counting on me spending this Christmas with him."

Cici said, "You spend every weekend with him. You can

have *lunch* with him whenever you want. I see you twice a year!"

"Now, Mom, you know that's not true. Besides, he's gone to so much trouble, arranging the trip to Aspen—"

"Aspen?"

"At Christmas. He's got this great condo there, and he's going to teach me how to ski, and we've got invitations to all the A-list parties. Say!" she exclaimed suddenly. "I've got it! Why don't you come, too? No kidding, Mom, this condo is huge, and there's plenty of room. That way I'd get to spend the holidays with both of you!"

And not miss a single A-list party, Cici thought, but didn't say. She couldn't quite keep the sarcasm out of her voice, however, as she replied, "I'm sure your dad would love that. Isn't he bringing his girlfriend?"

Lori hesitated. "Oh," she said, slightly subdued. "I guess that wouldn't work."

"No, I guess it wouldn't."

"I'm sorry, Mom. I really will miss you. But you understand, don't you? If he hadn't gone to so much trouble . . ."

Cici swallowed hard. "Yeah, sweetie. I understand."

"And don't be mad at me about school, okay? I promise to buckle down next semester."

"I love you, baby."

"Love you, too, Mom."

Cici punched out another set of numbers while she pushed back her bangs with her other hand, leaving a swipe of soot across her forehead. She had been cleaning out the fireplace when the mail arrived. Outside her window a tame deer munched on bright red sassafras leaves while a wild border collie raced around and around the sheep meadow in endless circles for no apparent reason. A squirrel hung upside down from the bird feeder, and Bridget, with her hair tied up in a yellow paisley scarf, rushed outside to chase it with a broom. And on the other side of the continent, in the land of palm trees and movie stars, a man who smelled of expensive cologne and silk sheets answered the telephone with a brusque, "Yeah, this is Richard."

She didn't even bother to pretend to be calm. "I have to get a letter from the freakin' *university* to find out my daughter is flunking out of college?"

"Who is this? Cici? How did you get this number?"

"I gave birth to your child. That entitles me to your cell phone number."

"Listen, babe, this isn't a very good time—"

"Don't you 'babe' me! What in the hell are you *doing* out there? Did anyone ever explain to you that the word *parent* is also a verb?"

"Okay, sweets, I'm about to lose you. Coming up on a tunnel here—"

"There *are* no tunnels in Los Angeles!" she screamed. Lindsay came in through the front door, and gave her a look of undisguised concern. Cici turned away, lowering her voice. "I swear to God, Richard, if you hang up on me—"

"Okay, okay, let's just do this. I've got lunch at Spago in ten minutes and Mel Gibson waiting in my office."

"Jesus!" Cici blew out an explosive breath and turned around again. Lindsay, sorting through the mail that remained on the entry table, raised both eyebrows in question. Cici fanned her face with her hand and tried to sound—and, for Lindsay's sake, to look—calm. "That kind of talk might impress a twenty-year-old but it does nothing for me. Did you even *know* she had two incompletes and one failing grade last semester? Doesn't it bother you that you just paid for half a year of exactly zero course credits?"

Lindsay patted her arm sympathetically as she left the room, and Richard replied, "Oh, come off it, Cici. Like Lori is the first kid to ever have a little trouble with school."

"She was an honor student when she lived with me. Did you know she changed her major?"

"Again?" But before Cici could even question that, he said, "Last I heard, that was not grounds for expulsion from UCLA. In fact, some people actually encourage young people to explore their options in college. Some people even think that's what college is for."

"I happen to think college is for getting an education!"

"Remind me again why we're not still married?"

"Did you know she's in love with one of her professors?"

He chuckled. "Not exactly the kind of thing a girl tells her dad, sweetheart. Although from what I can tell, Lori's in love with a new guy every week."

Cici felt a stab in her heart because she did not know this, and because Richard didn't even care, and because even though she knew perfectly well that this was all a part of being young, she didn't want her baby to grow up without her.

She said, "And you're letting her go to Italy with this guy in the spring?"

That piece of information apparently gave him pause. Obviously, he had not bothered to make the connection between the professor, the change of major, and the trip to Italy. And that was exactly the problem.

Then he said, "Come on, Cici, by spring she won't even

remember this guy's name. Could you lighten up just one time?"

There were a dozen things she would have liked to have said in response to that; no, a hundred. It was with the greatest possible effort that she let it go. She said instead, "I want Lori to come home for Christmas."

"So tell her."

"I did. She said you had made other plans."

"What can I tell you, babe? Sounds like she's made her choice."

"You call that a choice? Aspen, celebrities, skiing, A-list parties? She spends her entire life without a father, and all of a sudden there you are, offering her the world. What's she supposed to do? For crying out loud, Richard, it's the damn sports car all over again!"

When Lori got her driver's license, Cici had promised to match dollar-for-dollar the money Lori had saved from her after-school job toward the purchase of a car. On her sixteenth birthday they had gone shopping for a used Honda, only to arrive home to find a brand-new sports car sitting in the driveway. Happy Birthday from Dad. Worse, Cici had had to be the one to tell Lori she could not keep the car. Lori had eventually forgiven her, but Cici had never forgiven Richard for once again making her the bad guy, and forcing her to ruin her daughter's sixteenth birthday.

Richard sighed into the phone, managing to sound both impatient and sympathetic at the same time. "I don't know what you expect me to do. I can't make Lori want to spend Christmas with you."

"No, but you can give her a better choice. Cancel the Aspen thing."

He laughed.

"I'm not kidding, Richard. I need to see Lori, to talk to her. She needs to be with me, in the real world. You've got her so turned around and upside down out there she doesn't even know who she is anymore."

"She knows enough to realize she'll have a lot more fun in Aspen with me than in the middle of nowhere with you. Sorry, babe. She's made up her mind."

Cici was quiet for a moment. "All right, you leave me no choice. Lori invited me to spend the holidays with her at your condo in Aspen. I'll be there on the twenty-second."

Now it was his turn for silence. "Not funny, babe."

"Oh, and if you're worried I might cramp your style—you know, all the hot-tub parties, the clubbing, the après-ski with Heather or Tiffany or Brittany—don't give it another thought. I promise you to dedicate every waking moment to doing *nothing* but cramping your style. After all, what kind of man would invite his daughter on a Christmas ski vacation and expect to have anything but family time? Lucky for you, I'm going to make sure it's all family, all the time, for you this Christmas."

His voice was cold. "You wouldn't dare."

Her voice was colder. "You were married to me for four years, Richard. You want to rethink that?"

Silence. Then, quietly, "You had her for twenty Christmases, Cici. All I'm asking is one."

Almost, she felt a stab of remorse. But this was their only child they were talking about, and her future was at stake. "Not this one," she said firmly. "Call off Aspen. And not one word to her about this conversation."

"You are a cast-iron bitch, you know that?"

"Thank you. I'm glad to know I've still got it."

She hung up the phone, and was surprised to see her hands were shaking. But she had done the right thing. She was almost certain of it.

❧

"I'm out of practice being mean," Cici sighed, and held out her glass as she took her place in the rocking chair. "It's not as much fun as it used to be."

"The first of the merlot," Lindsay announced, filling each of their glasses. "And I don't see what's mean about looking out for your daughter's best interests. That's your job."

"I don't like the person I turn into when I'm dealing with Richard."

"It's probably a good thing you divorced him then, huh?" said Bridget.

"If Richard had any balls at all, he'd drag that Professor Jeff out behind the science building and beat the shit out of him." Lindsay sat down in her rocker and stretched out her legs.

"I don't think you're allowed to do that in California," Bridget pointed out.

"I'm not sure blackmail is the best way to deal with a dispute over child-raising approaches," Cici said unhappily.

"Darling, your child is already raised," Lindsay said. "I think that's the problem."

And Cici agreed, "I think so, too."

They were silent for a while, rocking.

"Umm, I love merlot in the autumn," Bridget murmured, tasting it. She was bundled up in a thick chenille sweater, a mohair scarf, and a wool throw against the chill of the dying day, but none of them was willing to miss the last few rays of the brilliant sunset.

"To everything there is a season," agreed Cici. "Chardonnay in the summer, merlot in the autumn, cabernet in the winter."

"Hot chocolate before you know it." Lindsay shivered elaborately and buttoned the top button of her fleece jacket as she sank into her rocker. "Boy, the temperature sure drops once the sun goes behind the mountains, doesn't it?"

"We won't be able to do this much longer," Bridget agreed regretfully. And then she brightened. "But we've got plenty of fireplaces. And there's nothing better than sitting by a fireplace with a good book in the winter, is there?"

"How cold is it supposed to get tonight anyway?" There was a worried note in Lindsay's tone. "Do you think Noah will be warm enough?"

"He has a fireplace, too," Cici reminded her.

"We should have sent him more blankets," Bridget said.

"If we do that, aren't we encouraging him to stay?"

"Well, we can't let him freeze!"

"Kids," Cici said and sighed again. "Whoever knows what's right?"

"I should have brought it up this afternoon," Lindsay said unhappily. "I really blew my chance. There he was, talking to me, practically opening up to me . . . I should have found a way to talk to him about school, about his home situation, about what he was going to do with winter coming . . . I let him slip through my fingers."

"I don't know what you could have told him," Bridget said, "except to go home. And knowing what we do about his home, I wouldn't feel right about that."

"Me either. That's the problem." Lindsay sighed. "I'm a teacher. I'm trained in crisis intervention. I should know what to do."

"I'm a mother," Cici said glumly. "I've *lived* in a constant state of crisis for twenty years. And I still don't know what to do."

Lindsay leaned across and clinked her glass with Cici's.

"Richard's right, you know," Cici said after a moment. "I can't make Lori come home for Christmas if she doesn't want to. She's over eighteen, an adult."

"I'd love to know who decided that," Bridget said.

"Some man, probably."

"Up until about four hundred years ago," Lindsay pointed out, "boys in Europe were considered adults at age thirteen."

"Yeah, that was when they only lived to be twenty-five."

"Before dying of syphilis," added Cici.

"In some tribal cultures today, girls can get married at age nine."

"That's sick."

"I'm just saying."

"You shouldn't be allowed to call yourself an adult until you prove yourself to be one."

"By building a log cabin?"

"Or making a quilt?"

"Or going to war?"

"Or having a baby?"

And Lindsay said quietly, "Or living in the woods all by yourself because you've got no place else to go?"

Bridget said, rocking gently, "Our children are so very lucky."

Cici sipped her wine silently for a time. Then she said, "I

don't think you should be allowed to be an adult until your mother says you can."

The other two laughed softly. "I'd vote for that."

"Me, too," Bridget said. "I would have emancipated my two at age twelve."

Cici said, "What if she doesn't want to come home?"

"What if," Lindsay said abruptly, "we let him sleep in the dairy?"

Cici said, "What?"

And Bridget said, "Who?"

Cici said, "There's no heat in there!"

"It's better than what he's got now."

Bridget added, "What about your art studio?"

"It would be just for a little while. Until he finds something better. We'd take it out of his wages."

"Heaven knows, there's plenty for him to do around here," Bridget admitted.

"He's an awfully good worker," Lindsay agreed, a little anxiously.

"I have to admit, I'd sleep a lot easier myself, knowing he wasn't freezing to death out there in the woods," Bridget said.

"Maybe we could even get some space heaters out there," Lindsay said.

"I say we do it," said Bridget.

They both looked at Cici.

She said, choosing her words with obvious care, "This isn't the 1920s, you know. You can't just pick up a hobo off the road and let him sleep in your barn."

"I think if he was a serial killer he would have done something about it before now," Lindsay pointed out.

"And it's not like we don't know him," Bridget added, "or that no one in the community knows him. He's a good kid. Kind of," she had to add, honestly.

"We're aiding and abetting a truant and a runaway. That's got to be illegal."

"Like keeping a wild deer in a pen isn't?"

Cici shrugged uncomfortably because the pen, after all, had been her idea. "That's just temporary."

"So is this," Lindsay insisted. "Besides, I can get him back in school, I know I can. All I need is a little time."

"Sounds like a big project to me," Cici said. "I wouldn't get my hopes up if I were you."

Lindsay said nothing, and neither did Bridget. This was one contingency—unlike pets—that was not covered in their joint venture agreement, but they all knew it must be a unanimous decision.

At last Cici sighed, shook her head, and said, "Oh, why not? We already adopted a dog, a flock of sheep, and a deer. What's one more?"

Bridget grinned and raised her glass. "This is starting to feel like a real home."

"Or a zoo," muttered Cici.

Lindsay sank back in her chair, her broad smile all but lost in the shadows. "I'll tell him in the morning."

But in the morning, there was a light dusting of snow on the ground, and Noah was gone.

16

In Which Ghosts Come in from the Cold

They did the responsible thing. They reported the boy missing. They called everyone they knew to make inquiries. The only response they received was surprise at their concern. As it was explained to them over and over again, this was the way he lived. There was nothing for them to worry about. He'd turn up again sooner or later.

Finally even Lindsay had to admit defeat. "Damn it," she said, pushing her hair away from her face with both hands in a gesture of utter frustration. "Damn it, damn it, damn it."

"We've done everything we can," Bridget reassured her gently.

"I know that," Lindsay replied. "Just . . . damn it."

Cici said, "We paid him close to two thousand dollars over the summer. What did he have to spend it on except cigarettes? If he saved even part of it, he should be okay until he gets another job."

Lindsay managed a dry smile. "He probably used it to buy

a ticket to Florida. He's hanging out on a beach somewhere right now."

"In which case he's better off than we are," Bridget observed.

Cici said, "He has a father, Lindsay."

"A father who didn't even know he was missing."

"There's really nothing more we can do."

"I know," agreed Lindsay heavily. "It's just . . . a shame."

There was nothing anyone could add to that.

With Noah gone and winter breathing down their necks, there was more than enough to occupy their attention, and very little time left over for brooding. They spent two entire days filling bushel baskets with pecans and black walnuts, then couldn't face the prospect of shelling them. Bridget came up with the idea of passing them around to all the neighbors who had shared garden produce with them, but that still left almost a bushel of nuts for them to dispose of, which Bridget decided to store in the barn.

"They'll attract rats," Cici warned.

"Good," said Bridget. "Then we won't have to shell them."

Keeping the house heated was almost a full-time job in itself. Every morning a day's worth of wood had to be brought inside and distributed between the fireplaces and the big furnace in the cellar. Four times a day, someone had to go downstairs and load more wood into the furnace, and they devised a rotating schedule for furnace duty so that the chore was shared equally. Although at first they had enjoyed the romance—and the warmth—of keeping a fire going in the kitchen and living room fireplaces all day, they soon found it was easier to simply put on another sweater. The charm of carrying armloads of wood upstairs to their bedroom fireplaces faded fast, and reminded them that this house was built in an era when everyone had servants.

The issue of servants was raised more than once as the shorter days forced them to spend more time inside and to notice, as they had not when most of their time was spent on the porch or in the yard, just how much work it took to clean a house that size. Dust accumulated almost as soon as it was wiped away, windows grew foggy from the invisible ash that the wood furnace circulated, and simply mopping all the floors was a full day's job.

Additionally, they each had projects that they were anxious to finish before winter settled in full-time. Cici had finally finished restoring and regrouting the tile in the sunroom, and spent her mornings (when it was too cold to paint) cutting and nailing trim and her afternoons (when the sun had heated the room so that the paint wouldn't thicken) carefully painting around the 152 divided windowpanes. It was so cold in her workshop that sometimes she would have to dash inside, strip off her gloves, and hold her hands over the fireplace or the kitchen stove until the circulation returned to her fingers and she could hold the tools again.

Lindsay took on the completion of her art studio with a determined ferocity that both impressed and alarmed the other two. She hired Farley to run an electrical line to the building, and Sam to install a series of baseboard heaters. Cici had been right about there being a water line already serving the building, but it had broken long ago. Rather than hire a plumber to dig up the semifrozen ground and make the repairs—a process that could take weeks—Lindsay hauled bucket after bucket of soapy water from the house to scrub the grimy windows and scour the floors. On one memorable occasion, she even climbed up on the roof to scrub away the years of accumulated muck from the skylights while Cici and Bridget held the ladder and passed up cleaning supplies and called up words of advice and concern.

She hung fluorescent shop lights from the rafters and whitewashed the dark wood walls. The interior fairly sparkled with bright winter light. She hung hooks on the walls to hold her tools and built shelves for her supplies. She moved in easels and rolls of canvas and paint boxes and art books. It was with a sense of almost defiant satisfaction that she began stretching and priming canvases. She had moved here to paint, and paint she would.

Bridget turned the small sitting room off the kitchen into a sewing room, and set about designing draperies for the tall front windows. She had found a scrap that wasn't too mildewed in the box of fabric they'd uncovered in the dairy loft, and sent it to Paul in Baltimore. He had been able to find a modern-day equivalent of the rose damask that was far more practical and much less expensive than the original, and shipped twenty-five yards. Now that everything had been preserved that could possibly be preserved, Bridget had time to begin the painstaking process of measuring, hemming, lining, and pleating the fabric into draperies.

Farley brought a dozen pumpkins when he came to run the electrical wire to Lindsay's studio, and the women spent an afternoon carving jack-o'-lanterns and setting them up to line the front steps, and another afternoon turning the leftovers into pumpkin pies.

And that was where the mystery began.

They baked four pies. Two they wrapped and put in the

freezer. Another they sent home with Farley. Another they enjoyed for dinner—or at least they enjoyed three pieces of it. When Bridget went to cut herself a slice for lunch the next morning, the entire pie was gone.

She would not have thought much of this—although it did seem odd that Cici and Lindsay could finish off an entire pie between breakfast and lunch—if it hadn't been for the ham. Bridget baked a small ham for dinner with the spiced apples they had preserved from their own tree. The next day, they all enjoyed ham sandwiches for lunch, and Bridget decided to use the leftovers in a casserole for dinner. But when she went to get the ham that evening to prepare the casserole, there was no sign of it—not even the plate upon which it had sat.

"I think it's the ghost," Lindsay said, when Bridget told the story. "It left us presents all summer, now it's taking some back."

"The ghost giveth and the ghost taketh away," Cici agreed. "I just wish it would give back the wood-handled screwdriver I left in the sunroom. That was my favorite one."

"Oh, sorry." Bridget produced the screwdriver from her jeans pocket. "I used it to pry open a stuck drawer. And you didn't leave it in the sunroom, by the way, you left it in the pantry."

Cici accepted the screwdriver with an odd look. "I haven't been in that pantry since we moved in. Are you sure that's where you found it?"

"Okay, this is starting to get weird," said Bridget, and Lindsay hummed spooky music under her breath.

"Maybe you accidentally tossed out the ham when you were clearing the table," Cici suggested.

"And maybe you were sleepwalking in the pantry," Bridget said.

They looked at one another for a moment, baffled. And so they remained, until the night of the mouse.

Cici was just snuggling into bed in her flannel pajamas, glasses perched on the end of her nose, breathing a sigh of sheer pleasure as she turned the first page of a brand-new issue of *Home Remodeling and Decor* magazine, when there was a tap on her bedroom door. She looked up as Bridget poked her head inside. Her eyes were big.

"I think there's something in my room," she said, half whispering.

Cici removed her glasses. "You think? You don't know?"

"It's making noises," she said urgently. "It might be a mouse. Will you come check?"

Cici said. "Me? I don't know anything about mice."

Lindsay's face appeared at Bridget's shoulder. "What's going on?"

With a last longing look at the magazine, Cici tossed aside the covers and thrust her feet into slippers. "Bridget has a mouse."

Lindsay grimaced and made a small *eek!* sound.

"I told you storing those nuts would attract rats," Cici said as they crossed the wide hall to Bridget's room.

There was alarm in Lindsay's voice. "Rats? I thought you said a mouse."

"Nuts in the barn don't cause mice in the house," Bridget said firmly, but she didn't look as confident as she sounded as she eased open the door to her room.

The three women stepped inside, standing carefully away from baseboards where mice liked to run, and looked around. Bridget's room, with its cabbage rose wallpaper and lace-trimmed counterpane, was quintessentially Bridget. There was a Queen Anne writing desk and a silk wing chair with a pie table drawn up before the fireplace. Neither one hid a mouse. There was a gorgeous rose-patterned wool rug—which once had been the centerpiece of her formal living room—anchoring a brocade chaise and a skirted lamp table. Lindsay bent to peek under the chaise, and Cici flicked aside the ruffled table skirt. No mouse appeared.

Suddenly Bridget lifted her hand. "Listen!" she whispered.

Lindsay said, "I don't—"

And then everyone heard it. A squeaking, shuffling sound, followed by what sounded like a basketball bouncing directly overhead. All three sets of eyes turned toward the ceiling.

"That's no mouse," Lindsay said softly.

"It's in the attic," Bridget whispered.

"Could be a raccoon," said Cici, "or a possum."

Bridget said, "We can't just let it stay there."

Lindsay looked uneasy. "Why not?"

This time the sound they heard was more of a rhythmic thumping, occasionally punctuated by a crackling, crunching sound, like something trying to chew or claw its way through the ceiling. Bridget's eyes were filled with horror. "Because I can't sleep in here, that's why!"

"You can sleep in my room," Lindsay offered.

"Good. Glad that's settled." Cici turned to leave the room, but Bridget caught her arm as something clattered overhead, louder than any of the sounds that had occurred before.

"Cici, we can't just ignore that!"

"Well, what do you want me to do?"

Bridget scrambled in her nightstand and came up with a flashlight, which she handed to Cici. "Go up and have a look?" she pleaded.

Cici looked at her for a moment, then snatched the flashlight away. "Why do I have to do all the hard stuff?" she demanded.

"Because you're the bravest," Bridget said.

"And you know how to use tools," Lindsay added.

"We'll come with you," Bridget added quickly, clutching Lindsay's arm.

Cici gave the two of them a withering look. "On one condition. If it *is* a raccoon, we are not adopting it."

"Promise."

"Absolutely."

On the way out of the room, Bridget grabbed an umbrella from the closet—"For self-defense," she explained—and they made their way up the attic stairs in close formation. Three steps from the top, Cici stopped suddenly. "The light is on," she whispered, looking around at them with a question in her eyes. "Did either of you—?"

Both shook their heads adamantly. And just then there was another creaking, scraping sound, like someone moving furniture.

"Oh my God," Lindsay breathed. "It *is* a ghost!"

Bridget and Lindsay, melded together as one, would have fled back down the stairs at that moment had Cici not grabbed the belt of Bridget's robe. "This was your idea," she hissed. "Come on."

Inch by inch, they crept to the top of the stairs.

Nothing had changed since their last visit. A single bare bulb with a pull string switch hung from a rafter in the center of the room, spreading a feeble pool of light toward the shadows of the vast space. Slowly, Cici swept the beam of the flashlight across those shadows. Already they had discovered there was nothing worth exploring in the space—a few cardboard boxes filled with things like aluminum cookware and moth-eaten sweaters, a picnic table, some folding chairs. Except that now one of those chairs was unfolded in front of the back windows, and upon it stood a person.

Lindsay's hand clamped down hard on Bridget's. Bridget's nails dug into Cici's arm. Cici gasped and dropped the flashlight. All three of them dived to the floor to try to rescue the light, and it was Lindsay who found it first. Cici grabbed it from her and aimed it with both hands toward the window. The figure on the chair held a spray bottle in one hand and a cloth in the other, and as they watched in disbelief, she sprayed solution on the window, then wiped it clean with smooth, deliberate strokes. It seemed to take forever. And the women, suspended in the moment, felt as though they had stumbled down the rabbit hole.

At last the figure on the chair stepped down stiffly, holding on to the windowsill for support, and turned to face them. "Ya'll sure have let the place go, ain't you?"

Lindsay whispered, "Oh my God! Our ghost does windows!"

Cici, still gripping the flashlight with both hands to keep it from shaking, moved the beam slowly up the form. Sturdy work boots, laced halfway up. Baggy dungarees cuffed up to reveal a red plaid flannel lining, and over them a navy blue skirt that reached past the knees. A navy peacoat covering an oversize green plaid flannel shirt with the band of a pink thermal undershirt showing at the neck. When the flashlight reached her face, the woman squinted and shielded her eyes, demanding, "What you trying to do? Blind me?"

It was, after all, a woman, with pink scalp showing beneath the short gray curls, and enough wrinkles on her face to make her age anywhere between sixty and a hundred. Cici lowered the flashlight, but only to the woman's chin. "Who are you?" she demanded, proud of the fact her voice hardly quavered at all. "What are you doing here?"

"Name's Ida Mae Simpson," the woman replied, and there was a marked belligerance in her voice. "This is my place. Who the hell are you?"

In the moment of stunned silence that followed, Bridget suddenly gasped, "Of course!" She surged forward, but Cici shot out an arm to stop her. "Ida Mae Simpson," Bridget repeated to Cici. "You know, the Bible?" She turned to Lindsay. "The housekeeper, remember?"

Lindsay said carefully, "But Bridget . . . she's dead."

Bridget looked slowly from Lindsay back to the stranger at the window. "Oh my goodness," she breathed, eyes growing wide again. "That's right."

The three women stared at her. She stared back, scowling. "Do I look dead to you?" she demanded.

"What you look like," said Cici, "is a trespasser. Do you want to explain what you're doing in our attic?"

The woman puffed out her chest and lowered her scraggly brows even further. "I ain't never trespassed on anything in my life, young lady. Just who do you think you are, talking to me like that?"

Lindsay held up a quick pacifying hand. "Maybe," she suggested, looking hopefully from one to the other of them, "we could all talk about this over a nice cup of tea?"

❧

They sat at the kitchen counter while Bridget brought water to boil and poured it into four mugs with tea bags.

"We heard you were in a nursing home," Lindsay said, placing the sugar bowl on the counter.

"Didn't care for it," replied Ida Mae, easing herself up onto a kitchen stool. "Ain't ya'll ever going to get any furniture? You poor or something?"

"Or something," said Cici, placing a mug of tea before the older woman, and handing Lindsay a second. "So you just walked out of the nursing home? With no place to stay?"

"I've got a place to stay," she replied, squaring up her shoulders again. "Been staying here just about all my life."

Bridget paused in the act of taking her own seat at the counter. "Do you mean to say . . . you haven't been living in our attic this whole time have you?"

"Stayed with my sister some," replied Ida Mae. "She's dead now. Children sold her place. Sometimes I stayed in my old room downstairs. But with you all tramping in and out, hauling firewood and such, weren't much privacy. So I made myself a pallet upstairs. Warmer there, too." She looked at them curiously. "Don't ya'll know about the gas heaters?"

Cici said sharply, "Gas heaters?"

She nodded. "Mr. B had 'em put in every room about fifteen, twenty years ago, even the pantry. You know how old people start to get cold," she confided, as though it were a secret. She added, "They're set in the wall, so as not to disturb the historical. But all you have to do is lift up the grate to light 'em."

Lindsay said, "Grate?"

And Cici sank back in her chair. "So *that's* what all those vents are for!"

Ida Mae fished the tea bag out of her cup, wrung it out with her fingers, and set it on the counter. "Never did learn to like tea made from a bag." She grimaced as she tasted it.

"So it was you who left Emily Blackwell's recipe book out for me," Bridget said with a note of wonder in her voice, "And the labels—"

"And the landscape map?" interjected Lindsay.

"I know where lots of things are," replied Ida Mae smugly. "And ya'll need all the help you can get. I turned the power on for you, too, that day you was too foolish to find it for yourself. I don't hear no thanks for that."

Cici said, "And you just walked into our house one night and put a record on the gramophone?"

The old woman shrugged uncomfortably. "How did I know you was t' home? Sitting around in the dark like that on the front porch. Besides, I missed my music. I wanted to hear the old place singing again, like it used to when Mr. B was alive."

They just looked at each other, hardly knowing what to say.

Then Bridget said, "Wait—did you take the pie?"

"And the ham?" added Lindsay.

"And leave my screwdriver in the pantry?"

Ida Mae shrugged, and did not even have the grace to looked abashed. "Didn't think you'd mind," she said. "You had plenty." She took a sip of the tea and wrinkled her nose. "Your pie coulda used more ginger," she added, stirring sugar into the tea.

Bridget looked at Lindsay. "Amazing," she said.

Lindsay looked at Cici. "Unbelievable."

"That would be one word for it," agreed Cici, and she looked at the strange old woman sitting beside her at the counter. "What I don't understand is why you had to keep sneaking around like that. Why didn't you just come to the front door and introduce yourself?"

Ida Mae Simpson looked slightly indignant. "Why, I had to see what kind of folks you was first, didn't I?"

"But," exclaimed Lindsay, "you've been living in *our house*! Without our permission! Don't you see that's just–just—"

She looked helplessly from Bridget to Cici and Bridget supplied, "Wrong."

Ida Mae did not react at all.

Cici took a calming breath. "Okay," she said, "you said you had nieces or nephews. Do you happen to know any of their phone numbers?"

She shrugged. "Got no need to call them. They're up in Michigan somewheres."

Bridget suggested, "Maybe you have relatives around here?"

"Nah. Outlived them all."

"Oh," said Lindsay. "Congratulations...I guess." She looked from Cici to Bridget with an exaggerated lift of her eyebrows, telegraphing a question. Cici gave a small shrug of her shoulders in return, and Bridget reached out to gently cover Ida Mae's hand with her own.

"Now, Ida Mae," she said. "You know you can't stay here. You must have some place else to go."

"How come?" demanded Ida Mae. She scooped two large spoonsful of sugar into her tea and stirred it sloppily. "How come I can't stay here? Always have, ain't I?"

"Because," explained Cici patiently, "we own the place now."

"You might own it," returned Ida Mae, "but it's plain you

can't take care of it by yourselves. I been doing for Mr. Blackwell nigh onto forty-five years. Now I'll do for you. Cook your meals—"

"I do the cooking," Bridget explained with a smile.

Ida Mae sniffed. "With my recipes." She tasted the tea, gave another grimace, and set the cup down. "Keep the place tidy," she went on, "dusting and mopping and such as that, keep the silver polished—"

"We don't have any silver," Lindsay said, and at the look Ida Mae gave her, she felt compelled to apologize. "Well not much, anyway. Not enough to worry about polishing . . ." she trailed off.

"You girls live like squatters," said Ida Mae. "Ain't you got no menfolk?"

"Well," Bridget began, but Cici cut her off firmly.

"I really don't think that's any of your business," she said. "And I've got to say I'm not all that comfortable with the thought of your spying on us all these months, much less with your opinion on how we live."

Ida Mae said, "What are you, a lawyer or something?" Then she shrugged. "I guess it don't matter. You don't hardly need a man half the time anyhow. But they're nice to do for." There was, with that last, an almost wistful look in her eye, and Bridget patted her hand again.

Cici drew in a breath. "Look, Miss Simpson . . ."

"It's Miz," corrected Ida Mae. "Miz Simpson. But you can call me Ida Mae."

"Fine. Ida Mae, we appreciate the offer, but we can't afford a housekeeper, and—"

"Don't need your money," replied Ida Mae proudly. "I got my pension."

"Oh." Cici glanced quickly from Bridget to Lindsay. "Still . . ."

Bridget said suddenly, "Cici, Lindsay, could we talk?" She jerked her head toward the door. "In there?"

They left Ida Mae placidly stirring more sugar into her tea as Bridget firmly closed the pantry door between them.

"She doesn't have any place to go," Bridget insisted in a whisper.

Cici's voice was incredulous. "You can't be serious!"

Lindsay offered, "You've got to admit, it would be nice to have help keeping this place clean."

"She's got to be a hundred and three years old!" Cici said. "How much help could she be?"

"She's lived here all her life," Bridget said. "And now she's homeless, all alone, feeling useless . . ."

"We're not talking about a flock of sheep, here," Cici said, "or a dog or a deer. She didn't just come with the house."

"In a way," pointed out Lindsay, "that's exactly what she did."

"And you don't find it the least bit creepy that she's been living here all this time without our knowledge, coming in and out as she pleased, eating our food . . ."

"*Creepy* is a strong word," said Lindsay uncomfortably.

"She was taking care of us," Bridget pointed out. "Making sure we had what we needed . . ."

"We can't keep her," Cici said. "We can't be responsible for a crazy old woman who goes around living in other people's houses."

Lindsay looked at Bridget, her expression apologetic. "You know she's right, Bridge. We don't know anything about this woman."

"Except that she broke into our house," pointed out Cici.

Bridget said, "Well, would you look at this?" Kneeling, she had located a metal vent below the shelf that held dry goods. Her fingers found a catch, and the slotted metal swung open. The other two women bent to see a fairly modern gas heater.

Cici murmured, "I wonder if it's natural gas or propane."

And Lindsay said, "Who cares? We can be warm again!"

Cici looked at Bridget, and Bridget said hopefully, "It might be nice, having someone around who knew how the place was put together."

Cici said, "Come on, Bridget, you know she can't stay."

And Lindsay added, "We're going to have to call around and find someone to take care of her. Those nieces and nephews in Michigan."

Cici sighed. "What this house really needs is a full-time social worker."

Bridget folded her arms. "Well, we can't do anything tonight."

"You mean—let her stay here?"

"It's thirty-six degrees outside. We can't toss her out!"

"It's not like we don't have the room," Lindsay pointed out. "She's been living here for months and we didn't even know it."

"Besides," said Bridget, "as far as she's concerned, I think, she's the one who's letting *us* live here."

As though on cue, there was a sharp rap on the door, and Ida Mae poked her head in. "If you ladies are about finished hashin' it out, I think I'll turn in. Oh, and I'd appreciate the return of my Bible, if it ain't too much trouble. I'm pleasured to do some reading before I doze off."

Bridget said quickly, "Oh. Yes, I'll bring it right down. And some extra blankets, too."

When she was gone, the three women looked at each other for a moment, hesitant, uncertain, defensive. Then Cici sighed and shook her head in resignation. "Just until morning," she said.

❧

But in the morning, they were all awakened by the aroma of fresh coffee, breakfast casserole with sausage, and homemade yeast rolls with cinnamon and honey. The sky was barely pink as, one by one, they wandered into the kitchen, their expressions varying from confusion to astonishment as they took in the breakfast counter set with bright place mats, silverware and plates, and cups and saucers instead of their usual coffee mugs. There were glasses filled with juice at each place setting, and presectioned grapefruit halves in the center of each plate.

Lindsay said, wide-eyed, "Uhh . . . is it Christmas?"

Ida Mae poured grits into a blue earthenware bowl. " 'Bout time you lazy bones got out of bed. Food's getting cold."

Cici said, "Are those grits?"

Lindsay practically sank into her place at the breakfast counter. "Yeast rolls! Those are yeast rolls!"

Bridget looked around uncertainly. "Gosh, Ida Mae, you shouldn't have gone to all this trouble. This is really too much."

Ida Mae took the breakfast casserole out of the oven and set it on the trivet in the middle of the counter. "Good breakfast, good day," she declared firmly. "Eat up."

Bridget took her place between Cici and Lindsay. "Wow, all this food."

"Yeast rolls," said Lindsay, taking one. "She made yeast rolls for breakfast!"

"They take two hours to rise." Bridget's tone was a bit defensive.

"I haven't had grits since my birthday." Cici helped herself.

"I didn't know you liked them that much," Bridget said.

"Is this real sausage in the casserole?"

Bridget looked at Lindsay. "I thought you were trying to lose weight."

Lindsay elbowed her in the ribs, hard. "She made *yeast rolls.*"

Bridget hesitated, then smiled. "I guess if I'd been out of a kitchen for as long as she has, I'd make yeast rolls, too." Then she called to Ida Mae, "Oh, don't bother getting the cream out. We all take our coffee black."

Ida Mae poured cream into a pitcher and set it onto a small tray beside the sugar bowl. She carried the tray to the counter and set it down deliberately in front of Bridget. "In my kitchen," she told her, "you put the cream and the sugar on the table when you serve the coffee."

Bridget drew in a breath to respond, but this time it was Cici who elbowed her in the ribs. "Just like in a restaurant," she said cheerily. "Grits, Bridget?"

The breakfast was delicious, but how could it not be, when the main course featured sausage? When the ladies got up to clear the table and load the dishwasher, Ida Mae shooed them away in no uncertain terms. She didn't trust "that damn dishwashing contraption" and preferred to do the dishes by hand. Furthermore, she didn't want anyone—not even Bridget—hovering around in the kitchen while she did.

On the way out of the kitchen, Lindsay grinned and gave

Bridget a high-five. "Looks like you've got the day off," she said. "Good deal."

Bridget said, "I just hope she doesn't wear herself out." She looked back over her shoulder, her expression unhappy and concerned. But her words seemed almost an afterthought as she added, "Poor thing."

Lunch was a rich beef stew, which Ida Mae refused to allow Bridget to help her prepare. By the time Bridget was ready to start dinner, a pork loin was already roasting in the oven and Ida Mae was shelling pecans for a pie. No, she didn't need any help with the pecans. No, there was nothing Bridget could do.

Cici located the underground gas tank, and by mid-afternoon had the gas company out to fill it, and to inspect and light all the heaters in the house. Within an hour the big old house was as toasty as any modern apartment.

"All the heaters are on thermostats," Cici reported, practically chortling with delight. "We can just set them once and never worry about them again. Of course, we'll still want to keep the wood furnace going to save on gas, but no more hauling in wood four times a day. Do you know what this means? We can live like normal people! We can be warm in any room we want to—even the sunroom! Why in the world didn't Ida Mae show up before now?"

Dinner was served in the formal dining room, where the huge walnut table had been spread with a white linen cloth, and the sconces on the wall, now served by propane gas flames, glowed with freshly polished brass and brilliantly cleaned glass globes. The chairs, which Lindsay had spent the afternoon rescuing from the dairy loft, gleamed with lemon oil and beeswax. The napkins were ironed, and the pork loin was served on a bed of fresh rosemary and parsley cut from the garden.

"I feel like I should leave a tip," Lindsay whispered, self-consciously pressing out the wrinkles in her jeans.

"She's auditioning," Cici pointed out. "She wants us to see what she can do."

"Well, as far as I'm concerned, she's got the part," said Lindsay, scooping out a generous portion of horseradish mashed potatoes.

Bridget smiled stiffly and said nothing.

❧

Three days later, Bridget had plenty to say.

Ida Mae did laundry, Ida Mae washed windows, Ida Mae dug a silver candelabra out of a box in the attic, polished it until it looked like a museum piece, and placed it in the center of the dining room table where she insisted they dine every night. She stripped the sheets off the beds every morning—often before the women who were sleeping on them were even dressed—and replaced them with freshly washed and ironed ones. Yes, she ironed sheets. She also ironed tablecloths, napkins, and dish towels. She polished the banister and waxed the stairs to a dangerous sheen. Using an ingenious mechanism none of the women had suspected before, she lowered the chandelier over the staircase, removed all the prisms, washed them in soapy water, and rehung the whole. The light that was thus refracted sparkled over the entire first floor.

On the other hand, she never lost an opportunity to criticize the ladies' taste, decor, or personal habits. She insisted on breakfast at dawn, lunch at noon, and dinner at seven. At first this was a novelty, like being on a cruise ship, but no one really expected to keep to the schedule permanently. She didn't like the way Cici dressed or the way Lindsay wore her hair, and worst of all, Bridget was banned from her own kitchen.

"The woman," Bridget muttered, flinging herself into her front porch rocker a little after five on a cloudy, cold afternoon, "is making me crazy. We've got to do something." She thrust out a half-empty wineglass for a refill. "Hit me, Lindsay. You know the worst part? I hate eating at seven. By seven I want to be soaking in the tub, up to my neck in bubbles. Why do we have to be on her schedule?"

"I feel like I should put on a dress to go to dinner," admitted Lindsay, filling Bridget's glass.

"We used to eat at seven back in the suburbs," Cici pointed out.

"That's not the point. We don't do that anymore. We eat when we're hungry and we drink when the sun goes down and then we go to bed. This is what we *do*."

Cici gave a half shrug, and sipped her wine. "She's a good cook."

"Obviously, she's never heard of cholesterol," added Lindsay.

"I kind of like living in a world where the cook doesn't know about heart disease."

Bridget bristled visibly. "I never heard any complaints before."

"Oh, Bridget, come on—"

"I didn't mean—"

"When we bought this place," Bridget said, her voice stiff with hurt, "I thought it was clear I was going to do the cooking. If you don't like the way I do it . . ."

"Are you kidding me?"

"Bridget, you can't be serious!"

"Hold on." Cici held up a hand for peace. "Bridget, I don't think there's any argument that Lindsay and I both love your cooking and appreciate the fact that you've been willing to take it on." Lindsay nodded vigorously. "And even though it has been nice being waited on these last few days, I for one am not all that interested in learning to live like a nineteenth-century woman of leisure. And I definitely can't keep eating like this three meals a day."

Lindsay murmured her reluctant agreement. "But come on, Bridge. Hasn't it been kind of nice, having help in the kitchen? When I think of all the peeling and slicing and blanching and preserving we did this summer—"

"Help?" exclaimed Bridget. "I'm not even allowed to set the table!"

Cici nodded and held out her glass for a refill, which Lindsay obliged. "She is a bossy old woman," she agreed. "And set in her ways."

"With way too much energy for a person of her age," added Lindsay. "Could someone clue her in to the fact that no one irons anymore? Maybe she should take up golf."

"Well, she's worked all her life," Cici said. "I know how I'd feel if someone told me one day I just wasn't needed anymore."

Bridget thought about that for a moment, and sighed. "Yeah, me, too, I guess."

"What she needs to understand," said Cici, "is that you're the chef. She's just the sous chef."

Bridget brightened a little. "Right. Sous chef."

"Of course," added Cici, "it's not like she's going to be here forever. As soon as we find her relatives . . ."

"No one I've talked to ever heard of her relatives," Lindsay said, "not even Maggie. Besides, what are we going to do if we find them? It's not like she's sick, or incompetent. We can't just call them up to come and get her."

Cici sighed. "I'd just feel better if she had some place to go, that's all."

"If she had some place to go," Bridget pointed out, "she wouldn't have been living in our attic."

"I wonder how old she is, anyway," mused Lindsay. "She's got to have some terrific stories about this place, but every time I try to draw her out, she brushes me off."

"The worst part is," Bridget said, shivering in the wool throw she had tossed around her shoulders, "it's forty-five degrees out here and we're sitting on the front porch because this is the only place we have to talk."

"It does feel weird, having someone else live here. I liked it better when it was our house," admitted Lindsay.

Cici said, "It's *still* our house. We own this place. That means you, too, Bridget. And if she's making you unhappy, then she's got to go. It's that simple."

"Go where?" asked Lindsay. "We're back to that again."

They were silent for a while, rocking.

"She's a good housekeeper," Cici admitted at last. "After all these years, I guess she's got the routine down. And with everything else we have to do trying to put this place back together, it's nice not to have to worry about mopping and dusting."

No one could argue with that.

"To tell the truth," Lindsay said after a moment, "I kind of like having ironed sheets. It reminds me of when I was a little girl, staying at my grandma's house."

"And the price is right," added Cici.

"But she's making me crazy," Bridget said.

Lindsay sighed. "Managing servants is an art." When the other two stared at her, she added, "So I hear."

Cici said, "We'll have a meeting, lay down the ground rules for her. If she can't abide by them, she'll have to find another job. It happens all the time."

Lindsay said, "Not when you're a hundred and five."

"Stop saying that, Lindsay," Bridget said. "She can't be more than . . . well, seventy or eighty."

"Right," agreed Lindsay. "That makes a huge difference."

Bridget said, "Anyway, I'll talk to her. We'll work something out."

"Sous chef," Cici reminded her.

Bridget said, "Right."

At that moment the front door opened, and the screen door creaked. Three heads swiveled to see Ida Mae standing there, scowling at them. "Supper's in half an hour," she said. "I ain't calling you again."

She started to close the door, but Bridget spoke quickly. "Will you join us for a glass of wine, Ida Mae?"

Ida Mae looked from one to the other of them, her fierce expression unaltered. "My mama always said," she replied archly, "that a sip of sherry at Christmas, or on the birth of a child, is all a lady requires."

She turned to go inside, while Lindsay mouthed, eyebrows raised, *Sherry?* And then they heard her mutter, just before the screen door slammed, "Bunch of damn alkies."

Cici looked at Bridget. "Are you sure you don't want us to talk to her?"

Bridget sighed. "No. She's my problem. I'll handle it. Really."

Lindsay raised her glass to Bridget. "You've got your work cut out for you," she said, and Bridget sighed as three glasses clinked together.

"Cheers."

17

In Which Bridget Has a Very Bad Day

Bridget talked to Ida Mae.

"Breakfast was delicious," she said, "but we really can't have you getting up before dawn to cook for us. We can make our own breakfast, really."

And: "Really, Ida Mae, you work much too hard. We can change our own beds."

And, firmly, "We're really not accustomed to sitting down to three formal meals a day. We're all watching our figures, you know. From now on I think it would be better if you let me take care of the cooking."

None of it made one bit of difference.

"You're too nice," Cici told her. "You can't be sweet to somebody like that. You have to speak up. Let me talk to her."

To which Bridget replied irritably, "For heaven's sake, Cici, you can't fix everything. I'll take care of it."

But clearly she could not. If Bridget got up at six a.m. to

make muffins, she would find cinnamon rolls already baking. If she chopped chicken breast for a salad, she would find Ida Mae had already used it for a casserole by the time she returned. If she wanted to spend the afternoon making banana bread, Ida Mae would choose that very time to bake a cake.

"Well, there *are* two ovens," Lindsay pointed out, which only annoyed Bridget further.

"That's not the point," Bridget snapped in return, and Lindsay lifted her eyebrows.

"Just trying to be helpful," she said.

Bridget apologized, Lindsay shrugged it off, and Bridget felt even worse. For as much as Cici and Lindsay tried to understand, their paths hardly ever crossed that of Ida Mae. It was Bridget who was constantly tripping over her, and now she was even causing Bridget to be short with her friends. And of course, the more irritable Bridget became over the whole situation, the guiltier she felt, and the harder she tried *not* to take it out on Ida Mae.

So when Ida Mae tossed out the pecans Bridget was toasting for salad, calling them "burnt," Bridget smiled and held her tongue. After all, it had been Ida Mae who had shelled the entire bushel of pecans, bagged, and frozen them. When Ida Mae went behind her, salting the stew, Bridget pretended not to notice, and when Lindsay and Cici raved over Ida Mae's chicken and dressing with cracked cranberries, thinking Bridget had prepared it, Bridget just smiled and gave Ida Mae all the credit. But it was the matter of the draperies that broke the camel's back.

"They're gonna fade," stated Ida Mae flatly as Bridget,

after two hours spent hand-pleating and hanging twenty-five yards of lined brocade damask, stepped down from the ladder and regarded her handiwork proudly.

Bridget turned slowly to stare at Ida Mae. Ida Mae flipped back a corner of the drapery to examine the lining, and sniffed. "Too flimsy," she pronounced. "Sun sets through this window all summer long. Won't last a season."

Bridget said, "I had this fabric special-ordered from New York to match a swatch I found stored in the dairy loft."

Ida Mae turned down one corner of her mouth derisively. "I don't know what you found, but there ain't never been anything like this hanging here. Miss Emily weren't no fool, you know. You should've asked me before you spent your money." She shrugged and flicked the corner of drapery away. "You need to call them others if you want to eat. I'm making broccoli quiche and it won't keep."

Bridget said, very evenly, "I was going to make soup out of that broccoli."

"What for?" Ida Mae was already leaving the room. "Nobody likes soup."

And that was it. "Ida Mae, wait a minute."

Ida Mae turned.

Bridget's hands closed at her sides. She drew a breath, but she didn't think about her words. She simply said them. "I know you're used to running this house," she said. "I know you like doing things your own way. But this isn't your place anymore. It's mine, and Lindsay's and Cici's. And in our house, we change the sheets once a week, not every day. We have cereal and fruit for breakfast, and sometimes I make muffins. We make our own lunch when we get hungry, and we have dinner when it gets dark. And oh, one more thing.

I'm the cook. I prepare the meals. I bake the cakes and the pies and the breads, and if I want to make soup, we have soup. I'm the cook. That's what I do. Do you understand?"

Ida Mae regarded her levelly. "How long have you been the cook here?"

Bridget blinked. "Well, since we moved in. When we bought this place, we decided. I was going to be the cook."

Ida Mae nodded, although there seemed to be less understanding than pity in the gesture. "I've been the cook here for forty-five years. Now, I'm taking the quiche out of the oven. You want to set the table?"

Bridget almost let it go. She caught her breath, bit her tongue, started to turn back to the draperies. And suddenly the words that were boiling up inside her would be suppressed no longer; she actually pushed her fingers against her temples to try to stop them but they burst out of her, heedless. "Stop it!" she shouted. "Just—stop it!"

Ida Mae turned to her, startled.

"Listen to me," Bridget said, breathing hard. "You're the intruder here, don't you get that? This is not your house! You're lucky you're not in jail for trespassing! I live here! I own this place! I'm in charge!"

And suddenly she caught herself with a gasp, a lurch that actually caused her to grip the back of a chair for support as her words suddenly echoed back at her and hit her like a slap. For a moment she couldn't believe that was her voice. Her fingers went to her lips as though to recapture the words and send them back. But it was too late.

And, in truth, she was not entirely sure she wanted to.

She found her breath, and somehow she even managed to straighten her shoulders. She looked straight into the other woman's eyes and she said, albeit somewhat stiffly, "I'm sorry. That was rude. I didn't mean to hurt your feelings. But..." Another breath. "I think what I was trying to say is that I know what it feels like to need to be in charge of something. To be needed. And—that's probably why you and I keep bumping heads. Because we're so much alike. But for you, it's just a job. For me, it's—well, it's why I'm here. Cici has her building and her restoration, Lindsay has her art, but all I have is the kitchen. That's all I know how to do. That's all I can contribute. Can't you understand that?"

Ida Mae looked at her for a long time, and Bridget couldn't be certain whether it was contempt or pity she saw in the other woman's eyes. Then she said, "It ain't just a job."

She moved toward the door, then stopped and dug into her apron pocket. "Here's your mail."

Bridget stared at her for a moment, then stepped forward and snatched the envelopes out of her hand. "We change the sheets once a week," she said again, tightening her fingers on the envelopes as though that could stop the shaking in her voice. "We make our own breakfast and lunch and we eat in the kitchen, not the dining room, and we don't use tablecloths and linen napkins. And I'm the cook!"

Ida Mae left the room without responding, and when she was gone Bridget flung the mail to the floor in a fit of temper. Almost immediately she felt her face flush hot, and she looked around guiltily. Quickly, she knelt to pick up the envelopes from the floor.

There were three birthday cards, which made her smile and went a long way toward soothing the tension of the previous confrontation. She felt rather foolish, in fact, and thought she probably should try again to apologize to Ida

Mae. And then she opened the statement from her health insurance company, which was routine this time of year, and she forgot about Ida Mae entirely. Because there was nothing routine about this statement at all.

She dialed her insurance agent in Maryland.

"You can't be serious," she said, after her agent had patiently explained to her—twice, in fact—that there had been no mistake. "You can't just suddenly double my premium for no reason."

Computer keys clacked in the background. "I'm showing here you have a birthday coming up."

"So? Everyone has birthdays. That's a good thing, right?"

"Well, you're moving into a new age bracket. The rates are different."

"I've been a customer of yours for almost thirty years!"

"And you did have significant claims last year."

"That wasn't me, that was my husband."

"I understand. But you were on the same policy."

She took a breath, lowered her voice, and clutched the phone tightly. "Listen, Reggie, you've got to do something. I can't afford this. I'm a widow, I don't have a job, I haven't budgeted for this. There's got to be something . . ."

He said sympathetically, "This is the most economical plan we carry. I wish I could help, but I really don't know what to say. A woman your age can't afford to be without health insurance. Would it help if we broke down the payments into monthly installments?"

She told him she would have to think about that and let him know, thanked him for his time, and hung up, feeling shell-shocked. And then she picked up the telephone again.

She didn't know why her fingers dialed Kevin's office

number. Perhaps she was simply conditioned, after all those years of marriage, to turn to a man when things went wrong. And her son was the only man she had left.

The thought humiliated her, and she almost hung up. But then it was too late. "Kevin, hi!" she exclaimed brightly. "It's Mom. How are you?"

He was fine, working hard, had just gotten a big case, was glad to hear from her, and how were things going with the house?

"Oh, great," she assured him, and hoped her voice was convincing. "I love it here. You should see the colors of the mountains. It's like something out of a painting. Of course, things are a lot more expensive than we thought they would be . . ."

"They always are." He sounded preoccupied, and she thought she heard him murmur something to someone while his hand covered the phone. "Listen, Mom, is there something in particular you called about? Because I've got a meeting in a few minutes, and—"

"I don't mean to keep you," she apologized quickly. "Gosh, I guess I'd forgotten how quickly things move in the outside world." She laughed, a little falsely, and then said, "Thank you for the birthday card, darling, it was so sweet of you. I wish you could be here."

"Me, too, Mom, I really do. Listen, I'm going to have to—"

"Actually, I just wanted to ask you . . ." Her heart started pounding as she looked at the numbers on the paper. "Well, it's about this health insurance premium I just got in the mail. It's twice as much as the last one. And I could barely afford that! Are they allowed to do that? Just double your payments like that without any warning?" She hoped her voice didn't sound too stressed, but she couldn't help it. She was stressed.

"I guess they're allowed to do whatever they want, Mom. Did you talk to your agent?"

"He said he couldn't do anything. Do you think I could get a cheaper policy?"

"Probably not. Listen, you're about to turn sixty, right? Premiums go up at that age. But the good news is you only have five years until you're eligible for Medicare."

Medicare. She smiled weakly. "Well, that is good news. All I have to do is hold on for five more years."

He hesitated. "Mom, I'd love to help you out, but with what I'm already doing for Katie there's not much left over at the end of the month as it is."

She blinked. "What? What did you say about Katie?"

The silence was heavy with self-recrimination. "She didn't want you to know," he said in a moment. "So don't let on, okay? I've been sending her a little every month, to help with the rent."

"Which you wouldn't have to do if I'd moved to Chicago," Bridget said slowly, "instead of buying this house."

"Well, it sounds like things are not working out as well as you'd hoped on that end, either," he said. "So maybe by the first of the year you'll reconsider."

She said absently, "Yes. Maybe."

"In the meantime, if you need help making the insurance payment, I guess I could scrape together a little . . ."

"Don't be silly," she said quickly. "Don't you dare. It's not even due for a couple of months. I'll think of something by then. It's no big deal, really."

"Well . . . happy birthday, again."

"It's not until Tuesday. But thank you anyway. Wish I could see you. Maybe at Thanksgiving?"

"Sounds good. I'll let you know."

She smiled into the phone. "You're a wonderful boy. I'm really proud of you."

"Good to hear you say that, Mom. Let's talk soon, okay? We'll make plans for the holidays."

"You bet. Take care."

"Bye, Mom."

"Bye, Kev." But even after he had hung up, she stood there holding the phone to her chest, staring at the bill, thinking about Kate, until Lindsay came in from her studio, rubbing her hands together against the cold and inquiring about lunch. Bridget smiled quickly and pretended everything was all right, but it wasn't. And it was about to get worse.

❧

Every afternoon around four thirty Lindsay put the fawn, who inevitably had been named Bambi, into his pen for the night, while Bridget fed the dog and checked on the sheep. Cici had fashioned a lean-to against the side of the house with two pieces of plywood and some tarp to provide the deer a refuge from the weather, but Lindsay worried it wasn't enough.

"Noah said they can freeze," she said. "What are we going to do when it snows?"

"Noah is a teenager," replied Cici, tacking down a corner of the tarp with a finishing nail. The wind whipped a strand of hair across her face and she used her shoulder to push it away. "We'll put him in the barn at night when I get the roof fixed. Meanwhile, he's a deer, not a house pet. He'll be fine."

Lindsay stroked the nubby head while the deer nibbled a carrot from her hand. "Maybe I should get more hay."

Cici started to reply, but they both turned at the sound of a cry. It was Bridget, running across the yard toward them. Her jeans and her shoes were spattered with mud and her jacket flapped open behind her; her face was taut with distress. "Cici! Lindsay!"

They hurried out of the pen and Bridget reached them, gasping. "We've got to call a vet. It's Bandit, he's not moving, and his eyes are all rolled back—"

"Bandit?" parroted Lindsay.

"The dog?" said Cici at the same time. Neither of them could remember what the dog's current name was.

Bridget shook her head, grasping Cici's arms. "The sheep. His breathing is funny, he won't move, he's really sick, Cici, and I don't know what to do!"

Cici said, trying to calm her, "Okay. Okay, show me. We'll see what we can do."

"I'll try to find a vet," Lindsay said, running toward the house.

"Call Farley!" Bridget yelled. "He knows about sheep!"

Lindsay waved affirmative, and Bridget grabbed Cici's hand, tugging her toward the meadow.

Farley arrived less than five minutes later, bouncing across the yard in his pickup truck, and screeching to a stop at the gate. The sheepdog, with ears pricked forward and eyes fixed on the downed sheep, didn't even bark when he slammed the door. Cici and Bridget, kneeling helplessly over the muddy mound of tangled wool, straightened up with visible relief as Farley strode through the gate.

He stood over the animal for a moment, chewing his tobacco thoughtfully, then spat on the ground. "Sure looks bad, don't he?" he commented.

Bridget said desperately, “I don’t know what happened. They all looked fine this morning . . .” She gestured to the remainder of the flock, which was contentedly plucking at the sparse blades of winter grass a few dozen feet away. “You don’t think it’s contagious, do you? Like hoof and mouth disease or something?”

Farley grunted, noncommittal, then grasped all four of the sheep’s hooves and flipped it over to its other side. The animal bleated in protest, then was silent. Farley bent for a closer look. “Right here’s your problem.”

He parted the wool to reveal a gory-looking wound in the sheep’s side. Bridget gasped and lost color, and Cici brought her hand to her mouth, looking away.

“Probably ran into a stick or tore itself up on barb wire,” he said. “Sheep’re stupid critters.”

He straightened up. “Want me to shoot it for you? Got my rifle in the truck.”

Both Cici and Bridget cried, “No!”

He gave them a long and unreadable look, then tugged at the bill of his camo cap, spat on the ground again, and said, “Bring my tractor by in the morning, dig you a hole. Cost you ten dollar.”

He started back toward the gate, and Cici saw the despair in Bridget’s eyes. She rushed forward. “Farley, wait. If you could help us get it to the barn, out of the cold, until the vet comes . . .”

Another look. But all he said was, “Your barn’s got a hole in it.”

“I know, but it’s better than being out here on the damp ground, and it’s getting dark. Please?”

He shrugged, and between them they managed to get the

wounded animal into the back of his truck. Bridget climbed in back with the sheep as Farley drove to the barn, the sheepdog trotting behind.

Cici quickly cleaned away as much of the debris as she could inside the barn entrance, and dragged a bale of hay from the stack they kept in the shed to use as mulch. The animal showed an encouraging surge of energy when they got him out of the truck, bleating in protest and shaking his head as they led him into the barn. But as soon as they got him inside, he collapsed on the hay, eyes rolled back and sides heaving. Bridget wrung her hands in distress.

Lindsay ran up just as Farley was driving away. "I called the vet," she said, looking anxious as she took in the scene. "He's out of town for the weekend. He'll be in first thing in the morning, but meantime his service gave me the number of the emergency clinic in Staunton."

"That's okay," Cici said quickly. "We can get him in the back of my SUV—"

Already Lindsay was shaking her head. "I called them. Cats and dogs only. I'm so sorry Bridge. I don't know what else to do."

Bridget drew in a breath, pushed back her hair, and straightened her shoulders. "We'll just do the best we can, that's all. I'll get some water, and some towels."

"I'll try to block up some of these holes to keep the draft out," Cici said.

And Lindsay quickly volunteered, "I'll get some more hay."

They worked by flashlight for over an hour, but it became increasingly difficult to convince themselves their efforts were anything but futile. The poor animal was barely breathing, and a closer examination of the wound revealed it to be much more serious than they had at first thought. The ten-inch long gash was deep enough to reveal viscera, and oozed a thick yellow black fluid that made even the strongest-stomached among them woozy.

"Bridget, come inside," Lindsay urged at last. "We'll call the vet again first thing in the morning. I don't think there's anything more we can do now."

Bridget shook her head, hugging her arms. "No, I think I'll stay awhile longer."

"But it's getting cold."

"I should have fixed the hole in the roof before now," Cici fretted. "I knew winter was coming. I should have gotten this place airtight. You could have put the whole flock in here at night, and the deer, too. That way they would have been safe."

Bridget's smile was strained as she patted Cici's arm. "It's fine for now. Don't worry about it."

"At least come in and have some supper," Lindsay said. "I'll stay while you eat."

Bridget shook her head. "I couldn't eat anything."

They both looked down at the suffering animal, and knew how she felt.

Cici said, "Well, we'll need some blankets."

And Lindsay added, "I'll bring out a couple of those battery-operated lanterns we got in case of a power outage."

Bridget caught each of their hands as they turned to go. Her eyes were glistening in the pale beam of the flashlight Lindsay had propped up against a crate on the opposite wall. "You guys . . . are the best. I know the sheep were my idea, and you didn't even want them, and now . . . you're just the best. Thank you."

Lindsay put an arm around Bridget's shoulders. "We might not be all that crazy about the sheep," she told her sincerely, "but we love you. All for one and one for all, right?"

Cici slipped her arm around Bridget's shoulders, too. "Oh Bridge," Cici whispered, with genuine pain in her voice, "I am so sorry I can't fix this."

"Well, there ain't no good in all of you just standing around here," declared a harsh voice behind them. They broke apart to see Ida Mae standing at the door in her flannel-lined denims and barn coat, scowling. She held a steaming basin in one hand and a thermos in another. "You two." She jerked her head at Cici and Lindsay. "Go on and get them blankets and lights. And when you're done, get back inside and eat yourselves some supper. Nothing for you to do here.

"You." She thrust the thermos at Bridget. "Drink this soup and move out of my light. This here poultice needs to be put on while it's hot."

Lindsay said heatedly, "Now wait just a minute—"

And Cici demanded skeptically, "What's in that poultice?"

Ida Mae stared them down. "Either of you know anything about farm animals?"

When they simply looked at each other uncertainly, Ida Mae sniffed. "That's what I thought. Now get on out of my way."

Reluctantly, they stepped aside, and Bridget, still clutching the thermos she had automatically taken from Ida Mae, watched anxiously as she applied a greasy-looking yellow cloth to the open wound. "Do you think that will help?"

Ida Mae looked up at her sternly. "Better than doing nothing, ain't it?" And when Bridget, swallowing hard, nodded, she turned back to her ministrations, muttering, "All this fuss about a damn sheep. Never seen the like in my life..."

For the next hour, Bridget moved back and forth between the house and the barn, fetching the sharp-smelling poultices that Ida Mae kept warm in a big speckled pot on the stove. Cici and Lindsay brought folding lawn chairs and lanterns and old blankets and more hay. It was good, for a while, to feel useful and empowered, but eventually there was nothing more to do but wait. Bridget was able to persuade Lindsay and Cici to go back to the house, and, reluctantly, they did.

Wrapped in a heavy scarf, hat, and gloves, Bridget sipped soup from the thermos and watched Ida Mae apply the last poultice to the wound. Then the old woman settled back in her lawn chair and the three of them—she, Bridget, and the sheepdog in the corner—kept vigil.

After a moment Bridget said awkwardly, "Thank you... for the soup."

Ida Mae said nothing.

Time passed. They sat in an oasis of thin yellow light while the night stacked up in layers outside the building, as thick as cotton and as black as soot. Bridget thought she had never known a heavier stillness, a deeper silence. Nighttime in the country muffled every breath and swallowed everything that stirred. The living creatures who had sought shelter inside the big old barn seemed small indeed, and very fragile, in comparison to the vastness of the night that pressed down on them outside.

Bridget said softly, "Do you think... he has a chance?"

Ida Mae got up, made a fuss about rearranging the poultice, and sat back down, muttering, "Damn fool city women, coming out here thinking you know how to run a farm. What ever made you buy this place, anyway? You don't belong here."

Bridget closed her eyes slowly, releasing a breath. "You're right. We don't. I don't know what we were thinking... what I was thinking. I guess... I don't know, I guess I never realized before how used I was to, well, to being taken care of. All my life, I thought I was this independent woman. I was on all the right committees, made speeches for all the right causes, traveled all over the world with Cici and Lindsay. I had my little part-time job, I made all my own decisions, but... there was always someone there to fall back on when things went bad. My husband, Jim..." She drew another breath, and it was a little shaky. "Funny, how after so many years of marriage you don't think about how much you depend on the other person until... well, until they're gone." Quickly, she touched the back of her gloved hand to the corner of her eye, and went on, "And then of course there's just the whole *system* in the city. Your doctor, your pharmacist, your plumber, your vet... there's always someone there. You never have to find out... how much you can't do."

She looked down at the empty thermos cup in her hand, and carefully set it on the ground. "I don't know what I was thinking, coming here," she repeated tiredly.

Ida Mae said, extending her hand, "Give me some of that soup."

A little surprised, Bridget handed over the thermos. Ida Mae unscrewed the top, and took a few sips. Then she said, "Nice dog."

Bridget followed her gaze toward the dog, who had not

moved from his position in the corner with his head on his paws since they had brought the sheep in.

"I had one like that when I was a girl," she went on. "Smartest dog I ever knew. Never stopped going, always into something. Called him Rebel."

"Rebel," Bridget repeated, smiling a little. "I like that name."

Ida Mae sipped from the thermos in silence for a while. Then she said, "What the hell is a sous chef, anyhow?"

Bridget looked at her, startled. "Umm . . . it's like an assistant cook."

"The girl that peels the potatoes," said Ida Mae, nodding. "I had me one of those, back in the day. Had a girl to do beds and laundry, too. There used to be some parties in the house like you never seen." She lifted one shoulder and finished off the soup. "After it was just Mr. B to take care of, we didn't need so much help."

She fixed Bridget with a steady look. "You girls now, you need a lot of help."

Bridget sniffed, and tried to smile, and blotted her eye with the back of her hand again. "Yeah. I guess we do." And then she added gently, "It was nice of you to bring the poultices . . . even though you knew they weren't going to do any good."

Now it was Ida Mae's turn to look surprised. But almost immediately she regained control of her expression, and averted her gaze.

They sat like that, in a silence that no longer seemed quite so oppressive, for close to an hour. Then Ida Mae got up one more time and bent over the sheep. Bridget watched her, with dread building in her chest, until the older woman straightened up again.

"I reckon you can go on back to the house," she said, without looking around.

Bridget stood slowly. "Is it . . . ?" She couldn't finish, and Ida Mae merely put both hands to the small of her back and arched her shoulders, working out the kinks.

Bridget took a long, steadying breath. "Okay," she said. "Okay, it's life on a farm. I understand that." She made herself walk over and look down at the lifeless form on the barn floor. "See that little smudge of black around his eye? Like a mask. That's why I called him Bandit." And before she could stop them, tears were rolling down her face, splashing on her muddy boots. She tried to stop them by pressing her fingers to her eyes, but it was no use. "I know you think it's stupid," she choked out, trying not to sob. "I know I'm just a city girl and it's just a sheep, but it was mine, my responsibility, and it shouldn't have died . . . I should have done something. I would have done something if I could have! It shouldn't have died! It's not fair when things die! It's just not . . ."

And then she was sobbing, great heaving painful sobs that wracked her chest and hurt her stomach, and Ida Mae just stood there, quietly, until she was too tired to cry anymore. Then Ida Mae said, "I buried a husband and two sons. I guess we got something we can agree on. It's not fair."

With an effort, Bridget lifted her swollen, burning eyes to focus on the other woman. "How do you get over it?" she asked hoarsely.

"You don't," Ida Mae replied simply.

The two women looked at each other for a long and gentle moment, and then turned and began to silently gather up the towels, the blankets, the basin of used poultices. When her arms were full, Bridget turned to the sheepdog, who had not moved from his vigil in the corner.

"Rebel," she said, and the dog lifted its head to look at her. So did Ida Mae. Bridget smiled faintly, tiredly. "Come on, let's go." She patted her thigh and the dog got up and trotted to the door. "It's been a long night."

❧

Two days later, Cici and Lindsay surprised Bridget with a birthday cake after supper. They brought out birthday hats and noisemakers and sang "Happy Birthday" and gave her silly presents that made her laugh.

"Of course we didn't make the cake," Lindsay felt compelled to explain, scraping a last dollop of icing off her plate, "Ida Mae did."

"Well, it was delicious." Bridget smiled at Ida Mae as she came to collect the cake plates. "Thank you, Ida Mae."

"You all gonna be wanting coffee this time of night?" asked Ida Mae with her customary tact, and of course no one admitted that she did.

"Good," said Ida Mae. She stacked the cake plates on the corner of the table and folded her hands across her stomach. "'Cause I got something to say. I ain't getting any younger, you know, and I have a mind to take it easy in my remaining years. I can't be running up and down them stairs changing your beds every day, or hanging out your linens to dry or doing your ironing, either. So if you want your sheets changed more than once a week, you need to do it yourself."

Her eyes went from one to the other of them, and they said not a word.

"And another thing," she went on, "I can't keep up with all

this cooking at my age. I figure Sunday dinner in the dining room is about all I can manage, but during the week, you're gonna have to do for yourselves. Now, I don't mind helping out now and again, keeping the place tidy, peeling potatoes and the like, for my room and board. But I ain't no machine, you know. You all are just going to have to learn to do for yourselves, and if you don't like it, now's the time to say so."

There was an immediate chorus of understanding and agreement from Lindsay and Cici, but Bridget didn't say anything at all. She simply stood up, walked around the table, and hugged Ida Mae. At first Ida Mae looked startled, even embarrassed, as though she didn't know what to do with her hands. But Bridget did not back away, and eventually Ida Mae lifted her arms and patted Bridget uncertainly on the back.

"Thank you," Bridget said again, softly.

Ida Mae grasped Bridget's shoulders and stepped away. "Well," she said gruffly. "How about doing up them dishes, then? I got to get to my resting."

"I'll be happy to," Bridget replied, smiling. "But first, we were going to have a glass of wine by the fire. Maybe you'd like to join us—for a sip of sherry?"

Ida Mae looked at her for a moment, her eyes narrowed fractionally. And then she smoothed out the folds of her apron, tilted her chin, and pronounced, "I don't mind if I do... just this once."

Winter
Home

18

In Which an Ill Wind Blows No Good

It got cold, and then it got colder. The brilliant cobalt days and vermilion sunsets gave way to lead-streaked skies that spit icy particles of snow. Almost overnight the last of the yellow and orange leaves shuddered off the trees and left nothing but bony protrusions along the spine of the mountaintop. The lawn turned brown with dead leaves that accumulated faster than they could rake them, and the ragged, withered seed heads of a few forlorn flowers were all that remained of the perennial beds.

"Why didn't anyone tell us how much colder it is in Virginia than in Maryland?" Lindsay complained, shivering in a turtleneck, sweatshirt, jacket, wool hat, and gloves as she came in from packing the last of the mulch around the roses—now so bleak and forlorn-looking it was hard to imagine they would ever bloom again.

"I just wish the sun would shine again," Bridget said, searching through a book on horticulture. "It's the grayness

I can't stand. Do you know if we're supposed to do anything to the raspberry bushes for the winter?"

If they had thought about it at all, they had all imagined winter as a time of rest and respite, of baking brownies on a snowy day, sitting before the fire with a book, soaking in a bubble bath, and curling up in bed beneath a downy quilt while the big old house stood sturdy against the storms that raged outside. In reality, it took a lot of wood to keep the fireplaces cozy, even with the gas heaters, and someone had to haul in the wood and sweep up the ashes. Brownies would have been nice, but Ida Mae had confiscated the kitchen in order to make her fruitcakes, and they didn't dare complain because with all the fruitcake batter they sneaked during the day no one had much interest in brownies. The house was indeed sturdy, but it was big and the windows were only single-paned, and bubble baths weren't nearly as much fun as they might have been in a house with a little more insulation and few less cross-drafts.

And then came the morning when Bridget turned on the burner to heat the pancake griddle, and nothing happened. After a frantic check of all the house's various switches and gauges, Cici came in from outside, blowing on her fingers, and reported, "The propane tank is empty. We'll have to get someone out to fill it today."

Bridget stared at her, aghast. "We just had it filled last month!"

Cici nodded. "Good thing we can still heat with wood."

"But that cost us two thousand dollars!"

"It's a big house," agreed Cici, looking unhappy. "And trying to keep it warm isn't easy."

"But—we can't spend two thousand a month on propane!

That's not even counting the cost of electricity for lighting and the water pump and—"

Cici just sighed. "I know. I guess we didn't count on that."

It turned out there was a lot they hadn't counted on, not the least of which was how much preparation was required to winterize a farm. The leaves had to be raked and the constant rain of twigs and sticks that fell from the trees had to be gathered for kindling. Shrubbery and fruit trees had to be pruned. The flower beds had to be cut back and the vegetable garden plowed under (Farley: ten dollars). The roses had to be pruned and mulched and the concrete garden ornaments had to be sealed. The outdoor water system had to be drained, the faucets covered, and the pipes that led to the house had to be insulated and wrapped with heat tape. The wisteria had to be cut back, and the grapevines tied. And then, of course, there were the outbuildings.

Cici was determined to get the barn weathertight for the livestock, despite the fact that the sheep had survived at least one winter with nothing more than the lean-to in the meadow, and the deer presumably had managed with even less. J&J Lumber delivered an alarming stack of plywood, six-by-sixes, roofing paper, and shingles, and Cici ran an extension cord for her circular saw from the workshop to the barn. Piece by piece, she replaced rotten siding, repaired sagging hinges and broken latches, and shored up fallen beams. Every night she gave a cheerful report about how well the work was coming and how much she enjoyed it, but Bridget and Lindsay were not fooled.

Lori had not called, and every attempt Cici made to reach her daughter went straight to voice mail. Once upon a time, in another life, Cici had exorcized her anxiety with a cell phone and a BlackBerry. Now she did it with a hammer and nails.

And then one day Lindsay came into the kitchen where the other two were warming their hands before the fire after a morning of dragging limbs out of the yard in a bitter wind. The expression on her face was strained. "That was Reverend Holland on the phone," she said, with a vague, uncertain gesture back toward the foyer where the telephone was located. "He thought we'd want to know—since we'd asked before, and everything—that the trailer where Noah's dad lived burned to the ground this morning."

Both women dropped their hands and looked at her, stunned. The wind-rouged spots of color on their faces suddenly seemed a stark contrast against paler skin.

"He . . ." Lindsay cleared her throat. "The dad, that is, was found a few feet away, dead from smoke inhalation. It looked as though he tried to get out, but too late."

"Dear God," said Bridget softly. "How awful."

Cici said, "Noah?"

Again Lindsay cleared her throat. "Apparently he's been living at a campground not too far away. The sheriff tracked him down to tell him about his father, and tried to get Noah to come to one of the shelters. But he ran away." She stopped and shook her head fiercely as though trying to free herself of the images inside her head. "What kind of place is this anyway? Alcoholics left to burn to death in their trailers, children living in campgrounds . . ."

Cici and Bridget enfolded her in their arms, but no one knew what to say. And when Lindsay, furiously scrubbing hot tears out of her eyes, muttered, "I hate this place," they didn't know what to say to that, either.

❧

Thanksgiving was fast approaching, but none of them was very interested. Bridget's children hoped to make the trip to Virginia for Christmas, but Kevin had to work and Katie really couldn't afford it; they hoped she understood. In fact, Bridget was relieved. A small turkey, soaked in bourbon and served with sausage dressing, would be fine for just the three of them. Ida Mae had already made the pecan pies.

Lindsay raked leaves and stacked kindling and pruned trees with a ladder. Bridget painted trim and tied up grapevines and spread bale after bale of hay over the frozen muddy meadow. The days were short and dark and filled, not with things they wanted to do, but with things they had to do. All of them were cold and tired, and in the backs of their minds, teasing and dancing like a playful imp, was the knowledge that, in little over a month, their contract would expire. Not that any of them seriously considered reneging on the deal.

Not really.

But a restlessness was rising within them like an arctic wind, fueled by disappointment, discouragement, and uncertainty. It was not something they could define or contain, or even understand most of the time. What had begun as a grand adventure was not so much fun anymore, and the cold, gray twilight came earlier every day. No one talked about it. But they didn't sit on the porch anymore, and most nights, gathered around the fireplace, they were too tired to talk at all.

And then, two days before Thanksgiving, something happened that changed everything.

❧

In the unwritten Rules of Sisterhood, there are very few occasions upon which it is acceptable to lie to your best friend. When she accidentally waxes off an eyebrow an hour before her dinner party, for example, of course you tell her that, as long as she combs her bangs down, no one will notice. When looking into the face of her newborn infant whose squashed-down features remind you of something from the cast of *Alien*, or after listening to her eight-year-old butcher the violin for two hours at his first recital, everyone can agree that discretion is always the better part of valor. However, Lindsay was almost certain that making a date to meet an old boyfriend for lunch was not among those Acceptable Occasions for Lying to Your Best Friends. And she was still not entirely certain why she had done it.

Nonetheless, when Shep called, she had barely even hesitated. She put on a skirt, swept up her hair, dug out earrings from the bottom of her jewelry box. She used hand lotion and shaved her legs. She told Cici and Bridget that she was going to Charlottesville to get an early start on her Christmas shopping, and she even hid a pair of high heels in her purse so that she could change when she got in the car. And then she went to Staunton to have lunch with Shep.

They met in a little street-front restaurant with chintz tablecloths and waitresses wearing Battenburg lace aprons, and were seated before the fireplace. Shep kissed her cheek in greeting, and told her how wonderful she looked. Lindsay hoped he wasn't lying, because she had gone to a great deal of trouble to look like anything other than what she was—a woman who hadn't seen a hairdresser in six months, who only wore lipstick on Sundays, whose hands were rough and calloused from digging in the dirt, fighting back undergrowth, and wielding tools that had nothing to do with a paintbrush or palette knife. Shep, of course, was as elegantly good-looking as ever, turning heads with his expertly barbered silver hair and his crinkled green eyes.

"Not much to this town, is there?" he commented as he held her chair, and Lindsay had to laugh.

"Are you kidding? This is the big city!"

He had told her on the phone that he was driving through the Shenandoah on vacation, which was probably a lie because it was too early for the ski resorts to open and there were certainly more hospitable months than November for vacationing in the mountains. But she had pretended to believe him, because the alternative would have been not to see him at all. And she was glad she had done so. Because seeing him was like a sudden welcome breeze, bringing with it the taste and the smell and the feel of everything she had left behind . . . movie theaters, walks along the harbor, coffee shops, bookstores, symphony concerts, sailboat rides. They talked about the crab cakes at Finos, and tailgate picnics on Saturday afternoons, and they laughed over the escapades of her former students, and he brought her up-to-date on mutual friends and colleagues.

"They miss you," he told her, warm green eyes smiling tenderly as he reached across the table for her hand. "We all do."

She said, "I miss them, too." She was surprised to find that was the truth. The simple, achingly genuine truth. "I miss a lot of things." She let him hold her fingers atop the rose print tablecloth for a moment, then she returned her hand to her lap.

"So," she said with determined pleasantness, "how is Estelle? Didn't she come with you?"

He sat back, his gaze steady. "We're divorced," he told her. "As of June."

"Oh." She didn't know why she was suddenly so tongue-tied. "Well, I'm—that is, I hope . . . I'm sure it was for the best."

He nodded. "I guess you figured out I'm not really up here on vacation."

She reached for her water glass. "You didn't really drive all the way out here just to tell me about you and Estelle?"

"That was one reason," he admitted. "The other one was . . ." A slight pause, and his eyes drew her in. "To offer you a job."

❧

Lori called just as Bridget and Cici were finishing lunch—egg salad sandwiches and tomato soup from a cup that they ate leaning against the countertop because every other available surface was occupied by chopped candied fruit, nuts, bowls of eggs and brown sugar, and mounds of flour made the color of pale sand by the generous addition of spices. The kitchen smelled like mace and allspice and warm baking sugar as Ida Mae took yet another sheet of perfect brown loaves from the oven.

"How many of those do you make every year, anyway?" Cici asked, watching as Ida Mae placed each loaf on the cooling rack.

"Enough," replied Ida Mae succinctly. "Wouldn't be Christmas to some folks without my fruitcake."

Cici and Bridget exchanged a glance, wondering how many of those fruitcakes ended up being secretly shipped off to other deserving relatives by their recipients. And then Bridget said, with a sudden mischievous look in her eyes, "Ida Mae, would you mind making a couple extra for me? I'd like to send some to my friends in the city." She grinned at Cici. "Wouldn't Paul and Derrick get a kick out of that?"

"Lotta work in a fruitcake," Ida Mae grumbled.

"I'll help of course," Bridget volunteered.

"And they ain't cheap."

"I'll buy the ingredients."

Ida Mae added with a sly glance at the two of them, "But it's the wine that makes them special."

Bridget's eyebrows lifted. "Wine? Ida Mae, you put *wine* in your fruitcakes?"

Ida Mae gave her a disparaging look. "Don't you know nothing? It ain't a fruitcake unless you wrap it muslin and soak it in wine for a month. That's why you have to start baking them so early."

She went into the pantry and returned after a moment or two with a bottle of red wine, brushing the dust off of it with her apron. Cici said curiously, "Where did you get that?"

"Mr. B always let me put some by every year for my fruitcakes, back in the day," replied Ida Mae defensively, holding the bottle close as Bridget came to look at the label.

"Good heavens," she said, "this is Blackwell Farms wine. Ida Mae, can I see this for a minute?"

Ida Mae surrendered the bottle reluctantly. "Don't you go thinking about chugging it down," she warned. "It's for my fruitcakes, and I'm getting low."

"Don't worry," Bridget assured her. "Look at this." She

showed the label to Cici. "Blackwell Farms Shiraz, 1967. Can you imagine?"

"I never claimed to be a wine expert," Cici said, wrinkling her nose, "but doesn't it go bad after forty years?"

"I read somewhere that they found a goatskin of wine from ancient Greece in a cave and it was still drinkable," Bridget said.

"Well, I think the grapes of ancient Greece might have been a little more durable than the ones in Virginia. This probably turned to vinegar twenty years ago."

Ida Mae snatched the bottle away. "It did not. People used to pay good money for this wine."

"Oh, I'm sure it's fine for fruitcakes," Cici said quickly.

Bridget added, "I'd love to have the label when you're finished with the bottle. Maybe Lindsay could frame it. It would look nice in the foyer along with the newspaper clipping and the landscape map, wouldn't it?"

Ida Mae shook her head and muttered something about city women hanging newspapers on the wall, and that was when the phone rang.

Cici answered the phone. Her daughter, with the frank lack of guile that Cici so adored about her, said, "Mom, I'm really mad at you right now."

And Cici replied, "I'm sorry to hear that."

"Daddy said he wants me to spend Christmas with you this year. He says he has to do business over the holidays and I wouldn't have any fun if I stayed here. But I don't think that's it. I think you two had a fight, and I ended up losing. I *always* end up losing, Mom."

Cici winced. "Lori, you know I never meant—"

In the background, Ida Mae started fussing about something to do with where Bridget had put the measuring spoons, and Bridget held up a hand for silence, her face turned in concern toward Cici.

Lori said, "Didn't it occur to you that I might *want* to stay out here? Maybe I have friends here, things to do, a *life*—even if I don't get to go to Aspen for the holidays, thank you very much! What's the point of going away to college if I don't get to make my own decisions? I'm grown-up now, Mom. You've got to let go."

Cici ground her teeth together, and squeezed her eyes briefly shut. In a moment she managed, "Honey, I never meant to deprive you of a good time. I want you to have different experiences while you're away. You're right, that's part of the point of going to college." With the very greatest of efforts, she said nothing about Italy. "But the other part is learning how to make *mature* decisions, and I'm just not sure that you've been making very good choices lately."

"So?" Lori challenged. "The point is, they're *my* choices!"

"Sometimes," Cici said carefully, "when we're in a new place, doing new things, it's easy to forget who we are. I just think it might be good for you to spend a little time away, thinking about things."

"I can think about things just fine on the ski slopes, thanks. And you don't have any idea who I am. What makes you think you can judge me?"

Cici could feel herself losing the battle to be reasonable. "I'm your parent. When I see you about to make a decision that could ruin your life, it's my job to pull you back."

"I'm not going to ruin my life! And who are you to talk about making bad decisions, anyway? You gave up a great career, a gorgeous house, an entire *life* to go live in the backwater of Virginia and raise goats!"

"Sheep," Cici corrected shortly. "And I don't think I appreciate your tone."

"You don't even have toilets! Come on, Mom, just because you're into this crazy menopausal fantasy about life in the country doesn't mean I have to be sucked into it. I'm young! I want to go to Aspen!"

For a moment Cici did not know what to say, and the silence between them stung. Then she said, coolly, "We have toilets."

Lori puffed out a breath. "I'm not your little girl anymore, Mom. You can't do this to me."

Cici exclaimed, "For crying out loud, I'm not planning to lock you in the attic and slip you food through a slot in the door. It's just ten days at Christmas with your mother, for Pete's sake!"

Lori said, "I'd rather be locked in the attic."

Cici pressed her lips together, wound the cord of the telephone tightly around her index finger, and then let it drop again. At last she said quietly, "You're right. I guess you're not my little girl anymore. Because the girl I knew would never talk to her mother like that."

"Mom, come on . . ."

Cici shook her head briskly, as though to clear it. "Look," she said, "I can't force you to come home. God knows, I can't force you to want to. But the door is open, and you're always welcome."

"Mom, don't be mad . . ."

"I'm not mad," Cici sighed, "just disappointed. We'll talk later, okay?"

"Does that mean I get to stay here for the holidays?"

"It means," Cici answered tiredly, "you get to decide."

Bridget's face was full of sympathy when Cici hung up the phone, and Cici spread her hands in resignation. "Well, I guess I really screwed that up."

Ida Mae, scraping batter in a loaf pan, commented, "Spoiled kid. Don't surprise me none."

Bridget shot her a quelling look, and turned back to Cici. "I'm so sorry. She's not coming home for Christmas?"

"She thinks I'm throwing away my life," replied Cici, and lost the effort to temper that with a smile. "Who knows? Maybe she's right."

"Oh, Cici," Bridget began, but Cici stopped her with an upraised hand.

"No, it's okay. I'm just a little annoyed with her right now. I'll get over it." She took her coat from the back of a chair and started toward the door. "I'd better get back to work. The wind is really kicking up out there and I want to get the roof patched before the temperature drops tonight."

"I'll be out in a minute to hold the ladder."

Cici waved her off. "Stay here where it's warm. I'll call you if I need you."

And because Bridget knew Cici liked doing things by herself, she did.

❧

"It's called the Renaissance School of the Arts and Sciences," Shep explained, "and I'm the new administrator. Our first classes don't start until September of next year and already we have a two-year waiting list." His smile was that of a man who had waited too long to share a secret as he deftly undid the elastic loop on a file folio and pulled out a large color brochure.

"Just look at this place, Linds." He spun the brochure around and unfolded it for her. "Everything is state-of-the-art. Pre-K through twelve, student–teacher ratio ten to one, a computer lab NASA would envy... I could go on, but you can see for yourself."

Lindsay's eyes grew wide as she turned the pages of the expensively produced promotional piece. "An entire school devoted to the arts," she said, her voice filled with wonder.

"And sciences. Our philosophy is a balanced education—which means every student will be exposed to a full curriculum in the arts. And I'm interviewing now for a director of Visual Arts."

Lindsay tore her eyes away from the brochure to look at him, astonished. "You don't mean... me?"

"I can't think of anyone I'd rather have," he told her. "Our program directors are all working teachers, not out-of-touch academics with too many letters after their names and too little classroom experience. This is a school run by teachers."

"I love this school," Lindsay said fervently.

"All our program directors are required to log twenty hours a week in the classroom, so it's not as though you'd be giving up teaching, either. But think about it, Lindsay. You'd get to develop your own visual arts program—design the curriculum, choose the textbooks, equip the classrooms, hire your teachers—all from scratch. And the pay... well, let's just say that condo overlooking the harbor you've always wanted doesn't have to be a dream anymore."

She sank back against the chair, regarding him with a puzzled half smile. "So. Did you just pop out of a magic lamp or something? Are you going to disappear after my third wish?"

His expression softened, and he reached again for her hand. "It depends on what your third wish is."

This time she withdrew her fingers before he could clasp them. "This can't be about us, Shep. You know that."

He said, "That's not why I came here. I miss you. I want you to come home. But I'm offering you this job because I want the best for the Renaissance School."

She drew in a breath, released it. "I'd actually be teaching art."

"You'd have a full office staff and two teaching assistants."

"And a condo on the water."

He smiled.

She thought about her light-filled studio in the dairy barn, and how hard she had worked scrubbing the stone floors and whitewashing the walls, and how, even with the electric heaters at their highest setting, she could never get the temperature above sixty-five degrees these days. She thought about jogging along the waterfront and going to hear a real symphony, and taking in a movie whenever she wanted. She thought about cable television and high-speed Internet. And all she could say softly was, "Wow."

He said, "Your contract would start in January. Would you like to see a copy?"

The waitress came by to clear their plates, and asked if they would like to order dessert. Shep turned the question to her.

Lindsay looked at the woman helplessly. "I don't even know the answer to that," she said.

❧

The first thing Cici had noticed about life in the country was how different the men were from those in the suburbs. When she went into the hardware store they didn't hover around, asking what she was looking for, following her from aisle to aisle as though afraid she might break something. When she went into the lumber store they didn't stop their conversations or look at her as though she had just stepped off a spaceship, as she had half expected. When she purchased PVC pipe they didn't ask if she was meaning to run hot or cold water through it, as though she didn't know there was a difference, and when she ordered a stack of two-by-fours no one asked if she meant to use them indoors or outdoors, and when she bought a box of nails no one questioned whether she had meant to get galvanized.

What they did instead was simply ignore her. She was an intruder into a world that smelled like male sweat and hunting boots, tobacco juice and machine oil, and they could not, in good conscience, acknowledge her existence with anything more than the barest courtesy. Cici began to like it that way.

Jake Senior and Jake Junior—the two Js of J&J Lumber—along with the clerk, the loading assistant, and the guys who hung around the woodstove in the office of the lumber store, grew used to seeing her once, sometimes twice, a week. They would tip their hats to her, silently help her load supplies, and occasionally take a reluctant, almost unavoidable interest in her work, as in:

"You ain't gonna try to dovetail them joints by yourself, are you?"

And, "If you're going to be cutting all that ash, you're going to need a couple of new saw blades, too."

And, "Now, if you want to try matching the hinges that are already on that door, there's a fellow with a salvage yard over in Hendersonville . . ."

What they never did, and what she appreciated to the point of amazement, was ask if she needed any help, surreptitiously slip her their business cards, or offer their opinions about what was or was not too big a job for her to take on. It seemed to her the questions they sometimes asked about the progress of her projects were laced with an underlying hope that she would eventually break down and admit she was in over her head. But Cici thought that was a small price to pay for their lack of interference in her affairs.

So she was caught off guard when, as she was buying the materials to repair the barn roof, Jake Senior inquired, "You all planning to stay the winter, are you?"

Cici replied, surprised, "Where else would we go?"

He shrugged. "Winters can get kinda rough around here. Bound to get lonesome out there all by yourselves."

To which she had just grinned and returned, "Thanks, but we're not pilgrims landing at Plymouth Rock. We'll be fine. Put that on my account, will you?"

But now, climbing the shuddering ladder in a wind so bitter it made her gasp, she thought about that. Hadn't there been a lost colony of settlers in Roanoke? Hadn't one theory been that they had all frozen to death over the winter? Hadn't another been that they had eaten each other to keep from starving? How deep did the snow get around here, anyway?

Maybe it was a little crazy for the three of them to plan to spend the winter in a hundred-year-old house in the middle of nowhere with no central heat and water that came from a spring. Not to mention no television or Internet or anything at all to keep themselves entertained. Already the short days and cold nights were making them irritable. What would happen when their driveway was under two feet of snow and Lindsay couldn't just jump in her car and drive to Charlottesville and Bridget couldn't get to the library to check out books and she, Cici, couldn't even get to Family Hardware? And how much colder could it *possibly* get, anyway?

A sudden gust of wind actually shook the ladder as she reached the top of it, and blew her hair across her eyes, blinding her. Her heart thudded in her chest and she grasped the roof eave to steady herself. She could hear the limbs of the trees creaking, and the wind sounded like the screech of a jet engine as it sang across the mountaintops. She wondered if this might be a job better left for another day. If she hadn't been so upset with Lori, she might have come to that conclusion sooner.

But the wind died down and she pulled herself up onto the roof. She had gotten the last piece of plywood decking on the roof by pulling it up into the loft with a rope, then pushing it through the hole and up onto the roof. All that remained for her to do was to position the plywood over the hole and nail it down. That would suffice as an emergency measure until she could get back up there with the underlayment and shingles.

Keeping to a careful crouch, steadying herself with her hands, she eased across the roofline. The hammer and nails were positioned beside the plywood, and she moved them out of the way. She got her fingers beneath the heavy sheet of decking, rocked it to its side for better maneuverability, and stood up.

Suddenly, from out of nowhere, there was a huge, thundering, crashing sound. Cici whirled, the wind caught the sheet of plywood and whipped it against her chest, and that was the last thing she remembered.

❧

The house shook. Bridget screamed and automatically covered her ears with her hands. Ida Mae dropped the empty bowl she was carrying to the sink, and it shattered on the kitchen floor. In the subsequent silence there was nothing but the sound of the wind roaring across the roof and the frantic barking of the dog outside.

"What was it?" Bridget cried.

"You check the front, I'll check the back," Ida Mae returned tersely.

They went their separate ways, opening doors, peering out windows. In a moment Ida Mae called, "Come look here! It's a tree down! Took out half the conservatory!"

But when Bridget came racing across the house her face was pale and her eyes were wild and she barely noticed the tree limbs protruding three-quarters of the way into the sunroom. "Oh my God, it's Cici!" she cried, snatching a blanket from the linen shelf. "Call 911!"

❧

Shep said, "Obviously, I expect you to take your time thinking about it. It's a huge move. And a huge investment for the school, too, so everyone has to be sure. It's a five-year contract; I'd need to present the Board with a preliminary proposal for your department by the first of the year."

"Wow." Again Lindsay simply stared at him, and again he smiled.

"You've said that a lot."

"Never meant it more." She took a breath. "When do you need to know?"

"In two weeks." And before she could speak, he raised his hand. "I know. Wow."

It had been so long since her cell phone had rung that at first Lindsay thought the ring tone—Beethoven's First—was part of the background music from the restaurant. It wasn't until Shep raised an eyebrow and looked pointedly at her purse that she exclaimed, "Oh!" and fumbled for the phone.

As she listened, she felt her face grow cold and her lips become numb. She was already standing, her napkin fluttering to the floor, as she said, "What hospital?"

Shep stood, too, concern on his face. She snatched up her coat. "I'm on my way."

"Lindsay, what is it?" Shep said. "Can I—?"

She was already out the door. She didn't say good-bye, and she didn't look back.

19

Mixed Blessings

The three of them lounged on Cici's four-poster king-size bed, fat pillows plumped under their heads, watching a delicate mist of snow drift down outside. A fire crackled in the marble fireplace, scenting the room faintly with warm hickory. Heavy-lined polished cotton draperies in a Victorian rose pattern were pulled back gracefully from the three casement windows, framing a view of frosted mountains against pale gray sky. A rose wool shawl was draped casually across the arm of a delicately carved rocking chair in front of the fireplace, and a skirted table near it held a vase of yellow roses. The scene was much as they had dreamed about all those months ago when they first walked through the big sunny rooms: cozy winter afternoons and cheery fires, stacks of books and a pot of tea nearby, afternoon naps with nothing to disturb them but the tinkling sound the snow made on the roof. Except, of course, that Cici's arm was in a cast, her chest was tightly taped to stabilize three broken ribs, and two pins held together her broken collarbone. And the yellow roses had come to her hospital room with a card that read, "Get well soon. We love you, Bridge and Linds."

"Is it just me," Cici said, gazing bleakly out the window, "or is living here less fun than it used to be?"

Bridget laid her head lightly against Cici's. "When I think of what might have happened to you. Do you realize how lucky you are?"

Cici winced. "Not feeling all that lucky right now."

"I still don't see why you won't let us call Lori," Lindsay said. "She has a right to know. She should have been with you in the hospital."

"Don't be silly. I was home before she could have gotten here. There's nothing she can do, and besides, after that fight we had, it would just seem like a play for sympathy."

"That's ridiculous."

"Probably. But you promised you wouldn't call her."

"Don't worry. If that's what you want, that's what you've got."

"It's ironic," Bridget said after a moment. "We cut down the hickory tree. We trimmed back the poplar tree. But it was an oak tree that went through the window."

"Not the whole tree," Lindsay pointed out. "Just a big branch."

Farley had come over with his chain saw and removed the majority of the tree branch, and boarded up the hole with plywood. Cici hadn't been able to make herself look at the wreck of her sunroom since she had been home.

"Well," she sighed. "At least oak makes good firewood."

"But who's going to cut it?" Lindsay said.

"On the other hand," Bridget said, trying to sound positive, "if the branch hadn't crashed into the house I might not have come outside to look for you for hours."

Cici gave her a dry look. "If the branch hadn't crashed I might not have fallen."

Bridget's expression fell. "Mixed blessings," she agreed.

Lindsay took a deep breath. "There's something I have to tell the two of you."

They looked at her curiously.

"That day—the day of the accident," Lindsay said, "I didn't go to Charlottesville to Christmas shop. I went to Staunton to have lunch with Shep." She held up a staying hand before either of them spoke. "And before you ask, the reason I didn't tell you was because I was embarrassed."

"Oh, we wouldn't ask," Bridget assured her.

"I'd be embarrassed, too," Cici agreed, and they both watched her with carefully reserved judgment, waiting.

"He has a new job," Lindsay said, "as administrator of a new charter school for the arts. He offered me a position."

"In Baltimore?" Cici said.

Lindsay nodded.

Bridget said, "Wow."

"That's what I said," replied Lindsay.

Again they waited, watching her, trying to read answers on her face. "And?" Cici prompted finally. "What did you tell him?"

Lindsay shrugged. "Nothing. I was hardly even listening." A quick smile. "After all, I don't see how I can teach school in Baltimore when I live in Virginia, right?"

It was meant to be reassuring, but they both noticed she didn't quite meet their eyes when she said it.

There was a shuffling and a clattering at the top of the

stairs, and Ida Mae edged the door open, her shoulders sagging under the weight of a laden tray. "Got your lunch," she announced, and it sounded like a challenge. "Although why you think I should be hauling food up and down them stairs at my age . . ."

"That was sweet of you, Ida Mae," Cici said as Lindsay and Bridget hurried to help.

And Bridget insisted, taking the tray, "You didn't have to make lunch, Ida Mae. I was coming to do it."

"Yours is on the stove," she told Bridget. "Besides, I didn't make it. Some of them women from the church brought by casseroles. Damn busybodies. Like we can't do for ourselves." She reached into the pocket of her apron and brought out some envelopes. "Some cards came in the mail, too."

"Which church?" Bridget wanted to know, and Lindsay took the cards.

"Oh look, Cici, all these cards. Isn't that nice?"

Cici smiled weakly but did not reach for the cards. "Maybe I'll look at them later."

Lindsay hesitated, then left the mail on the bedside table.

Bridget said, "Do you want me to set your lunch up on the table here by the fireplace? You know the doctor wants you to get up four or five times a day."

Cici said, "It's too cold to get out of bed. And it really hurts my back to sit in that chair. Do you mind?"

"Oh honey, of course not." Bridget fussed with pouring her tea and arranging the legs of the bed tray across Cici's lap, and Lindsay tucked a napkin into the top of her pajamas. Ida Mae stirred up the fire.

"It looks good," Bridget said. "Are those pimentos?"

Lindsay said, "Do you want me to read the cards to you while you eat?"

"You two go down and get some lunch," Cici said. "I'll be fine."

Bridget squeezed her hand and Lindsay kissed her hair. "Make sure she eats," Bridget said to Ida Mae and Lindsay gave her a worried look before she closed the door.

"Well then," said Ida Mae, straightening up from the fire and giving her a smug look. "Guess that'll teach you. The roof ain't no place for a lady."

Cici picked up her fork, set it down again, and leaned back against the pillows. "Will you take this away, Ida Mae? I'm really not very hungry."

"You're feeling sorry for yourself, is what you are. And you're not going to let that food go to waste—even if it ain't as good as I could've made myself."

And, since it was apparent that Ida Mae was going to stand there, glaring at Cici with her arms folded across her chest until Cici ate her lunch, Cici took a couple of bites of the chicken casserole and drank some tea.

"That's my pie there," Ida Mae said with a curt nod at the slice of pecan pie on the tray.

Cici tasted it, and tried to smile. "It's really good."

"Made it for Thanksgiving," Ida Mae pointed out. "Of course, nobody was here to eat it, thanks to you falling off the roof."

"It wasn't my idea, Ida Mae." Cici put down the fork, balled her napkin atop the tray, and leaned back against the pillows again.

Ida Mae took the tray and set it on the floor by the door. "I reckon you girls'll be selling out, then."

Cici, trying to get comfortable, grimaced as she shifted her weight against the pillows. "What makes you say that?"

"Plain as day, you bit off more than you can chew." She shrugged. "A place like this, it's way too much for a bunch of women to keep up with. Costs a lot, too. Sit up."

Cici eased herself forward and Ida Mae snatched a pillow from behind her head, pounding it with her fists. "And none of you've got jobs. Couldn't help noticing. Sit up." She replaced the pillow. "You got insurance?"

"Why?" asked Cici warily. "Are you going to sue me for ruining your fruitcakes?"

Ida Mae sniffed. "Your friend, Miss Priss, she don't have none."

Cici stared at her. "Bridget?" Ida Mae refused to call any of them by their proper names. Lindsay was Red, Cici was Miz C, and Bridget Miss Priss. None of them had yet determined whether this familiarity was a sign of contempt or respect.

"Can't afford it," Ida Mae informed her with a nod, "and her kids won't help her out. Shoulda thought about that, I say, before you come out here and start climbing up on roofs."

Cici didn't even bother to correct the non sequitur. She was too stunned, and worried.

Ida Mae picked up the lunch tray. "You better go through your mail, too," she advised over her shoulder, just before she opened the door. "There's more in there than get well cards."

When she was gone, Cici reached for the stack of envelopes on the table, wincing a little with the effort, and thumbed through them until she found the particular piece that Ida Mae must have been referring to.

"Oh, crap," she said wearily, when she had read it.

It was a notice from the bank, reminding them that their loan was coming due and payable in full in less than three weeks.

❧

In another couple of days, Cici was up and around, and feeling strong enough to face the damage in the sunroom. The three of them had to bundle up in coats and scarves to venture into the room, which, due to the many gaps and leaks around the plywood patches, was almost as cold as it was outside.

For a long time Cici just looked around. An entire wall of windows was either missing or shattered. The paint was scarred. Bark, sticks, and debris littered the floor, along with a dusting of snow that had blown in or drifted in through the six foot, plywood-patched hole in the roof. When Cici brushed the snow away with her foot, she saw jagged cracks running through the painstakingly restored tile.

"All that work," Bridget said softly, and the compassion of regret was rich in her voice.

"One step forward, two steps back," Lindsay agreed sadly. "It's always something."

And Cici said, "It's going to cost a freaking fortune to replace those windows."

Bridget touched her shoulder lightly. "Let's get out of here. I'm freezing."

But Cici didn't move. She looked around, her face filled with disappointment and her posture defeated. "Look," she said quietly at last, "I know you guys didn't sign up for this." A plume of frost wisped in the air as she blew out a breath.

"I'm the one who said we could whip this place into shape in a year, I'm the one who did all the figuring, I'm the one who got your hopes up. Well, the year is almost over, we're in so much debt I don't know how we're ever going to get out, and this place isn't much closer to being fixed up than it was when we started. We've got a hole in the roof and a loan coming due, and it looks like I figured wrong. I'm sorry."

"Cici, come on—"

"Cici, it's not your fault—"

Cici shook her head, eyes squeezed tightly and briefly closed as though to block out their words. "No. Listen, just the other day I was telling Lori how, when we're away from home and we get all caught up in the excitement of a new lifestyle, we sometimes forget who we are, and we make bad decisions." She looked at each of them somberly. "Well, we all have a really big decision coming up, and I think it's important that we take some time to remember who we are, and what we really want, before we make it. This last year—well, it's been kind of a whirlwind, dealing with one thing right after the other, and we've been so caught up in all the new things that have been happening to us that, well, I'm not sure we've ever really stepped back to see the big picture. And the first thing we probably should take a long, hard look at is money. Things could get a lot worse, financially, and judging from what we've seen so far they probably will."

Again, there were quick murmurs of protest, and Cici held up a firm hand for silence. "Now, don't you see that's just exactly what women do, and exactly why we're in this mess today." Her voice was tight, bordering on harsh, and every word was clipped with frustration. "We just don't face the facts. We say money doesn't matter as long as we're happy, money doesn't matter as long as we're together, we're not going to let money affect our friendship, there are more important things in life than money... well, maybe there's some truth to all of that but I'm here to tell you if I'd been a little more practical about the money part of this—if we all had—we'd probably all be sitting at home on Huntington Lane right now, surfing the Internet and watching *Oprah*, and turning up the thermostat whenever we liked. And if we don't take a good, hard look at what we're doing now, this time next year we might all be doing hair in a trailer park somewhere, and I'm not kidding."

There was a moment of stunned silence, then Lindsay said, sounding a little hurt, "We're not children, Cici. We knew what we were doing."

And Bridget added, "I'm the one who got you both into this. If anyone's to blame—"

"Oh, Bridge, no one's to blame." Cici ran a hand through her hair with her free hand, and now her expression was simply wretched. "The thing is, since I've had some time on my hands the last couple of days, I ran some figures, and it's not a pretty sight. I made copies for you both."

She drew another breath, winced, and touched her broken ribs, and added, "Anyway, we've got a few weeks before we have to make a decision. I think we should make each other a promise. Let's use that time to think about what we, individually, really want, and not talk about it with each other. And, speaking for myself, whatever you decide won't make me love you any less, and I mean that. You'll always be my best friends, so don't even let that come into the picture."

"Oh, Cici, same for me."

"You didn't even have to say that."

"Then can we promise?" Cici insisted. "No talking about it, just thinking about it, until January first?"

Lindsay looked at Bridget. Bridget looked at Lindsay. They both looked at Cici, and promised.

But the moment of tenderness was shattered almost before it had begun by the sound of Rebel racing across the yard and barking at the top of his lungs, followed almost immediately by a cavalcade of tires crunching on the gravel drive.

"What in the world?" They all turned to peer out the remaining bank of windows that faced the east side of the house. Two ladder trucks, equipment clattering, pulled up in front of the barn, followed by two pickup trucks with silver toolboxes in back, and a mud-spattered SUV. Doors opened and slammed, men in beards and hunting caps, flannel-lined jumpsuits, and leather work boots piled out of the vehicles and began to congregate in their yard, peering up at the barn roof, wandering around toward the sunroom. Cici recognized Jake Junior and Jake Senior, Jonesie, Sam and Deke, a deacon from the Baptist church, and two of the men who liked to hang around the lumber yard office, chewing tobacco and spitting into a coffee can. And, of course, Farley.

She whispered, "Oh, my goodness" and hurried out to greet them.

❧

"Morning, Miss Cici," said Jake Senior, and nodded politely to Lindsay and Bridget, who had followed Cici out with puzzled, rather alarmed looks on their faces.

He turned and shouted, "Junior, Nathan, why don't ya'll get started cuttin' up them limbs for firewood?" They waved a confirmation, and took a chain saw out of the back of one of the pickups. Deke and Sam started unhooking a ladder from one of the trucks.

He turned back to them. "Sorry it took us so long to get out here, but we was waiting for the snow to ease up. Hear you got yourself a little bit of a mess."

Cici looked from one to the other of the men, feeling almost as lost as Bridget and Lindsay. "Well . . . yes, I guess you could say that."

"Brought a sheet of tin to patch up your barn roof, fix her up good as new. Hear you lost a few windows. Why don't you show me what you got?"

Too stunned to argue, Cici led him through the house to the sunroom. Along the way they picked up Ida Mae, who said, "I'll put on a pot of coffee. You tell your boys to stop by the kitchen when they want some."

"Farley nailed up some boards to keep out the weather," Cici explained as they reached the wrecked sunroom. "I really don't know what more we can do until I'm able to get out and try to find some windows. Although where we're going to match hundred-year-old windows, I don't know."

Ida Mae said, "Why don't you use the ones that are in the attic?"

Cici stopped dead and turned to stare at her.

"Used to be," Ida Mae explained, "there was windows in the ceiling here, too. I remember Mr. B used to grow oranges and lemons here. Then the last time the tree fell on it—"

Cici said, incredulous, "The *last* time?"

"They decided to put a real roof in," Ida Mae went on as though she hadn't been interrupted, "and put what windows was left up in the attic."

"Yeah, I remember that." Jake already had his tape measure out, pulling measurements from top to bottom and side to side. "Fifteen, twenty years ago, weren't it?" He peered up at the ceiling, tested the sturdiness of a stud half exposed in the wall. "Don't look like any structural damage was done, but 'pears there might be a little rot up there in the rafters. I'll check it out. We got plenty of four-bys and three-quarter-inch ply out in the truck and a roll of roofing fabric. You want me to go up and look at them windows? If there's enough, it won't take us but a couple of hours to get 'em in, as much help as we got."

"I—thank you, yes, that would be great but..." Cici hardly knew what to say. "This is awfully nice of you, but, well, the thing is, I really don't think we can afford to have all these repairs done now, and the plywood will hold through the winter..."

He was already shaking his head, shuffling his feet, looking embarrassed. "Don't you worry about it, Miss Cici. I'll just put the materials on your bill, and you pay when you can. The labor, well, that's just being neighborly."

And then she really didn't know what to say. And because she was afraid that if she tried she would start to cry, she just said, "Um, I'll show you the way to the attic."

❧

"It was just like a movie," Bridget said wonderingly.

"From the 1950s," agreed Lindsay.

The work crew had stayed until dusk, and in that time had repaired the barn roof with weathertight seals, patched the sunroom roof with new decking and asphalt fabric, and replaced and caulked all of the broken windows. All that remained to be done was the cosmetic work.

"I never thought—" Cici stopped, and shook her head as though to clear it. "I never expected anything like this."

The supper dishes were done, Ida Mae had gone to bed, and the three women sat on the sofa in front of the living room fireplace, their feet, dressed in wool socks and fleece-lined slippers, propped up on the coffee table in front of them. They shared a fringed throw for warmth, and, in deference to Cici's pain medication, they sipped hot chocolate instead of wine.

"Ask and you shall receive," said Bridget, raising her cup in a toast.

"More or less," qualified Lindsay.

"Well, look how much money we saved on replacing the windows," Bridget pointed out. "They were stored up in the attic all this time."

"Yeah, but now we're going to have to replace the entire roof on the sunroom," Cici said, "and maybe the kitchen." When the men had pulled up the broken part of the decking to replace it, they had discovered water damage beneath the shingles, with at least one rotten rafter. The patch they had put in place would hold until spring, but no longer. "And if we restore it with glass the way Ida Mae said it used to be, we're looking at a major expense."

"There's no getting around it," Lindsay said with a sigh. "This place is a money pit. We just lucked out this time."

Cici looked from one to the other of them, her expression somber. "I think there's a reason why most balance sheets don't include a line for 'luck.'" She swung her feet to the floor, careful not to jostle her ribs, and picked up a small sheaf of papers from the coffee table. "I'm sorry," she said, and handed a paper to each of them. "But you guys needs to know. I was going to show you this this afternoon, but then we got distracted. The top figure is what we have left in the household account. The bottom one is how much we owe right now. Below that is what it costs to maintain this house for a year. And below that is a breakdown—realistic, this time—of what it's going to cost to continue the restoration."

All were silent for a time, studying the sheet. Finally Bridget cleared her throat. "Well," she said, and nothing more.

Lindsay looked up, her expression grim. "We can't afford this place," she said simply.

Bridget had the stunned look of someone who had just walked into a plate glass window. "Cici, I know you've been really depressed lately . . ."

Lindsay said, "Depression didn't make up these numbers, Bridge. I just . . . I don't think I realized it was this bad."

Cici said, "I sold real estate for thirty years. I've seen this happen over and over again. Clients make an emotional decision about a house with absolutely no idea about what it will really cost, and before you know it they're drowning in debt. I of all people should have known better. I am just . . . so damn sorry." There was such a ferocity to her tone that Lindsay immediately turned and hugged her, and Bridget reached across to squeeze her knee.

"For the last time, this is not your fault," Bridget said firmly. "We'll figure this out."

Cici pinched the bridge of her nose between her thumb and forefinger, but could not prevent a tear from trickling from the corner of her eye. Lindsay wiped it away with her little finger.

"It's okay," she said softly. "Really."

Cici sniffed, and tried to compose her expression. Bridget handed her a tissue. "I hate being such a bummer," she said. "Especially after everything turned out so well with the sunroom and all."

"Cici, you should be proud of the relationship you've built with those people," Lindsay said. "All this time, Bridget and I never knew. But you've really made quite a reputation for yourself."

Cici almost managed a smile. "Well," she said. "That's something, isn't it?"

"We should do something nice for them," Bridget said. "Bake them cakes or something."

"Well, it is that time of year."

" 'Tis the season."

"If you can believe it."

They picked up their mugs again and were silent for a moment, letting the gloom and the tension of the past drain away, losing themselves in the taste of chocolate and the popping and crackling of the fire. Then Cici said, unexpectedly, "Can you remember what we were doing this time last year?"

Lindsay stifled a chuckle. "What we were doing this time every year. Making ourselves crazy getting ready for the Christmas party. Decorating, baking, shopping, building, nailing, stapling, measuring, cutting..."

"Not to mention," added Bridget, "packing up thirty years' worth of living into boxes to get ready for the move."

"It doesn't seem like a year," Lindsay said thoughtfully. "A lot has changed. We've changed."

Bridget looked at her. "Do you really think so?"

Lindsay gave her a tolerant smile. "Do you really think

that a year ago, you could have raised a flock of sheep or put up a hundred and thirty-seven jars of preserves all in one summer?"

"And do you really think you could have been Mama to a deer?" Bridget returned with a grin.

Cici said, "I know I've changed. I used to think being rich meant having a new Lexus in the garage every year. Now it means having a shed full of firewood in the winter."

They all smiled agreement at that.

Then Cici said softly, "I miss it, you know. The Christmas parties, the neighbors, the gossip. The way old Mr. Millicker used to get drunk and break down in tears halfway through "Auld Lang Syne" and the way Carol Evans would always take off her panty hose in the middle of the party and hide them at the bottom of the bathroom trash can. Why did she do that, anyway? Did she think we wouldn't find them?"

"I miss Bridget's canapes," Lindsay said wistfully. "Remember that year you made fried green tomatoes with shrimp remoulade? And it was fun, you know, coming up with a different theme every year, planning all the food and the decorations to match . . ."

"Remember the year we did Pacific Rim?" Cici said. "Now *that* was a challenge."

Lindsay shuddered. "Those hideous illuminated palm tree yard ornaments."

"Oh my God." Bridget sat up slowly, placing her cup carefully on the coffee table, and turned to face them. Her eyes were big with the promise of a dawning idea. "We have to do it," she said. "That's exactly what we have to do!"

Lindsay blinked. "What?"

And Cici said, "Pacific Rim? Are you kidding? I didn't like it the first time."

"No, no, no, no." Bridget was practically bouncing up and down with excitement now. "A party! We have to have a Christmas party! It will be our thank-you to the neighbors for helping today, and all the people who've worked on the house—it'll be like a, what do you call it? When your house is finished and you give a party for all the craftsmen who helped build it?"

"But our house isn't finished," Cici protested, confused.

"Our house will never be finished," added Lindsay.

"And—listen to this! We'll invite all our friends from the old neighborhood for a house party! Isn't that what we bought a house with all these bedrooms for? Isn't that what we promised we'd do when we moved here?"

"All these bedrooms don't have beds," Lindsay pointed out uncertainly.

"But we have a loft full of furniture! Can you think of a better time to get it down and dust it off?"

"Bridget, it's three weeks before Christmas." Cici's tone was reluctant, though she was clearly trying not to dampen Bridget's enthusiasm. "Who's going to drag all that furniture out of the loft and up the stairs? I have a broken arm. I can't even make a bed, much less put one together. Besides, by this time most people already have plans . . ."

"Cici Burke, you know perfectly well that no one worth knowing has ever missed one of our parties!" Bridget retorted. "We'll get Farley to help with the furniture. And so the timetable is a little short. It's not like we have anything else to do!"

"Actually," Lindsay said, and a slow, speculative light began to spark in her eyes as she looked around, "can't you just see that staircase draped in live garland? And those windows?"

"With burgundy velvet ribbon," Cici suggested.

"Not just ribbon, but fabric. Giant bows! I really am going to have to go to Charlottesville now. I hope there's enough velvet left in the town for what I have in mind."

"We could get a fourteen foot tree in that corner," Cici speculated.

"We could get a twenty foot tree in the corner," Bridget corrected, "and a fourteen foot one on the landing at the top of the stairs."

"But a cut tree, not artificial," Lindsay said, warming to the concept. "Everything has to be authentic to the period—exactly as it would have been in Victorian times."

"Except for the candles on the tree," Cici cautioned.

"Right. No burning down the house. Oh my God, can you imagine what we can do with the mantle decorations?"

"Piles of sugared fruit and glass beads."

"I can make lace angels for the tree," Bridget said, "and upholster foam balls with leftover drapery fabric."

"It's a big job," Cici said, still trying to remain cautious. "Three weeks, a whole house to furnish and decorate and get ready for overnight guests . . . all that cooking and cleaning . . ."

Lindsay said abruptly, "I want to do it."

"So do I," said Bridget.

Cici looked from one to the other of them, and a slow grin spread over her face. "So do I."

They raised their cups in a toast to seal the deal. "To the best party ever," declared Bridget.

"The best ever!"

"Hear, hear."

And yet, like a silent echo that none of them could completely ignore was the knowledge that it might also be their last. Perhaps, deep down, that was exactly why they wanted so badly to do it.

20

The Lights of Home

The pall that had seeped into the house with the first frost of winter began to vanish over the next days, exorcised by the scent of cinnamon and cloves, the sound of excited, purposeful voices, and the nonstop buzz of activity. Farley was engaged to bring the stored furniture down from the loft, and Lindsay, Bridget, and Ida Mae set to work with lemon oil and polishing cloths. Cici started making phone calls, and to her utter amazement, almost everyone she invited from the old neighborhood accepted their invitation. As their friend Paul put it when she reached him at the office, "Well, darling, of course we've been holding the date. We simply assumed our invitation had been delayed in the mail."

"They want to come," Cici told the other two at lunch, still not quite able to keep the disbelief out of her voice. "Everyone wants to come! Already we have eight confirmed to stay the weekend, if you can believe that, and that's not counting Katie and Kevin. Where are we going to put all these people?"

"Katie and the girls can share my room," Bridget said, munching on a grilled cheese sandwich and barely glancing up from the recipes that were scattered across their newly rediscovered kitchen table. It was a gorgeous old chestnut piece, perfect to seat four, that had been rescued from the dairy loft. When Ida Mae positioned it in front of the big walk-in fireplace in the kitchen they knew it had always been there. "We'll put the kids in sleeping bags on the floor. They'll love it."

Lindsay said, "I don't suppose Lori . . ."

Cici shrugged her good shoulder, and an almost purposefully neutral expression assumed its place on her face. "I told her she could decide. I'm not going to beg."

"She's going to be missing a hell of a party, that's for sure."

"We've got that little room off the living room that no one ever uses," Bridget pointed out. "We could put someone there."

"And there's always the sunroom," added Lindsay. "Now that it doesn't have a hole in the roof anymore. And as far as that goes, we could sleep five or six in the art studio if we had to."

"This thing is going to be huge," Cici said, sitting back heavily in her chair.

Bridget grinned. "I told you people would come!"

And while they reveled in the anticipation of reuniting with all the friends they had left behind, the local people all felt they had to counter the ladies' invitation with one of their own: There was the Baptist church Christmas Pageant, the Methodist church Fellowship and Christmas Social, the Women's Club Charity Ball, the Mayor's Open House, the Downtown Association's Annual Luminary and Caroling, and of course the Lighting of the Tree on the town square. It did not occur to them to refuse a single invitation or pass up one small-town event. Who knew if they would ever get another chance?

They held true to their promise not to discuss the future until after the first of the year. But each of them understood, in her own private fashion, that this was more than just a Christmas party. It was also a way of saying good-bye.

Ida Mae threw herself into preparation for the event, polishing windows and banisters and stair treads and chandeliers, liberally dispensing advice and opinions on everything from the placement of the furniture to the holiday menu, working with the energy of a woman half her age.

"This is nothing," she boasted, "compared to the parties Mr. B used to give. He'd have one, two hundred people in here for Christmas. Why, I remember one Election Day we had cars parked all over the sheep meadow and down the highway a mile. Had to send the buckboard to fetch people to the house from their cars. Now there's a party. Of course," she allowed, "I was a lot younger then."

"We have got to get her something really nice for Christmas," Lindsay whispered to Bridget, feeling guilty.

"How about a trip to Aruba," Bridget hissed back. "Permanently?"

Five dozen cookies were baked, wrapped, and stored. Bridget shipped off a fruitcake to Paul and Derrick with a card signed with a smiley face. Lindsay ran off two dozen more cards on her computer, each featuring a black-and-white photo of Ladybug Farm on the front, encased in a full-color Christmas wreath complete with pears and calling birds.

Inside was a Christmas greeting and directions to the house. It was signed with three red and black ladybugs.

Even with one arm in a sling, Cici had no trouble turning fifty tiny terracotta flowerpots into silver candleholders, spraying several hundred pinecones gold, and hot-gluing sheet moss and potpourri onto foam cones to make natural Christmas trees for the mantle collection. She designed topiaries made of chicken wire and sturdy tree limbs to line the front steps, and Lindsay filled them in with evergreen and holly berries, then decorated them with tiny white birds that she had bought at Family Hardware for a dollar a dozen.

The bedlam of the mall at Christmastime was replaced by the chaos of Cici's workshop, where miles of cedar, spruce, and fir boughs were being painstakingly woven together with baling wire, sprayed with a mixture of wax and water, and hung to dry. An old sled that Bridget found leaning up against a wall in one of the barn stalls was sanded down, painted bright red with silver runners, and hung beside the front door surrounded by evergreen. Cici glued sleigh bells to a cracked leather mule harness and Lindsay used it as the center of a wreath for the front door. An ash bucket with a hole in the bottom was sprayed silver, stenciled in gold, and used to hold a vase of holly in the bathroom. Though they worked from first light in the morning until well into the night, they never ran out of ideas, or of things to do. It was as though the house itself was telling them how it wanted to look for Christmas.

Bridget found a green checked fabric stamped with red ladybugs, scanned the pattern into her computer, and used it to make labels for the jars of jam that were stored in the pantry. She cut squares of the fabric and tied it around the lids of the jars with bright red yarn. Everyone who came to the Christmas party would leave with a jar of gaily decorated Ladybug Farm jam.

Cici spent all day bouncing around in Farley's pickup truck, surveying the potential Christmas trees on their property. Finally she decided on a cedar for the downstairs and white pine for the landing, both because of their abundance on the property and because of their rapid rate of replenishment... and because she knew, without ever having been told, that those were exactly the choices generations of Blackwells had made before her. Farley cut the trees and hauled them inside, huffing and puffing and grunting as they all helped him maneuver the pine up the stairs, and they paid him ten dollars. The huge cedar spread its boughs across the corner of the main parlor and the giant pine looked down upon them from the front landing, and suddenly the rooms did not seem so sparsely furnished anymore. The house was starting to look like a home.

Day by day the rooms, once cold and filled with nothing but potential, began to transform themselves into a Victorian Christmas card. Mantles were draped with velvet and lined with evergreen and stacked with displays of gold Christmas ornaments in crystal vases or sugared fruit in wooden bowls or small topiaries covered with dried rosebuds and decorated with cinnamon sticks and lace. Living wreaths, suspended by velvet ribbon, hung from every window. Evergreen garland wound up the long bannister, tied with fluffy burgandy velvet bows that were centered with clusters of silver and gold ornaments. Living garlands draped every doorway and sprays of evergreen adorned every surface. The Christmas trees came to life with hundreds of tiny white lights, bouquets of pale pink and blue dried hydrangea that Lindsay had preserved from their own garden, and angel shapes cut from lace and stiffened with starch.

Ida Mae delivered her fruitcakes. Bridget kept the ovens going day and night, baking meringue cups, cheese straws, cranberry bread, and layer cakes. Ida Mae made the sausage stuffing and Bridget made the sweet potato casserole. Bridget made a bourbon glaze for the ham and Ida Mae made bite-size zucchini tarts from scratch. Without even noticing it, the two women worked effortlessly together, creating a menu that was based, not so much on a plan, but on dishes they loved. And in the process, the meal grew more and more extravagant.

Then it was Christmas Eve.

A twenty-pound turkey was roasting in one oven while a ham baked in the other. Casseroles, cookies, breads, and pies that had been prepared and frozen weeks ago now thawed on every available kitchen surface. Lindsay was putting the finishing touches on the dining room table centerpiece while Cici went through the house arranging candles on holders, floating them in crystal bowls, nestling them among the greenery. A delicate snow was drifting down outside the windows and dusting the garden paths with white, while inside the entire house smelled like Christmas dinner. Lindsay had set up her stereo system in the entrance hall, and the strains of holiday CDs were coming through the speakers, which were disguised by miniature Christmas trees.

"Okay." Lindsay read from her checklist. "The fireplaces are clean and laid with fresh logs. We'll light the fires first thing in the morning so they'll be nice and cozy by the time people start arriving. The buffet is set up with plates and silverware and all the glasses are washed. Punch bowls ready to be filled with eggnog. Party favors stacked on the foyer table, ready to give out when people leave."

"Candles ready to be lit," added Cici, reading from her own list. "Peppermint bath salts in every bathroom. Boy, am I glad we went with two water heaters. Pillows fluffed, candy bowls in every bedroom, towels rolled and decorated with sprigs of holly. We'll bring in the fresh greenery for the tables and mantles tonight, so it won't get too dried out before we light the candles tomorrow."

"Presents are wrapped for the kids," Bridget chimed in, drying her hands on her apron. "Cookie platters are ready to be set out. Ida Mae is frosting the Christmas cake now. Cheese biscuits are rising, the ham is ready to be carved, turkey is basting. All we have to do in the morning is—"

And then the phone rang.

The plan was for Kate to fly into Washington with the girls today, and drive to Virginia with Kevin in the morning. When she heard her son's voice, Bridget inquired happily, "Did Kate get there okay?"

He said, "Mom, the Chicago airport's been snowed in since early this morning. They've canceled all flights. There's no way Kate's getting out of there."

"Oh, no." Bridget sank back against the wall, and the disappointment in her voice caused Cici and Lindsay to interrupt their checklists and turn to her in concern. She put her hand over the receiver and told them, "Kate's flight was canceled."

To Kevin she said, "It won't be the same without them, but at least you'll be here for Christmas."

"I hope so," he replied, and it took her a moment to realize that he was serious. "If this storm keeps on the way they're saying, the roads are going to be pretty bad. They're already talking about closing parts of 1-95. Can you believe that? At Christmastime? What a mess."

Bridget blinked. "What storm? What are you talking about?"

"The same storm that hit Chicago. Don't you listen to the news?"

"But . . ." She looked out the window to make sure. "It's barely snowing here!"

"Wait for it," he replied grimly. "Mom, this is serious stuff. It's like a real blizzard, and the whole East Coast is bracing for it. You have got to get a television."

"We have televisions," she told him, still disbelieving, "just no reception. Listen," she told him firmly, "if the weather does turn bad, you stay off the roads. Don't take any chances. It's not that important."

"I know it's important to you," he told her. "But don't worry, if this thing plays out the way they say, nobody's going to be on the roads. Katie said she'll call you tomorrow. Merry Christmas, Mom."

She wished him Merry Christmas and hung up, then turned to Lindsay and Cici, looking worried. "I think we'd better turn on the radio," she said.

Throughout the afternoon they listened to the dire predictions from the Weather Service of the storm that was scheduled to arrive later that evening, with winds up to forty miles an hour, snow accumulations of at least a foot, and temperatures below zero. Outside their windows, however, the snow had stopped with little more than a pretty lace-work of white left on the ground and the trees.

"Maybe it will miss us," Cici decided, stirring rum into the eggnog with a wire whisk. "Or fizzle out before it gets here."

"Maybe," Lindsay agreed, looking uneasy. "But just in case, I think I'll go ahead and put Bambi in the barn."

"Maybe I'd better get the sheep in, too," Bridget said, going for her coat. "Just in case."

Twenty minutes later Lindsay returned, her cheeks red with cold and her hair tangled by the wind. She shivered and stomped her feet as she shrugged out of her coat. "The temperature is really dropping," she told Cici, warming her hands before the flames of the kitchen fireplace. "The thermometer on the porch says twenty degrees."

"Where's Bridget?" Cici had become quite adept at folding one-handed, and she looked up from the stack of napkins she had almost completed.

"Oh, that stupid dog. I guess he was mad because Bridget wanted to bring the sheep in early. Every time one of them would try to go through the gate he'd chase it off. We finally got all the sheep in the barn but then the dog ran off. She's out there calling him."

Cici looked at Ida Mae, who was rolling out piecrust dough into a big circle. "If it does get below zero, like they say, and with the wind and all, do you think the sheep will be all right in the barn? They won't freeze, will they?"

Ida Mae sniffed. "What're you going to do? Bring 'em in the house? It wouldn't surprise me none, come to think of it." She dusted a cookie cutter in flour and began to cut Christmas tree shapes in the piecrust. "Sheep don't freeze, but people do. If I was you, I'd bring in some more firewood before the wind blows snow all over it."

Resignedly, Lindsay reached for her coat again. "You're probably right."

"I'll help you," Cici volunteered. "I can't carry it, but I can stack it."

Lindsay filled the rolling cart with firewood from the shed and pushed it across the yard to the cellar door, fighting the wind all the way, where she dumped it for Cici to stack inside by the furnace. With the third load, she caught Cici's good arm and, shouting a little to be heard above the rising wind, said, "You've got to see this."

She pulled Cici outside and pointed toward the mountains—except that there were no mountains. There was only a solid sheet of blackish gray as far as the eye could see.

"Good God," Cici said, astonished. "There *is* a storm."

They hurried to finish stacking the last load of firewood, but an early dusk enveloped them before they were halfway through. They had to turn on the overhead light to see the furnace as Lindsay added fresh logs and opened the damper for more heat. They locked the outer door against the storm and hurried upstairs.

"Can you believe it?" Lindsay demanded, stripping off her gloves as they came upstairs. Ida Mae had already turned on the lamps and the overhead chandelier, and the Christmas tree glittered like a sky alive with starlight. "I mean, can you *believe* it? It's Christmas, for Pete's sake! We give one party a year. We've worked twenty-four/seven for almost a month. We have two tons of food that's going to go bad. Everyone we know is supposed to be here and we're in the middle of a freakin' blizzard!"

"Come on," Cici said. "The roads could be fine by tomorrow afternoon. I'm sure they have snowplows here." She started toward the kitchen. "Bridget?"

Ida Mae was taking two bubbling fruit pies with Christmas tree crusts out of the oven as they came in. "For heaven's sake, Ida Mae, stop cooking," Lindsay said irritably. "There's a blizzard coming. No one is going to make it to the party."

Cici said, "Where's Bridget?"

"Ain't here." Ida Mae took a handful of sugar and sprinkled it over the tops of the hot pies, forming a glistening crystal glaze.

"What do you mean, she's not here?" Cici's voice was tight with alarm. "She didn't come in?"

"Came in," replied Ida Mae, not looking around, "put on her boots, went out again. Looking for that dog."

The annoyance faded from Lindsay's face as she looked at Cici, and then at Ida Mae. "How long ago?" she demanded.

Ida Mae shrugged, carefully transferring the pies, one by one, to a cooling rack. "Fifteen, twenty minutes ago."

Cici looked out the window, but saw only her own tense, scared features reflected back against the black windowpane. "Did she take a flashlight?"

Ida Mae turned to look at them, and understanding slowly began to kindle in her eyes. "Not that I saw," she said.

Lindsay turned without a word and left the room.

When she returned, bundled in her hooded parka, knit cap, Burberry scarf, fleece-lined boots and gloves, and carrying a heavy flashlight, Cici was similarly attired, holding a flashlight of her own. Lindsay said, "Cici, stay here. It's starting to snow. You could fall. I'll find her."

"If you think I'm going to sit here and wait you're crazy,"

Cici replied curtly. "And the longer we stand here arguing about it the longer Bridget's out there in the cold. No one goes alone. Are you ready?"

So they plunged out into the cold, holding onto each other for support against the icy, gusting wind, following the path their crisscrossing flashlight beams traced across the yard. They reached the fence of the sheep meadow and shouted, "Bridget!"

They tasted snow on their tongues, and felt it pelting their faces. Their flashlights picked up fat, swirling flakes against the stark night landscape.

Cici leaned close to Lindsay and gestured with her flashlight. Lindsay nodded, huddled down inside her downy jacket, and plodded onward, following the fence line, shouting for Bridget.

The snow fell harder, slanting in sheets, then whirling and spinning in the vortex formed by their flashlights, blinding and disorienting them. It drifted across the ground with the vicious wind, dragging down their boots. To get their bearings, they had to stop frequently and look back at the house, which glowed like a beacon through the fog of snow. Cici's half-healed ribs stung with the effort of every gasping breath, and the clumsiness of her plaster-encased arm made the constant struggle for balance even more difficult. She cursed her infirmity even as she felt a thread of panic begin to wind itself through her. What if they couldn't find Bridget? What if she were hurt, lying broken at the bottom of a ravine somewhere? What if she couldn't even hear them call? What if...

"Wait!" Lindsay clutched her arm and stood still. "Listen!"

The snow had a voice, spinning and hissing and spitting in their faces. The wind had a voice, low and rumbling. Even the trees had a voice as they groaned in the storm. And yet, intermingled with all these voices, almost but not quite a part of them, was another voice: small, distant, half swallowed by the night. And it was human.

"Bridget!" screamed Cici, and Lindsay joined in with all the power in her lungs. *"Bridget!!!"*

Another sound, words indistinguishable, whipped by the wind, seeming to come from the depths of the woods.

"We're here!" Cici cried. "We're coming!"

Lindsay caught hold of Cici's jacket, pulling her forward, and they stumbled into the woodline. The scant shelter offered by the trees buffered the wind and offered a measure of relief from the driving snow, and this time when they called out they could hear the reply, faint but definitely Bridget's voice. Lindsay wanted to surge forward but Cici held her still.

"Wait!" she cried, clearing the snow from her lashes with a swipe of her hand. "Stand still, keep calling. We don't know where she is, but she can see our flashlights. Bridget!" she shouted, and held her flashlight straight out into the darkness. "Follow our lights! We're here!"

And still faint, but now distinguishable, "Stay there! I see you!"

They stood still, clinging to each other, shouting until their voices were hoarse and the beams of their flashlights trembled with their cold and exertion, until at last a form materialized in the swirling sea of snow. They stumbled toward her as she fought her way to them and they fell into each others' arms, gasping, shaking, clinging to each other.

"Oh my God, I was so scared!" Bridget sobbed. "It got dark and I couldn't see anything. I lost the path—"

"It's okay, Bridge, we're here, it's okay—"

"Thank you, thank you for coming for me—"

"Look Bridget." Cici had to practically shout in Bridget's ear over a sudden roaring blast of wind, and she grasped her shoulder and pulled her around. "You're almost home! We can see the house from here!" Sure enough, winking in and out with the motion of waving tree limbs and driving snow, were the lighted windows of Ladybug Farm. "Just hold on to my coat. The storm is getting worse. We have to get back!"

Lindsay wound her arm through Cici's, and Bridget twisted her fingers into the belt of Cici's coat. Their flashlights barely penetrated the tornado of twisting, spinning snow as they plunged forward, heads bent to the wind, eyes narrowed against the stinging snow and the winking, glittering promise that was home.

And suddenly, like a mirage that disappeared just when it was within reach, the house was gone.

They stumbled to a stop, disoriented, three lone figures on an endless plane of floating white, feeling, for a moment, almost weightless in the depth of their isolation. Then the wind roared again, buffeting them against one another, and Lindsay shouted, "The power must be out!"

Cici nodded, trying to shield her eyes from the sting of the snow with her hand. "We're not that far from home!" she replied. "We just have to keep going straight!"

"How do we know what straight is?" Bridget cried.

But they knew they had to keep moving, and move they did, clinging tightly to each other and fighting the wind step by infinitesimal step. The flashlights were almost useless, unable to penetrate more than a few inches in front of them and revealing nothing but driving sheets of snow, which, in certain terrifying moments and with no other reference points, actually seemed to be falling upside down. They were lost in a valley of white noise and white air, air so thick with snow it was hard to breathe, air that clung to their clothes and their exposed skin and weighed them down, yet they pushed forward, unable to talk, unable even to think, swimming through the thick white night and holding on to each other, just holding on.

Cici swung her flashlight before her like a blind man with a cane, and suddenly something knocked the light from her hand. Her cry was swallowed up by the wind like her light was swallowed up by the snow and she stumbled forward, hitting something solid. Lindsay caught the collar of Cici's jacket and shouted something Cici couldn't hear. Bridget wrapped her arm around Cici's and, flattening herself against the solid plane, began to inch along its surface. Suddenly the plane gave way and they fell, as one, out of the white and roaring vortex into peace.

Cici literally fell to her knees while Lindsay and Bridget struggled to close the door on the violence of the night. When the other two sank to the straw-covered floor beside her, the shaking beam of Lindsay's flashlight picked out the details of their own barn.

Weathered gray walls and plank floor. A deer munching hay in one of the stalls. A corral of sheep at the far end of the barn and there, just across from them, curled up in a nest of hay, a peacefully sleeping sheepdog.

For a long time, there was nothing but the sound of their ragged breathing, the shuffling and soft *baaing* of the sheep in their corral, and the whistle of the wind, sounding tame and far away now, outside their walls.

Then Cici gasped, "Is everyone—okay?"

Bridget just nodded, and Lindsay gulped for air. "How about you?"

"I don't think," she managed, "I've ever been so scared in all my life."

Bridget grasped a handful of straw and flung it furiously across the room, where it dissipated harmlessly in midair. "You *stupid* dog!" she cried.

The other two, still gasping for breath, stared at her in shock. Bridget covered her face with her hands, her shoulders shaking and her voice choked. "I'm so sorry," she sobbed. "I'm—so sorry!"

They both moved to her with words of comfort, and she lifted her chapped, tear-streaked face to them, fending off their reassurance. "Not just about tonight. I was stupid and you could have frozen to death coming out there looking for me. You didn't have to do that but you did, but it's not just that—it's everything." She started sobbing again, and the words were difficult to understand. "You wouldn't even be here, either of you, if it weren't for me. I know you agreed to buy this house because of me . . ." She scrubbed at her eyes with a gloved hand, but that only seemed to make the tears flow faster. "You had good jobs, you had lives, and now you're stuck out here freezing to death on Christmas Eve in a blizzard with a bunch of sheep and a st–st–stupid dog and you've lost all your money and Cici has a broken arm and . . ."

"Bridget." The astonishment in Cici's voice was absolute. "Bridget, are you kidding me? Is that what you really think?"

"Nothing worked out the way we planned, nothing," Bridget gulped. "We were supposed to make our dreams come true and we didn't even come close. We didn't even get started. All we did was mortgage our future and waste a year of our lives!"

Lindsay gazed at her in disbelief. "I don't know about you, but the last thing I feel is that I've wasted anything this past year. In fact... it was probably the best year of my whole life. I wouldn't change a thing."

Bridget choked a little on her sobs, looking at Lindsay through wet, swollen eyes. "But—what about Shep, and your new job?"

For a moment Lindsay looked confused, and then she shook her head. "I called Shep to turn it down the day after Cici came home from the hospital." She hesitated and added honestly, "It's not that I didn't think about it. He painted a pretty picture. But... somehow I just couldn't see myself in it."

"Don't you see, Bridge?" Cici said earnestly, gripping Bridget's gloved hand in her own. "Maybe our dreams didn't come true, but we got better ones. How can you say this year was wasted? Do you know what I was thinking the whole time I was in the hospital? I was thinking what might have happened to me if you hadn't been there. I could have fallen off a roof anywhere, any time, and what I was thinking was how lucky I was that it happened here, and now, with you two to take care of me. You guys..." She squeezed Bridget's hand, and then Lindsay's. "You're my family. And if we hadn't bought this house together, I don't think I ever would have realized that."

"Ditto," said Lindsay softly, and touched Cici's cold cheek with her gloved hand. She looked at Bridget. "Honey, don't you see? This is not about the house. It's about who we've become because of the house. And I can't go back to the person I was before, even if I wanted to."

"We're a family," Cici repeated firmly, "and in a family none of us does without the necessities of life—like health insurance—when the others can help her out." Bridget looked surprised, and then embarrassed, and Cici went on quickly, "Look, I know we said we weren't going to talk about this until the first of the year, but..." She drew a quick, short breath and looked from one to the other of them. "I for one have seen my life flash before my eyes twice in the past month and I think I'm entitled to break the rule. Especially when I made it up."

She unzipped her coat, reached into an inside pocket, and drew out an envelope. "I was going to wrap this up for Christmas," she said, "and put it on the tree. But I think I'd rather have you look at it now. It's for both of you."

She handed the envelope to Bridget first. Bridget took off her glove, used it to blot her tears, and opened the envelope. Lindsay moved close, holding the flashlight and peering over her shoulder as Bridget pulled out the piece of paper inside. "Oh my God," she said softly.

It was a check, made out to the Ladybug Farm Household Account, for an amount slightly more than equal to what remained on their loan.

Bridget looked up at her. "But how did you . . . ?"

Cici gave a small, self-conscious shrug. "I asked Richard for a loan. I figured he owed me, anyway."

Lindsay said, staring at her. "But you said you would never do that."

"This was more important than what I said, or what I thought," Cici answered simply.

"I can't believe he just gave this to you," Bridget said, big-eyed, "after that fight you had over Lori."

Cici averted her eyes with a brief, slightly uncomfortable-looking shrug. "Well, he didn't exactly just give it to me."

Lindsay touched her arm. "You told him he could have Lori for Christmas."

"Oh, Cici." Bridget's voice was deep with the understanding of her friend's pain.

Cici gave a quick shake of her head. "Lori didn't want to come home, and I've known all along I couldn't make her. I just released Richard from his promise, that's all. He got to feel superior, and I got the money. I know it doesn't solve all our problems," she added, her tone growing a little anxious as she looked from one to the other of them, "but I figured it would buy us some time, give us a chance to make things better... if the two of you would consider staying, that is."

For the longest time, neither of them spoke. The wind rattled the barn door and the sheepdog looked up from his nap irritably. An icy draft whipped down the back of Cici's neck. And then, with slow, deliberate movements, Bridget tucked the check back into its envelope and returned it, silently, to Cici. Cici felt the ice settle in the pit of her stomach.

Then Bridget said softly, "And I thought I was the crazy one." She unzipped her coat pocket and brought out a flat gold box. "I did wrap mine," she said.

Cici lifted the lid, and Lindsay's flashlight beam fell upon the contents. They both stared, dumbfounded, at the cashier's check made out to the Ladybug Farm Household Account that was nestled against the cotton batting. "But... I don't understand." Cici raised her eyes slowly to Bridget. "Where did you get this?"

Bridget smiled, and that was when Cici noticed she was absently rubbing her ring finger on the hand from which she had removed her glove . . . and that her emerald ring was no longer there. "I decided there's no point in having memories of the past if they keep you from building a future. Jim would have been the first person to say so. I didn't know how I was going to convince you two to stay," she said earnestly. "But all you asked us to do, Cici, was decide what *we* wanted, by ourselves. Well, this is what I want, right here with you two in this great big old falling-down house. I don't have to go any further to find my dream."

Suddenly Lindsay laughed, and hugged Bridget fiercely, then Cici. She sat back on her heels, her expression rueful, and announced, "I cashed in my 401(k). Well, what was I saving it for, anyway? Another day in the nursing home when I'm ninety-two? I was going to surprise you on New Year's Day, like we agreed, but . . . Merry Christmas!"

Then they were all laughing, hugging each other, clinging together, and resting in the moment. When they recovered their strength, they faced the storm again, and, leaning on each other, crossed the last few yards toward home.

21

In Which Miracles Happen

Across the Eastern Seaboard, people awoke on Christmas morning to cold dark homes, automobiles buried in snowdrifts, loved ones camping out in airports and bus stations, and a frantic crew of television doomsayers anxious to bombard their viewers with every miserable detail. On Ladybug Farm, the two-foot blanket of snow that enfolded every dip and valley, that shimmered from the mountaintops and hung like heavy icing off the roofs of the outbuildings, was a portrait of serenity.

Inside the house, the wood furnace and the gas heaters poured out warmth, while the crackling flames in the fireplace filled the house with a cozy Christmas glow. Cici used their joint venture contract to start the first fire of the morning, declaring, "From now on, we run this place like a home, not a business proposition."

They enjoyed the Christmas breakfast they had intended to share with their early-arriving guests: a festive breakfast casserole with sausage and cheese, sticky buns, even the grapefruit halves with coconut and maraschino cherry Santa faces that Bridget had prepared for the grandchildren. For while city dwellers in totally electric homes struggled to make coffee on barbecue grills that morning, the gas ovens of Ladybug Farm were working just fine.

They had small gifts for each other, although the biggest gifts had been given the night before. They opened them while watching Rebel the sheepdog through the window as he bounded and sank across the snowdrifts, stopping every other minute to scratch and shake his head, furiously trying to wriggle out of the new red leather collar Bridget had bought him for Christmas. "He really hates that thing," Lindsay observed, to which Bridget replied complacently, "He'll get used to it. After all, we got used to him."

Lindsay's gift to Bridget was, in fact, a hand-painted portrait of the border collie, which made her cry, not so much for the subject matter but for the signature at the bottom. For Cici, Bridget had a set of antique woodworking tools, which left her speechless, and for Bridget Cici had spent her spare hours of the autumn putting together a birdhouse from the twigs and bark of the beloved poplar tree. For Lindsay, a nineteeth-century edition of Audubon's *Sketches of America*, which Cici had found at the bottom of a stack of old textbooks on a back shelf of Family Hardware. And, as Ida Mae came in to clear away the coffee cups and the wrapping paper, Bridget reached under the tree and brought out a bulky package.

"We didn't quite know what to get you," she explained, offering up the package. "I hope you like it."

Ida Mae grunted, "What's this?" and wiped her hands on

her apron. She took the present hesitantly, and unwrapped it as though she suspected it of being booby-trapped.

"We know how much you enjoy the gramophone," Lindsay explained as Ida Mae pulled out the stack of old records, some of them still in their yellowing jackets. "And Jonesie finally found these in the back of the store."

"We thought you could have the gramophone in your room, if you like," added Cici.

"Well, now, ain't that nice?" None of them could be sure, but they thought, as the old woman thumbed through the records, they saw the hint of a smile.

But it was gone as she declared gruffly, "Didn't have a bit of trouble figuring out what to get you bunch of lushes." She made her way back to the big tree, bent rather stiffly, and pulled from behind it a clumsily wrapped bottle. They laughed in delight as they peeled back the paper.

"Blackwood Farms Shiraz, '67!" exclaimed Lindsay.

While Cici said, "Ida Mae, how thoughtful! You didn't have to do that."

And Bridget added, "I thought this was for your fruitcakes!"

"It's my last bottle," she told them, and looked as though she already regretted the gift. "Don't drink it all at once."

"We'll treasure it," they assured her, and she shuffled back to the kitchen, muttering about all the work she had to do.

But perhaps the best gift of the morning was Bridget's phone call from her daughter Kate, who was safe and sound in her apartment in Chicago, enjoying Christmas with her girls and, it turned out, their dad. "I was going to tell you when I saw you," she said, sounding a little shy. "But, well . . . Dave and I are going to try to make the marriage work. No."

Her voice was firmer. "We are going to make it work. It's best for the girls . . . and for me. For us."

"Well." Bridget hardly knew what to say. "That's—why, that's wonderful news, Katie."

"I think I'm a little more grown-up, now," she said. "I know what's important."

Bridget smiled. "I'm so glad, Katie." But she couldn't resist adding, "And wouldn't we both have felt foolish now if I had moved in with you last year like you wanted me to?"

"Actually," Kate admitted, and Bridget knew how hard it was for her to do, "turning me down was probably the biggest favor you could have done me."

"Kids," Bridget concluded gleefully to the other two as she reported the story. "Sometimes if you just leave them alone they'll do the right thing in spite of themselves."

But there was the hint of a shadow in Cici's eyes as she congratulated Bridget. Although they had received dozens of phone calls from friends who still had phone service, apologizing for the road conditions and the necessity of missing the party and wishing them a Merry Christmas anyway, Cici's own daughter's good wishes were not among them.

Despite the frozen whitescape as far as the eye could see and the continual influx of regrets, Ida Mae continued to put tarts and casseroles in the oven and sauces on the burners, infusing the house with the heady aroma of cranberries, bourbon, cloves, onion, sausage, and sage. "Really, Ida Mae," Bridget insisted, "there's no need for all this. The party is canceled. You should take the day off."

To which Ida Mae replied simply, "It's Christmas, ain't it? You gotta eat." And she just kept cooking.

"You know," Cici decided, and there was only a hint of

wistfulness in her voice as she looked around at the gaily decorated house, "I'm sorry not to see all our friends, but the good thing about this Christmas party—even if it didn't actually happen—is that we finally got our house put together. Just look at this place! It's gorgeous. What we've been trying to do for almost a year we were able to finish in less than a month, thanks to this party. I say, good for us!"

Lindsay said, "That calls for a toast. Shall we open the wine now?"

Bridget pointed out dryly, "Even if it is the Party That Never Was, we've still got a lot of cleaning up to do. Work first, drink later."

And then, shortly before noon, as they were putting away the last of the dishes they had stacked on the buffet table and were starting to pack away the wineglasses, they heard a peculiar chugging sound in the distance. Rebel started to bark. The sound grew closer, and they went to the window to see Farley's beat-up blue tractor making its way down their driveway, the twin plow blades attached to its front pushing mountains of snow to either side of it. When the tractor curved around to their back door and stopped, the women rushed to pull Farley inside.

"Farley, what in the world are you doing out on a day like this?"

"How did you even get here?"

"Isn't the highway closed?"

He stamped his feet free of snow on the mat, took off his camo hat, and spat politely into his soda bottle before replying, "You're having a party, ain't you? Thought you'd need your driveway cleared." And he added, "No charge, being it's Christmas."

Ida Mae just gave them a smug look and went to take another casserole out of the oven.

And sure enough, before the hour was out there were other sounds along the road: ATVs roaring and SUVs churning and tractors belching black exhaust and a wagon filled with hay and cheering passengers drawn by two sturdy plow horses. They came wrapped in blankets and capes and red and green knitted scarves, bearing homemade cookies and cakes and gaily wrapped gifts and boisterous good wishes. "Lord, honey," declared Maggie broadly, sweeping off her coat and her snow boots, "it's gonna take more than a little blizzard to keep country folk away from a party!"

The ladies rushed to put on their shoes and reset the buffet and pour drinks and pass the serving trays, and in what seemed like less than an instant the gentle serenity of a snow-blanketed Christmas morning was transformed by laughter and chatter, by clinking silverware and sparkling candlelight, into a full-blown celebration. They came, and they kept coming, bringing with them gusts of icy air and roars of welcome, scattered snowflakes that melted on the heart pine floors, and small gifts: a framed black-and-white photo of their house from the 1920s, with the casual explanation, "Don't know how I ended up with it, but thought you might like to have it." A newspaper clipping about Judge Blackwell, a dance card with the name "Emily Blackwell" featured on it—"Honey, the stories my grandma told me about the parties they used to have in this house . . ." And other things, simple things—scented candles and bundles of fire starter, homemade preserves and woven pot holders—signs of respect, signs of welcome, gifts of love.

The leather tool belt they gave Farley made his eyes mist

over, and Bridget's, too. Sam brought his pregnant wife to admire the job he had done with their heating and cooling system, and Sonya the banker came with her husband and three big-eyed children, whom she kept warning not to touch anything as she wandered through the house munching cheese straws and admiring every nook and cranny. Plates were filled with ham and turkey and sweet potatoes and cheese biscuits and zucchini tarts and sausage dressing. Ida Mae discovered a Christmas album among her vintage records, and—without stereo speakers, without electricity—the strains of "Oh Little Town of Bethlehem" and "What Child Is This" were added to the happy cacophony.

"Do you know," Lindsay whispered to Cici in a brief free moment between greeting and serving, "I don't even know the names of half these people."

"Doesn't matter," Cici replied, and the smile that spread over her face was of pure contentment. "They're our neighbors now."

Bridget, sailing by with a tray of canapés in her hands and a smile on her face big enough to illuminate the entire, electricity-deprived Eastern Seaboard, declared, "Have you ever in your life had a better party?"

Cici was about to agree that she had not when the door opened again with a gust of snowflakes and a blast of cold air, admitting yet another head-to-toe bundled guest. "Oh-oh, that one's going to need hot cider," she said, and turned to make her way toward the drinks table.

Lindsay caught her arm. "Cici," she said softly.

And Bridget, too, stood still, holding the tray, staring at the newly arrived guest as she unwrapped herself. "Oh . . . my," she breathed.

Cici turned at Bridget's urging and watched as a snow-stiffened scarf dropped away from familiar features, a backpack dropped to the floor with a familiar shrug, an ice-encrusted toboggan cap was stripped away to reveal a cascade of fiery red hair. Feeling as though she was moving underwater, Cici made her way slowly through the laughing, jostling crowd toward her daughter.

Lori's eyes were big with wonder as she looked around, and her face was filled with delight. "Mom," exclaimed the girl who spent weekends in her father's Bel-Air mansion, who partied with celebrities, who had forgone a ski trip to Aspen to be here. "Look at this place!" She opened her arms expansively, her expression filled with disbelief as she tried to take in everything at once. "Why didn't you tell me? You're rich!"

A laugh bubbled up from Cici's chest and out through her lips, and by the time she had embraced her daughter in a fierce, one-armed hug, it had become mixed with hot, happy tears. "Yes," she declared, and couldn't seem to let go of Lori. "I am!"

Then, wiping her running nose with the back of her hand, laughing again when she couldn't find a tissue, touching Lori's hair, her sleeve, her cold face, she demanded, "How did you get here? Why didn't you call?"

To which Lori returned, "Why didn't *you* call? I had to hear that you almost died from a *stranger*? Your only daughter, and you don't think I'd be interested to know that you fell off a roof? What were you thinking?"

Cici stared at her, the tears and the laughter drying up into pure astonishment. "What? How did you know? Who called you?"

Lori unbuttoned her parka, shrugging out of it impatiently. "Some woman who said she works for you. Housekeeper or something. Like you couldn't call me yourself? Or get Aunt Bridge or Aunt Lindsay to call?"

Lori waggled her fingers at Bridget and Lindsay across the room, while Cici searched the crowd until she caught Ida Mae's eyes. The older woman gave her a superior look and a half nod, and turned back to serving punch.

"But it's not like I wasn't coming here for Christmas anyway," added Lori, and her eyes grew dark with concern. "Mom, are you okay?"

So many emotions were wrestling for first place inside her chest that all Cici could do, for the moment, was nod. She tucked a strand of hair behind Lori's ear, brushed a melting snowflake off her shoulder, and finally regained her voice. "How did you get here?" she asked again. "The airports are closed, nothing is running . . ."

"Well," replied Lori, and her expression livened with the excitement of the tale, "it was quite an adventure. I got out of Chicago on the last flight, I mean, the literal last flight, but can you believe when I got to Washington Dulles was closed? So they rerouted us to Atlanta, and I rented a car. I drove all night to get to Virginia, and then when I got to Staunton, well, I was lucky to get that far. I'm telling you, the snow was over my hubcaps, and that was even after I stopped and had chains put on."

By this time Cici's heart was in her throat as she tried not to think about her daughter, driving alone through a blizzard at night on an interstate that was by now either closed or about to be closed due to hazardous driving conditions.

"I bogged down about five miles outside of town," she reported happily, "but then I met this kid on a motorcycle—"

Cici couldn't help gasping, "A motorcycle?"

Lori nodded. "And when I told him where I was going he said he knew right where it was, so here I am."

Cici said carefully, trying to catch her breath, "You got on a motorcycle . . . with a stranger . . . in a snowstorm?"

Lori nodded, looking around curiously. "He said he was coming in. Of course, he had to push the bike most of the way up the driveway. Oh!" Her face brightened as the door opened again on a blast of sunlight and cold air. "There he is."

Cici turned around to greet the stranger, and then she started laughing again. She couldn't help it. She laughed as Bridget and Lindsay surged forward, exclaiming over the newcomer, and she laughed as she made her way over to the door to greet him, holding tightly to her daughter's hand.

"Noah," she said, beaming at him. "Merry Christmas. And thanks for bringing my daughter home."

He was wearing only a thin nylon jacket that was stiff with cold and moisture, and his hair was frosted with snow. His face was bright red, though whether that was from the cold or embarrassment over the fuss that was being made over him, it was hard to tell. He looked around uneasily. "Ya'll having a party or something?"

While Cici took Lori into the kitchen to warm up, Lindsay pulled Noah over to the fireplace in the big parlor, where he refused to take off his coat but stretched his hands out for warmth. "Noah," she said gently, "I'm so sorry about your father."

He didn't take his eyes away from the fire. "Weren't no account anyhow," he muttered.

She touched his arm. "You're not like him," she said softly. "You're worth something. You're worth a lot. And I'm glad you came back here, so I could tell you that."

He slanted her a look that flashed, for one brief moment, the first genuine emotions she had ever seen from him—surprise, and gratitude.

But it was gone as quickly as it had been there, swallowed in embarrassment and awkwardness as he shifted his scowling gaze quickly back to the fire. To cover, Lindsay punched his arm lightly and injected outrage into her voice that wasn't entirely feigned.

"You spent the money we paid you on a *motorcycle*?" she demanded. "Do you even have a license?"

His answer was a shrug. He said, without looking at her, "You still got that ole deer hanging around here?"

Lindsay hid a smile. "We do. We made a place for him in the barn like you said."

He grunted. "Maybe I'll go have me a look, after a while. Surprised somebody ain't et him."

"That's not going to happen," she assured him.

Again he slanted a glance at her. "You shore are the craziest bunch of women."

This time she didn't try to hide the grin. "We've been called worse."

And then she added, "We really missed you around here."

Flames patterned color across his face. "Oh yeah?"

"There's an awful lot of work piling up, with Cici being hurt and all."

He grunted.

She said nothing else. He stood there, warming his hands over the fire in silence, for the longest time. Then he said, without looking at her, "I reckon I might be able to help you out some."

"We were talking about taking somebody on permanently," Lindsay said casually, "to live on the place and help take care of things. Of course, whoever we hired would have to agree to a few rules."

"I ain't much for rules," he said warily.

"Like no smoking on the premises."

He shrugged. "Hell, I can't afford smokes on what you pay nohow."

"And staying in school."

He scowled fiercely. "What you running, a damn prison?"

She shrugged, and started to turn away. "Well, I have to get back to my guests."

He said, without turning from the fire, "Maybe I'll think about it."

She smiled. "Why don't you do that?"

She started to walk away again, and again he stopped her. "Hey," he said.

She turned.

He reached inside his jacket and brought out a slender cardboard tube of the size that might once have held a roll of paper towels. "Here." Awkwardly, he handed the tube to her.

She took it slowly, gently prying out the cylinder of paper inside, unrolling it. "Oh . . . Noah," she whispered. "It's beautiful."

It was a charcoal sketch of their house, painstakingly rendered in exquisite detail. The hydrangeas and clematis were in bloom and the hollyhocks seemed almost to nod in the breeze. Shadows stretched across the front porch, and three rockers awaited their occupants. Mountains swelled in the background and in the foreground a long drive wound toward a road. At the end of it was a hand-painted sign: Welcome to Ladybug Farm.

Lindsay looked at him, her eyes full, hardly knowing what to say.

"I kept a picture of it in my head," he said simply.

Lindsay had to look quickly away, before she embarrassed herself and him with tears, and she smiled as she carefully rolled the sketch and replaced it in its crude container. "Come on," she told him huskily, "let's get you something to eat."

❧

Cici and Lori sat on the floor beneath the Christmas tree, where Lori quickly emptied a plate filled with one of everything on the serving table, and drank two glasses of nonalcoholic eggnog. "Mom, this fruitcake is outrageous," Lori declared. "Have you tasted it?" She offered her mother a bite from her fork, but Cici held up a hand.

"No, thanks."

"Seriously, this doesn't even taste like fruitcake. It's like—I can't even describe it. You've got to have some. I think it's the best thing Aunt Bridget has ever made."

"Aunt Bridget didn't make it," Cici said quickly, "so don't you dare tell her it's the best thing she's ever made. Lori, you did tell your dad you were coming here, didn't you?"

Lori scraped her plate. "We had a talk," she told her mother. "The thing is, I think I'm kind of over L.A. Maybe I'll stay out here for a while, if it's okay with you."

Cici stared at her. "Okay?" she repeated blankly.

Lori gave a self-conscious smile as she licked her fork.

"Well, okay, I know you don't like to hear this, but... maybe you were right. A little right, anyway, about how you can get mixed up when you're away from home, and maybe I haven't been thinking exactly straight lately. It was all so much fun. It was a great adventure and I got to do some terrific things but... it just wasn't going anywhere, you know? And after a while that starts to get old."

For a moment, Cici couldn't even speak. Finally she managed, "What about Jeff?"

Lori couldn't quite meet her eyes. "Married," she said. "And boring."

Cici reached across and squeezed her fingers. "I'm sorry."

But Lori's heart, if it had in fact been broken, was recovering quickly. "So now that I'm here," she said cheerfully, "things are going to be different. Lucky for me you've got such a super place, right? I mean, who knew? Too bad you can't do anything about the weather."

Cici's own heart was so full that her chest couldn't hold the emotion, and the simple, quiet joy radiated up into her eyes and spread across her lips in a smile that she could neither explain nor contain. "I love you," she told Lori.

And Lori replied easily, "Love you, too."

"And I also hate that you're so young and cute you can go two days without sleeping and so damn skinny you can eat five thousand calories at one sitting without even belching. And," she added sternly, "I haven't even started telling you what I think about you driving a rental car across three states in a blizzard, or getting on a motorcycle with a strange boy. However," she added when Lori started to protest, "since it's Christmas, I thought I might skip the lecture and"—she reached under the Christmas tree and brought out Ida Mae's bottle of wine—"invite you to share a glass of Christmas wine with Lindsay and Bridget and me. This is the secret fruitcake ingredient," she told her. "Ida Mae gave us the last bottle for Christmas."

Lori took the bottle, regarding it with the respect it deserved. "It's older than I am," she observed in awe, reading the label. And she added with a sly upward glance, "Which, if you do the math . . ."

"Means you're still not twenty-one," Cici said, with an airy wave. "I know. But someone told me you're grown-up when your mother says you are. And this is, after all, a very special occasion."

The smile in Lori's eyes indicated she understood the significance of her mother's invitation, and appreciated it. "Thanks, Mom," she said softly.

"Cici!" Bridget was waving to her across the room, making her way toward her through the crowd. "Derrick and Paul are on the phone. I've got them on speaker in my room. They want to wish us all a Merry Christmas."

"We'll be back in a minute," Cici told Lori. "You can open the wine."

Lori offered her arm for balance as Cici struggled to her feet, and then, grimacing, brushed something out of her hair. "What is that?" she asked her mother.

Cici laughed as she saw the ladybug take flight. "Ladybugs," she told her. "The heat brings them out. You'll get used to them." And she winked. "You'll get used to a lot of things."

Paul was regaling Lindsay and Bridget with horror stories about the Christmas blizzard blackout as Cici came into the room. "It's like something out of Dante, truly," he told them. "I expect people to start eating each other any minute now."

Cici laughed. "Peace on earth, goodwill to men. Merry Christmas, Paul."

"Merry Christmas yourself," he returned. "There you are in the boonies having the time of your lives while we're freezing to death in the heart of civilization wearing every piece of Armani we own."

"You missed the best party ever," Lindsay assured him.

"Go ahead, break my heart."

"Bridget, you little minx, what we really called to talk about was the fruitcake." Derrick's voice now. "It was without a doubt the best thing—"

"Confection!" chimed in Paul.

"I've ever put in my mouth!"

"Ambrosia!" echoed Paul.

Bridget exchanged a lift of the eyebrows with the other ladies. "It has a reputation around here for being pretty good."

"And don't think for one moment we don't know why. Didn't you say it was marinated in a Blackwell Farms Shiraz?"

"That's right."

"My dears, Blackwell Farms was one of the chichi-est boutique wineries of the 1960s," said Derrick, who was a self-confessed—and occasionally quite annoying—wine snob. "In fact some people said their Shiraz rivaled that of some of the oldest wineries in France. Did you know a bottle of 1967 Blackwell Farms Shiraz sold at auction last year for over eight thousand dollars?"

The breath went out of Lindsay's lungs in a whoop. Bridget's hand flew to her throat. Cici stared at the phone as though it were a living thing that might, at any moment, spring at her.

"Did you say," Cici managed at last, "nineteen *sixty-seven*?"

And Lindsay choked, "Eight thousand *dollars*?"

"That's right. We looked it up on the Internet last night before we lost power. Thought you'd get a kick out of it."

Bridget whispered, "Oh my God!"

And Lindsay gasped, "Eight thousand dollars! A bottle!"

Cici stumbled out of the room, raced across the landing, and caught herself on the newel post before she tumbled headlong down the stairs. "Lori!" she screamed. *"Don't open the wine!"*

❧

The house was silent; the guests—save two—were gone. Noah had accepted, albeit reluctantly, the hospitality of one of their guest rooms, and Lori had fallen asleep almost as soon as she had sat down on the newly dressed bed to take off her shoes. The faint glow of kerosene lanterns was all that illuminated the windows of Ladybug Farm, but overhead a brilliant half-moon bathed the furrowed snowbanks and flat white seas that surrounded it. The snow had stopped, and above the sky was awash with stars.

They stepped out onto the porch, bundled up in coats and scarves, to breathe the crisp night air and admire the moon. They each carried a glass of wine—not the Shiraz, which, thanks to Lori's inability to find a corkscrew, was safely locked away on the top shelf of Cici's wardrobe—but a nice California cabernet. From somewhere deep within the bowels of the house came the faint strains of the gramophone version of "Silent Night" as Ida Mae enjoyed her Christmas gift in the privacy of her own room.

Bridget said softly, "Some Christmas, huh?"

Lindsay repeated, wonderingly, "Eight thousand dollars."

"Remember what Derrick said," Cici cautioned. "Collectibles can be tricky. We shouldn't start spending the money yet."

"But still . . ."

"Yeah," Cici sighed, sipping her wine and smiling into the night. "Still."

"That Lori," Bridget said, smiling across at Cici. "She's really something, isn't she?"

"And how about Ida Mae, going in my address book and calling her?"

"We're going to have to keep our eyes on her," Lindsay said. "She's a little bit of a busybody."

Bridget made a face at her. "You *think*?"

Cici chuckled, and the other two joined in. And then Lindsay said, "Good news about Noah. Reverend Holland says he thinks he can arrange a temporary guardianship as long as he lives here, and if it works out, I can set up homeschooling. I think the reason he never wanted to go back to school was because he was so far behind, and embarrassed to be in class with the little kids."

Cici shook her head, grinning. "Imagine, raising a teenager at your age."

"Not exactly raising him," Lindsay said defensively. "Just—helping him out. Besides, he knows he's here on the we'll-see plan. It might not work out at all."

"It'll work out," Bridget said contentedly. "He's a good kid. And you have your classroom back."

Lindsay smiled and sipped her wine. "Yeah, I guess I do."

"All those people, coming in the snow," Cici said after a time. "Can you believe it?"

"I still don't know half their names."

"You will," Bridget said contentedly, "before long. After all, they're our people now."

"What a day," said Lindsay.

"What a year," agreed Bridget.

Cici raised her glass to them. "Merry Christmas, by the way."

They touched glasses. "And a very happy New Year."

And so it was.